The Oerken Leaves

Book I
Of the Trilogy

THE WHOLE CREATION GROANS

The Oerken Leaves

Book I
Of the Trilogy

THE WHOLE CREATION GROANS

By

Thomas Clayton Booher

Tome Publishing

Maryville, Tennessee

ISBN 978-1-928672-05-1 Revision 2

Published by Tome Publishing
909 Brown School Rd
Maryville TN 37804
beyondbusiness@charter.net

Cover design by Andrea Truan

Contents

Contents (continued)

Acknowledgements

When I finished the first draft of *The Oerken Leaves*, I did not realize how far it was from completion. To bring it to its final revision required the critique, prodding, and encouragement of friends and strangers alike.

My daughter Carrie and my son Thomas were foremost in this. Carrie encouraged me to give writing a try. After I started, she gave valuable advice and much needed reassurance, and was instrumental in getting the early drafts into the hands of others who provided frank discussion of the strengths and weaknesses of the book. Thomas (perhaps a future writer himself) provided stimulating ideas which helped me to sort out foggy details. He wrote the synopsis for the back cover, and he constantly pushed to get the next chapter finished. I might still be working on the book if it were not for him.

My wife, Kaye, patiently listened to the doubts that sometimes came when I got my head out of the clouds and had a realistic look at the quality and style of the book. Just to hear her say that she liked what she read was a great encouragement.

My Father, Walter Clayton Booher, has always been a believer in my abilities. As a son, I value his opinion highly, and in this endeavor, it was both heartwarming and encouraging. I cannot thank him enough.

Thanks to Sandy Good, a retired school teacher, who read the manuscript and provided valuable observations.

The greatest source of constructive criticism came from the Knoxville Five: Anthony Donohue, age 11, Andrew Donohue, age 13, Mariah Schaefer, age 14, Mary Nichols, age 15, and Timothy Weeks, age 16. Without a doubt, these are some of the most intelligent youth I have ever encountered. From the youngest to the oldest, their perceptive analysis was well beyond their years. I look forward to their efforts on the second and third books.

I must extend my gratitude and deep appreciation to Chase Moureau and his sister, Christian. In spite of busy school schedules, they took the time to read the book and provided valuable recommendations. As with the Knoxville Five, I look forward to their help on the two remaining books.

The enthusiasm of Spencer McCoy was a great encouragement, especially in the early going. If some, even the tiniest minority of those who read this book, should endorse it with as much passion as he, I might actually believe the book to be as good as he thinks it is.

Much thanks to Tammy Henderson who donated the book cover. Thanks to Andrea Truan, the illustrator, who did a superb job on the cover design.

My publisher, Deborah Taylor, and her mother, Linda Denyer, who is also the editor, put in many long hours. Needless to say, without their work, the book would have gone nowhere.

Prologue

B illy pulled his wide brim hat lower and tucked his collar tightly around his neck. The cold rain had been pouring for nearly a half hour, and he still had over three miles to go. His only companion was Willie, an old mule, who mindlessly pulled the wagon over the ruts and stones of Old Oak Road.

He had been delayed in Hampton that evening for nearly five hours, waiting for the delivery of a new plow that had at last found its way from Raleigh. Billy had spent the early part of his evening at the Brickhouse Eatery, gazing through dusty windows across the street at the rail station. At 9:00 PM, the eatery closed and Billy had nowhere to go but the station itself. It was lit by a few kerosene lamps, and even inside, the April night air was quite damp and chilly.

The plow was made by a reputable company that had been in business since 1883, over twenty years. It was expensive, but the advertisement, he recalled, guaranteed the plow to last for 'three generations of sturdy farm horses.' He would have waited until the morrow to pick it up, but he was fearful that it might not be properly delivered and thus nowhere to be found once he arrived. And now, he was trudging his way slowly back to Cameron through a furious storm that had come from nowhere. His mule looked like it was fording a river as it labored through the downpour. Blasts of heated, steamy breath spouted from its nostrils.

"Wouldn't yeh know it," Billy muttered to himself. "Jus' my luck to have my goods arrive late, and on a night like this." He shuddered as he thought of how far he had yet to go.

A bolt of lightning lit up the gray, fuming night sky, and for an instant Billy saw the outline of an extraordinary tree that towered above all the others in the forest. His spirits immediately rose. He knew the tree. It was the Grand Oak that marked the Griffin Farm. He hadn't realized he was so close to the farm.

The sight of the Oak gave him an idea that brought new hope. He could take refuge in the barn. He knew the owners, Robert and Virginia. They would not mind at all given the fierceness of the storm. Besides, he thought with self-contempt, he knew he wouldn't disturb them. Everyone in the county who was in their right mind was surely nestled warmly in bed.

"Ho! Willie!" he cried through the harsh, lashing noise of the deluge, "Ho...To the right, now...to the right!" He tugged on the rein in his right hand, and at first, he thought Willie was going to turn stubborn and continue down Old Oak Road. But Willie must have thought better of it and relented. The old mule suddenly turned his head and made his way onto Griffin Farm.

By one of the flashes from overhead, Billy caught sight of the mud-ridden lane that Willie had just pulled them onto. It led to the house and barn. A little way ahead, the lane split in two, each branch going its separate way around the Grand Oak. If it were not for the flashes that had been increasing over the last several minutes, he would have had a difficult time seeing and staying on the lane.

Billy was about to wipe his brow with a drenched sleeve when suddenly, directly in front of him and Willie, there came a piercing, ear-splitting, explosive crack. Billy instantly dropped the reins and covered his ears as he screamed out an oath. A violent shudder swept through the ground and air, and Billy felt like he had been rammed in the chest with an invisible log. He fell backward into the wagon, and Willie immediately sat back on his haunches, hee-hawing madly.

Billy struggled to turn over as he was wedged between the

wagon and his new plow. He managed to get his hands on the rim of the wagon wall just behind the seat and weakly pulled himself up. His ears were ringing and his heart pounded so hard, it hurt his chest. He peered over the seat and found himself looking right over the top of Willie's head and between his ears, as though he were looking through the sights of a shotgun.

The Oak was gone. He knew it was gone because it lay in two halves, each half glowing a dull red, like coals in a fire, hissing and belching large globs of steam under the onslaught of rain. His eyes went wide, and he uttered another oath.

"Willie!" he yelled at the top of his lungs, thrashing the reins madly from behind the seat. "Willie! Get up! Get up, you darn fool. Get up and get us to the barn before another'n turns us into a well-done side o' beef."

The mule didn't budge as he snorted and trembled, too frightened to move. Billy pulled himself onto the seat and slid down to the wheel and jumped off. He slipped over the mud and lunged toward Willie. Grasping him roughly by the mane, he began to shake the mule when suddenly, he stopped.

The smoking halves of the Oak lit up once again under another flash high in the sky, but there was something different this time. Billy squinted, his brow and eyes furrowed under the brim of his hat.

Another flash. He saw it...for sure this time. Billy let go of Willie's mane and stepped closer toward the smoldering Oak. He rubbed his eyes with his wet hands and took another look.

"Drat this rain, can't see for sure now..."

Another flash removed any remaining doubt. Something large and roundish lay near the stricken Oak. Billy trembled a bit at thoughts of what it may be. Had it fallen from the sky? He involuntarily looked straight up and immediately regretted it as big drops of rain splattered and stung his eyes. Billy jerked his head down quickly and covered his eyes with both hands, rubbing vigorously to clear them.

He scolded himself for thinking that whatever this was had fallen from the sky. But where could it have come from? Curiosity overwhelmed him. He forgot the misery of the rain and hurried back to the wagon. Stepping onto the wheel, he hoisted himself up alongside the wagon seat. Pawing along the wooden boards under the seat, his hand fell on something wrapped in an old towel. He grabbed it and jumped off the wagon. In the pouring rain, Billy wasted no time and unfolded the cloth, hunching over it as much as possible to keep it dry. With the object unwrapped, Billy held it in his hand with the towel over it. He could make out the shape with his calloused fingers.

"Knew it was still here," Billy muttered. It was his 'Ever Ready Flash Light', dry and hopefully working. He pointed at Willie and pressed the button. It flashed and lit up Willie's rear for a few fleeting seconds, then faded. He would have to wait a bit for the battery to recharge before he could use it again.

Looking beyond the mule, Billy saw the dim outline of the mystery object near the stricken tree. He moved forward and came alongside Willie's head. The mule snorted, still on his haunches. Billy paid him no mind and began to step cautiously.

Steam rose in thick billows from the smitten oak in spite of swirling gusts. The object was closer but still obscure. Billy pointed the light and pressed the button. The object brightened; it looked stone cold as the rain splattered and ran down its sides. The light went out and the object became dark again.

Billy had to know what this was. He took three more steps and the steamy air from the smoldering tree began to cuddle him with warmth. Another step. The object was very close now. Billy gave it another flash. It was large, with a curved surface, as if it had been carved out of a big rock.

Rock? Billy had heard about things falling from the sky, hot things, called meteorites. Was this what destroyed the tree?

"Naw," Billy answered himself, "'Twas lightning fer sure.

But..." The question remained, where did this come from?

Billy stooped down a little to get a closer look. He thought about trying another flash, but knew the batteries weren't ready yet.

Billy jumped and the light almost slipped from his hand. Several very loud thunderclaps reverberated in the sky during a prolonged fusion of flashes which revealed something new. Billy caught only a glimpse. He stepped close to the rock and pressed the button of his Ever Ready with his thumb. The beam was not yet full strength, but it was enough.

On the rock lay two leaves. They were green, like leaves that had just burst from the bud. But they were not tender leaves. They were large and full, but most fascinatingly they were green - enchantingly green, like emerald.

Billy reached to pick one up but as he did so, another bolt from the angry sky struck no more than a hundred feet from the wagon, and once again, Billy staggered as he clasped his ears with his hands.

He took a quick glance in the direction of the house. Though it was still a downpour, Billy could tell that there was not a single light within. Surely, they would be up and out on the porch, lanterns lit. Surely, no one could have slept through this.

Another bolt landed, this time no more than a hundred feet in the other direction. Billy forgot about the leaves. He had to get out of there. If ever there was a place on Earth that was under the wrath of God, this must be it!

"Willie! Get up! Get up you darned mule!"

Chapter 1

The Mystery of Griffin Farm

At the edge of a two-lane country road there is a bright yellow mailbox with an address painted in large, bold, black letters that reads:

R. N. Eaton
1854 St. Andrews Church Rd.

The mailbox is at the end of a long, narrow driveway that winds one hundred fifty feet from a house on a cul-de-sac. The house is large, two stories, with red brick and many tall arched windows that run across the front and back. It is the home of Robert Nelson Eaton, his wife Melanie, and their three children.

With little help, Mr. Eaton had built the house by himself. After finishing the basement, he and his wife moved into it and lived there while he worked on the rest of the house. It took three years to complete, and all the while Mr. Eaton was thinking of their yet-to-be-born children. He included lots of closets and nooks and crannies that they could hide in while playing a good game of hide-and-seek. It was a game he liked to play when he was little.

When they finally moved out of the basement, they were ready to have children. They wanted three of them and almost got their wish all at the same time. The oldest were fraternal twins. A few short years later another came along. The twins were named John and Josephine, and their younger brother, Matthew.

John was born with dark brown hair and brown eyes like

his father. Josephine took after her mother who had blonde hair and blue eyes. Matthew didn't take after either his mom or dad. He had curly light brown hair and hazel eyes. As he got older he sprouted a few freckles.

The house prominently stood on the brow of a hill which was a good thing. When it rained very hard, especially during some of the ferocious thunderstorms that passed their way, the ground didn't become soggy. For some of the neighbors, who all lived downhill from the Eaton's, the back yard could become a shallow pond.

If you turned left out of the Eaton's driveway, you didn't even get to the next mailbox before it wound to the right and started to drop quite severely. If you turned right out of the driveway, you had to go only two mailboxes before the road likewise began to drop.

Not far away there were forests where some of the trees were thick and tall. But where the Eaton's lived, most of them had been cut down. The front lawn had some shade trees here and there. The back yard had more trees - mostly maples, pines, and a few oaks. It also had a huge Formosa tree in the very middle surrounded by a large pen where two basset hounds spent most of their day sleeping or gazing at each other with sad, droopy eyes. Around the house and along most of the edge of the driveway were plants and flowering bushes that bloom only in the late spring or early fall.

Hide-and-seek was a game that John and his brother and sister used to play a lot, but it has been years since they've last played it. Even so, they still do a lot of things together – a lot more than most brothers and sisters do. They are usually off somewhere, riding their bicycles in the neighborhood or to the woods.

They're not the kind of children that are likely to get into trouble because they mind their parents rather well. Of course, no kids are perfect, and these three are no exception. They can stumble into trouble with the best of them. When they do, it's easy to tell by the way their parents call their names.

Josephine goes by "Josie" except when she's in trouble and then she's addressed by her full first name which is always pronounced "joh seh FEEN" (the last syllable is stressed much harder and louder than the first).

"Josephine! Why are there dirty dishes still in the sink?"

"Josephine! Finish your homework and let Matthew alone."

For John it's a little different. Since the name John has no nickname (except maybe *Jack* which John doesn't like) he's called by his full name, John Michael Eaton, whenever he's in trouble.

Matthew goes by Matt but, like the others, that changes abruptly when he needs tending to. Then he's addressed by just his first and middle name. Why Mom and Dad don't just say "Matthew!" is a puzzle to them. They reckon that *Matthew* doesn't grab your attention, and it wouldn't have the same one-two punch as "MATTHEW HENRY!" The way John figures it - it's like the difference between a single-barrel and two-barrel shotgun.

John and Josie are thirteen years old, and Matt is ten. September 9th is the birthday of the twins. Matt's is October 24th, about the time when autumn starts to turn really cool. Sometimes Matt's birthday comes during what Mrs. Eaton calls "Frosty Moon" week. That's the week when the cooling weather of early fall changes at the snap of your fingers, and the night air becomes downright chilly - so chilly that John, Josie, and Matt can see their breaths in the mornings while waiting for the school bus. The frosty air means they have to start wearing sweaters and coats, and it won't be long before they'll have to keep track of gloves. Gloves are always a bothersome thing for John. He's always forgetting where he's laid them.

The furthest thing from their minds is chilly frosty mornings with sweaters and gloves and, most of all, school buses. John and Josie have just finished eighth grade and Matt, fifth grade. It has been almost a week since the summer vacation started, and this is the first Tuesday evening of the summer break. The sun still has a good hour and a half before it will sink behind the trees that run along the creek at the back of the lot.

On this Tuesday evening, most of the other kid's dads and moms have already come home from work, and quite a few have finished with supper. Mr. Eaton usually doesn't get home till about 6:00 PM. When he pulls into the driveway and gets out of the car, there is often the distant sound of lawn mowers to the left and right. For Mr. Eaton, that is one of the nice things about where they lived. There were lots of houses around but none really too close by. The sputtering roar of the lawn mowers wasn't a nuisance. Sometimes it was even comforting. It was a sign that everybody was about their own business, that everything was normal, and everything was going along just fine; no problems, no worries - unless high grass can be considered a worry, which for some it probably was.

Mr. Eaton, and the whole family for that matter, was looking forward to a nice meal - it was meatloaf night, a family favorite. It had been fifteen minutes since Matt's Dad had gotten home from work, and Matt now had his eye on the clock in the living room. He heaved a sigh. It was 6:13 PM, time for supper. Matt didn't need a clock to tell him that. Twice, he had gone to the entrance of the dining room and stood there, his stomach gurgling like the bubbles in a water cooler. At the evening meal, the dining room became sacred ground, and no one was allowed to enter and sit down until Mrs. Eaton announced that supper was ready.

He looked across the big brown mahogany table where five empty chairs were neatly pulled up under it. The table was loaded: two aluminum bread pans of meatloaf, two gravy bowls, a very large bowl decorated with pink flowers and holding a mountain of mashed potatoes topped by a giant glob of butter. There was corn, peas, home-baked bread, two butter dishes, and a jar of seedless blackberry jelly.

Matt felt another pinch in his stomach. His mouth had been watering for several minutes as the wondrous aromas from the kitchen wafted through the hallways, permeating every cubic inch of the first floor. A big, dark chocolate cake sat on the counter in the kitchen next to the oven, but Matt wasn't even thinking of that right now. He just wanted to get to the meatloaf...and the mashed potatoes - with gravy and butter. It was cruel, Matt thought - all that food right there, in front of starving eyes, just out of reach.

"Mom," he whined, "When are we going to eat?"

His mother was in the kitchen. He could see her through the door at the other end of the dining room. She had just rinsed her hands and dried them on her apron which she always did just before she took the apron off. That always meant one thing.

"Supper time!" Mrs. Eaton called out merrily as if no one had a clue that it might be time to eat. It was, in fact, like the starting gun in a foot race. Matt dashed into the dining room, yanked his chair out and jumped into his seat. Right in front of his eyes was the magnificent pile of steaming mashed potatoes with yellow rivulets of melted butter streaming down the sides. He could taste it. Another grumble gurgled loudly in his stomach, and he was about to call for John and Josie to hurry up when he heard thumping footsteps charging down the hallway. John raced in with Josie barely a step behind him.

"I won!" John taunted, "Too slow again."

"No fair, you cut me off at the door."

"Should've gone faster."

"That's enough, you two. Sit down and get ready for the blessing." Mrs. Eaton had stepped in from the kitchen with Mr. Eaton just behind. Matt watched in agony as everyone took their sweet time to sit down. But he did have one thing going for him. It was his turn to ask the blessing which was perfect because he could make it short and to the point.

After everyone sat down, he closed his eyes and as quickly and reverently as possible prayed, "Thank you, Lord, for this food. Amen." His eyes popped open, and he lunged for the big silver spoon stuck in the potatoes.

Mr. Eaton frowned. "A little short wasn't that?"

"That's all we need, ain't it?" Matt defended. "Isn't the blessing really just to be thankful for our food?"

"Say *isn't it*," Mr. Eaton corrected, "there's no such word as *ain't*. And yes, that's what the blessing is all about, but there are lots of other things we can be thankful for."

"Now Bob," Mrs. Eaton interjected softly, "I've noticed the hungrier you are the shorter your blessings. Think there's any connection?"

Mr. Eaton shrugged his shoulders. "Wwellll...You're probably right...New rule everyone. Blessings have to be at least two sentences - in addition to the *amen* that is, which really isn't a sentence anyhow."

Matt was vindicated and didn't waste any time getting down to business. He had his plate filled in under a minute and started putting it away quite efficiently. Matt's appetite was hefty, and his round face and belly showed it.

Matt eyed John between spoonfuls. Now John was different. John could eat as much as anybody, even more, but he never showed it. True, he was always moving, always active. He liked to climb trees or scale that side of the porch which doesn't have steps. If there's a wall and there's any chance at all to get to the top without a ladder, he'll climb up and pull himself over, instead of going through the gate. He especially liked to climb the rainspout that led from their bedroom window to the ground. In fact, Matt thought, there probably wasn't anything that the Eaton's owned that John hadn't tried to climb up, jump over, hang by his legs from, or straddle. Most of all, the thing that John liked best was to ride his bike. He never seemed to wear out.

"But still," Matt thought, "he sure eats a lot."

Conversation was at a minimum. Except for Josie's exposition on how her softball team lost the last game of the season because of a bad call at third base, and John's observation that there were thirteen strikeouts, which may have had something to do with it, not much was said. Mrs. Eaton mentioned something about the Women's Circle from the church to meet at their house, and Mr. Eaton reminded John that the lawn needed mowing. Other than that, especially after Mr. Eaton put a stop to John and Josie's debate over the softball game, the eating passed in relative quiet.

Soon, however, the eating slowed down. The chatter began to pick up after the bellies had filled and the food had lost its savor. Everyone was finished except for John who was still going at it like he had just sat down.

"Josie, please pass the gravy to your brother," said Mrs. Eaton.

Mr. Eaton slipped on his reading glasses and quietly picked up the Hampton Herald which he began to read.

Josephine picked up the green gravy bowl and passed it across the table to John. John took it and laid it next to his plate which already had seen two helpings of meatloaf and potatoes and just about everything else.

"John, tell your sister thank you." Mr. Eaton lowered his newspaper and his glasses to make sure John heard him. John complied with the request, but after his Dad pushed his glasses back on his nose and lowered his eyes to the newspaper, he made a face at his sister. Josie mimicked the same face.

Mrs. Eaton got up to cut the cake. Silence followed with Mr. Eaton deeply engrossed in an article. Josie and Matt were watching John shovel the last several bites into his mouth.

"Don't you even chew?" Josie asked with a mix of repulsion and wonder.

"Sure, I chew, just like you, only faster," John replied matter-of-factly.

Josie and Matt watched John's chin move up and down and counted the number of times he chewed before he swallowed.

"Four," Matt said.

"Yeah, I counted four, too," Josie said.

"Now John," Josie began, "four chews aren't enough. That means a piece of meatloaf this size," she picked up a cube about two inches on a side, "is still in pieces about this big..." Josie cut off about a fourth and held it up.

With the food shoved into one cheek so that he looked like he had mumps on one side, John answered, "That's not quite right, but close. Besides, I don't put that big of a piece in my mouth at one time. You might, but I don't."

Josie's eyes grew wide, "I don't eat like that - you're the pig..."

"Joh-seh-FEEN!" Mrs. Eaton called loudly from the kitchen. "Stop calling your brother a pig. That's not nice - you know that! Bob did you hear that? Say something."

"Uh-huh," said Mr. Eaton as he continued reading not sure whom he was talking to.

"So," Josie said, looking at John, "where did you go this afternoon? Richie came over to play catch, but you were gone." Josie suddenly frowned disapprovingly. "You weren't at that old library were you?"

John shook his head. "Nope. I haven't been there since school's let out. What did Richie want?" John glanced back at Josie with a glint that tipped her off he was up to something. She was immediately wary.

Slowly she began, "Well, he just wanted to play catch. But he...uh...left after I told him you weren't around."

"Left? Hmmm." John acted as if he were deeply puzzled at this. "You mean he left right away, of course."

"Of course," Josie replied defensively. "He left right away. Since you weren't here, you know, he went home...or somewhere...I don't know. He didn't say."

John's puzzlement turned to feigned surprise. "You mean he didn't hang around for awhile?"

"Of course not!" Josie said emphatically. "Why wouldn't

he leave right away? You weren't here, remember?"

"Well, you know," John said slowly and distinctly, "I think he really came over to see you."

Mr. Eaton lowered his paper and glasses again and looked over at John. Mrs. Eaton stopped fussing with the cake and did the same. They didn't know their thirteen year old daughter had any admirers.

"You hush...John!" Josie hissed, making her lips and jaw as immobile as possible. She was flushed. She knew it was probably true but didn't want anybody, especially Mom and Dad, to know about it. She glared at John. But she could tell that Mom and Dad were now looking at her. John was poker-faced; no need to let on he might be up to something.

"Well, er..." Josie stammered and looked down at her plate. It had nothing on it, except a piece of meatloaf. She thought about scooping it into her mouth with the hope that her mouth would be too full and she wouldn't have to continue talking. But the thought was nauseating. She was stuffed. There was no way she would get it into her mouth and swallow it without really feeling uncomfortable - or worse. She would have to keep talking.

John cleared his throat. He stabbed a piece of Texas toast, pulled it off the fork, looked up and said, "You know, Richie has been coming around a lot. Let me see..." John paused. He looked up as if to mentally count and continued, "In the last week I think we have played catch four times. Today would have been the fifth. Richie has never come around to play catch, or do anything, before the last week of school. That was when you were helping him with his math, right?"

Josie's eyes were pleading with John to keep his big mouth shut.

"I think he likes you." John looked across the table at Josie with a faint smirk. "And," he said, as he raised his eyebrows, eyes twinkling, "I think you liked helping him."

Matt sat silently, mindlessly chewing on some bread while

his eyes followed the conversation. This was getting good.

Josie raised her voice from a hiss to an audible whisper. "Well...you know he was having a tough time all year long and especially with final exams and all."

She paused and looked at her mother. With a little more volume she said, "I don't mind being nice to him. But I don't - you know - like him."

She looked at her Dad. "I mean, he's nice and all, and I kinda like him, but I don't really like him." For effect, she wrinkled her nose and grimaced. She hesitated and then sputtered, "Oh, you know what I mean!"

She gave Matt a sharp look who suddenly stopped chewing. Mouth full, he mumbled, "Meeff? Whaff?" He chewed off another piece of bread.

"You know what," Josie said acidly.

His eyes became wide as silver dollars and with bread sticking out of his mouth, he protested, "Whaff arf you lookin a' meeff for, like I ftharted it."

Dad got the picture. It was awkward for Josie to be nice to a boy, especially around two brothers who sometimes liked to tease her. Josie was mature, and she knew girls and guys that age shouldn't pay much attention to each other. But Josie liked math. Math came easy, and she never had to put much effort into it. And she did like helping others with it. She often helped Matt.

Mr. Eaton decided to change the subject. He looked at Mrs. Eaton and said, "Melanie, did you know that someone mysteriously disappeared from the old farm down the road?"

Talk about changing the subject! John looked up at his Dad and immediately forgot about Richie and Josie. Josie looked up too, half interested and half hoping it would divert the conversation away from her and Richie.

"You mean the old Griffin Farm, the one that's been around for years, since before World War II?" asked John.

"Since before World War I," Mr. Eaton said. "In fact,

according to this article, it was around before the Revolutionary War."

"But how would anybody know what happened way back then?" John responded in wonder. "I mean, that was a long time ago. Nobody lives there anymore. The farm house, the barn, the cows and pigs or whatever they had, are gone. You wouldn't even know there was a farm there if it weren't for the silver sign."

The old farm site had one of those silvery signs that documented the historic landmarks around the city of Hampton. Most of the signs lined the streets of the old downtown section - the historic part of town. This one was four miles west. The Eaton's and their neighbors lived a little over a mile from the place. The farm was a landmark because it was host to General Longstreet who marched through those parts on his way north in 1862.

"Well, according to this newspaper article," Mr. Eaton continued, cocking his head slightly and pointing to the article with his glasses for emphasis, "that old farm had something very unusual happen to it a long, long time ago. Let me see if I can find it here." He put his glasses back on, ran his finger down the print and stopped.

"Yeah, here it is."

Mr. Eaton read out loud:

> The Fergusons, Angus and Mary, moved from Bonneville, Virginia to Hampton, North Carolina in 1838 and bought the farm from the Griffins. They had three children, Henry, born in 1842, Ginny, born in 1844, and George, born in 1849. George died a year later from pneumonia. The Fergusons worked the farm until 1854 when they simply and inexplicably disappeared.

Mr. Eaton peered over the top of his paper and glasses to see the reaction. Everyone's eyes were fixed on him. He continued reading.

The Fergusons had three household slaves and a few farm hands, who were immediately suspected of foul play. But suspicion soon dispelled. The slaves were deeply shaken and saddened at the grim disappearance. The farm hands likewise were visibly distraught. The Fergusons had taken good care of their workers, often including them in the festivities and celebrations of the family and holidays.

No one knows what really happened to them. There are many theories, but none can be proven. One theory was that the Fergusons were actually in deep debt to their lenders and simply left, leaving their debt behind. The lenders would not comment at the time, which added mystery and some credence to the theory. But years later it became apparent that the financiers themselves had mishandled the monies of not only the Griffin Farm, but also of many of the other, more affluent, businessmen in the town. Hence their silence.

Another theory is that there was an unknown enemy either inside or outside the family who did away with them and disposed of the bodies so thoroughly that they were never found. But this has generally been rejected since the Fergusons were not known to have any enemies.

John sat fixed in his chair. This was fascinating stuff. Josie looked over at him and rolled her eyes. John was always fascinated by such things. Not because they were grim or dark or morbid, but because John loved a good mystery, especially real-life ones.

Josie wanted to say something, but she was afraid if she spoke it might break the spell and bring them back to Richie again. She would rather have gone without food for a week than let that happen.

Mr. Eaton folded the paper quickly and laid it down. He looked up and said, "The article says that if you're interested in learning more, the library has a well documented account by Louis Montgomery in his three volume work, **A History of North Carolina**. The account itself is in Volume II, entitled "From the Revolution to the Civil War." He was looking at John now. He knew that John would check out the story himself as soon as humanly possible.

Josie relaxed. No one thought any more about her and Richie. But she still couldn't believe John had made such a big deal about it, right in front of Mom and Dad, too. The more she thought about it the more she fussed inside.

Everyone got a big piece of chocolate cake; John had two, and a glass of milk. Mom had tea, and Dad had coffee with his cake. John noticed that Josie was quiet. By now, he thought he probably should have obeyed Josie's eyes when he heard them say, "Keep your big mouth shut!" Maybe she would cool down later.

John and Matt finished brushing their teeth. Josie had already finished and was crawling into bed. Her bedroom was at the top of the staircase and to the right, at the end of a hall that ran from one side of the house to the other. The boys' bedroom was at the other end. The bathroom and some closets were along the hallway.

When John was done he went to Josie's door and knocked.

"If it's John stay out," Josie chanted, "Anybody else can come on in."

John pushed the door open and peeked around the corner to where Josie sat on the bed brushing her long, blonde hair. She did not look very amused. No doubt about it, she was still miffed about what John had done at supper. Matt went in and John followed.

"Aw come on Josie; I was just teasing," John said in a whiny voice.

Mimicking the same whine, Josie said, "Yeah? Well it didn't seem like you were just teasing." In her normal voice, she spoke grumpily, "You know I don't like Richie. I mean I don't have, you know, feelings and all." She was even embarrassed to talk about it using such words.

"Yeah," John said with a tinge of guilt, "I know. I shouldn't have done that and I guess I'm sorry. I mean if it really embar-rassed you that much..."

"Well it did! And you know it did! If Dad hadn't started talking about that weird story about the Griffin Farm, I don't know what I would have done." Josie sat with her arms crossed and a really serious frown on her face.

"Okay, okay, OKAY! I'm sorry. I won't do it again." Josie didn't look convinced.

"I'll tell you what," John said, "I'm going to check out that story at the library tomorrow. You know, look it up in that history Dad told us about."

"Yeah, so what?"

"Well if I find anything cool about it, I'll let you know."

Josie was dumfounded. "And that's supposed to make me feel better? What do you expect to find that would make me feel better? Oh yes, I can see it now,

The Fergusons were tending their
farm and minding their own business,

> when Shorty, their diminutive cousin who was a weapons collector, showed up at their front door and said, "SUR-PRISE!", as he accidentally blew them away with a forty millimeter cannon left over from the French and Indian War, which he brought over to show off."

Matt howled. "No, No! Wait! It wasn't the cannon. It was the chickens. The cannon scared the chickens, and they over-ran the farm in a stampede and destroyed everything in their path."

"Ha, Ha, Ha, very funny you two." John was annoyed.

"Look, you have to admit, this is really something cool. Someone...well really, a whole family, who once lived only a mile from us, mysteriously disappeared...as in vanished into thin air, never, ever to be seen again. If that's true, isn't it possible it could happen again? I mean, c'mon, it's so close to where we live, where our house stands this very moment, where we ride our bikes..."

"All right, all right, I get the picture," Josie said with annoyance and anxiety. She thought there was probably not much, if anything, to the story. She knew from a school report she had to do last year on famous tall tales that there were such stories of people disappearing, but they turned out to be false. They were made up by some who went around the country propagating the stories for their own fame.

And no matter. Whatever it was about, even if it really did happen, happened a long time ago. And nothing more had come of it for over one hundred fifty years. Still, just the thought that it might be true. If the family were living there now, they would be neighbors, and the children would probably be their friends; somebody they would see almost every day, especially during school.

"But I don't see how that would make up for what you did

tonight." Josie's eyebrows rose. "You were mean!"

John's shoulders dropped. He liked to tease his sister sometimes, but he could see this time that it really hurt. Unlike most brothers and sisters, John and Josie got along well. Sure, they had little tiffs, and they teased each other. But John didn't like to make anybody feel bad, especially Josie...or Matt.

"I'm sorry, Josie." He sounded like he meant it. "I really didn't mean to make you feel bad."

It was tempting for Josie to keep the grudge going, but she knew it would make John feel bad. She really liked John even though he was her brother. He usually was a pretty neat guy. He was probably the smartest of the three. He was the one who always ventured to do the things that didn't sound like fun, but after he did them, they turned out to be really super.

Josie looked away and then back again. The frown relaxed. "I guess it's okay."

John did one of his heart-attack mimes in which he slumped backwards, put his hand to his chest, and panted as though he had just finished the one hundred yard dash in ten seconds flat. It meant he was relieved.

Josie giggled. "But forget about telling me what you find about the Griffin Farm. I don't think I really want to know." Her voice was serious. "If it really did happen the way the newspaper said...well, I just don't like to think about such a place so close to us. It's too weird and creepy."

Given the delicate tension that had marked his brother and sister's conversation, Matt had been pretty much just listening. But now he suddenly spoke up.

"Well I want to know. How many kids like us can say they live near a place where something mysterious and famous happened?"

"It's not famous, only mysterious...and weird," Josie said. "Before that article in the newspaper, there probably wasn't anyone in all of Hampton, or Lee County for that matter, that ever heard about it."

That made John think out loud. "Yeah, and now everyone's going to try and get their hands on that book." He looked anxious. Of course, his fears were exaggerated. But it was possible, maybe even likely, that two or three readers out of a circulation of about twenty-five thousand would go for the book. He might not get to it. Not right away. Hopefully, it was in the reference section. At least then, no one could check it out of the library.

John started to speak again, but no one said anything more that night about the Griffin Farm or the book in the library. Their little meeting was broken up by their father's bellowing voice from the bottom of the stairway, "John Michael Eaton and the rest of you, you better move at the speed of light and get into bed!"

The library was on Harris Street, next to Trinity Presbyterian Church of Hampton, North Carolina. That was the church John and his family attended. It was about a four-mile trip into town if you followed the main roads. Instead, John took some bike trails that cut through woods and fields, which kept him off the roads until he got to town. After that it was only ten blocks to the library.

John had planned to get there by 9:00 AM, when the library opened. But at 8:00 AM, his mother made him mow the back lawn, which took one hour and forty-seven minutes exactly. It was a big lawn, and he had to do a lot of it with a push-mower. It took another thirty minutes to put the mowers away and wash up. Grabbing his book bag and cap, he jumped on his bike and set out with every intent to set a new personal record.

It was 10:43 AM when he rode up to the side entrance. Not many cars were in the parking lot, which was a good sign. He was still worried about someone getting to the book first.

He parked and chained his bicycle next to another that looked vaguely familiar.

He heaved the book bag over his shoulder. He always carried it around, especially to the library, as long as it didn't get in his way. In it were two thick spiral notebooks, some pens, pencils and erasers, a pencil sharpener, a dictionary, three library books (one of which was overdue), and a New King James Bible, the Pocket Companion size, which was too big to fit in a pocket. In the front pouch there was a digital camera, a cell phone, a small zip-lock plastic bag that held five paper clips, a pack of gum, four very thick rubber bands, six stone-hard paper spit-wads the size of a large pea, and eighty-one cents.

John came through the side door and passed the main desk. The librarian looked up and smiled at him. John smiled back, hoping he didn't look too guilty because of the overdue book in his pack. He whisked by the computerized electronic card catalog and went straight to the reference section.

It was small; eight shelves, mostly encyclopedias, biographies, periodicals, magazines, and newspapers. Everything was in alphabetical order by title. The shelves weren't very wide, so John easily scanned the book spines as he stood in front of them. When he came to the H's he quickened his scan but suddenly stopped cold. There was Montgomery's three volume history minus one volume, the second. Someone had beaten him to it.

Anxiety swept over John. He went to the end of the shelves where he could get a good look at the section's reading cubicles. Whoever had it would still be in the reference section because all such materials could not be taken to the other parts of the library. There were four cubicles arranged in pairs in a square. A cubicle had only one open end where a reader would sit with his back to the rest of the library. The reader couldn't see over the sides or back of the cubicle unless he stood up. This gave a sense of isolation and minimized distractions. But it also made it difficult for snooping.

No one was sitting in a cubicle on the side where John stood, and there were no books in them. He squatted down to see the legs of anyone that might be sitting in one of the far cubicles. There was no one there. Maybe they were taking a break and left the book. That would make it easy to see what was in the cubicle.

John started to move but suddenly stopped. He saw a familiar face – one he didn't like. It was the face of Brutus Malroye, and he looked like a relic from the Fifties. He was dressed in a black leather jacket, wore sunglasses, and had greasy jet black hair combed straight back on both sides to form a 'ducktail.' What was he doing in a library, of all places? Worse, what was he doing in the reference section? Brutus was an oversized, crude bully who had flunked first and fourth grade. He did and got whatever he wanted.

Brutus's real name was Bruce, but he only went by Brutus. It was a nickname he liked very much. John had a few run-ins with him which always ended with John backing away. John wasn't afraid of him though he probably should have been. John did not like fighting. To hurt someone, even a super-jerk like Brutus, didn't seem right. Brutus called him some pretty bad names because he thought John was chicken to fight.

Once, in seventh grade, while John was walking with his friends to a morning class, Brutus and a couple of his goons were heading in the opposite direction on the other side of the hall. John didn't notice because the halls were always crammed between classes. Just as they passed, Brutus jumped out and nailed him in the stomach. It was so unexpected, John didn't know what happened. He doubled over and could hardly breathe. He managed to look back and saw Brutus and his friends pointing at him and laughing as they disappeared in the school crowd.

John ducked back. He desperately did not want Brutus to see him. Concealed behind the bookshelves, John could observe Brutus by looking through the space between the tops of the books and the shelf just above them. He saw Brutus walk over to one of the cubicles on the other side. He expected him to sit down, but instead, Brutus hesitated momentarily to pick something up. Then he started for the very shelves that John was hiding behind. John's confusion instantly cleared. Brutus held Volume II in his grubby hand, and he was going to return it to its vacancy.

John ran like a track star to the other end of the aisle between the shelves, making the turn to duck out of sight just in time. Very carefully, he peered around the corner to peek back. Brutus stood in front of the other two volumes, his sunglasses pushed back onto his greasy black hair, the vacant book open in his hand. John thought he was writing in the book but then realized he was jotting something on a piece of paper that lay on the page. Having done that, Brutus crumpled the note, stuffed it into his pocket, and slid Volume II into its vacant slot on the shelf. Then he turned, slipped the sunglasses back down over his eyes, and walked straight out of the library.

In a panic, John bounded to get the book before anyone else could jump out of nowhere and snatch it up. As sometimes happens when a book has recently been used, John opened the book at exactly the same page where Brutus had been reading. John mentally noted the page number and took a seat at the nearest cubicle.

He re-opened the book and found the page that Brutus was on. On the left hand side there was a pen and ink drawing of a barn and farmhouse. The caption under the drawing read, "The Old Griffin Farm, circa 1898." On the right page a new section began with a bold-face title that read, "The Mystery of Griffin Farm."

John placed the book at the back of the cubicle so that it stood upright. Then he opened his book bag and took out a rubber band and his digital camera. John paused, rose from his chair a little, and looked around to see if anyone was watching or might be coming his way. There was no one, so he sat back down. He placed the rubber band around the book to hold it open and took a snapshot of the pages. John mainly wanted to get a picture of the drawing on the left side, but he included the page on the right as well. There was something about the picture that was familiar, but he could not quite place it. Having done that, John put the rubber band and camera back in his book bag and began to read. A few minutes later he jumped up, hastily closed the book, returned it to the shelf, slung the book bag over his shoulder, and bustled out of the library.

Chapter 2

The Old Oak Tree

John quickly unlocked his bicycle. The one that was there when he first arrived was gone. He knew now it belonged to Brutus. John pedaled hard to race back home. After a feverish twenty-five minute ride, he coasted into the driveway where the car was parked. Josie and Matt were sitting in the back seat waiting for Mom to come out of the house. John let the bike fall onto the grass next to the car. He was huffing and puffing vigorously.

John fell on the window, "Josie! Josie!"

His chest was heaving, and he was barely able to get his words out.

"I..." (gasp) "...found something."

Josie shot straight up in her seat. John's clammy hands were cupped around his face and pressed against the window. His breath was hot enough to form a small misty patch on the glass. Josie's face screwed up into a dark scowl.

"You scared me! And you're smudging up the window!"

John opened the door and stooped over to look in. His speech was still broken with quick breaths. "Josie! I found something..." (pant, pant) "...about the Griffin Farm," he repeated.

Josie's scowl disappeared as she leaned back, closed her eyes, and groaned. "John," she said with irritation, "I really don't want to hear anything about that place. You know what I told you last night."

"Yeah, I know, but you've got..." (quick breath) "...to let me show you this." John was pointing behind him with his thumb.

Josie opened her eyes and stretched to look over his

shoulder. Nothing there except the bike on the ground. "Show me what? I don't see anything."

"Not here, inside...on the computer."

"*Oh bother!*" Josie thought.

"Joooohhhhhn," she protested in a sing-song way, "I really, really, REALLY, don't want to see anything about that creepy story."

John took a deep breath. "Josie, look, it's really important; you've got to believe me." John's words were so tense that Josie had to look him square in the eyes to see if he was just putting her on.

Their mother stepped out of the front door onto the porch, car keys in hand. When she walked up to the car, she looked at John, smiled, and said, "Hey, where've you been? We're going to Jackie's Grill for lunch. Want to come along?" Knowing John and food, she fully expected him to jump directly from his spot into the car. He didn't.

John was breathing a little easier. "Uh...no thanks Mom," he said hesitantly.

Food! The word echoed in John's brain. Thick burgers that looked exactly like the ones pictured in the menu behind the serving counter. Ah! Such burgers - packed with two (or three) patties, big slices of tomato, onions, pickles, ketchup, and mustard, all carefully and gently stacked between two halves of a toasted sesame bun. Except possibly for Matt, John was probably the biggest fan in Hampton of the burgers from Jackie's Grill.

"Oh man," he thought. The temptation was terrific. But he suppressed a moan knowing that what he had to show Josie and Matt couldn't wait. Raising his eyebrows admonishingly, he shot Josie a stern look.

Josie closed her eyes and shook her head. Why couldn't John just take *no* for an answer? She really didn't want to hear any more weird news about that farm. She knew that look. It was the same look he had about a week before Christmas once, when he found where all the presents had been hidden. Josie didn't believe him, but sure enough, he had found them. But that wasn't creepy. That was fun. They weren't looking for people who vanished like ghosts.

Her next thought sent a tingle down her spine that almost made her shudder. What if she went along with it, just for now? Would it hurt? Maybe John was over-reacting. And yet, that look...those eyes. What if John was really on to something? She might be sorry if she missed it.

John's eyes narrowed.

"Mom, I don't think I want to go either. I'm really not hungry. I'm still full from breakfast." Josie wasn't lying. Jackie's Grill had only two sizes of burgers, large and super large. She really wasn't ready for a Jackie's Burger.

Their mother looked at Matt through the car-door window. He was frowning now. No burgers? No fries? No soda? If they didn't go now, how long would it be? An hour? Two hours? With horror he thought they might not go at all!

"I'm hungry!" Matt snorted. "I want to go. Let them stay if they want to."

That morning he had skillfully avoided breakfast knowing they were going to Jackie's. He had erected three large cereal boxes around his place at the table so no one could see he wasn't eating anything. He had put a little milk and a few Fruity O's in his bowl just in case anyone looked.

Matt's fears were realized.

"Well," Mrs. Eaton said, "it won't be any fun if we don't all go. I have to do some shopping anyway. Maybe we can go when I get back, say in about two or three hours?"

The computer was in the basement where there was now only a laundry and cooking area, as well as a little office where Dad did such things as pay the bills, write and print the church bulletins, receive and answer emails, or do some "research" as he called it. Mr. Eaton taught an adult Sunday school class and used some Bible study tools he found on the internet to prepare his lessons. John planned to download the pictures from his camera to the computer and view them on the screen.

"John, what's this about?" Josie asked impatiently. Matt was beside her, his stomach beginning to rumble. John's fingers were furiously pecking the keyboard and clicking the mouse.

"You'll see," he said, "just one more click and...there."

The screen went blank for a second and then a beep sounded with a message box telling him the slide show was ready. John pressed another button and the first picture appeared. It was their grandma and grandpa, ages eighty-four and eighty-seven respectively, smiling and standing arm in arm with white dogwoods in full bloom in the background. John had taken that a couple months ago. There were several more as he clicked from one picture to the next: the ball field, a black cat, a white dog, a turtle, twelve crows huddled on a high power wire, a garbage can (with garbage; Josie's jaw dropped slightly as she muttered "yuk"), a quartz rock, an anthill, his bicycle, the front tire of his bicycle, the seat on his bicycle, the car parked in the driveway. A few more clicks and the picture with the library book appeared.

"Look there, at the drawing."

Josie stared at the book in the picture. It sure didn't look like any of the books in their bedrooms or in the bookcase upstairs in the living room.

"John, where did you get this picture? Did you take this at the librar..."?

"Look at the drawing!" John snapped.

Josie could not believe John had shot and smuggled out a picture of a copyright protected reference book from the library. Shaking her head she said, "If Mom and Dad knew about this you'd be in real trouble mister!"

John closed his eyes to control himself. "Will you PLEASE, just look at the picture!"

Josie, arms folded, reluctantly turned her attention to the picture. It was a fine pen and ink drawing with exquisite detail. There was a barn to the right, a farmhouse to the left, some bushes around the house, and somewhere between the house and the barn stood a huge tree. The trunk appeared to be about four to six feet in diameter and at least seventy feet in height. It was taller than the highest point of either the house or the barn. The lowest branches were a good fifteen feet above the ground. Down the right side of the tree, on the trunk, there was something that Josie could not quite make out. She leaned a little closer to the screen.

"What's that on the tree?"

John said, "Let me show you."

He moved the mouse pointer next to the tree. Then he pressed the mouse button as he moved it diagonally down and across the lower portion of the tree. As he did so, a box appeared and expanded to surround the tree trunk and lower branches. John clicked a button and the image disappeared. Another moment, it reappeared but now the part that had been in the box filled the screen with perfect detail.

"It's a ladder," John said.

Indeed, there was a ladder that ran up the side of the tree from the ground until it disappeared into the branches. Josie counted sixteen rungs.

"So this is what you wanted to show me?" She glanced at Matt who was really getting hungry now. Looking back at John she said, "What's so neat about that? Haven't you ever seen a ladder attached to a tree before?" Josie thought a moment and realized that she couldn't remember herself ever seeing a ladder nailed, tied, or otherwise fastened to a tree.

"Yes," he said with emphasis. "Yes, I have."

Now that took Josie by surprise. "Where? I haven't seen any trees around here that have ladders nailed to them."

"There is one, but not exactly in the neighborhood." John clicked another button and the image went back to its normal size. He drew another box around the right page of the book and enlarged it. The words, "The Mystery of Griffin Farm," stood boldly at the top of the page.

"Well...where?" Josie said. She tapped his shoulder to make sure he was listening.

"At Griffin Farm, of course."

Immediately a bunch of questions jumped into Josie's head. "Griffin Farm? What are you talking about? How do you know? When were you ever at Griffin Farm? Why were you ever at Griffin Farm? Nobody goes there. It's just a lot of woods and thickets and roots overgrown with vines." Then she mentally froze. She had just thought of the real question, the only question that mattered.

"John Michael Eaton, don't you try and say that whatever you saw, wherever you saw it, is the same thing as in the picture." Josie was holding up her hand as if to put up a stop sign. Matt's eyes shot up and landed on John. John's face was as solemn as a pallbearer's.

"That's exactly what I'm saying."

As soon as Brutus left the library he rode his bicycle back to his house and went inside. He took off his black leather jacket and changed into a black T-shirt with a pocket where he placed his sunglasses. He gathered a few other things so that when he came back out he had a backpack, canteen, and a small collapsible shovel called an entrenching tool. It was standard issue in the U. S. Army. Soldiers use it to dig foxholes.

Brutus put his sunglasses back on and started pedaling. From his house Brutus headed five blocks south on Penn Street, the street he lived on. Then he turned right onto Lafayette Street and pedaled another ten blocks. At the end of this street was an old-fashioned icehouse still in use. Between the icehouse on one side and a laundromat on the other, there ran a sidewalk that led to a dirt alley in the back. On the other side of the alley was a creek, and on the other side of the creek there were woods and an opening where a trail began.

Brutus dismounted and turned his bicycle down the sidewalk. The passage between the two buildings was narrow and dark. As he came out onto the alley in the rear, a cat darted out from under a porch and then quickly stopped at the corner of the icehouse. It crouched and looked back at Brutus. Brutus picked up a stone and threw it at the cat. The stone missed and the cat disappeared around the corner.

Brutus pushed his bike to the edge of the creek. There was a small bank and the water was shallow. He eyed several sandy spots which would make the passage to the other side simple. Brutus stepped down into the creek pushing his bike at his side. He quickly made it across and up the far bank. He got back on his bike and disappeared into the trees.

Brutus knew the back trails almost as well as John. After about twenty minutes of easy pedaling he came upon another trail that branched to the right. It showed no travel. It was lightly covered with dry pine needles. There were sandy splotches intermingled with red clay dirt. Roots crisscrossed the path like thin knotty ropes coming out of the ground on one side and slithering into the dirt on the other. Tree branches protruded overhead to form a leafy canopy. He took the new trail. It would carry him not to St. Andrews Church Road and the silver sign, but in the other direction, deep into the woods.

At first, the path wasn't bad; the roots were tucked close to the ground and the sand was firm. But it quickly became a sandbox. Pedaling was no longer possible. Spider webs stretched from one side to the other like flimsy, silver nets. If he weren't careful, a root just under the sand would trip him.

He went on like this for about ten minutes and then stopped. He took the crumpled paper note that he wrote in the library out of his pocket. On it was a crude map of what used to be Griffin Farm.

According to this map, there was a road that passed in front of the house, barn, and tree. But this road was on the west side of the house. St. Andrews Church Road ran along the east side of the official site of the farm.

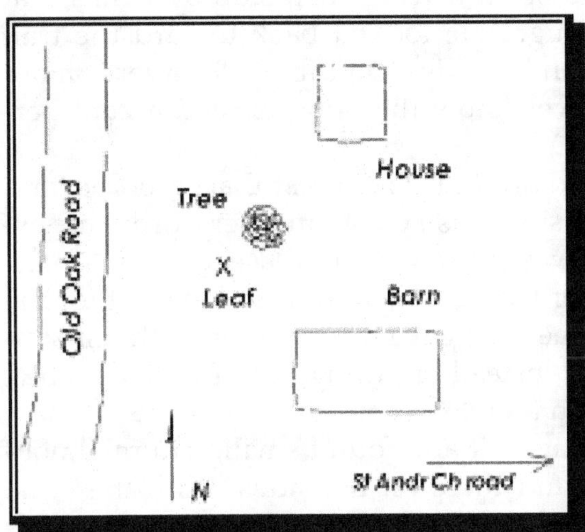

Brutus, after taking his sunglasses off and stuffing them into his shirt pocket, began to look around. He was looking for anything that was different about the lay of the woods and terrain. To the left, the ground gradually sloped downward. The trees were thick with pines, and with a few hickories, oaks, and maples mixed in. The floor of the forest itself was carpeted two or three inches deep with the same reddish-brown pine needles that were on the trail. To the right, the trees were fewer and the brush not quite as thick. Brutus intently studied this side of the trail.

After a few minutes, he began to sense there was a change in the way the ground appeared about thirty feet into the woods. He left his bicycle on the trail and began to work his way into the brush. At first, it seemed that he was wrong about any difference. The brush and vines were thicker than he thought. As he pushed his way through, he had to duck under thorny branches or step around a hanging vine or over a root or rotting log. Now that he was in the middle of the tangle, he could only see about four or five feet to his front and sides. He was about to give up and go back when, without warning, the ground fell away and he stumbled headlong.

Cursing, he picked himself up and looked at his palms. They were scuffed up a bit, but there were no cuts or any broken skin. When he looked about, he found himself on a relatively clear swath of ground straddled on each side by banks that were about two feet high. He looked back toward the trail where he left his bike and could see nothing. Observers on opposite sides would never know the other existed except perhaps by sound.

Brutus again looked around. The forest that stood beyond the bank on the other side was sparse and very ordinary except for an object that was entirely out of place. It was a single, large rock about four or five feet high, roundish except for the top, which was flat. The rock gave the impression that it simply rested on the earth instead of jutting out of it, like a bowl turned upside down on a table.

Brutus made his way to it and found small, natural, knob-like protrusions here and there on the sides. With these, he was able to step up and pull himself onto the top. From his hands and knees he stood up, and Brutus immediately saw what a difference this made.

This side of the bank was very grassy with patches of bare earth here and there. To his left and right were two distinct areas, noticeably different from everything else. These stood out in relief from the grass and bushes that surrounded them. They were extraordinarily and unnaturally rectangular.

Brutus pulled out his map again and began to piece things together. If the hollow he fell into was the Old Oak Road and the mounds were the house to the left and the barn to the right, he was looking at the ruins of Griffin Farm. The only problem: this was not where Griffin Farm was supposed to be. All the local historic maps placed the farm at least another mile to the east and much closer to St. Andrews Church Road. This place likely had few human visitors for several years, perhaps decades.

Brutus looked at the map again. The X that was labeled "Leaf" would be just about where he was standing atop the boulder. Brutus climbed down and took his backpack off, tossing it on the ground in front of him. He removed the entrenching tool from its clip and unfolded it to lock the handle and shovel in place.

He tentatively traced the perimeter of the rock crouching down every now and then to get a closer look where it met the ground. Then he began to work his way around the rock, probing the dirt just underneath it. About half way round, the point of the shovel hit something that sounded like metal.

Brutus dropped excitedly to his knees and feverishly began to scrape away the earth with the tool. He was soon using his hands to clear the dirt from something wedged between the ground and the rock. It was silvery and smooth. He scraped away about an inch of dirt from above and below the object so that he could squeeze his hands into the small gorge. He had only enough room to grasp the metal with his fingertips.

Twisting and prying, it began to loosen. He sat down and placed his feet against the rock so that he could brace himself with his legs as he tugged. Through the tips of his fingers, Brutus could feel it give. He paused, got another grip, and started pulling again. It gave way all at once, and Brutus fell sharply backward.

As he lay on his back, Brutus held in his hands a flat silvery object that looked like a light metal box about the size of a book. Along one side there were small hinges, and on the other side, a clasp which was clearly intended to lock the box. But there was no lock. The clasp held the cover to the box tightly but did not keep it from being opened.

Brutus now sat up and got back to his knees. Much of the earth had fallen from the box. There was something on one side that appeared to be an engraving, but there was still a stubborn layer of dirt that made it difficult to read.

Brutus took his canteen and poured water on the box. He

rubbed over it with his thumb and smeared it. With a little more water the dirt became a thin, dull film, and some of the letters became legible. Another rinse and the film washed away revealing distinct and precise characters. Inscribed into the metal were words which included names that were familiar to his family:

Oak Leaf #1
Robert Malroye
May 17, 1904 A.D.

Brutus reached into his backpack and pulled out another silvery object that was identical to the one he just dug up. It too had an engraving that read:

Oak Leaf #2
Virginia Malroye
May 19, 1904 A.D.

Brutus set them on the ground side by side. He took a deep breath, wiped the sweat from his face with his shirt, and opened the boxes; first the one he pulled from under the rock, then the other he had carried with him. Inside each box there was an oak leaf pressed between two panes of glass. Carefully he took out the panes and held them up for inspection, but the light was dim and the location was shadowy. He looked around and saw, just a little way off, a beam of sunlight that shot down through the trees. He moved to the ray and raised the two encased leaves up to the light, one in each hand. Then he brought the two glass sets together and placed the one over the other. He held them so that light shone down through the glass directly onto his face. As he did so, he saw that the leaves were green, translucent, and identical in shape and venation.

With the panes still held upward toward the light, Brutus's concentration was broken when he sensed a rumbling under his feet. He looked down with his arms still in the air holding the glass cases. His right foot was on a barren patch of earth, the other in grass. Next to his foot on the bare dirt were twigs, sticks, dry leaves and anything light and small, vibrating and dancing across the surface.

Brutus dropped his arms and was about to turn around when a loud crack from behind jolted him. Instantly, he felt stinging pellets of stone and rubble strike his back. He fell forward to his knees, the encased leaves still in his hands. Another loud crack and Brutus was pushed forward and fell flat on his face. The glass cases dropped from his hands to the dirt.

"What the..." Brutus's words were cut short by a third more powerful thunderous crack. The ground was shaking now. Like a giant flood lamp, a light was turned on from behind, so brilliant that the earth and woods around him turned into shades of gray. His own shadow was the only thing that stood out, and it seemed jet black by comparison.

He pushed himself to his hands and knees but lost his balance and fell to his side. He was now looking toward his feet and beyond where the rock had lain. Fissures had split open its sides. From these cracks bright, glowing smoke shot out. A beam of light thousands of watts bright shot upward out of the top. And that noise! There was a blasting, deafening sound, like a trumpet held inches from his ear.

Brutus desperately clawed and pulled and pushed with his hands and feet to get away from the terrible light and sound, but to no avail. As if his feet and legs were in the clenches of a giant invisible hand, Brutus was dragged helplessly toward the rock. His sunglasses fell out of his shirt pocket.

Brutus caught sight of a faded gray rabbit to his right. It dashed into pale, bleak thickets a few yards away. Those thickets immediately seized his attention. Logic left him. A place to hide! A haven! A fortress! He must reach them at all cost. He began wildly flailing and grabbing for weeds and blades of grass, pebbles and sticks and dirt...anything to pull himself away from that terrifying light and noise.

Suddenly, with a jerk, he was yanked upright to his feet and flung around to face the horrific sight. Resistance was impossible. A powerful force curled its fingers around him and began pulling him, his feet helplessly dragging and the toes of his shoes carving narrow furrows in their wake.

Brutus threw up his arms to cover his face. With earth still clenched in his fists, a silent scream emanated from his mouth. Brutus was sucked into the light. The instant he hit the beam he shot upward like a rocket and was gone.

The trumpet blast fell silent and the light beam went out. The pebbles and sticks stopped dancing and the ground once again was firm and solid. Smoke swirled above and around the rock so thickly it was impenetrable.

Several minutes later, from out of the thicket, the rabbit appeared. It sat quietly and calmly. His deep black, colorless eyes were fixed on the sight. The smokiness was clearing and where the brilliant light beam had risen from the rock there was now a solid dark shaft. It was moving in an upward direction, thrusting itself from the ground and rock.

The rabbit continued to wriggle its nose but remained motionless. Another rabbit hopped forward and sat down quietly on its haunches next to him. Through the haze the rabbits watched the rugged, dark shaft take on more distinguishable features. It became thicker at its base. The creaking and grinding noise of wood and rock rubbing together vibrated through the air and ground. The rock itself broke up and tumbled away. When it all stopped, there appeared the unmistaken features of large tree roots entering the ground from the base of a thick trunk. Around the roots lay the broken rock in pieces. The upper portion was still too smoky to reveal any branches.

The rabbit noses stopped wriggling. One put its front paws to the ground, turned and momentarily faced the other. With a jerk, it turned again and scurried off into the woods. Neither did the other bother to stay. It turned away and in two jumps it was also gone.

"Now look at the other page," John said. Josie was stunned. Matt forgot about his growling stomach. Together, he and Josie leaned closer to the screen. The page filled the screen, and Josie easily saw the boldface section title at the top of the page that introduced the topic of the mystery of Griffin Farm. Out loud, she began to read:

> Part of the mystery of Griffin Farm, as it became known to the inhabitants of what was then Moore County, involved an oak tree that had become a landmark. The grand oak stood one hundred three feet in height, and its trunk measured sixteen feet, seven inches around. It had survived two fires, one in 1857 and the other in 1883. In the second fire, all flora within a radius of a quarter mile of the tree was utterly burned to ashes. The fire destroyed the barn, and severely damaged the house.
>
> One night in the spring of 1904 at about 12:30 A.M a severe thunderstorm passed through the county and in its path encountered Griffin Farm. During the storm, an enormously powerful bolt of lightning...

Josie looked up at John, "Remember the storm?"

It had become known by the three as 'The Storm.' That spring there had been a storm so bad that some of the neighbors' houses had been damaged by wind and by trees that had been snapped in two. They had gone up to the boys' bedroom to watch. That view was always fascinating, because it looked out to the south where the rains usually came down like a curtain flowing across the land.

This was an especially powerful storm. The rain pounded against the window, and streaks of lightning splintered across the sky. It was daytime, but it was so dark outside that the room felt like a gloomy cavern, and they were looking out over the world from its mouth.

Then it happened. A giant bolt struck about a mile away, somewhere in the distant woods. It was so powerful and so loud that it lit up the bedroom and literally shook the house.

Josie gulped and looked back to the screen. She continued slowly:

> ...an enormously powerful bolt of lightning struck the tree so loudly that some of the townsfolk from nearby Hampton, a distance of four miles away, reported that they were jolted out of their sleep. One said that he instantly sat upright in bed with both eyes wide open.
>
> The current owners of the farm, Robert and Virginia Malroye...

Josie stopped again. "Isn't that the name of that kid they call Brutus? You know who I'm talking about?" Matt cast a dark look at Josie on hearing Brutus's name.

"Yeah, and guess what? He was at the library this morning reading this very book. He got there before I did."

"Brutus? At the library? Reading this book?" Josie was pointing at the computer screen.

"Yeah. Keep reading."

Josie found her place and resumed:

> The current owners of the farm, Robert and Virginia Malroye, had been visit-

ing family in nearby Cameron and returned home late the following morning. When they arrived, they found the oak split down the middle with each half lying flat on the ground in opposite directions. At the base of the tree, a boulder about five feet in height was resting against the remnants of the oak's roots. Lying on top of the rock were two identical oak leaves, still green, unwhithered, unfaded, and unscratched. The other leaves, whether still attached to the tree or scattered over the earth, had either burned or shriveled.

The two surviving leaves were taken by Mr. Malroye and pressed between glass and locked away in silver cases. It was said that for many years afterward, on the anniversary of that unfortunate night, Mr. and Mrs. Malroye would take the encased leaves from their boxes and, in memory of the grand old oak, set them on the sill of their front window with a burning candle. On one such occasion, the oak tree briefly appeared in its original stately form for a few minutes and then vanished.

Josie had come to the end of the page.

Chapter 3

Once Upon a Starliner

Josie eyed John curiously and said, "Brutus must know something about this from his family history. Why else would he be in the library looking at this?" She was pointing to the screen.

"Yeah, he must know something we don't know," John replied. "But Brutus in a library? I don't get that."

"Maybe he's not stupid like everyone thinks he is." Matt, as usual, had been quietly taking in what his older brother and sister were discussing. This thought just popped into his head and jolted him into saying it out loud.

John thought a moment and then shook his head. "How can that be? He was going through first grade for the second time when we started. I remember first grade. He would just sit there at his desk and daydream. He never knew what was going on."

John suddenly looked disturbed and frowned. Cheerlessly, he continued. "All the kids started making fun of him. Not to his face, but he could tell they didn't like him. Then there was that day the teacher had him go to the blackboard to print out the list of spelling words. He kept getting letters mixed up. I can see where you might mess up words like 'bumblebee' and 'automobile', but how can you mess up 'cat' and 'dog'? Jack Godfrey started laughing. Brutus turned around and screamed at him to shut up. He threw the chalk and just missed his eye. The teacher sent them both to the office. Remember Mr. Briggs? The gorilla with the black, thick framed glasses who always wore a yellow plaid suit and a fire engine red tie?"

John was gravely shaking his head. "Boy-oh-boy! I hate to think what happened in that office. They both came back and looked like they had been threatened with a death sentence."

Josie thought about what John said. "Yeah, I had forgotten about it until now. I remember you talking about it. I was in the other first grade class and never really saw what happened."

She pondered the part about mixing up the letters. "Actually, that sounds like dyslexia. I'll bet that's what his problem was...and might still be. I don't know if it ever goes away."

"What's Dixie Lecksie?" Matt asked.

"Dis-LECKS-see-ah, D-Y-S-L-E-X-I-A," Josie spelled. "It's a problem some people have. When they read words, they get the letters mixed up. They write them that way, too."

"You know," John said, his mood perking up, "I read something about dyslexia just last week; it was in the newspaper. People who have it may seem to be stupid, but they're really smart. They think in pictures instead of words and numbers. But the newspaper said there are ways to learn to read and write just like normal people."

"But why is he so mean?" Matt asked. For Matt, Brutus was about as friendly as a mad dog and a Doberman at that.

"Well, if you were laughed at every day at school, you probably wouldn't be too nice either." Josie said.

"Or maybe he's just mean," John said. "Maybe it's automatic. Maybe deep down inside he is just plain nasty." John thought of a Bible verse that said the heart is deceitful and incurably wicked.

"Yeah, but isn't everyone like that? Why should Brutus be any meaner than the rest of the world? Or why isn't the rest of the world like Brutus?" Josie mulled this over a second or two and then looked at John.

"Not sure. I think everyone *is* like everyone else. Maybe there is no difference, and we're all the same deep down inside, in the heart. It's just that some of us show our true nature more than others."

Matt spoke up. "I know what else makes someone mean and nasty."

"What?" said John and Josie in succession.

"Hunger. H-U-N-G-E-R. I am starving. My stomach is growling. If I don't get some food SOON, you're going to see a mean and nasty little brother."

Matt finished his tomato soup and crackers. John and Josie had none. Josie took Matt's bowl, spoon, and glass and put them in the sink where she had already placed the pan in which she heated the soup.

"Okay Matt," Josie said with an abrupt look, "I fed you, but you have to clean up." She was standing by the sink and facing Matt at the table. She held out a dishcloth for him.

"Can't we use the dishwasher?"

"No! I want the kitchen to be the way we found it. It's just like boys to leave a mess for the women in this house." John and Matt looked at each other as if someone told them a funny joke, but they weren't allowed to laugh.

Matt didn't like to wash dishes by hand; even so, maybe this wouldn't be so bad. There were only a few, and the soap and water were already in the sink. All he had to do was dip the dishes once, maybe twice; swipe them with the dishcloth, and then rinse. It would be as easy as pie. Matt got up, went to the sink, and took the dishcloth from Josie's hand.

"I'll dry," Josie said, and she turned back to the counter where the dish rack stood.

John spoke up. "It'll be an hour at least before Mom gets home, you know. We can be back in time."

Josie whirled around. "Back from where?" The look of disbelief on her face already told John she knew what he meant.

"Look," he said, leaning back in his chair and shoving his cap back a little on his head, "we could be there in twenty minutes. I know a shortcut through the woods. That would give us twenty minutes there and twenty minutes to get back before Mom got home."

Matt was happy to hear the news about his mother getting back. One bowl of tomato soup and a few crackers were no substitute for a big burger. And there was no way he was going to tell his mother he had already eaten. He just hoped his brother and sister wouldn't blab.

"John, just exactly what do you think you'll find..." Josie stopped in mid-sentence. How could she have forgotten that John said he had already been there? Not only that, he said he saw the tree with the ladder, just like the one in the pen and ink drawing.

"John," Josie said quietly but firmly, "I think you're nuts."

"Thank you Josie," John quipped, "that's the nicest thing anyone has said to me all day."

Matt chuckled. Josie turned and looked sharply at him. He immediately thrust his hands back in the dishwater and became as sober-faced as a kid on his way to Mr. Briggs' office.

Josie looked back at John. "It's not funny. Let's assume that everything we've heard or read about this place is true. You could be walking along and...phhhhttt...you're gone." Then, with a really puzzled look, she asked, "Why would you ever go to Griffin Farm in the first place?"

"My bug collection."

"Your bug collection?"

"Yeah. It was about a month before school let out, and everyone was working on their collection. I wanted to find some bugs that were different, so I figured if I go way out in the woods I might find just that...something different. Everyone has bees, wasps, ants, beetles, flies...that's all we have around here. I wanted something that would make the teacher's eyes bug out when they saw it."

Matt chuckled, "Hey that's a good one John; eyes bug out for a bug collection."

Josie ignored Matt. "So you decided to go to Griffin Farm to look for bugs?"

"Not exactly." John shrugged his shoulders. "I just took off and ended up at Griffin Farm. It *is* kind of neat there, you know? You can see the ruins of the house and barn."

"And the tree?"

"Well, sort of..." John was less emphatic about the tree than before.

"John, did you see the tree or not?" Josie stood with her hands on her hips, just like their mother. Matt stopped swirling the dishcloth on the plate and cocked his head in John's direction.

"I saw it, that's for sure. But only on the way into the woods, not on the way back out. I would have stopped to get a closer look, but I still had too much work to do on my collection. There were a lot of vines and brush around. It would have taken too much time." Disappointedly he said, "I really didn't find any special bugs. Just a few that I didn't have yet; some termites and a big yellow garden spider, the size of..."

"John! Hello, anybody there? I get the picture. What about the tree?"

"Oh yeah...right," John said distractedly, his thoughts still on the spider. "Well, when I came back I took a different trail which brought me by the ruins of the barn and house. And that's the puzzling thing about it. The tree that I saw was just like the one in the drawing. But it wasn't where the ruins were. It must have been much deeper in the woods than I thought. A half-mile, maybe even a mile deeper."

"You said you saw it at Griffin Farm. Now you're saying it was about a mile away?" Josie was confused.

"Yeah, well I guess I meant it was near Griffin Farm. When I saw the drawing with the tree between the house and barn, I just kind of put everything together in the same basket."

"Why do you think it's the same tree as in the picture?"

John thought a moment, doubt rising in his mind. "I don't know, I just have this feeling about it. Now that I think about it more, it doesn't make as much sense. But I know somehow there's a connection. And still, it looked exactly like the drawing."

Josie breathed a little easier for the first time during the conversation. To her, it was beginning to look like this was more myth than reality after all. She had an idea that would put an end to it.

"Tell you what. I think this is just a fairy-tale. But to prove it, I'll go with you, and we can see for ourselves."

John's face cracked a big smile as he jumped up to grab his book bag and start for the door.

"BUT..." Josie said loudly. She held up her hand like a traffic cop. "But, not right now, it's too late. Mom will be back soon, and we don't want to get anyone suspicious."

She looked at Matt and in an unnaturally sweet, sing-song voice said "We'll all go to Jackie's Grill and act like everything is normal."

Looking back at John, she finished with her arms crossed, "THEN...when we get back this afternoon, we can go."

"All right!" Matt shot his fist into the air like he just scored a basket. The dishcloth was still in his hand, and water streamed down his arm and onto the floor. Josie groaned. Matt didn't care. His mind was on the burgers, not the adventure they were about to begin.

––––––––––––

The kitchen clock read 3:12 PM when they all got back from Jackie's Grill and an extra unscheduled stop at the food store. Mrs. Eaton was going to be busy that afternoon with the Women's Circle from the church. That was why John had to mow the yard that morning. The Circle was to meet at 4:00 PM.

After giving the three a little work to help her get ready, she told them they could take their bicycles and do whatever they wanted. They just had to be back by 5:30 PM so they could help clean up while she got supper ready.

She never worried about them. The neighborhood was a good one with nearly empty streets. Their friends had bicycles too, and they all would spend hours just riding around. Sometimes they would stay at one of the houses and play games or watch TV. John would call and let their mother know what was going on. And if he hadn't gotten in touch with her, she would call him.

By 3:35 PM they were all three on their bicycles heading down the driveway. They stopped at the end of the lane next to the yellow mailbox. The road was clear, and they went straight across and up the little bank on the other side.

Here, they were at the corner of a ten-acre field that had recently been planted with tobacco. In a few months the tobacco would grow three or four feet high and be ready for picking. The tobacco pickers would start at the bottom of the plant and over a week or two, work their way to the top. The leaves would be placed on tobacco sleds - long flat trailers pulled by trucks - and hauled off to the tobacco barns. In the tobacco barns, they would be cured or dried by heated air. But now, they were small, green leafy plants that lay between deep furrows. Long rows of green dots covered the field.

Running along the edges of the tobacco field was a well-worn trail used by the tobacco workers. The trail ran along the same side as St. Andrews Church Road, but it also turned and ran along the side that was perpendicular to the road. It was this part of the trail that led to the other side of the field where the woods began. It was ideal for bicycles. John was the first to make it to the wood line with Matt and Josie right behind.

They all dismounted and entered the woods single-file. No noticeable trail was present, but the forest was thin. Pushing their bikes through the woods was easy, and soon they came to a trail that ran from left to right. John got back on his bike and headed down the trail to his right. Matt and Josie followed. Another six minutes and they ran directly into the dirt road that led from the silver sign on St. Andrews Church Road down to the Griffin Farm. For obvious reasons it was named 'Old Griffin Farm Road.' To John's surprise, the road looked like it had recently seen traffic. He took a left that put St. Andrews Church Road and the silver sign to their backs. Matt and Josie trailed. Two minutes later, they were at the old farm site and the ruins. Josie and Matt pulled up beside John; Josie on his left and Matt on his right.

They all looked about, left and right, scanning the site for a large, towering oak tree.

"Well, I don't see any oak tree here," Josie said, "not even a little one." She was right. The only trees around were pines.

They could clearly see the ruins. If all the tourist brochures and history books were right, the house and barn had been built on what was left of the solid stone wall foundations right in front of them.

To Josie's surprise, roots and vines didn't overrun the ruins as she had imagined. Instead, the foundation walls had been cleaned up and exposed to show exactly what they must have looked like a hundred-fifty years ago. Just two years earlier, there had been discussion by the city council of restoring the farm as a matter of historical interest, but it was voted down. Instead, the council agreed to clean up and maintain the site as it now stood.

There were several signs posted around the area identifying different features of the farm. John, Josie, and Matt parked their bikes and forgot about the tree as they went from sign to sign. One silver sign stood by what looked like a large, round, flat stone. The stone covered a well that had dried up in 1918. The sign noted that the last bucket of water drawn from that well was on November 11th, the day the armistice was signed which ended World War I. Other signs identified locations for such things as chicken coops, corrals, and a family garden. Except for the signs, no one would have guessed they ever existed.

One sign which John liked read: "Doghouse. In 1828, the

Griffin family inherited a sheep dog, Michelangelo, who had been sent from England. Its enormous doghouse, which had two stories and a balcony, covered 128 square feet. The dog slept here day and night. The farm had no sheep."

Their musings were broken up when they heard the sound of a car backfire as it came down Old Griffin Farm Road. The rumbling sound of the heavy car on a road made of dirt and stone grew louder as it drew nearer. It came into view and pulled in just behind their bicycles. The car, vivid red with gleaming chrome, looked really old and yet, at the same time, it looked really brand new. The glistening grill at the front of the car resembled the nose of an airplane propeller without the blades. John remembered seeing a car like this in one of his Dad's books, *Popular American Antique Cars*. He was pretty sure it was a Studebaker. John didn't know how old it was, but it had to be at least fifty years old.

An elderly gentleman was behind the steering wheel, and an elderly woman sat next to him. He wore a cap, had wire rim spectacles, and was smoking a pipe. The woman wore a white shawl over a dress that was covered with pink flowers. On her head she wore a wide brimmed hat piled high with flowers. John wondered how the hat fit on the lady's head and inside the car at the same time. They both had white hair. It was the whitest hair that John, Josie, or Matt had ever seen. Both the lady and the gentleman were smiling broadly. The old man spoke first.

"Hey there," he said. His voice was high pitched and raspy. "How are yeh young'ns doin' today?"

"We're doing fine, sir," said John. "How are you?" John was polite but Josie could tell he wasn't sure what to make of this oddly dressed, elderly couple showing up in an antique.

"Oh, we're fine, we're fine, Amy 'n me." The woman nodded her head and smiled even wider revealing beautiful pearly-white teeth. The elderly man continued. "Tain't this place somethin', a genuine piece of hist'ry for these here parts, yeh know." He cleared his throat uneasily and continued in a more serious tone, "So, yer kids interested in hist'ry, eh?" His smile remained fixed.

John caught a glance of Josie and Matt who looked like they were witnessing man's first encounter with Martians. He responded hesitantly.

"Just a little, sir. We live just down the road and thought we'd come and take a look and see for ourselves." The man glanced at his wife and looked back. His smile faded just slightly. John noticed it. He decided he should keep talking.

"Well, sir, we've heard about this place for years, and we've never really seen it. Up close I mean. School's let out, and we didn't have much else to do. We have to be back home soon to help our Mom clean up from a get-together. She and some of her friends from church are meeting at our house." John finished on an upbeat note.

"Well," the man interrupted, "you'nes must be interested in at least a little hist'ry, ain't yeh?" The tone of his voice said he was eager to hear John answer in the affirmative.

Josie jumped in. "Excuse us sir, but we really DO have to leave now."

The old man held up his hand, "Whoa there. Now...jus' hold on ther missy. I kin see your spishus of us. You'nes don't need to be afraid of us." He was shaking his head, "We're interested in hist'ry too, ain' that right Amy?"

The lady leaned toward the driver's side to look more directly out the window. "Oh yes," she said, smile gone and wide-eyed, "You'nes don't need to be afeard of us. We're interested in hist'ry right earnest like. Why we drop in here...I mean...drive this way most chances we git."

The old man gave the woman a stern look, but he quickly recovered and broke into an even larger smile. "Amy means we come here as often as we can, which ain't too often seein'...uh..." the old man fumbled for words "...seein' how's our car is so old 'n all."

"Old?" John said. "Sir, your car looks like a pristine classic. It looks like you went back to the Fifties and drove it into the twenty-first century right out of the showroom. This car must be at least fifty years old. Nobody drives these anymore."

The woman turned to her husband and said, "Amos! Didn' I say not to git this'n. That's jus' what I said, and you wouldn't listen."

The man brought the forefinger of his right hand up to his mouth and made a loud "SSSSHHHHHHH." The elderly woman sat back, arms crossed, and eyes straight ahead piercing the windshield. He slowly looked back at John with a very nervous smile.

"Sorry...pardon the missus. It's jus' somethin' about this place that makes us both...well...a little edgy. Let's jus' say we're not quite our ol' selfs 'round here."

The old man's wife sounded off with a hefty, "Hmmph." Amos ignored her.

"Sonny," he began with a certain resignation in his voice, "Amy and me must be goin' now, but if you'nes really wants hist'ry, yer got ter look fer it a lot deeper than here."

The elderly gentleman gestured with his pipe as if to mean he was talking about a place beyond the ruins of Griffin Farm and deeper into the woods. John looked in the direction he gestured, and it was farther to the west. It was the same direction he came from when he was heading home from his bug hunt.

The gentleman started to roll up his window. Just before it closed up, he looked at John and winked, "Air condishinun. Comes extra," he whispered. He grinned like he was the only one that had it.

The woman knocked him hard on the arm and said, "Amos! I heard that. You know better..." The old man quickly lost his smile. Just before the window closed tight John could hear him say "All right, all right, I'm mindin'."

The old gentleman gunned the gas. The engine roared and

the wheels spun furiously, kicking up dirt and stone momentarily before they took hold. The driver turned the wheel hard to the right, and the car kicked up a rooster's tail as he did a one-eighty and sped back onto Old Griffin Farm Road and out of sight. A second or two later they heard the car back-fire followed by a loud boom like thunder.

They all looked at each other and started running to see what happened. When they got to the road the only thing they saw was a small mushroom cloud of blue smoke and no car in sight.

"Now that was weird," Josie said. "I'll bet that's not in Montgomery's history."

John didn't know what to say. The only words he could get out were, "Air conditioning?"

Josie looked at John, confused. "What did you say?" Matt was wondering what he was talking about, too.

John looked at them both, "Just as he was closing the window, the old man whispered that he had air conditioning."

"So, what's so amazing about that?" Matt asked.

"That was probably a 1950 Studebaker Starliner." John said. "Nobody had air conditioning in 1950...at least I don't think so." Then John thought out loud, "So that's why he winked and grinned. He probably is the only one with air conditioning where he comes from."

"Okay. I'm done," Josie said. "I don't want to hang around here anymore."

John wasn't listening. "What do you think he meant when he said we have to look deeper?" he asked pensively.

"Who cares? I don't want to find out. I want to go home...now!"

Matt didn't say anything, but he looked like he wanted to go home too.

"Look," John said as if coming out of a trance, "I'm not sure what that was all about. But we still haven't proven anything about the tree."

"Yes we have." Matt ran over to a silver sign that briefly related the legend of the old oak tree. "This is where the tree must have been. And if that's so then there's really no more tree."

Josie agreed. "You know that anybody who knows anything about this says the tree was destroyed by a lightning bolt."

"Okay," John said, "then what did I see? Look, the old man pointed in that direction when he said we would have to look deeper. I think he means we have to go deeper into the woods. And that's the direction I came from when I was on my way back from the bug hunt."

"But how do you know you came from that way?" Josie objected.

"There's another trail that picks up on the other side of these ruins. That's the one I came back on. If you want to be absolutely certain, I say we go down that trail and see for ourselves. We could be there in just a few minutes. If the tree's there we'll see it easy. If it's not, we turn around, and I won't say anything more about it...ever."

Josie moaned, "I know I'll regret this, but if you promise with a cross-your-heart-and-hope-to-die sort of thing, we can go. How about you, Matt?"

Matt didn't want to go but neither did he want to sound like a fraidy-cat. "Well...Okay. But make him say it first."

John raised his right hand and made the cross-your-heart vow.

John had found the trail on the other side of the site, and they were moving along quickly. After about three minutes, the ground became so sandy it was almost impossible to pedal their bikes, and they could only trudge along. They dismounted and after another five minutes, came to an intersection of trails. John stopped. Sweat ran down the side of his face.

"What's the matter?" Josie asked.

"I'm trying to remember which way I came from. I think it was from the right, but I'm not sure."

"You mean you don't even know if this is the way you came back?"

John started to answer, but Matt yelled, "Look!" and pointed down the trail to the right. Almost out of sight but still recognizable was a bicycle parked on its kickstand.

"Are you kidding me?" said John. "Who else would be down here?"

They all turned their bikes and headed down the trail toward the abandoned bike. It took a minute before they reached it, but John recognized it before they got there.

"I know whose bike this is."

"Whose?"

"Malroye's," John said with conviction.

"What?" Matt and Josie said in unison.

"How do you know?"

"It's Brutus's bike for sure. I saw it this morning at the library. He took his bicycle to the library, and I parked right beside it when I got there. When I came out, it was gone. Brutus took his bicycle when he left."

"That means only one thing," Matt said in a squeaky, frantic voice, "He's around here somewhere, and he'll probably punch us all out!" They all quickly ducked down pulling their bicycles with them. "We better get out of here fast," Matt whispered as quietly as he could.

"No, no," John whispered back, "let's just listen to see if we can hear anything."

They listened. A dead tree branch fell to the ground not very far away and made them jump. Recovering, they became as motionless as three statues. A squirrel took no notice when it jumped out of a tree just behind them. Matt let out a yelp, but Josie quickly covered his mouth.

Many seconds passed and nothing that sounded like a human was heard. John got up. "I don't think he's here."

Josie got up, too. "He has to be around somewhere. He wouldn't leave his bike alone."

Matt decided to stay down.

"Look!" John yelled without warning.

Matt squealed again, "I knew it! I knew he'd find us!"

"Hush, Matt," John said, "it's not Brutus. Look over there."

Matt looked up at John who was pointing. He didn't look scared at all. He looked humorously stunned as if he just witnessed someone dive off the roof of a ten-story building into a glass of water. Matt got up and looked in the direction John was pointing.

On the right side of the trail there was a lot of thick brush mixed with vines and trees. Between the trees and beyond the brush, Matt could see something that looked like a tree - an extremely huge tree. In their excitement over the bicycle, they missed it when they first rode up. But now it was as plain as day. It towered high into the air, firmly rooted to the ground by its thick, dark, rigid, immobile trunk.

"Is that the tree you saw?" Josie asked.

"No," John said, "this one's bigger - way bigger."

John took another look around. "Yeah, I think this is where I saw the tree. It was just about the same spot."

"So what do we do now," Josie asked. "We've found the tree. So let's go home."

"Yeah, I still think Brutus is around." Matt moved closer to Josie, siding with her. John got the picture.

"Hey, not so fast everybody," he said. "We see a tree, but we don't know if it's THE tree."

"Aw come on, John, give it up," Josie moaned. "How are we going to tell if it's THE tree?"

"First we have to get a closer look."

"And then..."

"If it's the tree we're looking for it will have the rungs of a ladder on the trunk."

"How are we going to get to it?"

John didn't have an answer to that one. He turned about to get another look at the tree. Then suddenly, "There!"

Matt clasped Josie's arm and made her jump. "Now what?" he asked, almost whimpering. "Is it Brutus?"

Josie jerked her arm loose from Matt's hand. That little scare didn't help her mood.

"Right there," John said, pointing at a clump of bushes and trees just off the trail. "We will have to do it the same way Brutus did it. He left his bicycle here because he must have seen it too, and the only way to get there is through all that brush."

"I'm not going through the brush," Josie objected sternly.

"Then I'll go first. It looks like this is where Brutus must have started anyhow."

John had walked over to a place where branches had been bent back and broken, and where the vines were pushed out of the way. He stepped forward and began to follow the path Brutus forged. After a little while, Josie and Matt could only hear him but not see him. Another short while and John gave out a yelp muffled by the intervening brush as he fell into Old Oak Road, just as Brutus had done.

Josie yelled, "John, what happened? Are you okay?"

"I'm okay," he called back, "but you really need to see this."

Josie closed her eyes and shook her head. With no enthusiasm whatsoever she shouted, "I'm coming."

Matt couldn't believe his sister was leaving and fell in line right behind her. They made their way through more easily than John because a path by now had been cleared of the toughest obstacles. When they came to the edge of the bank that was part of Old Oak Road, John was waiting and helped them down. When they settled down and had a chance to get a good look, they couldn't believe their eyes. Because the area was much clearer on the far side of the road, they saw 'THE' tree, and it was even bigger than they imagined.

"What's all that smoke?" Matt asked.

"Don't know," said John curiously, "Looks like smoke or fog or something."

The air around the upper branches of the tree was heavy as the smoke wrapped it in thick, patchy blankets. And there, on the right side of the trunk, were clearly the rungs of a ladder that was somehow attached to the tree. Josie counted them. There were sixteen.

Before anyone could say anything more, John started off to the far bank and the tree. Josie had no choice. She knew she wasn't going to change John's mind. She followed and Matt was right behind her. They were soon all three standing under the tree.

At the base of the tree, thick roots ran deep into the ground. All around the roots were shattered pieces of rock, large and small. When they looked up into the tree, the branches were so thick and numerous that they could see no farther than the lowest limbs.

John walked over and stood next to the trunk where the rungs were. They were rusty looking, but not rusty feeling. They were shaped like large staples. The staple-rungs were hammered into the tree trunk. It wasn't easy to tell how deeply they were embedded, but they were solid. John belted one with his fist, and it didn't budge. Welded to the outer sides of the rungs was a long continuous bar of iron. The iron bar not only gave stability to the ladder, but also functioned as a railing so that it could be gripped to steady anyone who ventured to climb the ladder. John couldn't tell how far the ladder continued up into the tree. It just disappeared into the branches.

John looked back down at the base of the trunk. Among the shattered rock there was a small odd-looking shovel. He picked it up and looked at it inquisitively.

A flash of light as from a mirror caught Josie's attention. There was something on the ground, like polished metal, only a few yards from the tree. She went over to it.

"Hey guys, look at this," Josie said, holding up something that looked like glass. John and Matt scampered over to see what she had. It looked like a picture of a leaf except the leaf was real.

"Here's another one," said Matt excitedly. He stooped to pick up another framed leaf. John came over and held it up so he could get a better look.

"This looks just like the other one," he said. "Josie, let me look at the one you have." Josie handed it to him, and John lifted them both up and held them side by side. The two leaves were identical, and they looked fresh as if they had just been plucked from the tree.

"Hey, what's that over there?"

John looked in the direction where Josie was pointing. It was toward the ground near the base of the tree among the splintered rock. He could see some silvery objects near another greenish and roundish object, but he couldn't tell what they were. He hurried over to get a better look.

He recognized the green thing as a plastic canteen. But the silvery objects seemed so out of place, especially as they glistened, lying on the dirt in the middle of the woods.

"Looks like something flat," he said, "like metal tins; maybe aluminum."

John suddenly stooped down.

"Look!" he said excitedly, "there's something written on the outside." He handed Josie the encased leaves and picked up the silvery-looking boxes. He read out loud the engraved inscriptions on the covers and from them made the connection between Brutus and his family's past.

John stood up. "So," he said aloud, "Brutus's great, great, great, great grandparents must be the ones we read about. His family once owned the farm. And these are the leaves they found."

He traded Josie the silvery boxes for the leaves and held them side by side again. "Look at them; they're still green and fresh looking, just like the book said."

"So where's Brutus?" Josie asked.

"Maybe he's up in the tree," Matt said quickly.

Matt had forgotten about Brutus, but Josie's mention of him brought back the dread of his showing up. He shot his head back and looked up into the tree. There was no sign of him...yet.

"You think he climbed the ladder?" Josie asked, but then added wonderingly, "Wouldn't he know we're here? Why hasn't he come back down?" For the moment, Josie was more puzzled than fearful that Brutus might suddenly catch them.

"I don't know where he is," John said, "but I don't think he's around here. He would have been back by now, unless he's gotten himself lost." John was eyeing the ladder as he spoke. He walked over to it and with fascination looked up into the tree. Its branches were thick and dark. Not a single ray of light penetrated them.

John's cell phone started ringing to the tune of Beethoven's Ninth Symphony. He had forgotten to call their mother.

"Hello, this is John."

"John, this is Mom. Isn't it about time you kids should be thinking about coming home? The ladies are leaving, and I'll need some help to clean up. What are you doing? Riding your bikes?"

"Uh...yeah, we're riding our bikes. We're almost ready to come back. We might be a few minutes late."

"Well don't be too late. Your father will be home soon, and you know he doesn't like supper to be late. Everybody okay?"

"Yeah Mom, we're doing fine. We'll be home...soon. We're just about done."

"What are you doing?"

John didn't want to say, but neither did he want to lie.

"Well...actually we rode our bikes out to the woods, and we found this tree that looks like it might be pretty neat to climb. I was going to try it. It won't take long. We'll be heading back soon."

"Well, all right, but don't be long. And be careful, hear me?"

Mrs. Eaton was long past the stage of worrying about her kids falling out of trees. The tree climbing was not anything new. They had gone tree climbing many times before. And

John always kept his word when he said they would be home.

"I will Mom...love you, bye."

"Love you too, bye."

Turning to Josie and Matt, John said, "Okay, Mom just called, and we'll have to head back soon. I told her I was going to climb the tree and as soon as I'm done we'll leave."

Matt was glad to hear that. The sooner they left the sooner they would be out of danger of meeting up with Brutus. Josie wanted to leave right away.

"I think we should go now," she grumbled. "I don't like the looks of that tree. It's so dark up there. I've never seen a tree where you can't see some daylight through it. It's not natural."

"Not natural? Are you kidding me? What's more natural than a tree?" John lamely argued. He knew what Josie meant, but he didn't want her to give up so soon.

Josie wasn't buying it.

"Look," John pleaded, "Just let me get my feet on those branches." He was pointing upward. "I really want to see this before we head back. No further, I promise."

Josie relented. How long could it take to climb a ladder anyhow? Let John satisfy his curiosity and then they could get out of there.

John stepped on to the lowest rung and slowly began to climb. Josie and Matt watched in silence, holding their breath as he got closer.

Fifteen feet does not seem very far when looking up into a tree from the bottom of the trunk. Looking down from fifteen feet with no branches below you is quite a different matter. John was very uneasy as he stretched out to touch the lowest and nearest branch. When his fingers contacted it, he could tell that the branch was firm and steady. It had a nice grip, too. It was easy to hold onto. This gave John a little more courage to go on. Using the ladder and the branches, he pulled himself up higher into the tree.

He looked down at his feet. They were now even with the branches. Matt and Josie were craning their necks as they kept their eyes glued on John. They saw him take the final step upward and, except for his foot on the bottom branch, he completely disappeared.

"Okay," John's voice sounded from somewhere just overhead, "I made it, I'm coming back down."

John was about to take his first step downward when he looked up and saw something absolutely absurd. About ten feet above him and to his right, sitting on the branches as if they were made for it, was a tree house. And what a tree house! This one looked like a miniature cabin. It had a porch and door and above the doorway was an upper porch or balcony with its own doorway. At the very top, where the two sides of the roof met at the angle, was a sign. On it read, *Michelangelo*. It was the doghouse - the one he read about back at the ruins.

Even more peculiar than the doghouse itself was the reason why he could see all this clearly. There were two brightly burning lanterns that hung by silver ropes from nearby overhead branches, just opposite the porches. John had to let his brother and sister know.

"Josie! Matt! There's a doghouse up here!"

Josie looked at Matt uncomprehendingly. "Are you kidding me? Did he say a doghouse? In the tree?" The idea of a doghouse in a tree was so ridiculous it started to make Josie giggle. Matt grimaced in such a way as to suggest he thought John was losing his marbles.

"John, what did you say?" Josie called out chuckling uneasily. "I didn't hear what you said."

John's foot was no longer on the branch.

Very loudly, while enunciating each word, John bellowed, "THERE - IS - A - HUGE - DOGHOUSE - IN - THE - TREE." Then quickly, "It's Michelangelo's doghouse."

Matt didn't hear the 'Michelangelo' part. He stopped listening when he heard the word 'doghouse.' But Josie heard it all. She lost her laugh. Michelangelo? The Italian painter, sculptor, and architect? He had a dog, and the doghouse was in the tree?

"John, what are you talking about? Quit fooling around. That isn't funny. You need to come down now, Mom's waiting. We need to get back home."

John forgot about going back the moment he saw the doghouse. During Josie's admonishments, he had been inching his way toward it, and now he was just in front of it straddling the main branch that supported it. He could see into the door quite well. On a floor that was carpeted by a beautiful, red rug lay a hairy sheep dog, snoozing soundly.

John pulled himself up to the doorway and stuck his head through. The inside was empty. The walls, which were barren, had no windows. There was no furniture or doggy items such as a food dish or water bowl. There wasn't even a chew-toy. There was nothing inside except for the rug and Michelangelo. With some effort John pulled himself into the doghouse and stood up...barely. There was only an inch between his head and the ceiling. Except for the soft glow of the hanging lanterns, the room was rather dark. On the far side of the rug there was another door, slightly ajar. A glimmer high-lighted its open edge. John tiptoed past the dog softly, the rug dampening his footsteps. He nestled up against the door.

"John, come down right now! We have to get going!" Josie's voice sounded farther away, but it was clearly agitated and worried.

John couldn't answer for fear of waking the dog. He reached out and grabbed the door handle. With just a little push, the door slowly swung outward. As it did so, John's eyes grew wide.

Hovering in mid-space against the backdrop of a brilliant Milky Way Galaxy was the Studebaker and the elderly gentle-man and his wife in the front seat. The windows were down, and small puffy clouds of tobacco smoke lazily floated out into space.

The old man stuck his hand out the window and waved. "Hey there, sonny. It's 'bout time yeh got here. Amy an' me's bin waitin fer yeh most of an hour." John could see Amy's outline against the bright galaxy in the back window. She was waving at him. He feebly waved back.

The old man pulled his hand back in and seemed to fumble with something along the dash. A moment later, the engine turned over, and the car was idling like a well tuned motor. The gentleman put the car in gear and drove it up to the back door like a taxi does to pick up riders. He leaned out the window, patted the car gently, and said, "'Taint called a Starliner fer nothin'."

Chapter 4

Eskathoer

Inside the doghouse, Michelangelo stirred. John went back to the door and poked his head in. Until now, he had paid little attention to the dog. He knew only that it was an Old English Sheep Dog, the shaggy kind, with hair covering everything, including its eyes. As it lay in the flickering glow of the lanterns hanging in the tree, he could see that the tail wasn't docked, or shortened, which was unusual for an English Sheep Dog. What most impressed John was how really big the dog was. John stepped in to get a closer look.

Michelangelo was too lazy to wag his tail or move his head. He just lifted his ear to get a better reading on where the sound came from. John remained still and Michelangelo's ear flopped back down. John began to think the dog had gone back to sleep when the branch underneath the doghouse creaked loudly. Michelangelo jerked his head up and looked straight at John. The moment it saw someone standing in the doorway, it started flopping its tail up and down in a pleasant way.

"Okay," thought John, "He's wagging his tail. So, maybe he's friendly." Michelangelo rolled onto his belly and stood up. He yawned, stretched his front legs, and then his back legs. He walked over to John. The withers came up to John's waist. The dog's hairy face looked up at John, his pink tongue protruding through the wooly stuff in quick panting breaths. It was impossible to imagine how the dog saw anything. Michelangelo nudged his head under John's hand; it wanted John to pet it. John relaxed; the dog was big, but he was also friendly.

By now, Josie was downright frantic.

"JOHN!" she yelled shrilly, "QUIT FOOLING AROUND AND COME DOWN RIGHT NOW!"

She looked at Matt helplessly, her mind in a fluster. Frightening questions with equally frightening answers bombarded her brain.

"*What's going on up there; why doesn't he answer?*"

A little voice inside her head answered, "*The tree has him Josie; you were right about it. It's not a natural tree. It's swallowed him. He should have listened to you.*"

Josie shook herself. "*Stop that,*" she thought. "*Trees just don't swallow people. But why doesn't he answer...*"

"JOHN! COME ON! THIS ISN'T FUNNY ANYMORE. MOM'S WAITING. WE HAVE TO GO HOME...NOW!" From somewhere not far up in the tree a thunderous dog's bark echoed down.

"GGRRROOOFF! GGRRROOOFF!"

Josie froze. Matt was certain the ground underneath him shook. He wanted to run, but he couldn't make his legs move. A soft thunk just overhead made them look up. John's foot protruded from the leaves and branches and was resting on the topmost rung of the ladder. Matt and Josie ran over and, huddling together, peered up into the mysterious branches. The lower part of John's body came into view as he stepped down the first few rungs. He stopped, paused a moment, and then shouted, "Stay Michelangelo, stay!" A few more steps downward and his upper body came into view. He seemed okay. He looked down, and they could see his face. He was grinning.

"What was that?" Josie's voice was high-pitched and squeaky.

"Sssshhhhh!" John warned with his finger to his mouth, "That's Michelangelo. He's sitting at the door. I don't want him to try and come down, or he might fall out of the tree and get hurt."

Michelangelo barked again.

John hollered back up, "Stay boy, stay!"

He made his way down the ladder to the next-to-last rung,

jumped off, and landed right in front of Josie and Matt. He was still grinning. Somehow he had climbed down while holding in his hand three large golden envelopes that the old man had given him. He handed one to Josie and one to Matt. He kept the third.

Written lavishly on the front of each envelope, in large swirling script, was their name. In the upper left corner, in the same but smaller script, there were printed the words, ***"From the Office Of Lord Bigsley."*** Just below this was an embossed stamp bearing the image of two lions standing upright but facing opposite directions with their backs to each other.

John turned his envelope over and found it sealed with a large green and yellow stamp that had the same embossed image. John opened his envelope and took out a pastel yellow sheet of paper that was folded lengthwise in thirds. He unfolded it to reveal that, except for the signature which was written in bold strokes with a fountain pen and black ink, the letter was printed like a typewriter. He read the letter to himself:

> Mr. John Michael Eaton
> 1854 St. Andrews Church Road
> Hampton, NC
> USA, Planet Earth
>
> Dear Sir,
>
> A matter of urgency whose nature I cannot reveal at this time has compelled me to send you this letter. The matter of which I write is beyond my expertise and warrants the solicitation of help outside my jurisdiction. I have appealed to my superior who has granted me permission to seek such help as I deem necessary. Af-

ter consulting my advisors, I have decided to follow their recommendations. Therefore, I appeal to you and your sister and brother to allow the old gentleman and his wife, whom I presume you have already met, to bring you to me at great haste. These elderly folk are my long-time loyal servants and faithful friends whom you can trust completely. I assure you, your trip will be swift and pleasant and you will return to your planet in time to meet any obligations that you have hitherto committed yourself.

The same appeal is made to your sister and brother in the letters that they have received. However, I have required them to allow you to make the final decision, not only on this but also on all other critical issues that may arise should you respond to my request in the affirmative.

I implore you again to make haste and come to my aid.

Sincerely,

Winston Charles Bigsley

Lord Winston Charles Bigsley
Royal Governor of Brandenhelm Province
Cynthoeria, Planet Eskathoer[1]

Josie had finished her letter and Matt was still reading when

[1] Properly pronounced Ehs-kah-**theer**, but many native Eskathoerians like to pronounce it Ehs-kah-**thohr**.

John looked up from his. When Matt finished John said, "Well, what do you think? According to this we'll still make it home by supper."

Josie just shook her head in disbelief.

"Where did you get these letters?"

"Up there," John said, pointing to the tree. "They have given us ten minutes to decide. Otherwise, they've been given strict instructions to leave."

"And, who are *they*?"

"The old man and woman we saw back at the ruins in the Studebaker."

"They're in the tree?" Josie asked incredulously.

"Well, not exactly. I mean you do have to climb the ladder and go up into the tree to meet them. But when you see them, they're sort of...well...it's hard to explain. You really have to see it for yourself."

At that moment a car horn sounded from somewhere up in the tree. Josie and Matt bolted. They clung to each other, wide-eyed, looking up at the tree as though something horrible might fall out right on top of them.

"Now do you believe me?" John said with a good dose of smugness. "That's the first honk. We have five minutes." Josie had an arm around Matt's neck and was squeezing a little too uncomfortably.

"Wait a minute, John," Josie said with an unsteady voice and a sideways glance, "you mean there really *is* a car in the tree?" Josie's arm involuntarily squeezed a little tighter.

"Yes, the Starliner...and don't forget the doghouse."

"I don't believe this!" Josie shouted. She released Matt who was starting to feel faint. "That is ridiculous! How did it get up there, drive up the ladder?" Josie scorned, using her hand to mimic a car zooming up the side of the tree.

"Well, I don't think so," said John. "It's up there where the branches are and all, but it's not really *in* the tree."

Josie was too flustered to say anything at this point. She looked like she wanted to speak, but the words just seemed to catch in her throat.

"Look," John continued, "we haven't got much time. We have to decide now."

"Aren't you supposed to decide?" Matt asked, rubbing the back of his neck.

"Yeah," Josie blurted, and then reproachfully added, "the letter says we have to let *you* make all the decisions."

"That's not quite accurate," John said. "The letters say I am to make the final decision in this and all other 'critical' issues. But I'm not going to go unless you two come with me. We're in this together."

Josie looked at Matt, unconvinced of any of this.

"Okay," John said, "I know this whole thing sounds way out there, but have I ever lied to you? Ever?"

Josie and Matt honestly could not think of a time that John had ever lied to them about anything. In fact John was painfully honest. When John was younger, even if it meant a spanking, he would tell the truth.

"But I just don't get it," Josie lamented, "how can there be a car, a dog, and a doghouse in the tree."

Josie eyed the tree again with absolute distrust. It looked ominous, as if it could come to life like a monster and pluck them from the ground and gobble them up.

Matt, having gotten his air back, spoke up and surprisingly said, "As crazy as it sounds, I'd like to see what's up there. If it's really nothing, we can come back down. But if we *do* find something in the tree...Whoa!...Can you imagine what the kids at school would think when we tell 'em about a doghouse and a car in a tree?"

"Yeah," Josie snipped, "I'll bet I can imagine. They'd think we're nuts, and they'd be right."

"I want to see what's up there," Matt said firmly having completely forgotten about Brutus.

Josie shook her head, flustered and anxious. Matt was the last person she expected to side with John, especially on something as foolhardy as this. She was weak and had the same sickening feeling in her belly as on one of those rare mornings during school when she woke up and knew she had to face a test that day; not the little quiz with just a few multiple choice answers, but the monster one that had what seemed like a thousand essay questions. On those days, she didn't want to get out of bed, but she knew she would have to sooner or later because there was no way she'd get out of having to take the dreaded test.

She wanted to turn around and go home, but she knew that was going to be impossible. Two against one. She was facing the choice between being branded as a fraidy-cat or doing something that at this point in her life was the last thing she wanted to do. She'd rather face the monster test. But she knew she'd have to give in. Josie bucked up, put on a brave face, and looked at the whole thing philosophically.

"Well," she said, "This is really, really, REALLY crazy." She paused, mustering the nerve to keep going. "But it seems like every crazy thing John has done has somehow turned out to be pretty cool."

Then very reluctantly, she gave in. "Okay, I'll go up the tree." Frowning darkly, she warned, "But if this is a joke John Michael Eaton, you'll pay for this."

She turned on Matt and pointed her finger right at his nose, "You too, if you're in on it."

"Honest Josie," Matt said pleadingly, "I'm not in on anything. Let's just go before it's too late."

With a heave Josie said, "All right...let's go."

John hollered up into the tree, "We're coming! Don't leave yet!"

Two short honks of the horn told them that the elderly gentleman in the Studebaker heard them and would wait.

John took their letters and put them in his book bag. Then he led them up the ladder and into the tree. Josie stopped suddenly when she thrust herself up through the lower branches and saw the doghouse. It was palely lit under the lanterns and overwhelmingly uncanny. She couldn't believe her eyes. The house seemed to sit gingerly on the forked limbs of a thick branch that John was now straddling as he was inching his way toward it.

"What's the matter?" Matt called out from behind, his feet still on the ladder. Josie didn't answer.

"Come on, Josie! Don't stop!" Matt commanded as he patted her legs to keep moving. Josie must have heard him because she began to move again. Matt followed quickly. When he poked his head through the branches, he too saw the doghouse. He would have stopped to gaze, but Josie was now a good bit ahead of him, straddling and crawling along the branch. Matt didn't want to be left behind, so he pulled himself up and began to crawl, his knees pressed against the sides of the branch.

They made their way to the edge of the house, near the front door where Michelangelo was still sitting and panting. As John reached out to pull himself onto the porch, Michelangelo barked again, sat up, turned around, and went back into his house.

When they had dragged themselves onto the porch, John stepped inside the house while Josie and Matt simply stood at the opening and peered in. They saw the red rug, but there was no Michelangelo. The back door was open and a soft glow shone through the doorway giving the room an air of a city apartment dimly lit by a street corner lamp at midnight.

As dusky as it was, Josie was still dazzled by the rug's beauty. It seemed to have a radiance of its own. It was the purest, deepest, most splendid red she had ever seen. John turned and motioned for them to hurry. They walked straight across the rug and right through the back door onto another porch. There was no rail around it and no visible steps. It simply jutted out into black space.

The first thing that caught Matt and Josie's eyes was the vivid spiral galaxy as it continued its silent, lazy spin against the black heavens. Parked next to the porch was the Studebaker Starliner. Inside, the old man and woman were sitting in the front seat with the same broad smile they had when they first appeared at the ruins.

Michelangelo was also on the porch, but he was pawing at the back part of the car near the bumper. The old gentleman reached down somewhere below the dash board and pushed a button. Immediately, the trunk popped and slowly opened. Michelangelo hopped in.

"Do yeh mind closin' the trunk fer me?" said the elderly man who was still behind the steering wheel. He was addressing Matt. "Michael won't mind. He's jus' goin' to sleep till we git back."

Around and below the car was emptiness and blackness that fell away into nothing. It was like looking into a deep, cold well. It made Matt shiver to think of it. He moved stiffly with short, shuffling steps to the rear of the car and the open trunk. He carefully peered in. Michelangelo was sprawled out on his right side with nothing moving except the slow rhythm of his chest inhaling and exhaling. He was fast asleep. Matt stood as far from the car as possible while he brought the trunk slowly down and, as quietly as he could, pushed it shut until he heard the latch click. He paused to listen for Michelangelo stirring. Not a sound. Then he moved back to where John and Josie were standing.

"Well, you'nes goin' to stand there an' gawk or are yeh comin' along," the old man said with a chuckle. "An' before we git started let's introduce ourselfs proper. I'm Amos Buckwalter an' this here's Amy, my wife."

Amy nodded still smiling. "Oh, we're so glad you'nes decided to come. It's bin such a long, long time since we'nes had a chance to talk to someone like you'nes. Please. You'nes just git on in the back there an' make yerselfs comfy."

John opened the back door and poked his head in. He was astonished. The inside was big and roomy, with soft plush seats that sunk way down under the weight of his hand. He took off his backpack and laid it on the seat. Then he climbed in, scooting it across the seat as he went. Josie, whose spirits had improved a little, followed.

Matt was hesitant. It seemed to him that maybe his weight would be too much and the car would simply sink into the blackness. Gingerly, he stepped onto the floor board and allowed his weight to settle. The car stood firm. He pulled his foot back.

"Come on, Matt," Josie said, "I did it, you can too." She extended her hand to help him in.

Very cautiously, Matt took it, and in an instant Josie yanked him in. Matt let out a yelp and crouched on the seat, afraid he might slide back out and fall into the deep. Josie got up and reached over him to pull the door shut.

Once inside, Matt moved to the center between Josie and John where he felt a little safer. The three clustered together in the middle. John put the backpack on the floor.

"Excuse me, sir..."

"Amos. Please call me Amos," said the old man, looking at John through the rear view mirror which was about six inches high and two feet wide.

"Excuse me Amos, but are there seat belts?"

"Seat belts! Why yeh know that these ol' cars didn't have seat belts. 'Sides, this here's a smooth ride. Never stops too fast an' never starts too fast."

John wasn't so sure about that. He remembered the Studebaker's rooster tail back at the Griffin Farm site.

The gear stick was on the steering column. Amos moved it into first gear, let out the clutch, and floored it. The tires squealed while spinning on nothing.

"Sound effects. Had 'em installed last week," Amos said, barely concealing his enthusiasm.

The car backfired and lunged forward. Then there was a loud boom like thunder. The next thing John saw were the stars flying by like road signs at a hundred miles an hour.

The three couldn't see very well over the front seat. Amos with his cap and pipe, and Amy with her broad rimmed hat stacked with flowers, were like moving silhouettes. On the windshield John could see the reflection of many colored dash lights: reds, blues, yellows, oranges...way too many lights for any car he ever saw. He reckoned this was not like the Studebaker pictured in his Dad's book.

Amos and Amy talked about everything. In fact, they did all the talking. Amy especially. She would ask a question and before the three in the back seat had time to think of an answer she was off on another subject. Only twice did Matt or Josie get one or two sentences in. Even then, they were not sure if Amy heard them. She always started on something else before they finished.

Amy talked about everything: cherry pies (made from red, green, yellow and white cherries), the latest deodorant (Marlboro's Polar Air), her favorite brand of bread (Sherman's cracked packa peas and peanut bread), the best way to catch greenchniks (whatever they were, she never bothered to explain), and many other things.

After about twenty minutes, the one-sided conversation slowed down, and John had a chance to look around. He was in absolute awe. Out of the front window, between Amos and Amy, the galaxy that hung in space like a picture on a wall when viewed from the back porch of the doghouse, now loomed ahead. It was so much larger. In fact, it covered the entire breadth of the windshield and was getting visibly bigger by the minute.

Another five minutes went by and everything to the front and sides of the car was shimmering with the white dots of billions and billions of stars. This continued for another three minutes when the star-specks began to thin out. Not long after that the black sky began to resemble a very starry night on Earth. But here the stars were big and vivid and perfectly round, like ping pong balls. And there were at least three, maybe four times as many. John realized now how ordinary even the most clear starry night on Earth really was.

After a few more minutes in which there was little conversation, Amos spoke. "We're gittin closer. We'll be there in 'bout another ten minits."

Then he pointed out Amy's window.

"See that big bluish white star a'yonder?"

John answered in the affirmative.

"See that reddish spot next to it, on th' right?"

Again John answered, "Yes."

"That's my ol' stompin' grounds. Lived there a long time. But I was a restless soul. Needed adventure 'n all - you know, somethin' challengin'...like travelin'." Amy cast Amos a cautious look. He cleared his throat and began again.

"Well...yeah...right. Anyway, Amy and me met on Eskathoer and got hitched. The gov'nor, before he was the gov that is, was kinda what you'nes like to call the best man. We, the missus and me..." Amos patted Amy on the hand causing a slight smile to curl the left side of her mouth, "...we had to take special classes at the 'cademy at Smidgeons, you know, official stuff for folks who are in the government; not that we were top-level, mind yeh." In a lower, slightly mournful voice, Amos added, "Did real well at the 'cademy, 'cept English, which, wouldn' yeh know it, was the main reason we done went there."

That did not surprise John. But, English? Did he really say English? Of course he did. That is what they had spoken ever since they met back at the Griffin Farm ruins. But how was it that Amos and Amy spoke any English at all? More mystifying to John was why did they even look like humans? John ventured to ask.

"Amos, you and Amy aren't from Earth are you?"

"No sirree, Johnny, we're from that red dot planet I showed yeh. That was Framboozle. Pertiest planet this side o' the galiksee."

"Well, if you're not from Earth, why do you and Amy look like...uh, well...like humans?"

"Hyoomins? Is that what yeh said?" Amos snickered.

Amy turned suddenly and looked severely at Amos.

Amos immediately composed himself. And he really did try to control himself. But the more he thought about it the funnier the comment seemed. He sat rigidly, gripping the wheel like a helm in a storm, while little snickering belches escaped his lips every few seconds. But, alas, Amos couldn't hold it back any longer and burst into uncontrollable laughter.

"Hear that Amy?...Ha, Ha, Ha, Ha, Hee, Hee, Hee...Why d'we look like hyoomins? Hee, Hee, Ha, Ha, Ha ..." Amos went silent to catch his breath and then fell into another round of loud body-shaking laughter.

"An'...An'...An' I s'pose you'nes think we'd have arms 'n legs a'sprawled all over the place...AAAAAAAH HA HA HA HEE HEE HEE...An' eyes like a bug's...HOO HOO HEE HEE HA HA HA ..."

Amos was flailing his arms up and down like an octopus to mimic a multi-legged space creature. Amy grabbed the steering wheel to steady the car. Matt snickered at Amos's silhouette thrashing about and his howling high-pitched grandpa-like laughter. Josie got to laughing as well, and John sheepishly grinned. Amy relaxed when she saw them laughing.

It was difficult, but after a couple of minutes Amos settled down. "I'm sorry if'n I made yeh feel bad there laddy, but I just couldn' hold it in. Fact o' the matter is that me and Amy, well we *are* hyoomins just like you'nes. Well, almos' jus' like you'nes. Let's say we're close cousins. Practically from the same mold."

Matt spoke up. "Do you bleed when you get cut? Have you ever had a cold?"

"Yessiree, we kin bleed and we kin sneeze...Green blood tho'."

Amy's mouth went wide open. "Amos, you quit a'pullin his leg now." She looked back at Matt. "Nev'r you mind him sweetie, we bleed red blood too, just like you'nes."

John started to ask what he meant by being made 'practically from the same mold,' but he was interrupted. Amy reached over the front seat with a box in her hand.

"Take yeh one and put 'er on," she said. "Sunglasses. And don't worry none, they's polarized."

John, Matt, and Josie reached in and pulled out very large sunglasses and put them on. They may as well have put blindfolds on. Only the faintest of glimmers were visible. Amos and Amy also took a pair and put them on.

With Amos's outburst of laughter and everything else that was going on, John had paid little attention to what was outside the windows. If they had been able to see through their glasses they would have seen that they were now approaching the bluish-green surface of a planet at an altitude of about forty miles.

Suddenly, even through the sunglasses, John could tell that everything in front of the windshield turned white hot. They felt a blast of heat as if the door of a hot oven was opened. The front seat and dash lit up like day. The Starliner was starting its entry into the planet's atmosphere. Amos reached down and pushed a button. Another blast hit them, but this time it was ice cold air. Through the rear view mirror, Amos looked back at his three huddled passengers. He pulled his glasses down just enough to peer over the rims, "Told yeh I had air conditioning."

The mix of heat and cold was almost instantaneous, and it felt quite comfortable. As it turned out, the frigid air wasn't needed for long. The fiery blaze died out as quickly as it appeared. Amos reached down to push the button again, and the icy air stopped. Amy collected the sunglasses and put them back in the box.

The planet was now directly below them. Amos rolled his

window down and the air rushed in. It was clean and fresh and chilly. The three huddled even closer. Amy pulled her hat down tight with both hands.

"That ther's Eskatheer," Amos hollered above the blast. He had his arm out the window pointing downward. His sleeve rippled like a flag in a gale. "That's where weer goin'." He brought his arm back in and rolled the window up.

The surface was now brownish-green, and it stretched outward until it disappeared at the horizon.

Amos turned the steering wheel hard to the right, shifted gears, and tapped the brakes twice. The car hovered momentarily, and the front dipped down. Another second and they were in a free fall dive with the ground hurling upward to meet them. Through the front window they looked straight down onto the world of Eskathoer. They were in a nose-dive and speeding toward a city whose building tops and city blocks were rushing up at them. John, Josie, and Matt closed their eyes tightly and grabbed onto anything they could clutch - mainly each other - and braced for impact. Seconds seemed like minutes, but there was no crash. One by one they opened their eyes.

Amos shifted again and hit the gas. The car leveled out at fifteen hundred feet, and the building and streets now rushed by underneath them. They continued like this for another half minute when the city disappeared and open country lay below.

Amos brought the car down to five hundred feet. Lakes and forests, ridges, valleys, and open ranges passed quickly below the floor of the car. Through the front window, at a good distance, a lone mountain began to take shape. As they soared toward it, it grew bigger and bigger until they were able to see a structure like a radio tower with a red flashing beacon midway up the right side. Below this structure John faintly saw a road that wound down the side of the mountain. Amos turned the steering wheel slightly and lined up the car with the road.

Just as John thought they were going to do a fly-by of the tower, Amos tapped the brake hard, and the car fell directly onto the road. Now they were doing seventy down the mountain side passing cars traveling both directions. As Amos hugged the turns of the road, the three slid back and forth across the seat with the backpack tumbling at their feet. John muttered something about wishing Amos had installed seat belts instead of sound effects, but no one understood him.

The road finally straightened out at the bottom and turned into four lanes. But there were few other vehicles on it – only funny looking cars that looked like boxes. Amos slowed to fifty as they approached the off ramp of an exit. The exit sign read, "Governor's Mansion" with a large arrow pointing toward the right. Amos took the exit and came to an intersection where he stopped.

There was no traffic light. Over the center of the crossroads was a large basket suspended from a wire that spanned diagonally from one corner of the intersection to the other. There was a sign hanging over the side of the basket with the word "STOP" painted on it in large, bold letters. Amos waited for a minute while tapping his fingers on the steering wheel. Finally, he honked the horn. A man with bushy gray eyebrows and whiskers sat up and peered over the side of the basket. He was wearing a bright yellow uniform and an official looking hat. Amos explained that he was the traffic basket director, and they had to wait on him in spite of the fact that their car was the only one around.

The man in the basket pulled up the sign which read "STOP" and laid it in the basket. Reaching way down inside, the yellow-suited man pulled up a different sign and hung it over the side just like the other one. This sign read "GO."

Amos made a right turn. "That's McSuggs. Been doin' that fer years. Prob'ly the only one that does it anymore. We got rid o' traffic baskets like them 'bout fifty years ago. But McSuggs is a pers'nal friend o' the gov'nor and that's what he loves to do. Only thing he knows. Use t'be good at it, too."

They drove for another five minutes on a road that was colonnaded by trees on both sides. A wide driveway came into view on the right; Amos pulled into it quickly. Up ahead, a hundred feet or so, the driveway ended, and they were about to come to a stop before a huge wrought iron gate set in a solid, twelve-foot high, yellow brick wall. The gate was painted green. Welded onto it were the images of the two lions that appeared on the letters in John's backpack.

On this side of the gate was a booth which had two big buttons on the outside: a red button that said "PUSH TO OPEN," and next to it, a green one which said "PUSH TO CLOSE." Inside the booth there was a lady who wore a bright yellow long-sleeved gown that flowed all the way to the floor. Her golden blond hair was long but tied up with a yellow ribbon in a large bun on the top of her head. She was young and pretty. Amos pulled up beside the booth and leaned out the window.

"G'day there Miss Sanders. Nice t'see yeh again. Anything happen since we left this mornin'?"

The young woman did not smile, but she spoke very politely.

"Good afternoon Mr. Buckwalter, Mrs. Buckwalter. No sir...Ma'am. Nothing new to report. I received notice to alert the governor of your arrival immediately. I was also to inform him if you were able to accomplish your mission."

"We sure did there Missy. They're in the back. Yeh can take a look n'see."

The woman came out of the booth and opened the back door. She stooped to look in. When she saw John, Josie, and Matt, she smiled for the first time and spoke to them in a very pleasing tone.

"You dear, dear children. I am so pleased to see you!" She clasped her hands joyously as her eyes passed over each of them.

"The governor wants you to know that you are his honored guests. We hope your stay will be pleasant. And if I can do anything at all to help you during your time at the governor's mansion, just let Mr. Buckwalter here know."

With a delightful giggle, the young woman closed the door, walked back to the booth, and pushed the red button. The iron gate began to swing inward, a lion on each half-gate.

The three watched it swing open slowly. It made them feel special. An iron gate had to be there for only one purpose. To make sure only the right people got through. It was a privilege to enter the gate. You had to live there or be an invited guest.

But it also marked that stage of their journey with a sense of finality. They had reached their destination. What was next? Who knew how far away they were from home? And speaking of home, it sure did not look like they were going to get back any time soon. This had been in the back of John's mind for quite a while, and now it came to the surface again.

John leaned forward a little as he rested his hands on the front seat and asked quite abruptly, "Amos, when are we going to go back home? We did have a prior appointment; you know...supper?"

Amos looked at John through the rear view mirror, smiled, and said, "Not t'worry Johnny boy, yeh'll be back in no time jus' like the gov'nor promised."

John and his brother and sister looked disappointed but relieved. They did tell their mom that they would be home in time for supper. But the way it looked now, they would already be late. And yet, no sooner had they arrived here were they to leave again. Maybe this was not going to be much of anything after all.

The three discussed this quietly in a huddle while Amos and Amy pretended not to notice.

"John," Josie whispered, "maybe we can come back another time. Ask Mr. Buckwalter and see." Matt nodded in agreement.

John cleared his throat. Amos jerked his head up as if he

were not paying attention.

"Amos," John started, "We were just kind of wondering."

"Yes, Johnny boy?"

"Well, I know this trip must have taken a lot of gas and all, but...er...do you think we might be able to...you know...come again...just to visit?"

"That depends."

"On what?" Matt asked hopefully.

"Well, you'nes have t' be invited just like yeh were this time. Yeh have to git an official letter from the gov'nor. And that prob'ly won't happen unless there's a 'mergency just like now."

This made no sense to John. How can they take care of an emergency and be on their way back home in the next few minutes. The situation must not be that bad. Certainly, if three kids can figure it out, would it not be a no-brainer to the governor?

"Well," John said, "since we'll be leaving right away we thought..."

Amos interrupted. "Leavin' right away? Why you'nes'll be stayin' fer the night at least. Prob'ly longer. Prob'ly days; maybe ev'n weeks."

Josie spoke up this time. "But you just said we'd be back in no time."

"Indeed, I did there Miss Josie. And yeh will; all of yer will be back in *no* time."

Amos looked at three very puzzled faces in his rear view mirror.

"It's like this," Amos began, "when you'nes walked 'cross Michael's red rug, time stopped fer yeh, Earth-time that is. It's as if you'nes never was born. Time'll go on, fer sure, on Earth. But yeh won't be there. Yer parents won't have no kids. But, when yeh walks back the other way, it'll start back up; everything'll be normal. So when you'nes git back, no time will've gone by. Yer'll have plinty o' time t' git home. Jus' gotta make sure yer walks back across the rug. Ain't no tellin' what'll happen if you'nes don't."

Something now began to make sense to John. He had been wondering why Amos and Amy had not presented the letters at the ruins. But if they had left then, they would not have been back for days, maybe weeks. That would have made them really late for supper.

But what could possibly take days or weeks?

"Amos," John said, "Do you know why the governor needs us? What could we possibly do to help?"

"Well," Amos began, "me an' Amy can't divulge what it's all 'bout. The gov'nor hisself wants to explain."

It was about 8:00 PM.[2] The sun would not set for another two and a half hours so there was plenty of light. When the car came to a stop, the three slid over to the door window on John's side and pressed their faces as close as possible to get a good look.

They were now parked in front of a mansion bigger than John had ever seen or read about. A man dressed in a bright yellow tuxedo, a yellow top hat, and a yellow bow tie opened the door and with a smile gestured for the three to exit. With the help of the doorman they were able to tumble out of the car gracefully. Once out, they stood side by side craning their necks to look up...way up.

The mansion was five stories tall and at least two football fields wide. Josie counted sixteen chimneys just on this side. A colonnaded porch spanned the front of the building. There were five different stairways that led up to the porch - one in the center that led directly to the main door, and two on each side that led to secondary entrances. Matt counted fourteen pillars.

The entire structure was made of brick. Bright yellow brick. In fact, everything was one shade or another of yellow. The columns were alternately gold, lemon, and mustard. The banisters that led up the steps to the porch were amber. On the first floor along the porch were beige bay windows. There were

[2] It would be like 6:00 PM on Earth.

cheddar rain gutters and rain spouts and the welcome mats were the color of corn. The only exceptions were the roof, all the arched windows and their ledges above the first floor, and all the doors. These were emerald green.

Amos popped the trunk. Matt went to see how Michelangelo was doing. Sure enough, he was still sleeping. His nose twitched once or twice, and he was still inhaling and exhaling slowly. Amos called Matt around to his side and through the door window put something in Matt's hand.

"Matt, my boy, take this here milkbone an' put it right under his nose. It's like smellin' salts; wakes him right up."

Matt ran back to the trunk again and held the milkbone next to Michelangelo's big, black nose. Sure enough, Michelangelo's eyes popped wide open - so wide, you could even see them under the hair. Michelangelo shook his head and sneezed. Then with one quick snap he took the milk bone right out of Matt's hand and swallowed it in a single gulp. Michelangelo pushed himself up and jumped out of the trunk. Matt moved back around to the side of the car to stand with John and Josie again. Michelangelo followed and sat right next to him.

Amos and Amy had gotten out on their own and were standing close by. Another young man approached them. He was dressed like the first, except for the top hat and bow tie which were both emerald green. He took the Studebaker's keys from Mr. Buckwalter. The man politely stood while Amos gave him some parting instructions.

"Make shoor ye scrub 'er good 'n clean."

"Yes Mr. Buckwalter."

"And don't be cheap now. Give 'er th' hot wax warsh. An' check her oil; we just put over two-million light-years on 'er. Four-million round trip."

"Yes, Mr. Buckwalter, I will personally see to it."

"Thank yer, Stanley, I know yeh'll do a good job."

The young man got into the Starliner and drove it away.

John noted that he had to remove the hat to fit into the car.

The stairway had twenty steps to the porch. Amos and Amy started first. Mr. Buckwalter was a little slow but did quite well for his age, whatever that was. Mrs. Buckwalter was a little quicker. John and his brother and sister, out of respect, climbed the steps more slowly than they would have otherwise done, just to allow Amos and Amy to keep pace.

When they reached the porch, they faced a large door that appeared to be made of a polished wood whose natural color was a deep green, like grass. The door was fitted with a sparkling brass knob so big that John was convinced it would take two hands just to be able to grasp it. Etched into the surface of the door was the likeness of a roaring lion which faced them while sitting on its haunches.

The heavy door suddenly swung open, and they were greeted by a distinguished looking man not nearly as old as Amos, but at least twenty years older than the two young men they already saw in the yellow tuxedos. He was completely bald and clean-shaven. Like the others, he wore a tuxedo, but this time the tuxedo was emerald green and the hat and bow-tie were lemon-yellow.

"Mr. Buckwalter," the bald man said, "the governor wishes to see the children in one hour. In the meanwhile, they will be shown their rooms and given a chance to freshen up after their trip."

John was glad to hear that. He was hopeful of a bath. The bicycle, woods, and tree climbing back on Earth had taken its toll. They were led inside and asked to wait until the head maid could show them to their rooms. John had expected the same hues of yellow to predominate as it did outside, but the inside was completely different. It all looked very normal. All the colors were present and in superb coordination.

The vestibule was a large hall whose ceiling reached the bottom of the third floor. In the center hung a chandelier that held a hundred smokeless, burning oil lamps. The floor was a polished gray granite. A balcony ran around the vestibule along the second floor. On the far side of the hall, to the left and right, were stairways that rose in a wide sweeping spiral ascent and met at the top on the second floor. On the walls hung several paintings of various subjects and scenes: mountains, sea-shores, ships, cottages, floral arrangements, forests, meadow lands, farm houses, horses, dogs, unfamiliar and very strange looking animals (one picture had a cow grazing next to another animal that reminded John of a striped kangaroo with tusks and horns), and portraits of impressive and important looking people.

The house maid led the three up the staircase on the left to the second floor. Michelangelo followed. From the top of the stairway, they followed the maid down a hallway to a room whose door was on the left at the end. The maid unlocked and opened the door, gave John the key, and led them into the room. This room had couches and sofas, and several stuffed chairs each accompanied by a floor lamp. There was a large fire place on the far wall. In front of the fire place was a large, shallow bamboo basket lined with a soft blanket and fluffy pillow. Michelangelo walked over to the basket, stepped in, plopped himself down, and immediately went to sleep.

On each side of the fireplace were full length windows with drapes that reached the floor. On one of the walls was a full length mirror. The floor was a polished dark hard wood. There were doors to their left and right which opened up to side rooms. The room on the right had a couch, a sofa chair, a dresser, two closets, and a bed. This was Josie's room. The other door opened to a room similar to Josie's. But this one had two beds, one for John and one for Matt. Each side room had its own bathroom. The bathrooms were luxurious and as large as their dining room back home. The dressers and closets contained enough clothing to dress the three of them easily for a month without having to wash anything.

The maid, whose name they learned was Rosie (short for

Rosebud), asked if there was anything she might do for them before she left.

"Wow!" said Matt. He ran and jumped on a bed. It felt cool and soft like a cotton cloud.

Rosie laughed. "Sometimes I feel like doing the same thing. These are the best beds on the whole planet...maybe even the galaxy."

"Okay, everyone," John said, "we have only an hour to get ready so we need to get started." Turning to Rosebud, he thanked her, and she left.

"Matt, you can clean up first. Take a shower, and don't tell me you don't need one. And don't use all the hot water."

Matt needed no one to tell him to take a shower. The bathroom was so fascinating that he was uncharacteristically enthused about washing up. He really wanted to use the big golden bathtub that had a gentle whirlpool built in. But John strictly said to use the shower since they didn't have much time. Matt was content with that. He figured he could use it that evening before they went to bed. Matt went into the bathroom and closed the door.

"Have you got any idea what this is about?" Josie asked.

"No, I don't. But I do have a lot of questions."

"Like what?"

"Well for starters, now that we know there are extraterrestrials, why don't they look like extraterrestrials? You heard Amos. He said they were sort of human like us. How did that happen? What did he mean we were made practically from the same mold? The Bible doesn't say anything about people existing anywhere but on Earth. Why doesn't it say anything about extraterrestrials, since they do exist?"

"God doesn't have to tell us everything," Josie said.

"Yeah, but if He didn't intend for humans to know about it, why are we three, of all people, in on the secret?" John was flustered over this thought. "Don't you see Josie? This just doesn't happen. What makes us so special?" John was shaking his head slowly, trying to comprehend it all.

He continued in a humorously mocking manner, "Why, we not only know about it, but we have actually met them; not to mention the fact, of course, that we've been transported two-million light years to meet them on their turf, not ours."

Josie had no answer, and she didn't know what to say. "I don't know," she began slowly, her voice wary, "but I hope you're not going to embarrass us. We don't even know what the governor's like, and I wouldn't want to be rude."

John looked at her quickly. "I'm not being rude, I just would like to know what's going on. Don't you?"

Josie had a pleading look in her eyes. "Let's take it easy. I'm sure we'll find out why we're here. I've got a feeling that in time, not only the answer to this question will come, but also to questions we haven't even thought of yet."

John didn't respond for a moment, and then, "Yeah, you're probably right," he conceded. "The number one question is, what is this big problem that three kids like us are supposed to be able to solve?"

That question had been nagging John since they left Earth. The more he thought about it the more mystifying it became. In an hour or so, he was going to have the answer.

Chapter 5

Dinner in the Blueberry Room

The hour passed by quickly. Michelangelo was still snoozing. His only movement was to yawn and stretch while lying on his side. They had barely finished their showers and put on fresh, clean clothes when there was a knock on the door. Josie opened it to find Amos on the other side. He was dressed in a white shirt and a big purple bow tie. Bright red suspenders held up his short purple plaid pants. He carried a smoking jacket over his right arm and his pipe in his left hand. He wore gray and white saddle shoes, and his short pants revealed argyle socks. When he saw Josie he quickly shifted the pipe to his other hand and tipped his cap.

"Hello, miz Josie. Why that's a pritty dress yeh have on there."

Amos always complimented the ladies, especially his own wife. The color in Josie's cheeks warmed a shade or two.

"Thank you, Mr. Buckwalter...I mean, Amos." Josie cast a glance over Amos's shoulder and asked, "Where's Amy?"

"The missus has t' entertain some friends so she couldn't come t'night."

"Oh, well then...please come in."

"No thank yeh, miz Josie, but we haven't got much time. The gov'nor sent me t' fetch you'nes. He says he'll meet us downsteers in the Blueberry room. That's a dinin' room yeh know. We've got eight or nine of 'em. This one's the pertiest tho'. The gov'nor thought yeh might like a bite t' eat while he explains the whole story."

They were all glad to hear the "bite to eat" part, especially Matt. It was three hours past their supper time.

"What about Michelangelo?" Matt asked. He spotted the dog's slumbering body, partially curled up in the basket with one paw draped over the side. He was twitching a little. Matt wondered if he was dreaming.

"Aw, he kin stay there till you'nes git back. Just bring 'im a doggie bag. I'll send one o' the maids to take 'im out fer a walk whiles we're gone, if'n she kin git him t' wake up, that is."

Amos led them down the hall and the spiral steps to the vestibule where they met the head butler, Bentley. Amos asked the butler to arrange for someone to take Michelangelo for a walk. He agreed to do that and asked them to follow him. He led them by two's down a very wide hall that was lined with life-size statues. They were images of what must have been very important people dressed in various attire. One wore a toga and another a kingly robe. A few wore heavy fur coats. One, clad in a loincloth with his hand held across his brow to shield the sun from his eyes, was reminiscent of an American Indian. Others indicated that double-breasted suits were a popular style at one time.

Almost every figure wore a hat. Some were strange, but many of the hats looked like something found back on Earth: cowboy hats, top hats, three-cornered hats, and slouch caps like the kind a civil war officer might have worn. One of the figures looked like a trapper from the wild wearing a hefty fur overcoat. He adorned his head with what would have looked like a coonskin hat, but the stripes went the wrong direction.

A statue that particularly caught John's attention was a youth dressed like a heavily padded football player from the waist up, whose helmet completely covered his face. He was holding a circular racket whose diameter was about a foot, maybe a little more. At his feet was a sphere-shaped object about three-quarters the size of a soccer ball with stubby blunt spikes on it. The motion of the figure was frozen with the racket held in both hands above the youth's head poised to slap the object like a fly with a flyswatter. The engraving on the base of the statue identified the youth as "Polaris Xantham, Greatest Greenchnik Player of the Last Century."

The Blueberry room was midway down the hall on the right side. The entrance was an archway with no door. The smooth and shiny wood floor was black, like ebony. Along the walls were various objects: A grandfather clock, potted trees and plants, sofa chairs, reading lamps and coffee tables. In the middle of the room was a large dining table that could seat about thirty people. At the end closest to them there were five table settings; one on the very end and two on each side. Matt and Amos took the two nearest the entrance and John and Josie went to the two on the other side.

No sooner were they seated than a door opened at the far end of the room and a flourish of invisible trumpets sounded. Amos rose to his feet quickly and motioned for the others to do the same.

"It's the gov'nor, and he's shoor lookin' slick tonight. Look at 'im will yeh. Ain't seen 'im so decked out since the first inaugural ball." Amos was beaming.

In the doorway appeared a short, slightly plump man with grizzled hair, pork chop sideburns, and a monocle for his left eye. It was the governor, Lord Winston Charles Bigsley. Like everyone else around there (except Amos) he was wearing a tuxedo. This one had tails like the butler's. It was purple and blended superbly with his yellow top hat, red bow tie, and emerald and tan saddle shoes. When the trumpet fanfare stopped he proceeded with a slight waddle to their end of the room, took up his position at the end of the table, and gestured for his guests to be seated.

The governor cleared his throat audibly, opened his arms wide, and speaking in a tenor voice as if there was standing room only in the hall said, "My honored guests and dear friend, welcome to the evening meal." He stood for a moment, arms still open and poised to begin what Matt feared might be a long, windy welcome, but then simply said, "Let us dispense with the formalities, shall we?" A wide grin appeared. "Let's eat!"

Bentley walked to a door behind the governor and opened it, signaling that dinner was to be served. From this door came five servers each carrying a very large tray of food concealed under a domed silver cover. They quickly and deftly placed the trays in front of the five who were all now seated. Bentley had moved back to a position that was behind and to the left of the governor so that he could be out of the way of the servers.

The governor had ordered a meal to be prepared like one on Earth. He didn't know how his three guests would take to food they had never seen before. Upon removing the silver covers there was revealed large roasts. Each roast by itself would have sufficiently fed everyone present. In bowls of pink china were mounds of peas, corn, mashed potatoes, and dark, rich gravy. Another server came out with a large dish of butter and three baskets of bread hot from the oven. Behind him was another carrying a tray of large crystal goblets filled with a liquid that looked, smelled, and tasted like root beer. Everyone was eager to start, but they were waiting for the signal from the governor to begin.

The governor held up his hand. "Let us give thanks." He raised his eyes upward, as did Amos, gave a short prayer, and then announced, "Please help yourselves."

The three forgot all about the grave issue at hand and lunged into their meal. They had not realized how hungry they really were. Each one vigorously consumed the food that lay before him. Except for an occasional "Please pass the butter," or "May I have some more bread?" or "You've got to try these peas!", the meal went on with little conversation.

Josie complimented the chefs. "Lord Bigsley, this roast is out of this world!"

"Indeed it is, but how did you know it came from Prantathoer? That's over five billion light years away." The governor was bemused by Josie's comment.

Josie failed to get it at first but then realized that the expression she used was unknown in Eskathoer. She covered her mouth politely with her napkin and started to giggle. John had to explain.

"She means that the roast is so good it couldn't be from around here. Somebody out of this world had to make it. It's a common expression on Earth."

"Oh, how quaint that is," said Lord Bigsley with delight. "I shall have to start using it myself. Maybe I can get it placed in Lord Milo's **Interplanetary Dictionary of Unusual Words and Phrases**." Lord Bigsley was quite serious. He requested Bentley to make a note about it. Bentley dutifully took out a pad from an inside coat pocket and jotted a few scribbles.

As the meal went on, their hunger waned while the banter picked up and gradually turned to unimportant topics such as weather and hobbies and riddles. The governor was an excellent dinner conversationalist. His eyes sparkled with merriment. He spoke effortlessly and warmly and with such amiable expression that John and the others could not help but relax and feel welcome. As the end of the meal approached, everyone was carefree and pleasantly full.

"Gov'nor sir, do yeh mind if we take a doggie bag back fer Michael."

"Certainly, Amos," the governor said jovially. "The large roasts were intended to provide plenty of scraps for your dear hound."

Three servers came out and took away their food trays replacing them with the customary cup of coffee. Next to the coffee they placed a large crystal goblet in which was nestled the biggest and most delicious looking hot fudge sundae that any of them had ever seen. Matt nearly fainted at such a wondrous sight. They had been warned that dessert was coming, not that it would have made any difference for John. He always took care of dessert, especially something as hot-fudgey as this.

The chatter tapered off again as they concentrated on their sundaes. But as the end of the meal approached there was a change in the governor's demeanor. His mood became sober, and his mind was on something else. The merriment in Lord Bigsley's eyes had become gray. He turned to Bentley, who had waited patiently through the entire feast, and dismissed him expressing his appreciation for staying until the end of the meal. Bentley smiled, bowed slightly, and left the room promptly.

"Alas, my dear friends, we must now speak of serious things," he began in a solemn tone. "I have asked you to travel to this distant world because of something that has happened recently which has proven difficult for me to deal with."

Everyone stopped eating and looked intently at the governor.

"Let me start with the events of the past few days. And please, if I do not make myself clear, stop me and let me know. It is very important you understand the gravity of the situation."

The governor paused and looked at each one as if to give them an opportunity to ask anything now before he started. They all remained silent so he proceeded.

"Two days ago, something happened that hasn't been witnessed for at least one hundred and fifty of your Earth-years. An individual from your planet quite literally and unexpectedly dropped in on us. It happened on the back pasture. A lad of about fifteen Earth-years of age flew out of the grand oerken tree. I believe you have such a tree on Earth which you call..." Here, the governor paused for effect and then in a grave, monotone voice said, "...an oak."

At the mention of an oak, the three brothers and sisters looked at each other questioningly. The very first thing that came to their minds was Brutus Malroye. How on Earth, or as the case now was, how on Eskathoer, was Brutus going to figure in on this crisis? The governor continued as if he expected such a reaction.

"We had several official guests from the other provinces with their families. The children were engaged in a game of greenchnik when a blood-curdling scream came from the oerken tree. In a flash, the young lad which I hitherto mentioned, shot upward out of the top of the tree tumbling head over heels and, fortunately for him, came down on a lone haystack some thirty yards away. We rushed to see what happened and found the lad spread-eagle atop the stack, delirious, and ranting something about rabbits and thickets and smoke and a blasting, deafening trumpet.

"It took some time to calm him and coax him to come off the stack. The lad was very distrustful. He spoke in a most peculiar manner often using words that we are not familiar with. From the facial spasms and the guttural intonations, we gathered that some of these words were not, let us say, wholesome words. With such a nasty attitude I immediately became wary of where he may have come from."

The governor paused, closed his eyes, and pondered for a moment on how to continue with his story. He opened them abruptly and began afresh.

"Let me explain that the particular oerken tree of which we are speaking is unique among all trees of that kind in this world. This particular oerken is a portal, a gateway, through which one may pass from this world to another. And others may pass from their world to ours. Nothing magical about it. It is completely explainable through the laws of physics.

"You see, our Creator made many worlds inhabited by creatures in the likeness of his image. All of these worlds are interconnected so to speak. We can freely travel from one world to another, with one exception. Only by special permission and for extremely rare and unusual circumstances are we allowed to venture into that world. The exception of which I am speaking is none other than your world, the planet Earth."

John raised his hand as if to ask a question of his history teacher. Lord Bigsley was delighted to see this.

"Ahhh, yes, yes, I see that this has piqued your interest my little friend," the governor said with deep satisfaction. He nodded for John to ask his question.

"Why is our world off-limits?"

"That is an excellent question, but if you thought about it you would see that you already know the answer. Let me ask you a question. What is the most tragic thing that ever happened in the history of your planet?"

Matt spoke up. "The two world wars?"

Josie also responded. "The Great Flood of Noah's time. The whole world was covered with water and all civilization was destroyed. No one survived except Noah and his family. That sounds pretty tragic to me."

Lord Bigsley smiled. "Indeed that was tragic, but there is something that was far more tragic."

After hearing what Josie and Matt thought, John was relatively confident he knew what it was. "The fall of man," he said in little more than a whisper. More loudly, he explained, "When Adam and Eve sinned. If it hadn't been for that there would have been no flood and no world wars."

"Ahhh, there you go." said Lord Bigsley. "The fall of man. But I think that you do not even yet fully understand how tragic that single event was. You see, before Adam and Eve partook of the forbidden fruit, while they were enjoying the garden and daily fellowship with the Creator, there were millions of other worlds whose first parents were likewise blessed. But when Adam and Eve disobeyed the Creator, it was not just simply that sin entered your world. No indeed, the matter is much darker than that. Their sin affected the whole universe. Everything was cursed, not only your planet, but our planet as well. There is not a single world that has not been touched by the curse of Adam's sin."

John interrupted. "Do you mean Eskathoer is a fallen world

also? Is every world a fallen world?"

Lord Bigsley took a deep breath as he carefully considered how to respond.

"Yes and no." he began. "Before your parents fell, all men of all worlds enjoyed direct fellowship with the Creator. Life and labor were enjoyable. All was perfect peace and harmony. But with Adam's sin, no longer did we have immediate access to the Creator. And the physical universe itself changed. Because of that we suffer from many things just as you do. Hunger, cold, disease, and pain. Nature, as in your world, struggles for survival. Things wear out. Plans go awry. Ultimately there is death."

Oddly enough, Lord Bigsley smiled. "Indeed we suffer under the effects of the curse of your first parents' sin, but all is not utterly desperate. Though the curse of Adam's sin extended to the remotest world of the universe, it did not reach the heart of all men as it did in your world."

Lord Bigsley stopped suddenly and looked at the half-eaten desserts. "Tut-tut-tut, come now, please finish your sundaes. Let us all finish our desserts. I can explain as we eat."

Lord Bigsley picked up his spoon and took a big bite. The rest did the same. It lightened the mood a bit.

"'Scuse me sir," said Amos. "I'd like t' check on Michelangelo. One o' the maids is suppose to take 'im fer a walk while we're eatin', and I wanted t' make sure she was able to wake 'im up and git 'im outta the door."

Lord Bigsley was sipping from his coffee cup and motioned for Amos to go ahead and leave.

After one or two more spoonfuls, Lord Bigsley resumed.

"When the Adam of your world sinned, his very nature changed. He could do nothing but sin. Even his best intentions were mixed with evil. The reason Adam and Eve and their descendants were condemned to become such wretched creatures was because they and they alone were responsible for the entrance of sin into the universe. However, those of us in other worlds did not become so utterly sinful. In short, men and women in your world are evil at heart. Those of us in the rest of the universe are good at heart."

The three looked at each other in mild disbelief. The governor noticed and quickly spoke up.

"Now, please, don't misunderstand me," he said almost apologetically. "I'm not trying to...to...uh...hmm, what is that word?" Lord Bigsley stammered as his voice trailed off.

"Brag?" Matt guessed.

The governor cleared his throat in an awkward manner as if to distract them from his lapse of memory. "Uh...yes...quite... thank you."

"As I was saying, I don't mean to...uh...brag. Please understand that it is not that we always obey perfectly. But disobedience to our Creator's laws is quite uncommon. We are not prone to do evil as in your world, but rather to do good. And yet, we do face temptations from without, and we do not always resist them."

Josie looked up from her sundae and asked, "Does God forgive you? He will forgive us but only because His Son paid for our sins. And only if we trust Him to forgive us."

Lord Bigsley smiled. "Indeed God forgives us of any sin that we may commit. And because we are the victims of the curse of your first parents' sin and not our own, this forgiveness is consequently given to us freely as needed. What the Son did to pay for your sins was so infinitely powerful that it effectively covers our sins as well."

"So, I guess you can't enter our world because of its sin." John said.

"That is absolutely correct," replied the governor. "Though we are not prone to sin, we are not immune to it either. It is possible that if we were exposed to such evil influences as are in your world, we could change and become just like the Earth-dwellers. You see, it is still possible that we in the rest of the universe could turn in such a way as to become like mankind on Earth. And if that were to happen, I'm afraid we would have no second chance as you have."

"What do you mean?" Josie asked, confused over Lord Bigsley's statement.

"We have been extended forgiveness from birth. If any were to rebel against such grace and blessing, they would fall without any hope of recovery or rescue. They will have sealed their doom. It would be like the angels who, in their blessed state, turned away from the Creator. They have no second chance. They are eternally doomed.

"So now do you see? Our world, indeed the rest of the universe is not out of danger. That will not happen until the Son returns to your planet and renews the whole creation and confirms it in righteousness. For now we are safe as long as we stay away from your lost world and as long as those in your world do not come here."

John suddenly contemplated a disturbing thought. "What about Satan? On Earth, though God's angels protect us and fight for us, there are devils about. Satan himself walks to and fro on the Earth. He is even called the 'Prince and Power of the Air' which I've always heard explained to mean that our planet is under his immediate rule; like he has his own kingdom on Earth."

Here, John's voice strained a bit. "I hope, from what you've explained about the nature of men in this world, Satan has no kingdom here."

The governor nodded his head in acknowledgment of these facts. "There has been evidence that the great Deceiver has visited this world once or twice. We think he stays away because he is so occupied with your planet and that the rest of the universe is, much to his disliking I'm sure, too hard of a nut to crack - if I may use a saying from your world."

John breathed a little easier when he heard that. Now he was ready to ask one of the questions he posed to Josie earlier that day.

"But why did you bring us here? We're from Earth."

"Good point," Lord Bigsley replied agreeably. "And that brings us back to the grave issue at hand. We discerned that the young man was from your world. And from his behavior we sensed that the sooner we sent him back the sooner we would be out of any danger, however remote that may be. I really did not think he would pose much of a threat, but you cannot be too careful. As for you three, we knew that there might be some risk in bringing you here. But we were confident that you do not pose a serious threat as does this lad who landed on the haystack. We know that your hearts have been changed in a way that his has not."

"So why don't you just send him back?" Josie asked.

"That was our plan. After we had cared for him a couple of days..."

"Wait a minute," said John. "The name of this kid is Brutus Malroye, right?"

"Why, yes it is." The governor was apologetic. "I'm sorry not to have mentioned that yet."

"We kind of guessed that already," said John. "But you say that he's been here for a couple of days now."

"That is correct."

"But I saw him this morning, Earth-time that is, at the Hampton City Library. Then not long after Amos and Amy first met us, we found his bike in the woods. That was the last place he must have been." John paused, frowning over the thought of that. Then he looked at Lord Bigsley squarely and revealed, "But that wasn't two days ago. It was today."

"Sometimes," Lord Bigsley replied, "time becomes a little distorted during the trip. That would explain why he showed up here two days ago in our world but left only today in your world." The governor paused and then said quickly, "Nothing magical though. It's all quite reasonably explained through physical laws."

At this second mention about magic versus physical laws,

John and Josie quickly glanced at each other curiously, John frowning slightly. Matt seemed to take no notice.

"Yes...Well, then...So why don't you send him back?" Josie asked again.

"Yes," Lord Bigsley resumed, "after we had cared for him a couple of days, to make sure he could take the return trip, we decided to send him back. Two of our grounds keepers were given the task to move him from his quarters to the oerken tree. The lad, Brutus that is, put up a fearful fuss. Very melodramatic was he. He insisted we allow him to stay. He claimed that everyone in his world hated him and made fun of him. He didn't think he could live another day on Earth.

"Details at this point are not very clear. Somehow, he was able to struggle free and set off on a run. One of the grounds keepers ran after him while the other hurried back to alert us. But Brutus outran his pursuer and made it over the North Wall. Since then he hasn't been seen."

John broke in. "I don't understand, what can we possibly do, now that he is gone?"

Lord Bigsley answered. "We believe that once we find him, you will be able to convince him to return to your planet."

John suddenly felt ill at the thought of confronting Brutus. His stomach tightened with a dull ache reminiscent of the punch that Brutus gave him that day at school.

"Why do you think Brutus would listen to me? He hates me. He would sooner knock my teeth out than listen to anything I had to say."

"Ahhhh, but you underestimate yourself, John. While we were tending to him before he escaped, Brutus mentioned you by name. And it was not out of hatred but out of respect. He said you were the only one he ever knew that never laughed at him. And that is the reason we have sent for you."

John didn't know how to respond. He had no trust in Brutus. Brutus was villainous, a wretch who would sell his mother if it favored him. It mattered little what Brutus might have said; it would make no difference. John was convinced that under these circumstances Brutus would do anything, even the unthinkable, if he had to.

"Sir, I think you have made a mistake. I don't think Brutus will listen to me or anybody. And really, why does he need to be convinced to leave? Just find him and take him by force."

The governor shook his head. "No, no," he said grimly, "that is the dilemma we are facing. We cannot force him to leave now. Once he left the confines of this estate he had sanctuary status. He is allowed to stay in this world and travel anywhere he desires in Cynthoeria. There is no exception to that."

"But not even for someone from our world; couldn't you make an exception for that?" asked Josie.

Before the governor could respond, Matt interrupted. "You're sure he got away, right? I mean, he's not anywhere around here, is he?"

Bewildered at what Matt had just said, the governor spoke directly to him, "Why yes, he's clean gone. You sound as if that were a good thing, but I assure you it is not."

Josie knew what Matt was thinking. He didn't want to meet up with Brutus anywhere, including Eskathoer.

Josie responded, "Well, it's just that Brutus has the reputation for not dealing kindly with those he thinks are his enemies. And there aren't too many that don't fit the category of an enemy in his mind."

"Then you confirm our worst fears," Lord Bigsley said gravely. "Though he is a youth, his mischief could have serious consequences if he is not found and returned to Earth as soon as possible. At best, he will cause only minor inconvenience and discomfort for a few. But it's the worst that I fear. Left unfound and unrestrained the consequences could be disastrous."

Lord Bigsley looked John squarely in the eyes. "The fate of Eskathoer may hinge on finding and returning Brutus. For now, you are the only answer that we have."

John closed his eyes to take in what was just said. This was bizarre. The fate of Eskathoer. How ominous that sounded. Brutus could certainly be a troublemaker, but how could he have anything to do with the fate of a whole planet?

With anxiety mounting, John brought them back to Josie's question.

"But you still haven't explained why he can be allowed to run free in this world. Even if he doesn't do anything now, he could certainly be a troublemaker in days and weeks...even years to come."

Lord Bigsley smiled. "Ironically, it's because of another visit from your world that we have this law. As I said, Brutus isn't the only one from your planet that has found his way into our world. One day, roughly one hundred seventy years ago, our time that is, a family of four climbed out of the oerken tree. Their surprise gave them away as being from your planet. Everyone in the universe is aware of the oerken gate. Earth alone has been isolated from this knowledge. I think you can see why."

Matt offered his opinion in the form of a question. "Is it for the same reasons you don't want Brutus here?"

"Precisely," said the governor. "If the men of your world knew how to travel to the stars they would bring their evil with them. While one planet would succeed in resisting the malevolent ways of Earth-dwellers, another might succumb and fall into wickedness from which there would be no redemption. There would be war between good and evil on a cosmic scale. The whole creation would become a battlefield.

"This family was urged to return to your planet, but they too, as Brutus had done, pleaded to stay. But not for the same reasons. Unlike Brutus they had no enemies on Earth. Indeed we were able to confirm this. We also learned that they were of those few in your world whom we refer to as Overcomers."

"Overcomers? In our world?" John was befuddled at the terminology.

"Indeed, there are Overcomers in your world. In fact your family is in the camp of the Overcomers."

"But what do you mean by *Overcomer*?" Josie asked.

"You are puzzled at what I am saying, but you know very well what I am speaking of," said Lord Bigsley. "Those of you in your world who have come to know the grace of our Creator through his Son are in a constant battle against evil. Not only evil around you, but also the evil that remains in you. Though you do not always fare well in this battle, you will never utterly fall. Therefore you will ultimately overcome evil. Hence the name, Overcomer."

Josie spoke again. "So what about this family? What happened to them?"

"We appealed to our superiors who reviewed the case. They permitted Angus and Mary, the father and mother that is, and their children to stay on Eskathoer under a probationary status. During their probation, they were restricted to our continent, Cynthoeria. To ensure that status, a law was created that explicitly grants sanctuary to those who come to Eskathoer by way of the oerken. They are free to live, work, and, if they pass the probationary period, to die here if they so desire. The one place on Eskathoer where this sanctuary status is not guaranteed is the royal estate of the Governor of Brandenhelm Province."

Lord Bigsley held his arms outward in a way as to indicate that the grounds and building in which they were now seated was the royal estate he was speaking of. The governor continued.

"This is the only place where such sanctuary is not guaranteed because it is here where the oerken portal in this world resides. We serve as the gatekeeper and are given the discretion to return anyone to his world that we deem undesirable or dangerous. In practical terms, this means anyone from your planet."

Josie raised her hand.

"Then you can still send him back. He certainly won't pass the probation."

The governor acknowledged Josie's point. "Indeed we can but the probation period, by law, must not be less than a year. That's two hundred fifty-nine days a year with a leap year every eighth year. But since our days are longer than yours are, it comes to about three hundred forty-five Earth-days.

"Angus and Mary passed their probation. They lived out the rest of their days on a farm in the North Country. They were a fine family. If all from your planet were as gracious at heart as they were, there would be no need to isolate your world from the rest of the universe."

John was listening intently, but he was slightly distracted on hearing the names of Angus and Mary. There was something that struck him as familiar, but he could not quite place it.

Amos appeared at the doorway to the dining room. Michelangelo was at his side. Matt got up and ran over to Michelangelo to hug and pet him. As Matt stroked him, Michelangelo leaned in such a way as to ensure maximum benefit from each stroke.

The appearance of Michelangelo prompted John to ask, "Michelangelo is from Earth too, isn't he?"

"Indeed he is," said the governor. "He also came by way of the oerken tree. In fact, he arrived several years before Angus and Mary. And he wasn't alone so to speak. Michelangelo was so attached to his house that the house itself materialized in the oerken tree with Michelangelo inside it. Nobody would've known he was there if he hadn't awakened and barked. Why, he might have been whisked away to some other world if he had been left in the tree."

The governor chuckled. "Poor Michelangelo. We spent nearly two hours coaxing him out of his house. Finally, Amos showed up with a milkbone. Michelangelo perked up as soon as we stuck it under his nose. He came out of the house, and we had him out of the tree in a jiffy."

This made no sense to John.

"That had to be a hundred sixty or a hundred seventy years ago," he said. "I read about Michelangelo in one of those silver signs this morning..."

Josie interrupted. "He means the historical signs in our town. They're everywhere, especially in the old downtown part."

"Michelangelo was mentioned in a historical sign in your town. How intriguing," mused the governor. "But do go on," he said quickly, motioning to John.

"Well, the sign was all about Michelangelo and his doghouse. He came from England in the early part of the 19th century. Soooo...are you saying that you were alive that long ago?"

"Indeed, that is so," said the governor. "I am three hundred forty-three years old. Amos here is six hundred thirty-seven."

"Six hunert an' thirty-eight," Amos corrected. "An' many a folk 'round these here parts say I don't look a day over five hunert."

Amos patted Michelangelo on the head. Speaking to Lord Bigsley he said, "Pardon, sir, but the missus upsteers is expectin' me back kinda soon. Do yeh mind if'n I leave Michael with you'nes?"

"Certainly Amos," Lord Bigsley said. "And give Amy my regards. Wish she could have joined us."

"Thank yeh kindly, sir. But yeh know how womens are when they git t'gether; just a big ol' hen party. They ain't gonna miss a hen party fer nothin' yeh know." Amos gave Michelangelo another pat on the head.

"Indeed, I do Amos," said Lord Bigsley with a knowing smile. His wife was one of the 'hens' at the party.

Michelangelo yawned, stretched, and lay down on his side. He flopped his tail once and fell asleep.

"What about Michelangelo?" John asked again. "He's an Earth-dog. He's still alive. Shouldn't he have died a long time ago?"

Amos, about to step out of the room, heard what John had just said. He stopped at the door and lingered. Nobody noticed.

"He would have if he had stayed on Earth," Lord Bigsley said. "But this world increased his longevity, just like Angus and Mary's."

John pondered this as Amos sauntered back to Michelangelo. He reached down with the stiff manner of one up in years and gave the dog another affectionate pat on the head. Michelangelo dozed on, a slight twitch in a back leg.

"So, you're saying Angus and Mary lived out the rest of their days here."

Lord Bigsley nodded.

"Then, they must have been alive until just recently," John concluded.

"Oh yeah!" Matt was nodding his head like he just figured out the answer to a riddle. "Angus and Mary. Aren't they the ones that Dad read about in the newspaper article yesterday?"

"Yeah!" John snapped his fingers. "I knew there was something familiar about their names."

"How interesting, a newspaper," Lord Bigsley said curiously. "I am always amazed at how close all the worlds are in culture and customs. Regardless of the differences, there are so many things alike."

John repeated his question, "Angus and Mary must have lived until just recently, right?"

"It was only two years ago that they passed away," the governor said. "The children did a wonderful job with the funeral arrangements."

"The children?" John thought out loud. "Of course, they would still be alive." He placed his hand on his forehead like a detective pondering a new clue.

Looking up at the governor John said, "I'm not certain, but I think I know where Brutus may be trying to get to. I think he'll be trying to reach Angus and Mary's children. Although...since he doesn't know Angus and Mary have died, he may try to find their whereabouts first. Sooner or later he'll find out about them and head for the children."

The governor, noticing that Amos hadn't left yet, caught his eye. They exchanged puzzled glances.

"Henry and Ginny? Do you really think so?" The governor was doubtful. "Why would he want to go to them?"

John continued. "I'm not sure how all the pieces fit together, but some years after Angus and Mary disappeared from their farm, Brutus's ancestors came to own the same property. We read all about it this morning. I think he probably knows a lot more about this than what the history books tell us. There are probably secrets that his family's been keeping for years."

Amos was listening intently now, Michelangelo resting at his feet.

"That would explain why he was at the library this morning. He was looking for something in Montgomery's history to back up what he had heard of these secrets. And I think he figures that the disappearance of Angus and Mary had something to do with the oak tree. He may not be sure, but he's probably going to try and find out. When he does, he'll surely learn about their deaths and the whereabouts of the children. He'll get to them as quickly as he can. He'll talk them into giving him whatever he wants. Brutus is good at that. Besides, he'll have an advantage. They're human like he is and more prone to temptation than any one else around here. He probably thinks he'll have his best chance to get what he wants through them."

They were interrupted by the servers who came in and took away the empty goblets. The governor asked for another cup of coffee. The three declined the coffee. Matt asked for more root beer, and Josie and John had water.

Amos sat back down and asked for coffee. The governor gave him a look that plainly asked why he was still there.

"The missus won't mind," Amos said with a hint of uneasiness. "Seems to me we've done bumped into somethin' here, haven't we?" The govenor nodded sedately. He looked back at Josie. She continued where John left off.

"There isn't a whole lot we know about it, but sometime in the early 1900's, on Earth that is, there was an oak tree - a really huge oak tree - that became a landmark on the farm that Brutus's ancestors owned. The tree was struck by lightning and split down the middle. Every leaf on it was destroyed except for a pair that never withered or lost their color."

The governor held up his hand to interrupt. "Lightning? And leaves that never withered or lost their color. You mean they didn't turn like an autumn leaf?"

"Yes, two leaves," John said. "They were as green as leaves in spring. We found them this morning, near the oak tree. It was the tree we had to climb up to get to Michelangelo's doghouse. That's where we hitched the ride in the Studebaker with Amos and Amy. The leaves were somehow in glass like a window. I'm certain that Brutus had them before he ended up here on this planet."

"I believe," Lord Bigsley said, "I know how Brutus left your world and entered ours. But let me give you a demonstration and then an explanation."

Lord Bigsley stood up from his place at the table and walked over to the entrance to the dining room. On the wall, next to the doorway, there were three colored buttons – red, yellow, and blue – about the size of quarters. The governor pushed the red button, and the yellow and blue buttons lit up. He then pressed the yellow button, and a voice came over a hidden speaker.

"Yes, sir."

"Is this Bentley?"

"Yes, sir."

"How are you doing, Bentley?"

"Since I left the Blueberry Room, I must say I have done rather well, sir. I trust you are also doing well?"

Bigsley laughed flinchingly at Bentley's dry humor. "Yes, Bentley, I forgot you were here earlier. We've been having such an interesting conversation here. Which brings me to the purpose of my calling you up."

"Quite fascinating, sir. Can I be of any help?" Bentley spoke with stiff polite English, just like a well-trained butler.

"Yes, you can. Listen Bentley, this is important. I need you to bring the item in box 254 to us in the Blueberry Room."

"Box 254?" It was difficult for Bentley to speak without revealing his surprise and excitement.

"Yes, Bentley. Please bring it here immediately. It is very important. And be sure to take the usual precautions."

"Indeed I will sir. Anything else?"

"Just a couple of milkbones for Michael. Get the gravy-filled ones. Beef. I think he likes those."

"Yes, sir. I will be there shortly."

The governor pressed the blue button, and the speaker became silent. Then he pressed the red button, and the other two went out.

Time had passed quickly that evening. The sun had gone down. Their only light was from a large chandelier that hung over the center of the room. After several minutes, and some trivial conversation about Michelangelo's ability or inability to see because of his hairy face, the butler appeared in the archway with a large cigar box in one hand and a few milkbones in the other. The cigar box bore the name "Royal Beauties" on it. The cigars that it once contained had been "All Tobacco Grancheros in a Kimerin Wrapper."

The butler placed the box on the table in front of the governor and walked over to Michelangelo. He put the milkbones in his pocket, reached into his jacket, and pulled out a white silk handkerchief which he carefully unfolded and laid on the floor next to Michelangelo's nose. He took the milkbones back out of his pocket and gingerly laid them on the handkerchief. Michelangelo barely lifted his head off the floor and snatched up the tasty treats. He chomped twice and swallowed. He popped an eye open, which no one noticed, to see if there might be more coming. None were, so he plopped his head back down and went back to sleep.

Lord Bigsley sent for a candle from the kitchen and lit it. Then he asked Bentley to turn out the lights from the chandelier. Except for the light from the lone candle and the pale light of the three moons that shone through the windows in the hall beyond the archway entrance, the room was filled with empty blackness.

The candle flickered and cast a pale yellow hue across their faces. The governor opened the cigar box. The pleasant aroma of tobacco was still present. He reached in and pulled out a leaf encased in crystal. Though the candlelight was dim, it was not difficult to see that the leaf was pure green and shaped perfectly like that of an oak leaf. The crystal was set in a silver base so that it could stand upright on the table. The governor fidgeted with the crystal until he placed it exactly like he wanted it.

"I'll allow your eyes to become accustomed to the dark before I proceed with the demonstration," Lord Bigsley said softly. "It won't have the same effect if we don't wait."

They sat quietly for a few moments. The rhythm of Michelangelo's breathing was the only sound that broke the silence. It was amusing and comforting at the same time. Gradually, the figures of one another and the features of the room became perceptible though dark and shadowy.

"I think we are ready," the governor said in a hushed voice.

He placed the candle a few inches from the encased leaf on the side closest to him. Then he reached out and touched the top of the crystal case. The crystal glowed and about four feet distant from the encased leaf, there suddenly appeared the image of a tree. The tree looked very much like the oak tree back home. It was actually a replica of the oerken tree.

"That just means it's warmed up and ready to go," said the governor. The glow from the image was eerie and cast a pale, greenish hue. Bentley stood a little behind the governor and peered over his shoulder. His lips were tense with excitement and his eyes glued on the image.

The governor turned to Matt and in a low tone said, "Now place your hand on top of the crystal."

Matt did so. "It's warm," he said, "and I can feel a vibration."

"Now speak to the crystal. Say something that you are familiar with, something from back home on Earth."

Matt thought it was odd to speak to something as inanimate as a leaf stuck in some glass. But he thought about it for a moment and then, in a hushed tone so that he wouldn't feel too silly, he whispered, "Popcorn."

Nothing happened.

"Popcorn?" Lord Bigsley was taken aback. "Yes, popcorn...sure...why not?" He turned to his butler. "That is a good test wouldn't you say, Bentley? Something unknown on this planet."

The governor moved next to Matt and leaned close to his ear. In a soft, quiet, and articulate manner he said, "Now just say it again but this time louder, like a command. And concentrate, Matt. You can do it. Get a good picture of this...er...popcorn in your mind."

Matt closed his eyes, concentrated, and said loudly, "POP-CORN!"

Immediately the image of the oak tree vanished in a billow of yellow and pink smoke. They were now gazing upon a very large tub of popcorn, layered with butter, a large twenty-two ounce diet cola with straw, and a box of Sour Yummy Gummies.

"Whooooaaaa! Look at that!" Matt's eyes were fixed on

the biggest tub of movie theater popcorn he had ever seen.

The crystal no longer glowed. The governor picked up the glazed leaf, placed it back in the cigar box, and closed the lid.

Speaking in his normal voice Lord Bigsley addressed the butler. "Get the lights Bentley. Let us have a look at this 'popcorn'."

The lights came on. There was still a wisp of smoke in the air. "Would you look at that Bentley," Lord Bigsley said, "I do believe that is a tub of puffed packa peas our friend has created. I'm not sure what the rest is though."

"Created?" John asked. "You don't really mean created, like something from nothing, do you?"

"No, no, to be sure. We are bound by the same laws of physics as you are on Earth. No, indeed. What Matt has done is to harness the energy of the supercharged leaf in the crystal, and fashion, so to speak, this "popcorn" and this...er...well it appears to be a flavored liquid...and...mmmm...yes, and tasty too."

"So where did the popcorn come from?" Josie asked.

"Why from the energy of the leaf, of course," the governor responded. "By merely picturing the popcorn and the rest of these delicacies, Matthew was able to convert the energy of the leaf into matter. The matter assumes the form of whatever he imagines." Lord Bigsley smiled and quickly elucidated, "Nothing magical mind you. It can all be explained by physics."

"Um...Lord Bigsley...Sir?"

"Yes, John?" Lord Bigsley asked, a bit taken back by the faltering rhythm of John's words.

"Why do you keep telling us that it's not magic." John nodded toward Matt and Josie and added, "We don't believe in magic, you know."

The governor diverted his eyes downward, suggesting he was slightly embarrassed. "Well, my little friends, you are, after all, from that planet where there is so much...well...a lot of attention paid to such ideas." The governor looked at Amos and said, "Isn't that right, Amos?"

Amos wasn't expecting the governor to ask his opinion so pointedly, so he jerked his head up and in a fumbling manner answered, "Yes, sir. That's right sir." Then he looked at the three youngsters and cleared his throat. With a firmer voice, he began, "Let's just say we're wise to how fixed that there idea of magic and charms and spells, an' the whole lot is in yer world."

John chuckled. "Where did you get that idea?"

"Merlin," Amos countered. "Don't tell me you'nes never heard tell of Merlin, the so-called Wizard. I got plenty o' books from yer world that tells all kinds o'stories about wicked ol' witches, and sorcerers, and the like. And some of yer movies. Horrible things there, I tell yeh; makes me plumb shudder when I think of 'em."

Josie's mouth dropped open and Matt giggled a bit too rudely. After quieting Matt with a dark look, Josie answered, "Mr. Buckwalter, Merlin's just a myth. Even if some people believe in such myths, it's not like everyone is a witch or a wizard in our world. You read about them in make-believe stories, but everybody knows they're just for fun." Josie's smile faded a little, "Now, I have to admit you might have a point about some of the movies..."

A silent, awkward pause followed. John broke it. "So, Brutus imagined an oak tree?"

The governor seemed glad to speak about something else. "I don't think it was an oak tree in particular," he said eagerly. "You see, I think Brutus was just thinking of getting away from his world, not in any particular way; he just wanted to get away. And when he had the two leaves together, his desire was so powerful that he was able to quite literally leave his world. The oak tree that you found was probably the residual effects of the energy transformation."

John held up his hand, "Sorry, Lord Bigsley, sir, I don't

mean to sound...you know...stupid, but what do you mean by 'residual effects'?" John scooted to the edge of his seat. "The oak tree was pretty solid, I mean, we could climb into it just like a real tree."

"Indeed you are not stupid, my boy!" replied Lord Bigsley quickly to assure John that he thought no such thing.

"It's just that the unskilled use of the crystal and leaf can result in the formation of unintended objects. Sometimes, without the control of a disciplined mind, the leaves will produce something that they have been involved with in the past. That would explain, for example when Michelangelo arrived, how a replica of his house formed in the tree. Michelangelo's imagination, albeit a dog's, was responsible for that. I surmise that the special oak leaves that Brutus had must have been from the tree that whisked away Michael and his house many long years before."

The governor suddenly gazed down at Matt and with great admiration in his smile, he said, "On the other hand, you did a very good job lad. You produced exactly what you imagined." Matt smiled like he just won first prize at the county fair for the best model airplane.

"But as you saw in our little demonstration, the natural tendency for the leaf is to reproduce an image of the tree from which it came, an oerken tree, or as you would say, an oak tree."

Turning to Josie and Matt, John said, "Now I think I know why I saw the oak tree while hunting bugs."

"Bugs? You were hunting bugs?" The governor looked puzzled.

"Sure," John said, "we had to collect bugs for a school project. I went looking for them in the woods and saw this huge oak tree. At least, that's what I thought at the time. But I'll bet that is when Brutus found the leaves, or at least one of them; probably in his attic, or some such place."

"Yes, indeed," said the governor. "Just exposing the leaf to light, especially sunlight, reinforces its ability to cause objects to materialize or at least to produce an image of them, like a hologram. It is best to keep the leaf hidden away until it is necessary to use it. When Brutus found the leaf he may have examined it under light or left it somewhere in the light, say on a windowsill or under a lamp."

Bentley cleared his throat. Lord Bigsley looked up. Bentley motioned with a slight nod toward the grandfather clock. At the same moment, the clock rung once marking the half-hour. It was 11:30 PM (the hours on the clock went from 1 to 16, counter-clockwise, Earth fashion that is).

"Ahhh, yes Bentley, our friends are weary from their trip, and I have kept them far too long. We must wind things up here and allow them to get a good night's rest.

"Tomorrow we will begin. Brutus hasn't had much time to do anything yet. He's probably trying to lay low until he can get a chance to do some investigating. He knows we'll be looking for him. Since he doesn't know about the law of sanctuary, he'll be hiding. It may be a while before he finds out. That's going to make it more difficult for us to find him. Seems to me the very first thing to do is contact Henry and Ginny. Warn them."

The governor looked directly into John's eyes.

"Well John, will you do it?"

John was not sure what he wanted to do. He now knew the seriousness of the situation. He also knew Brutus. It could be very dangerous.

"Am I to go with you on the search, or am I to wait until you find him?"

"I prefer that you accompany us. The sooner we can persuade him to leave the better. That has a greater probability of happening if you're with us when we find him."

"But I haven't got a clue what I would say. I just don't think I can do or say anything that would make him change his mind. I may even make matters worse."

The governor thought about this for a moment. "Indeed, that is always a possibility. But we have to take that chance, if you believe in that sort of thing. Oh yes, there is one more thing I haven't mentioned yet."

"What?" the three asked in unison.

"There's another leaf out there."

Chapter 6

Puddle Bottom East

Earlier that day, before the three had arrived in the Starliner, Brutus had managed to escape. Brutus had been accompanied by two grounds keepers who acted as guards and walked him from the mansion to the oerken tree. They politely, but forcefully, directed him to the tree. One on each side, Brutus was firmly gripped by his arms so that he had little chance of escape. Even so, Brutus made quite a commotion, struggling to free himself and complaining loudly that he didn't want to go back.

It was not until they arrived at the oerken's trunk when the two men suddenly realized that they didn't know how they were going to get Brutus into the tree. It was obvious that Brutus was not going to willingly climb into it of his own accord.

As all three stood at the base of the tree, quite mum, not knowing what to do next, Brutus felt their hands loosen. That was all he needed. He shook himself loose and shoved them away as hard as he could. The moment he was free, he took off at a run. He gave little thought to what he was doing. He simply spotted the closest part of the wall that surrounded the estate and headed straight for it. It was the North Wall.

The North Wall was much farther away than Brutus had realized – a good three hundred yards away. Brutus sprinted. Surprisingly, one of the guards chased him. The guard looked clumsy, running with his hand on his hat to keep it from flying off. Brutus was able to stay ahead, and it looked like he was going to make it to the wall several seconds before the guard.

Fortunately, the North Wall at this point was not as high as the section by the front gate. With a running leap, Brutus was able to scale the wall and pull himself over the top. He fell with a solid thud on the other side.

"Oooohhhh," Brutus groaned as he continued to run, "what now, what now, what now…"

He had put only fifty yards between him and the wall. The keeper would be coming over it any second. Brutus had no idea where to go or where he was or what awaited him 'out there.' He only knew he wasn't going to be able to stay ahead of the keeper if he didn't get out of sight, and soon. About a hundred yards ahead there was a tree line marking the edge of a sparsely wooded forest. The trees were few with little concealment. He was running across open ground and the keeper most likely would make it up the wall before he reached the trees. But there was nowhere else to go.

The sight of those trees sent a surge of energy through Brutus. He picked up his pace and shot forward like a rabbit, running as hard as he could but, oh, how slow it seemed. He kept looking back expecting any moment to see an arm or a head appear at the top of the wall. His frantic imagination painted pictures of the man catching up to him, as if by magic, leaping over the wall to land just behind him.

In fact, Brutus never ran faster than he was running now. The ground was level and firm and the grass was short and dry. It provided good traction. He was more than halfway across and took another peek back. There was still no sign of the grounds keeper.

"*Hah,*" Brutus thought, "*that guy ain't in as good a shape as I thought he was. That pansy probably can't get up the wall. Why, I hope he falls and breaks an arm. Maybe I shoulda stayed and helped him over.*"

Brutus's lungs hurt as he chuckled at the idea. He reached the forest edge and hit the ground behind some brush. He lay on his back panting horrendously, but there was no time to rest. He turned over and raised his head a little to get a clearer view of the wall.

"*No one coming yet…wait…aaaahhhh…there he is on the wall;*

the freak's still coming. Why doesn't he give up? How am I gonna get rid of the rat?"

Brutus eyes darted around looking for a way of escape. If he got up, the grounds keeper would surely see him. If he stayed, the keeper might stumble into him. The grass was high enough that if he kept his body very low, he might be able to crawl out of there. Brutus began to crawl on his belly, inches at a time, toward a clump of trees where the grass was higher. If he could just get to the grass, he could start moving on his hands and knees. That would be faster. It might give him the chance he needed to get away without being spotted.

Brutus was too slow. He made it to the high grass just as the grounds keeper entered the tree line. He was afraid to keep moving for fear of drawing attention. Brutus mentally cursed his hunter and stayed on his belly.

The grounds keeper stopped. His yellow shirt was covered with large splotches of sweat. He took his emerald cap off and wiped his brow on the back of his sleeve. He looked around having no clear idea of what to do next. Cupping his hand around his ear he slowly turned his head this way and that, listening for a sound - the snap of a twig, a startled bird taking flight, a cough, a sneeze, anything that might give away the hiding place of the escapee. He heard nothing. The keeper was going to have to talk Brutus into giving up, provided he was still within earshot.

"Young man," the keeper called out sternly through cupped hands, "you might as well come out. You have no place to go. We don't mean you any harm. We're doing what is best for you."

"Yeah, right, you moron. You're gonna send me up that tree and right back where I came from. Why, you'd probably mess it up and put me right in the middle of a black hole. I'll bet you've done that haven't you...you knucklehead."

The grounds keeper tried again. "Now listen to me, young man. I have to warn you. You could get lost out here and then what will you do? "

"Yeah...hah...I'll take my chances. I'm smarter than you think I am. Call me a 'young man' will you? Do I look like I have no brains?"

"Others will be coming soon. There's no place to hide."

"Well, what do you think I'm doing now? I'm hiding from you ain't I?"

It struck Brutus that there was no siren or horn. This was as much of a prison break as there ever was, and there were no alarms coming from the other side of the wall. He figured no word had made it back yet.

A crackling noise came from the direction of the grounds keeper. It sounded like static from a radio. The keeper tapped something attached to his belt on his left side, and the noise stopped. Brutus glanced back but was unable to see what had made the noise.

"Yes, sir. This is Farnsworth, sir."

"What the...who's that weirdo talking to?"

"No sir, I haven't found him. I think he entered the woods about just where I'm now standing, but there's no sign of him."

"Who IS he talking to? I don't see a radio. These jerks must use mental telepathy or something. Wait...ahhh, I knew it. He's got something in his ear. I'll bet it's a miniature walkie-talkie. That stooge probably thinks he's real hi-tech. A showoff he is."

"What's that, sir?"

The grounds keeper pressed his fingers against the ear that had the plug.

"Yes sir, I understand. The law...what's that, sir?"

The keeper listened carefully.

"Yes sir...Yes sir, I'll return immediately."

Brutus wanted to jump up and dance. The grounds keeper took one last look into the woods before he turned and walked away. A minute later it was safe enough for Brutus to start crawling. A few short moments later he was able to stand behind a tree.

Brutus peered carefully around the trunk. There were enough trees and brush between him and the open field that no one was going to see him now. Brutus exhaled, relief gushing audibly from his lungs.

"Man oh man, if this ain't my lucky day," he whispered, still wary.

Eyeing everything around him in a full circle, Brutus decided it was safe for the moment, but he knew he better keep moving. He made another quick survey and noticed that behind him, the forest was thicker and suited for hiding, but he was afraid it might lead to nowhere. He wanted to get to a town. Not a big one; just big enough to blend in and snoop around. He knew they would be looking for him, but he felt he still had some time before he needed to worry about that.

He looked at his clothes. They were the same he had the day he came shooting out of the tree. How long ago was it? Two days? Three? Someone had taken them and mended a few tears and rips and washed them. What they had given him in the meanwhile were some really ugly garments. The lemon yellow was irritating. The shirt was too blousy; it made him feel like a sissy. And the pants were silky smooth. Not rough like his nice pair of jeans they had given back to him that morning.

When he got them back, it had raised his spirits, but now he wondered if they would make him too conspicuous. He had no idea what ordinary folk wore. Everyone at the Big House wore a yellow or green tux or gown. Everyone except that old screwball they called Amos, and his wife Amy. Now those two - they were misfits, they were.

Brutus looked toward the Big House to his left; and then he looked to his right. There he saw more trees. He cautiously made his way over, staying out of the open areas. As soon as he made it through the trees, he came to the clearing again, but at a different section. A quick assessment told Brutus this part of the clearing was out of sight from the North Wall, and he should be able to cross it unnoticed.

It sloped downhill and at the bottom there was a road wide

enough for two lanes. He couldn't tell if it was paved or dirt. The road wound its way into a little valley. Brutus followed the road with his eyes until he came to something. It was box-like and whitish with dark square spots on it like a building with windows. He figured it was about a mile away.

Brutus surveyed the ground around him and found a stick about five and a half feet in length, fairly thick and straight.

"No telling what kind of creeps are around here. I'll say this is my walking stick, but I'll crack a skull if anyone tries anything."

He took off at a run and quickly reached the bottom where the clearing met the edge of the road. The road was paved with a reddish-brown clay that was somehow baked as hard as concrete.

He figured he was going to have to steal some money, or whatever it was they used to buy things. Maybe they used no money. Maybe they traded, like furs for food.

Brutus moved onto the road and looked in both directions. Nothing was coming. The road was in extraordinarily good condition. No cracks, splits, or holes. The texture was gritty like fine sandpaper, but there were no loose particles. Brutus scraped his shoe across it. Not a single grain of the coarse surface budged.

He began walking along the road in the direction he thought would take him to the white building with the windows. Brutus had the habit of scuffing along as he walked but soon found this to be a problem. When his shoe made contact with the road it didn't slide but abruptly stopped. This caused him to stumble.

He moved to the grassy shoulder and picked up his pace. Everything seemed to be just like back on Earth. Birds took flight; animals scampered into the grass; insects buzzed nearby. And yet, it was different. None of the birds looked like any he had ever seen, except for a rather ordinary looking one which reminded him of a robin. Most of the birds were Earth-like in their size but not their color. Their plumage was colorful and vivid. Most were multihued, but some were a solid red or blue or orange from the tip of their beak to the end of their tail feathers.

Here and there a fluffy ivory cloud broke up the deep, deep blue sky. The sun shone brightly, but it wasn't hot. A gentle breeze picked up and jostled the flowers along the highway. They were gorgeous and rainbow-like, just as the birds, and had the scent of a light sweet perfume. Brutus traveled a little farther and then stopped for a moment to enjoy the aromatic breeze.

"Yeah, I think I could get used to this place. If I play my cards right, I should be around for a long, long time."

As pleasant as the thought was to make this world his permanent home, it brought him back to the reality that he would have a rough time making it come true. He walked a long way with this on his mind.

"Okay, Brutus, how are you going to handle this? All's you have to do is find them. They're kin you know. But, you got to be on your guard. Can't trust nobody. Not till you get to know them real well anyhow. But what are you going to do when you find 'em?"

That thought was perplexing.

"You gotta convince 'em you're kin. Yeah, you gotta convince 'em all right. They gotta trust you. Yeah, that's the ticket. It shouldn't be too hard. You gotta be real nice. You gotta smile and be cheery."

Brutus stopped and practiced a smile. It was uncomfortable.

"People who smile a lot must be bozos. Nobody ever has that much to smile about."

The thought of having to feign a cheerful spirit made Brutus faintly queasy.

"Ah, don't worry about it. You'll probably get plenty of practice before you find 'em. By that time you'll be a real pro. And when they see how much you know about 'em, they'll know you're telling the truth. They'll have to accept you as family."

Brutus was trudging along pretty well now. A sound from

the distance ahead alerted him that something was coming down the road. Brutus's first instinct was to run and hide.

"Whoa, hold on, no need to run yet. Nobody knows about you. This'll give you a chance to see how you look to the locals around here. Yeah, just keep walking. Look normal."

A peculiar looking vehicle came into view as it rounded the corner ahead. It was like a pink box with a row of windows all around it. Brutus was not sure if it had wheels.

The box drew closer and noticeably slowed down. This made Brutus unsure of his decision. Not knowing what else to do, he waved unsmilingly. The box came to a stop. It had wheels. A window on his side opened, and a woman with bright red hair peered out.

"Hello there. Any trouble?" The woman looked friendly enough.

Brutus smiled consciously. "No ma'am. This is my walking stick." Brutus held it up. "I'm just hiking." He held the smile uncomfortably.

The lady frowned. She looked him up and down quickly. "But why are you hiking along the highway? People normally use the walking trails."

"Well...uh...I'm not going far, just to the next town yonder." Brutus's smile was becoming unbearable.

"Which one?" the lady asked.

"Which one?" Brutus lost his smile. "Which one...well the one just down the road."

"Come on lady, how many towns can be the next town?"

"But which one? Puddle Bottom East or Puddle Bottom West?"

"Oh, oh, yeah...uh...Puddle Bottom...East?"

"Good, it's just around the bend. Puddle Bottom West is another two miles you know. I wouldn't want you to walk that far on such a busy highway."

"Lady you gotta be kidding me; you're the only car (or whatever you call that thing you're in) I've seen for twenty minutes. Oh,

ho, hoooohhh, yes-sir-ee, lady, I'll bet you have a really wild time around here. Lady you GOTTA BE A..."

"MORON!" Brutus blurted out. "Er...uh."

The lady with the red hair jerked back in surprise.

"Brutus, you blockhead, are you nuts; you gotta be nice...be nice...be NICE!"

Quietly and with great control Brutus said, "You are *more* than ever correct ma'am. I'll be off the road 'ere long."

"Hah, 'ere long.' A touch of class."

The lady regained her composure. How odd this young man was. Maybe he was afflicted by a strange disease that caused him to suddenly raise his voice and shout. Maybe he was one of those rare few in that world who was born with a malady that affected him the rest of his life. At any rate, he seemed to be otherwise in control of his faculties. And Puddle Bottom East was not far away. He would be there in another ten or fifteen minutes.

"You be careful now, young man."

"Yes ma'am, I'll get off the highway soon. Don't you worry, ma'am."

The woman looked Brutus up and down one more time and then rolled the window back up. The box lunged forward and then pulled away. The sound of the wheels on the sandpaper surface was like the swishing sound of tires driven over a wet highway after a light rain.

"Well, well, well now. Yeah, all right Brutus, that wasn't hard now, was it? Gotta hurry though. Gotta get to...uh...Puddle Bottom East...or was it West? Ahh, who cares. It's just around the bend. They'll have a sign."

Puddle Bottom East was a quaint little town of about 5,000 people - 4,763 to be exact. The main street was a right turn off of Yellow House Highway, so named because it was the closest and most traveled road that ran past the governor's mansion. Parking was permitted on only one side of the street during business hours, but which side depended on which day of the week. On Lurene, Lufene, and Torkene (Monday, Wednesday, and Friday) during the hours 8:00 AM until 6:00 PM in the afternoon, parking was allowed only on the left as you entered the town from the west. On Mirene and Brofene (Tuesday and Thursday) it was just the opposite. At all other times, one was permitted to park on either side.[3]

There were several smaller streets that crossed main street creating a dozen or so intersections. The seventh intersection traveling east was the largest and busiest and therefore the only one regulated by a traffic official. There were no traffic baskets. The manned baskets had gone out of style decades earlier and the city council never thought it necessary to install an automated basket.

Main street was paved with chimney red brick and lined with a variety of shops: three barber shops, a small grocery store, a bank, two delicatessens, a department store, a book store, a tobacco shop, and a pub to name a few. The names of the businesses were typically painted on windows and doors, but several appeared on a sign that hung over the sidewalk.

A stone wall about three feet high bordered the street. Every fifty feet or so there was a small flight of stairs that led from the shoulder - or parking lane, depending on the day of the week - to the sidewalk and shops. The sidewalks were made of hard wood and always in good repair. These were never deserted but neither were they crowded except for special occasions such as festivals and parades.

The townspeople were a cheerful sort. The women were very modestly dressed. Not a single skirt or pair of shorts were found. In fact, the scene was reminiscent of a town of the Old

---

[3] The Tuluthoer (original language of Eskathoer) words for the days of the week are still in common use. The English names are shunned because they are rooted too much in Earth's mythology.

West in the 1800's. Some ladies had bonnets, but most had no covering except perhaps a scarf or shawl.

Few men were on the street during the working hours. These were dressed appropriate to their profession. Some wore suits; others work clothes. The work clothes were not like the jeans that might be worn by farmers and factory workers on Earth. They were silky and smooth like the suits worn by office workers. But they were heavier and more durable and tailored differently. Most noticeable was that regardless of one's profession, blue collar or white collar, the appearance was always neat and tidy.

The traffic was light. All the vehicles were like the mobile box that Brutus encountered. Not a single vehicle resembled an automobile from Earth. Some had two rows of windows indicating an upper and lower deck. As tall as the two-deckers were, they were stable even when traveling at high speeds around the sharpest corners. Obviously, none were speeding in town.

Brutus decided he should get off the street to collect his thoughts. The first shop he came to was the tobacco shop. The sign that hung over the door read *Froodly Frisber & Sons, Tobacconists/Est. 2021.*

Brutus paid no attention to the sign and cautiously opened the door and entered. The air was sweet and thick with the aroma of burning tobacco. To his left by the doorway, stood an image of a cartoonish looking man in a cap and knickers, clenching a pipe between his teeth. In both hands lay an open box of cigars with a sign that read, "Take one, friend."

Along the walls on either side were glass-enclosed shelves that contained boxes neatly laid side by side and packed with cigars of all shades and sizes. On the floor in the middle of the shop was a glass case that displayed an assortment of pipes and tins of tobacco. Sitting on top of the case were two shelves holding wide glass jars containing a variety of pipe tobaccos. Next to the shelves was a scale used to measure the tobacco by the ounce. At the far end of the shop was a small humidor room with a sliding glass door. Inside, the walls were lined with shelves that held more open boxes of cigars.

In a corner to the right as Brutus entered, was a counter on which there sat an old-fashioned looking cash register. Seated on a stool behind the counter was a lanky gray-haired man wearing a red tweed cap and a pastel blue, silky smoking jacket. He held a large-bowl meerschaum pipe firmly in his teeth. Positioning the yellow flame of a matchstick over the tobacco-filled bowl, puffs of smoke squirted out of the corner of his mouth as he labored to get an even burn of the tobacco.

After several puffs, the old man shook out the flame and closed his eyes to enjoy the aroma. When he opened them he was surprised to see standing in front of him an oddly dressed lad supporting himself by a crude staff in his right hand.

"Why, hello there young man. What can I do fer yah?" The old man smiled sincerely.

"This is my walking stick, and I'm hiking," said Brutus.

The lanky man chuckled. "Well, I can see you got a big ol' walking stick, but why did yeh hike into my shop?"

Brutus had no special reason except to get off the street and figure out what to do next. He wished he had paid attention to the sign over the door. A tobacco shop was not an ideal place to find information. Especially with this old man. The only thing he probably knew was how to light up and smoke a pipe.

The clerk looked Brutus up and down, just like the lady on the highway. "Where did yeh get them britches, son? Don't think I've ever seen any britches like them there ones. Not that I been everywhere there is to go, mind yeh. Are yeh from outta town?"

Brutus forced a smile. "Yeah...uh...yes sir. I'm not from around these parts, sir."

"Whereabouts?" The old man nonchalantly blew another puff of smoke. He wasn't suspicious, just curious.

Brutus could think of only one place. "Puddle Bottom, sir, you know...uh...the other one." Brutus mentally fumed at himself for not remembering if it was East or West.

"Oh yes, Puddle Bottom West. So you've had a nice little walk I see. I guess those are some new type of walking pants. Strange though. Not sure what that material is. Looks uncomfortable."

The door opened and two men came in.

"'Scuse me lad. I'll be right back with yeh." The old man smiled again and moved from behind the counter to join the two that just came in. The register was unguarded.

"Hah, that fool. If I could just get behind the counter without that old man seeing me."

One of the men held up his hand and the clerk struck it with an open palm.

"Morning Froodly," the customer said to the clerk.

"Morning Filbus. You too Fratemore." The clerk struck the other man's hand likewise. Then he looked back at Brutus.

"Say, young man, what's your name?"

"Brutus, sir."

"Brutus. Nice name. But everyone that patronizes this here place has to have a name that starts with an 'F.' Any nickname in particular you like?"

"What a stupid thing; a nickname that starts with an 'F.' Come on play along; think of a name. Think, think..."

"Frankenstein?"

Froodly frowned. "That's a new one. Well, Frankenstein it is."

Froodly held out his arm in a flourish and bowed flamboyantly, "Gentlemen, I present to you...Frankenstein."

The other two men smiled and nodded. They were pulling out their pipes and getting ready to light up.

"Froodly," said Filbus, "have yeh got that new tobacco in? You know, the Rhoonan Valley Burley blend."

"Ah, let me check, Filbus."

"And check if you got any of the Shrappenau Kabandarsh blends in stock." That was Fratemore's favorite blend.

Froodly returned behind the counter and pulled out a leather bound ledger from a shelf underneath. He opened it somewhere in the middle and ran his finger down a column on the left-hand page. He stopped midway.

"Sorry Filbus," said Froodly, "nothing's expected for another week."

Froodly continued tracing the column and stopped a second time.

"Ah, let me see...yes, Jarvis Smeeks..."

Froodly looked at Brutus and explained, "Jarvis is really Fratemore. Have to use his real name for the books ya know."

Froodly continued. "Jarvis Smeeks, ordered 1 pound of S. K. on the 8th of Stantsor, this year, paid sum of 20 grankels, balance due: 5 grankels and 31 ponks."[4]

"And here it is my friend," said Fratemore.

"Ah, just pay me when it comes in, Fratemore, old boy."

"No, no, I have it here in my pocket. Take it. It'll save me a worry when I pick it up."

Froodly relented and took a pink bill and some coins from Fratemore's hand. He hit a red button on the register, and it opened silently. Brutus could not believe it.

"Why these dopes must be mental midgets. Trusting folks, aren't they. No bell. Oh yeah, is this going to be easy or what? If they'd just move away from the front of the store."

Froodly placed the bills and coins neatly in the register and closed the drawer. He whispered to Brutus that he would only be a few more minutes and asked if he could wait.

"Certainly, Mr. Froodly."

"Uh, you mean Frisber. My first name is Froodly."

The clerk smiled and walked back to the other two. And just as if Brutus willed them to do so, the long-legged clerk

---

[4] Ponk = 1/100 of a Grankel; Hamponk = 5 ponks; Domponk = 10 ponks; Jamponk = 25 ponks; Grankel = 100 ponks

(Froodly Frisber or Frisber Froodly, he couldn't remember which) turned the conversation to cigars and led the men to the humidor room. They stepped inside and closed the door.

Brutus ducked down and maneuvered behind the counter to where the register rested on the counter top, but he couldn't see it; it was too far forward. Brutus slowly raised himself up just high enough to get a line of sight across the counter to the humidor room. They were looking at some cigars on the third shelf and their backs were turned. Now was the time. Brutus reached up and hit the red button. The drawer opened silently.

The door to the tobacco shop opened and a third customer walked in.

"Are you kidding me? Does everyone have a smoking habit in this town?"

Brutus pushed the drawer shut and ducked down. The customer thought he heard something and glanced toward the register. He saw nothing and forgot about it when Froodly came out of the humidor room to meet him.

"Feebers, come on in, how are you doing today?"

They greeted each other with an open palm. Froodly looked at the counter.

"Why, where's Frankenstein?"

"Who?"

"Oh just a lad who came in a little while ago. Said he was a'hiking. Came all the way from Puddle Bottom West. Strange clothes. Odd that he came into the shop. Never found out why. Anyway, Filbus and Fratemore are here. We were looking at some Mandaroomas we just got in."

Feebers and Froodly walked back to the humidor room to join Filbus and Fratemore. It was getting a little tight so Froodly left the door open and stood in the doorway while Feebers, Filbus, and Fratemore looked over the cigars. Froodly's back was to the register.

Once again Brutus peered over the counter top. Keeping an eye on Froodly and his pals in the back, Brutus pressed the red button and the drawer slid open. Brutus raised himself a little higher to look into the drawer. There were green, red, blue, yellow, pink and white bills. He was careful to take only a few from each section. He had no idea how much they were worth because there was no denomination printed on them. The value was determined by the color.[5] He guessed that the value of the bills decreased from left to right so he took more from the stacks on the left than he did from the right. He left the coins in the drawer. No need to take a chance on dropping them.

Brutus slowly pushed the draw shut. He could hear Froodly and the gang jabbering away in the back of the shop. He ducked back down, crawled to the door, which he carefully and slowly opened, and sneaked through.

Once outside where he could stand up, he stuffed the bills into his pockets and started walking farther into town. That little heist boosted his confidence. He also learned something important. People around there were careless and far too trusting. Getting food and new clothes was going to be easy.

He came to the first intersection and found a small food stand at the corner. It was like a hot dog vendor in a big city except he was not selling hot dogs. Laid out on a grill were thick steaks of various sizes. To the right of the grill was a covered basket filled with fresh baked rolls. Along a lower edge near the basket of rolls were several glass bottles filled with a variety of sauces and dressings. A sign above the grill read, "Genuine Glanemoor Yank and Beef Steaks." On the grill were several cuts of familiar and not so familiar meat. Brutus figured the yank cuts were the orange pieces.

The vendor would often walk away from the grill to serve a customer through the window of their mobile box. During one of these, Brutus simply walked up to the grill, nabbed a steak, slapped it in the roll, and walked away before the

---

[5] Pink Grankel = 5 Grankels; Yellow Grankel = 10 Grankels; Blue Grankel = 20 Grankels; Red Grankel = 50 Grankels; Green Grankel = 100 Grankels.

vendor returned. He was observed by many, but no one objected to his behavior. It was as if the notion of theft was so foreign to the passersby that what he did was transparent; as if pilfering was such a virtual impossibility, his actions were automatically above reproach and as such no one gave it a second thought.

Even so, Brutus took no chances. He quickly moved to a doorway of one of the shops and stepped in. He stopped just inside and carefully looked back. The vendor had returned to the grill. He was standing with his hands on his hips as if puzzled. Brutus watched him physically count the steaks, scratch his head, shrug his shoulders, and then throw on another piece.

"Man oh man, this is going to be easy. Like takin' candy from a baby. Like shootin' ducks on a pond. Like..."

Someone tapped him on the shoulder. Brutus jumped and spun around quickly. He was face to face with a husky youth about four inches taller than himself. The other was wearing a bib apron and a hat that resembled a Kaiser roll. Across the front of the hat were blazoned the words "Village Yank & Beef" between two animal caricatures, of which only one had the resemblance of a cow.

The youth momentarily looked at Brutus curiously, then held up his hand like he was going to take a pledge. Brutus remembered how Froodly and the gang gave high-fives when they greeted each other. He thought it was just another stupid thing they did like taking nicknames that began with 'F.' Now he realized this was the customary way to greet someone, like a handshake.

Brutus shifted his walking stick to hold it against his body with his left forearm. He was holding the steak and roll in his left hand. He wiped his hand across his pants and returned the greeting.

"You're new around here, aren't you," the other youth said.

"Yeah, I'm new. I'm hiking and just passing through."

Brutus retrieved his walking stick with his free hand and held it up.

"Where from?"

"Planet Earth you dope! Man, why is everyone so nosey around here? Can't they mind their own business?"

"Puddle Bottom...West." Brutus was quite pleased he remembered this time.

"Oh, that's not too far, just a couple miles up the road. I pass by there on my way to and from work."

Pointing to the beef and roll in Brutus's hand, he said, "The doorway is a bad place to try and eat that. You need a place to lay that stick. Come in and sit down. That's what most people do."

Brutus was wary.

*"Whoa man, did this guy see me swipe the food? Look at those eyes. Yeah, I'll bet he was watching everything. But then...he doesn't really seem to be suspicious. Wait a minute...I'll bet he's trying to keep me busy while someone is calling the cops. Cops? Hmmm, I don't remember seeing any cops...anywhere. Man, this place is stupid **and** weird. How do they keep law and order around here?"*

"Sure, yeah, I can take a load off for a little while."

The phrase, "take a load off," was odd, but it only took a second to register. "Yes...take a load off...come on in. I think we have a seat by the window."

For the first time Brutus took a good look at what he had walked into. It was a little sandwich shop. In fact, it was owned and operated by the yank and beef vendor outside. Some of the customers were those who had picked up their food from the stand and came in to sit down and enjoy it. When they finished, they paid on the way out.

"My name is Bortamus Binger. I work here. What's yours?"

"Brutus Malroye," grunted Brutus.

Brutus wanted to say something to make Bortamus think he knew the ropes.

"But they call me Frankenstein down at Froodly's."

"Or is it Frisber's. Come on Brutus you gotta be sure about these things."

"Froodly's?"

"I mean Frisber's"

"Frisber's?"

Brutus strained to keep an even temperament.

"The tobacco store," he said coolly. "Down the street."

"Oh, you mean ol' Moodly"

"Moodly?" asked Brutus blankly.

"Yeah, Moodly Froodly. His real name is Froodly, but everyone calls him Moodly. He wishes everyone called him Froodly, but Moodly has stuck for years. He makes up for it by requiring everyone that wants to buy from him to use a nickname that begins with an 'F.' So he's Moodly outside the shop, but Froodly inside. Yes sir, ol' Moodly has his ways. But everyone loves the guy. He'd give his left rib if he had too."

"It's 'left arm' you numskull...'left arm'."

Brutus was listening, but he was getting edgy. He had plenty of other things on his mind. He knew he better finish up his business in Puddle Bottom East and get moving. It had been at least an hour and a half since his escape. Surely they would be looking for him by now. Brutus reckoned they would expect him to hide and stay out of the open. Least of all, to head straight for a town or village. He figured they were scouring the back roads and woods; and probably those walking trails mentioned by the lady with the red hair.

While Bortamus droned on, an idea formed in Brutus's head. This guy might be useful. He might know the whereabouts of Angus and Mary. He was certain they were around somewhere.

Well, fairly certain. His family had come into possession of the Griffin Farm, and many tales had risen over the oak tree. Most of them were probably embellished with exaggerated or purely made up features, but some probably had, at the very least, an element of truth. Perhaps some of them were more truth than fiction.

Many of these stories were about a distant Uncle Chester and Aunt Clara, who were by far the most famous of all in the oak-tree legends that surrounded the Malroye family history. Clara was a Malroye and married Chester Wilson in 1856. Chester was an educated and wealthy plantation owner who liked to travel. He had been to Europe, South America, Africa, and India. He was an expert in the history and archaeology of Mexican and South American Indian tribes such as the Incas and the Aztecs. At the time of their marriage, he had been staying closer to home and was studying the ancient past of the Indian tribes of the southwestern territories that later became Arizona and New Mexico. Chester published several books on his findings which, though not widely read, were highly acclaimed among scholarly circles.

Clara introduced him to the tale of Angus and Mary. In 1858, four years after Angus and Mary and their children disappeared, Chester, with his wife, had taken a trip that was literally out of this world. They claimed to have transported themselves to another planet through the oak tree of Griffin Farm. In that world, they had found the Fergusons.

That first trip, as the story goes, was almost a disaster. They arrived unnoticed on a huge estate and mansion during the festivities surrounding a peculiar game that they thought a little too rough. They mingled with the crowd but, speaking only English, they proceeded to say and do things that made them look odd, like foreigners.

Fortune, however, smiled on them. They perchance ran into an elderly couple who amazingly spoke English as well, a mystery that Chester and Clara were never able to explain; they simply said they asked no questions and played it safe. And nobody could really blame them. After all, if their story were true, what were the odds of finding anyone that would take them in, treat them like special guests and show them around?

Their ignorance turned out to be easy to excuse. It so happened that in the conversations, the names of a few planets came up; planets whose occupants found Eskathoer quite attractive for holiday breaks and vacations. That became their cover story; they were simply visiting from another planet and only planned to be around a few days.

After a while they were able to sneak in and out as they pleased. They never stayed for long, Earth-time that is. They claimed to stay a couple of weeks and when they came back it was as if only a few days had passed. When asked why they came back they simply said they became homesick. It was like taking a vacation to a far-off land. It was fun for a while, but they never felt like they fit in. After a time they just wanted to get back to home, sweet, home.

One of the rumors that had come down through the family was that Chester and Clara aged well. When asked, they pointed to it as evidence of their visits to this planet, because people there lived a long time - centuries. They reasoned that the atmosphere of that world had something to do with it, and it kept them looking younger than their years.

Uncle Chester and Aunt Clara claimed they knew what happened to Angus and his wife. They told stories of how Angus was very close with some pretty important people. They were not sure who these people were or how tight Angus was with them, but they knew he had something going on.

Chester and Clara did this for twenty-three years when, one day, for no obvious reason, they decided to leave and move to England. Some thought they had returned to this other world to stay, but that notion was always countered by the argument that there were too many witnesses who saw them get on the boat and sail out of Charleston, South Carolina.

Still, many thought it odd that Chester and Clara never returned to visit, nor ever wrote or sent word as to how they were doing. The day they sailed for England was the last day anyone in America ever saw or heard from them. In spite of the testimony of the witnesses who saw them off, the fact that no one had ever heard from them again was, for some, overwhelming evidence that they never went to England at all. There was even rumor that a relative on the Wilson side of the family sailed to England and searched in vain for them.

"Quit day dreaming," Brutus muttered to himself. He needed to focus his attention on more important matters than reflecting on his family's history. Perhaps Bortamus could be a step in the right direction. But this was going to be touchy. One cannot be too obvious.

"And don't forget to be nice, Brutus, old boy. Don't forget to smile. Be pleasant. Ahhh, blast it all! I'm going to hate this part."

Chapter 7

The Evil Within

When Brutus realized he was day-dreaming he found Bortamus staring at him with mild puzzlement. Brutus smiled, artificially, but slightly easier than any time thus far. He decided to begin with some light chatter.

"That...uh...that's...interesting, very interesting, Binger...I mean, Bortamus. Is Bortamus what you go by or should I use something else?"

"Everyone calls me Borty."

"So it's Borty Binger. Well, Borty, tell me, how old are you?"

"Sixteen. I'll be seventeen in three months. How about you?"

"Fifteen," Brutus answered in ho-hum manner, "I just turned fifteen two months ago...on April 16th."

"April?" Bortamus strained to associate that word with the calendar. "What do you mean April? It was Thransor two months ago."

Brutus had no idea there were only nine months on Eskathoer, and none of them had a name that even closely resembled any of the twelve months of Earth.

"Yeah, well...uh...April? Of course, I meant Thransor." Brutus's speech lost its drabness. It became light and falsely cheery.

"Sorry about that Borty. I've been reading about life in Kentucky...ancient Kentucky. It's a newly discovered kingdom of the old world, you know. Not much known about it. April was the name they used for Thransor."

Bortamus was impressed. "Hey, that's pretty good. So you're a history buff. I like history a little, if it's relatively recent. Those accounts from antiquity are boring to me."

Bortamus gestured toward Brutus's steak and roll. "Would you like anything to drink with that?"

"Yeah, sure, what have you got?"

Bortamus cited the flavors like a ritual, counting them off on his fingers. "We have cherry, grape, cintamor, orange, mongrina, lemon, and black licorice fizzes.[6] These are also available as a natural fruit juice."

"Black licorice? A fruit juice?"

"Sure. It's a favorite."

Brutus passed on the fruit juice and took a black licorice fizz. Bortamus left to get it and to fill the empty glasses of a few other patrons as well.

Brutus yawned. This little stop was making him tired. He felt like he hadn't slept for days. Brutus leaned his chair back on two legs and balanced himself against the wall. He rested his head and closed his eyes. He knew Bortamus would be back around. At first, as he drowsily mulled the situation over, he feared Bortamus was one of those who thinks everyone loves to hear him talk. He sorely wanted to keep Bortamus from getting started or the encounter might not end for a very long time.

However, as he contemplated further on which way he wanted the conversation to go, he came up with an idea of how he might get Bortamus to talk about things he desired very much to know. He judged that Puddle Bottom East was probably as close as any town to the Big House. The history of the two may have overlapped in some ways. If he could steer the conversation in the right direction, Bortamus might give him some ideas of which way to go next.

---

[6]A **cintamor** is a round fruit about the size of a small apple that grows on a tree. It is native to Cynthoeria and has a pale yellow-green center and a pink thin skin. Flavor: lemon-peach. A **mongrina** is a large purple berry that grows on a bush. It is native to Russophora (a Middle Eastern country of the Euthoran continent). Flavor: apple-orange.

But Brutus knew he had to be careful and not let Bortamus know that he himself was quite ignorant of any kind of history of that country or, for that matter, the whole planet. At the same time he knew it would be difficult to do so without taking the chance of making some statements or asking certain questions that might reveal such ignorance.

It was a few minutes before Bortamus came back with the fizz. The fizz looked like a cola and had a pleasing kick to it.

"So Borty," Brutus started with a half-yawn, "since you're from around here, and I'm an out-of-towner, can you tell me anything about this place; I mean as far as anything historical goes? Can you tell me...let's see...who the most influential person of Puddle Bottom East was in the last two hundred years? My personal favorite is Abraham Lincoln."

Bortamus thought a bit and answered honestly, "I don't think I've ever heard of him."

Brutus feigned surprise.

"Don't tell me you've never heard of Abraham Lincoln! The one who sent the yanks south and freed the cows?"

"No, that name doesn't honk a horn for me."

"Honk a horn, what the...oh, oh I get it, like 'ring a bell'."

"Well, let me tell you about it. Up until about 145 years ago, the yanks were allowed to graze anywhere they wanted to. But all beef cattle were required by law to pasture only in the ranges to the south. No cow was free to graze anywhere else. Cows weren't very popular at the time. Cows and yanks were segregated. Even in the southern ranges, cows weren't allowed to graze on the same ranges as the yanks. Can you believe that?"

"No, you're kidding me!"

"I am *not* kidding. What happened after that affects you even today."

"Me? Today? How?"

Bortamus was taking it hook, line, and sinker. Brutus's sleepiness had fled.

"Old Abe, who originally came from a country where cattle of any kind were allowed to roam freely, somehow hadn't gotten wind of this law. He naturally allowed the herds to graze together. This went on for a long time, but someone finally found out and the citizens were horrified.

"The town sent a team of inspectors to his farm to figure if this had any serious health consequences. But what they found was that the yanks prospered very well when there were cows around. They started growing bigger and tenderer and had the orangest of all meat. Nobody knew why. But it sure changed everyone's attitude.

"The law was changed and all the cows were free to graze anywhere they wanted, just like the yanks. And naturally, the beef and yanks were allowed to integrate. Cows and yanks for the first time, everywhere, grazed on the same pastures. If it weren't for good old Abe, you probably wouldn't be working in a shop today that specializes in beef and yank sandwiches."

Bortamus pushed his Kaiser roll hat back and scratched his head as he contemplated this marvelous story.

"Why, I don't believe I've ever read or even heard about that." He was absolutely pleased to learn of something new about his town. "You know, that is *so* amazing. Where did you ever find such trivia? You must have had to really dig around to find that story."

"Ah, not really," said Brutus with an air of self-importance, "You can find groovy stuff like that in old newspapers archived at the library."

On hearing the unfamiliar reference to 'groovy stuff,' Bortamus was about to ask Brutus if he had always lived in Puddle Bottom West. But someone waved from across the room, and he was called away to a far table.

"Man oh man," Brutus thought, *"ol' Borty boy is a gullible creature. Wonder if he's any smarter than those yanks they serve around here. Hmmm, seems smart enough, just gullible; which is exactly what I need."*

Bortamus made another round of drinks and cleared a couple of tables before he made it back to Brutus.

"Hey Brutus, you still here? I thought you'd be gone by now."

"Nah, I'm just taking my time. Been walking most of the day. Feels good to relax."

"Refill on the drink? Only half price."

"Sure, why not."

Bortamus quickly got the refill and brought it back to Brutus's table.

"It's about time for my break. Mind if I sit down?"

Brutus acted as though it mattered little if he did. "Yeah, sure, if you want to." He gestured toward a chair. Bortamus took off his Kaiser roll hat and laid it on the table as he sat down. Brutus felt self-conscious under the gaze of the yank and cow which were looking straight at him. He nonchalantly placed a napkin over the hat which Bortamus seemed not to notice.

"Borty, does the name Angus Ferguson mean anything to you?"

Brutus wanted to make sure he got the conversation started in the right direction. He expected Bortamus to respond by saying something like 'Ferguson? Hmmm that name honks a horn,' or, 'Angus? Odd name that is. Sounds a bit familiar though.'

Instead Bortamus replied, "Angus Ferguson? You mean *the* Angus Ferguson? Sure, you'd have to be from another planet not to know that name."

This caught Brutus off guard. He wasn't prepared to respond.

"Well...yeah...sure. What I mean is Mr. Ferguson was such a...a...a good citizen and all, I...uh...and since I was just asking about such influential men of the last hundred years, I mean, two hundred years or so, I...uh...I was just wondering if you...uh...maybe you thought he was a good candidate...or something."

Brutus felt like he had the word 'liar' tattooed across his forehead in capital letters. He concocted a facial expression intended to signal he was genuinely interested in knowing what Bortamus thought.

"Well, let me think about that one."

Bortamus pondered the idea as he absent-mindedly patted his nose with the rag he used to wipe tables down. "Yes, I think he'd be pretty much a good choice, seeing that he's responsible for English becoming the official language of the land."

"But," Bortamus countered, shrugging his shoulders to indicate that English was nothing remarkable, "nobody thinks much about it any more. Tuluthoer isn't spoken, as you know; except for a few things like the days of the week, months of the year, names of certain holidays and probably some other things we don't pay much attention to."

Changing his tone argumentatively, Bortamus continued, "Now I'm not saying switching to English was a good idea. But since it became so popular it was inevitable I guess. What do you think?"

"What do I think?" Brutus stammered, surprised by the sudden question. "Well, hey, after all, we're talking about English." Brutus chuckled nervously as Bortamus simply stood by expectantly, waiting for Brutus to elaborate.

"Seems to me," Brutus rattled off, "those gerunds and pluperfect tenses rank right up there with the subjunctives and imperatives of Tuluthoer. And how about versatility. Why with English, it's easy to talk about something in the past of the past. Or express it as finished and yet still future at the same time." Brutus wasn't sure what he just said, he only remembered snatches of sayings his fanatical sixth grade English teacher was fond of citing in class.

Of course, Brutus had no idea that was how English came to be spoken in Cynthoeria. He wondered if Uncle Chester and

Aunt Clara had known. But no matter. He needed to get to the point. He was going to have to take a shot in the dark. Well almost. He figured that if Chester and Clara were right about Angus having connections, there must have been periodic visits to the governor. And if people lived long lives in this world, the Fergusons would probably still be alive. The fact that Bortamus, a non-enthusiast for history, remembered Mr. Ferguson by his first name was evidence that they likely were still kicking.

"Do you think Mr. Ferguson still visits the Big House...I mean...uh...the governor sometimes?"

Bortamus was visibly stunned by this statement.

"What do you mean 'still visits?' And why don't you call him by his proper title, 'Vicegerent Ferguson?' Nobody calls him 'Mister.' That's so...you know...ordinary; even disrespectful."

For the first time in Bortamus's life a sense of suspicion and mistrust toward another adooma[7] faintly rose in his mind. He didn't like it and immediately shook it off.

Brutus had no answer. He wasn't sure what a vicegerent was, but he sensed it was something official like a vice president or a secretary of state. He feared this discussion was getting away from him.

Brutus had suspected Angus and Mary might no longer be alive, but he was not sure. For all he knew it might be they were just no longer in a position to keep in touch with the governor. They could be somewhere lazily rocking on a front porch watching the dogs play in the yard. Whatever it was, he had to think of something fast. He was going to have to come up with either a convincing retort, change the conversation, or get out of there immediately. He decided on a convincing retort.

---

[7] The word *adooma*, which is used interchangeably with 'human,' is one of those Tuluthoer words that have endured. A literal translation would be 'one like Adoom', who was the first man on Eskathoer.

"You're absolutely right, Borty. Of course, I meant no disrespect. Sometimes I think it's more honorable to be addressed with simplicity. It allows the name itself to stand out on its own merit. And obviously he no longer literally visits the governor. I meant in spirit, like when someone goes away for a long time but is constantly on everyone's mind back home."

Brutus gritted his teeth in anticipation of Bortamus's reaction.

"Of course, of course. That makes perfect sense."

Bortamus seemed strangely relieved at the explanation. In fact, to Brutus's delight, ol' Borty appeared to accept it without reservation.

Bortamus continued, "I'm certain he is much missed by the governor. I remember reading the eulogy he gave at Vicegerent Ferguson's funeral. It was published in all the newspapers. The governor considered the Vicegerent a dear friend."

Bortamus tilted his head slightly and grabbed his chin between his thumb and forefinger as a new thought came to him.

"Hmmm. Odd how they both passed away on the same day, Angus and Mary that is. They were in perfectly good health. They looked like they could live on another two or three hundred years."

Angus and Mary passed away? As in, kicked the bucket? Bought the farm? This was extremely disappointing news to Brutus. He suddenly realized how much he had banked on their being alive. The outlook was grim. A flustered expression took over his face.

Bortamus asked, "Don't tell me you don't remember? You've seen pictures of them haven't you? Everyone has. I always thought they looked quite well in spite of, you know, being from that dark world."

Brutus responded with a light-hearted chuckle as he was trying to think of what to say. "Well...uh...yeah, of course, I've seen pictures just like everyone else, but pictures can be tricky you know. Adds ten pounds, they say. I figured the pictures didn't tell the whole story. I figured maybe they drank and smoked too much. My guess is that a couple hundred years of hard drinking and smoking probably did a number on the body."

Brutus wanted to slide right under the table and out of sight as soon as he saw the look on Bortamus. *Drinking?* Absurd! *Smoking?* Ridiculous! No, it was stupid, stupid, STUPID!

"Did a number?" Bortamus asked, pondering the phrase. "You mean it was pretty hard on them?"

Nothing about the drinking and smoking. Maybe that wasn't such a bad come-back after all.

"Yeah, sure. Haven't you ever seen a drunk? They can be a real ignoramus you know."

Bortamus frowned. "A 'drunk'? I'm not sure what you mean."

"Sure, you know, a drunk," Brutus insisted, starting to feel uneasy again. "Someone who gets so loaded on beer or whiskey that they lose control. They start doing stupid things, dumb things, like get up on a table in the middle of dinner and start dancing and singing."

Bortamus chuckled at the thought of someone doing that. But he was still mystified by the question if he had ever seen a 'drunk.'

"I have never seen anyone 'drunk' as you call them. And my guess is that no one else here has ever seen such a one. Everyone knows that too much alcohol can have an unpredictable effect on you. But that's why nobody drinks much. You might do something that would be unkind or silly or even harm someone else. Who would ever want to do that? And how could you possibly think that Vicegerent Ferguson and his wife might have ever been in such a condition? They were well mannered, you know, very moderate in whatever they did."

Brutus had to think fast.

"Well, of course I don't mean I actually ever saw or heard of anyone really drunk," he said with mild exasperation. "Least of all Mr....uh...Vicegerent Ferguson. I'm just saying haven't you ever imagined what it would be like to see a drunk. Once I saw a dog drink a pint of beer by mistake. He walked sideways for an hour."

Bortamus thought that was very funny. He came back to the question about how Angus and Mary died at the same time.

"Well, here's what I think about Vicegerent Angus and Mary dying. I've heard that some medical doctors and scientists explain that it was as if they were like clocks and wound down at the same time. At precisely the same moment, they just quit living. The doctors were quite certain it was no mere coincidence, that it was because they were from Earth and the curse of their first parent's sin somehow triggered the countdown mechanism once they entered this world."

Brutus stifled a snicker and with a straight face thought to himself, *"Sin? Borty ol' boy you gotta be kidding me. These people believe in sin? And medical doctors and scientists to boot?"*

"Well, I guess that's a possibility. Do you think anyone really knows?" Brutus asked dispassionately.

Bortamus thought a moment and responded. "Probably not. But since they died rather young it's a sad thought that their children probably will be passing away within the next century. But they might live longer since they came into this world at a younger age."

Brutus stopped listening the moment he heard Bortamus mention the children. Of course, the children. How could he have forgotten about them? They would be a generation closer to him. And a lot younger than Angus and Mary would have been. This could work out much better than he expected. But how was he going to find them? He didn't have the faintest notion of where they lived. Bortamus probably knew. This might be his best chance. Somehow, he was going to have to weasel it out of him.

Brutus had lost the conversation and Bortamus was halfway through some point he was trying to make.

"...and besides, it's best to not remind them."

Brutus, in the most apologetic tone he could muster said, "I'm sorry Borty, what was it you said that was best to not remind them?" Brutus didn't have a clue who 'them' was.

"I was just saying that it's best to not remind the children, Henry and Ginny, of the loss of their parents until one was sure they were quite over it."

Brutus attached a sympathetic smile to his face as he sensed he could take advantage of Bortamus's point.

"Well it probably doesn't really matter," he said understandingly. "I imagine they want to pretty much keep to themselves. Having famous parents sometimes makes it rough with all the publicity, you know. I'll bet they allow no visitors to see them now. I wonder if anyone has tried."

Bortamus thought a bit and then said, "I'm sure the governor has visited them. Vicegerent Ferguson's whole family was always welcome to the governor's mansion. And the governor often visited them. It was like a home away from home, so I've heard. I've never seen it, but some say the house on the Ferguson Farm is like a small mansion. It's the biggest house in these parts...except for the governor's mansion, that is."

Brutus smiled again. This was exactly what he was looking for. "You know, it would sure be nice just to see it."

"You mean go to Lake Proskoonoh in Kittanning? That's over two-hundred miles north of here. You'd have to take the magnerail. A round trip would cost two or three red grankels. Once you get there, what will you do if you can't get in? That's a lot of money for a wasted trip."

"Trust me, Borty," Brutus said with a sly look, "I don't think it would be a waste."

Once Brutus knew what happened to Angus and Mary and where the children were, he had no more use for Bortamus. He abruptly ended the conversation and excused himself saying it was getting late; that he promised his mom and dad to be back before 6:00 PM. Bortamus wished him well and said he hoped to see Brutus around again, to which Brutus lied, "I'll stop in if I'm ever back in town again." Of course, Brutus had no intention of ever meeting up with Bortamus if he could help it. Bortamus was such a bore.

Brutus picked up his walking stick and decided against trying to leave without paying for his meal. However, paying for the sandwich was a little tricky. He made sure Bortamus wasn't watching before he walked up to the clerk. The sandwich and drink (with the refill) were seven grankels and forty-eight ponks. He first offered a green bill, but the clerk said one hundred grankels was more than he could handle at the time and asked if he had anything smaller. Brutus chanced a guess and offered a blue bill. The clerk accepted this and gave Brutus a yellow bill, two white bills, two silver coins that had a star stamped on them, and two smaller white coins that were stamped with an eagle or hawk or some kind of a bird. From this, Brutus figured that the yellow bill was worth ten grankels and the white bills were worth one grankel each.

Once he left the beef and yank shop, Brutus wasted no time. In just one hour, he had stolen a pair of pants and shirt from a small store two blocks away on a side street. It was easy. He took the clothes off the rack and went to a dressing room where he exchanged them for the clothes on his back. Then he stole a billfold that was a display and boldly but very discretely helped himself to the cash register before he finally made it out through a side door. He spent the next two hours mingling with the townsfolk and learning how to blend in.

It almost didn't matter, most walked by with a smile or a friendly nod. Even so, there were several who were intrigued by the stick he carried and asked if he was out of town and needed help, to which he responded, "I'm hiking and this is my walking stick." This usually brought a smile and an inquiry as to where he came from and where he was going. By the end of the fourth episode of these encounters, Brutus's confidence was soaring. He was able to talk his way in and out of most any questions that came up during the banter.

In between these meetings with the townsfolk, Brutus had a chance to think things over. He was certain he had enough money. From the way Bortamus talked, the red bills were worth quite a bit, and he had collected twelve of them. He also had quite a fistful of the other colored bills as well. These were all neatly tucked away in the billfold and safely stashed in a back pocket. He decided that, if possible, he would not steal anything more, except perhaps food and drink. He didn't want to stretch his luck too far.

He also had to decide if it was going to be safe to travel by train, or whatever the magnerail was. He thought about hitchhiking but that would require too much interaction with others. He thought about stowing away on a truck (he had no idea what they might look like) and ride it to Kittanning. But it would be difficult to locate one without asking too many dubious questions. He even thought about making the trip by foot or bicycle. But he would have to steal the bicycle, and he wanted to stick to his plan not to steal anymore. To go by foot would just take too long even if he knew exactly where he was going. It was undeniable that the only choice he really had was to use the magnerail.

Once he decided on the magnerail, he stopped a passerby and explained that he was new in town and wanted to know where he could pick up the magnerail. Brutus was fortunate he had not introduced himself as a hiker from Puddle Bottom West - that was the closest town, so he was told, that had a magnerail station.

Another problem he had to face was one that had been nagging him since he arrived in this new world. His body was on a twenty-four hour clock and he became very weary hours before anyone contemplated retiring for the night. Brutus was having an extremely difficult time adjusting. He wondered how Chester and Clara had handled it. He remembered no tales in which they mentioned anything about it.

Puddle Bottom West was only two miles away. He could walk there in thirty minutes, forty at most. But he was very wary of the road, and wanted to stay off it if at all possible. Hopefully, he would find a walking trail. The lady with the red hair in the pink autobox (Brutus could not think of any other term by which to call it) was a warning that traveling by foot along the roadways was very unusual.

Brutus wanted to stay out of sight leaving town. So he decided to get off of Puddle Avenue, which was the main street. He walked a couple of blocks south to Muddy Street and turned right to head west until he came to Jacamaw Street. This was the street that cut across Puddle Avenue and formed the intersection he encountered when he first arrived in town. Brutus took Jacamaw to Puddle Avenue. Because he was now on the edge of town there were fewer pedestrians. With a little patience and right timing, he would be able to leave unnoticed.

At precisely the right moment Brutus made his move and began to trudge back to Yellow House Road. He had traveled a short distance when he came upon a sign on the far side of the road that would have been an answer to his prayers if he believed in such a thing. The sign read:

Puddle Bottom Walking Trail
Puddle Bottom West, 1 1/2 miles

He didn't remember seeing it on the way in. This was good news. The walk would not only be shorter, but it would keep him from suspicion as a hiker. It was about 7:00 in the afternoon (which was roughly equivalent to 5:15 PM on Earth).

This would hopefully get him to his destination before the last magnerail out of Puddle Bottom West. He hoped not to run into any other hikers and especially anyone that might be looking for him. He was relatively confident that he would not. All the same, he would stay alert. Brutus crossed the road to the sign and entered the trail.

Brutus was making good time. The trail was easily traversed and at the pace he was keeping he would be in Puddle Bottom West in thirty minutes or less. He met no one coming or going. After ten minutes he came by a pool of water about thirty feet across which was remarkably clear and clean. Brutus tossed in a stone, and it fell to the bottom so quickly that the pool appeared to be only a few feet deep.

Brutus thrust in his walking stick and indeed it struck the bottom with only half the stick submerged. The bottom of the pool was not at all muddy but hard like stone and blue like the sky. There were a few large rocks jutting out of the water near the center of the pool. Lily pads idly floated here and there and the grassy banks came down to the edge of the water. Except for these, Brutus might have thought the pool was built by the city or perhaps by those who sponsored the walking trail.

He squatted down and put his hand in the water. It was cool but not chilly. Brutus took a handful of water and splashed it over his face. It felt very good. He reached in again scooping out enough with both hands to refresh himself with a few swallows. Brutus reached in a third time and was startled by a disturbance of the water near the bank on the far side. Something had clambered out of the pool and was slowly dragging itself up the bank. It was a large reddish-brown lizard.

Brutus quickly pulled his hand out of the water and fell backward. With dread, he glanced to his left and right to spot anything along the water's edge that might resemble the creature on the far bank.

A shadow passed over the pool. Brutus looked up and in the expanse above that little body of water he saw a dark, gloomy sky that harbored pale, gray clouds. To be sure, the sun was soon to set but this should have made the sky, if anything, pink. Brutus lowered his gaze back to the water. The pond had changed.

A chill swept over Brutus. The air was considerably cooler; actually, it was chilled, as if the door of a deep freezer the size of the sky opened from above. There was no wind, no rustling of leaves or branches. Just stillness, like a cold wintry forest plunged into deep silence where no living animal moved or bird took flight.

Brutus began to shiver. The air frosted his breath as it billowed from his nose and mouth. Only the pond escaped the freeze. It sloshed with a repulsive, muddy liquid at the bottom of which Brutus imagined nasty, slimy creatures. Here and there a bubble rose to the surface and ejected a stinking vaporous fume into the air.

Brutus sat on the bank surrounded by stench and gloom. There was no place to go, no rock to hide under, no hole to climb into. Brutus earnestly wanted to get to his feet and run from that cursed place, but he couldn't.

Then, without warning, a suggestion formed in Brutus's mind. He was urged, as if by an inner voice, to move closer to the lizard. This fancy, so utterly illogical, and yet unexplainably logical, grew stronger and stronger until it gave way to desire.

Brutus got to his hands and knees and began to crawl slowly along the bank above the murky pool. The lizard continued to fix its gaze on Brutus as it gradually turned its head and eyes to follow his movement. Brutus crawled a dozen feet or so when the reptile unexpectedly began to push itself slowly along the top of the bank toward him. A fearful chill struck Brutus making the back of his neck prickle. He halted his movement but the lizard continued to edge closer, slowly, smoothly, ever keeping its eyes fixed on Brutus.

The lizard had moved to within a few yards and stopped. Over the barren, frosty, tundra of the pond's bank, no sound was heard except the soft cracking sound of the willowy tongue whipping in and out of the lizard's mouth.

Brutus extended his hand toward the lizard. The beast stood still for a moment and then pushed itself once more. It moved now to within inches of Brutus's hand. It edged closer and closer, the snaky tongue all the while softly slapping the air. Brutus stretched out the back of his hand to within an inch of the creature's slippery tongue. Without breath, he continued to stretch it closer and closer until he came to feel the disturbance of the air against his skin.

Then the tongue struck. The moment contact was made, a loud, snapping, cracking noise like an electric spark pierced the air. A fiery, stinging sensation seared the back of his hand. Brutus involuntarily jerked it away and fell on his side. With his eyes closed and knees curled to his chest, Brutus cradled his hand and wailed. The stinging was intense. The pain deepened and his hand swelled as Brutus writhed on the ground. Out of desperation he dragged himself to the edge of the pool and plunged his arm deep into the foul water.

Astonishingly, there was relief. Not complete relief, but relief nonetheless. Brutus did not dare pull out his arm and held the wounded flesh there for a considerable while. After a time, the pain became bearable and Brutus ventured to withdraw his hand and arm.

Water dripped in big, stinking, gray drops. The hand itself was only slightly swollen now. Brutus held it up in front of his face, and he saw a red circular welt about the size of a dime. The red spot was extremely sensitive and Brutus dared not to touch it.

In all of his pain and bellowing Brutus had clean forgotten about the creature. He was facing away from the spot where the wretched beast had lain when it stung him. Brutus reeled around with his fists clenched, but the reptile was gone. He surveyed the immediate area, but there was no sign of it. The little beast had stung him and lumbered away. Brutus hastily judged that when he had made such a stir over the sting, the lizard was frightened and simply clambered away as fast as it could.

And yet, Brutus pondered the episode. He played it back in his mind. Certainly he was a fool for even thinking that the thing was friendly. The recollection of those eyes and that tongue began to make Brutus feel sick in the pit of his stomach. Especially that tongue. It was fascinating! Enthralling! But dreadful. Brutus shivered. It was a very, very dreadful thing, a scary thing, a thing of pitch black horror.

Brutus felt absolutely nauseous. The tongue was so beautiful and yet so repulsive at the same time. He knew deep in his heart that he was not a nice person. He knew that he cared little for anyone but himself. That never bothered him and didn't bother him even at that moment. But this was as if he had an encounter with pure evil; as if the epitome of all that was contrary to good resided in that beast with the yellow-orange eyes and the slippery, whipping tongue. He had come face to face with it and was drawn to it.

Brutus became sick. He stepped away from the pool, fell to his knees and vomited. He hated himself. How could even he have given in to such wicked beauty? He held up his hand. In clear view, on the back of his hand, was the mark of that little beast.

Brutus's mind began to thrash around with terrifying thoughts. What was the meaning of that mark, if it had any? He studied it closely. He could give no explanation, but there was a menacing thought that kept coming back to him; that the mark had somehow affected him, changed him, and would force the worst of all that he was to come out.

The presence of the mark was, as it were, a seal of ownership and possession, like the branding of a cow. Brutus firmly believed that the cursed creature had deceived him and laid claim to him by marking him exclusively for its own pleasure. And after it saw with satisfaction the pain it had caused, it deemed its work for the moment to be finished and simply left Brutus to ponder the consequences.

And yet, how absurd that notion was; a dumb cold-blooded animal purposely setting him apart, making him the target of an evil ambition. Brutus held up his hand once again. He feared that that stinging red mark would give him away, that he would have to conceal it or else he would be known truly for the foolish person he must be to allow such a ghastly thing to happen.

Reason. Common sense. Those words burst into Brutus's mind like an explosion. He had to be reasonable. The red mark could be explained away. He had no reason to fear it or fear that anyone would be suspicious of it. It would be gone in a few days, a week or two at most. He was a fast healer. Many a bruise or scrape or burn had marked him, and they were all gone except for the faintest evidence of an unnoticeable scar or discoloration of the skin.

Brutus forced himself to be reasonable. The lizard was probably one that was commonly avoided and for good reason. This taught Brutus a lesson. Trust no one and no animal; trust no living creature. There was much about this world he had yet to learn. He had to guard himself not to be so careless.

Brutus shook himself as if from a trance. He took a deep breath. The frozen chill of the air was gone; the winter barrenness of the wood had returned to its summer plentitude, and the stinking pool now sloshed with crisp, clear water. He took another deep breath and held it for a few seconds before he let it out slowly.

He felt much better now and his mind was clearer. The pain in his hand was little more than a dull pinch. The more he thought about it the more it seemed to be a trivial matter after all. He hastily concluded that his imagination had run wild and exaggerated the whole encounter. He had to put this behind him. He probably wasted a good half-hour, and he wanted to make it to Puddle Bottom West before that last departure of the magnerail. He was going to have to get back on the trail and get moving again. Brutus took one last look at the pool before he turned and made his way back to the walking trail. It was getting late. There was no time to lose. With a new sense of purpose, Brutus pressed on. He must make it in time. He must..."or someone will pay for this," he muttered.

Chapter 8

Trouble on the Commodore Mitchell

Brutus stood before a pale blue-gray stone building that had two large open doorways through which a fair amount of people passed. On the front of the building and over the doors was a large sign on which were written, in large golden letters, the words:

Magnerail Station #272
Puddle Bottom West

Though Puddle Bottom West was about five times larger than its sister town, it was not large enough to merit more than a medium size magnerail station. Nevertheless, this building was impressive. Its architecture was a replica of an earlier day when large stone blocks, high arched windows, and heavy wooden doors were the fashion.

The door on the right appeared exclusively to be the one used to enter the building. Brutus set off for the entrance and fell behind a woman and her two children, one of whom lagged a little behind the others. The mother and older sister passed directly into the main hall of the building and to the far side, leaving the younger sister to trail.

The little girl stopped a short distance inside the doorway as she stood in awe of her surroundings. Brutus could easily have gone around her, but he stood impatiently behind her. She finally noticed him and smiled. Brutus scowled so meanly that she turned and ran off to her mother who was still on the other side of the lobby. She tugged at her mother's dress and pointed back in Brutus's direction. Her mother was looking at a magnerail schedule posted on the wall and took no notice of what her daughter was trying to bring to her attention. Once the woman found what she was looking for, without glancing down, she grasped her daughter's hand and pulled her along as the three of them passed through a large doorway to the right.

The sun was now much lower in the sky and shone into the hall where Brutus stood holding his walking stick, like a staff, in his left hand. With the entranceway to his back, his shadow stretched out before him like a rubber band pulled to its limit. The ceiling was very high and made the hallway appear empty and cavernous. The sounds and noises of voices and footsteps traveled through the air as hollow, resonant echoes.

Brutus set out across the hall intending to examine the same posted schedule the woman had just consulted. On each step, the thump of his walking stick as it met the stone floor reverberated with a hollow thud like a soft mallet striking wood.

The schedule was simple and easy to read. In a matter of seconds Brutus learned that there was one more magnerail scheduled to leave within the next twenty minutes. Its destination was beyond Kittanning, but it did make a stop there.

At one end of the building, to the right as one entered, was a large booth where tickets were purchased. No one was standing at the window, and Brutus was relieved to know he would immediately be able to inquire. He walked over and stood just opposite the clerk on the inside of the booth.

The clerk looked up, smiled, and said, "Yes, young man, how may I help you."

Brutus did not like the "young man" reference. The recollection of how the groundskeeper at the Big House called out to him as "young man" came to mind, and it bothered him. There was something about those words that were very distasteful. Brutus puzzled over what that was when it suddenly came to him.

The words "young man" did not mean a man who was young. He took it as a thinly veiled way of demeaning him, as if at best he was an adolescent who was quite immature; or at worst, a little boy who needed constant attention. Had he not entered a new world on his own? Had he not escaped foolish adults who did not understand him? Was he not in control of his own destiny?

Destiny. The word had always made Brutus think of a distant object, so far away, it was not distinguishable. Brutus had never thought much about destiny, especially his own. It was something that was always out there, way off, in the future. Where he was going in life had never seriously crossed his mind on Earth. He simply wanted to get away from everything he had grown up in. It didn't matter where, and it didn't matter how.

But something was different now. On the trail he had strangely become possessed with the thought of his personal destiny. Since the lizard's sting on the back of his hand, he couldn't get that question out of his head. The more he contemplated it, the more he felt that his so-called destiny had taken a turn.

He now sensed a difference in his being. He became more fully aware of himself. He was older now. Or rather, he was mature like an adult. In fact, he perceived that he was more mature than most adults. It was hidden away from the eyes of those around him. He alone saw himself as no others were capable of seeing him. None of them understood this. Just as on Earth, they deemed him to be a foolish youth without direction. They were wrong, all of them. He was a unique being, a man better and different from all other men in that world. He wanted to be perceived as such. He was going to prove it. He wasn't sure how yet, but something within welled up, assuring him that he was on the road to great and marvelous things.

"Look at him," Brutus thought, "eyeing me as if I were an insect, a strip of bacon with no more importance than a stone."

Brutus looked back at the man in his ridiculous ticket-man hat and his silly shirt and tie that looked as old and dusty as the little pile of dirt he had swept in the corner and abandoned when the last passenger walked up to the window.

Brutus swallowed the nasty remark he wanted to make. He still had to be nice. That was more important than ever now. To be accepted as an adult was the first step, and he had to start acting like one. He remembered the look on the little girl's face when he scowled at her, how frightened she was. Would a grown-up have done that?

"Certainly not," Brutus said inside his head again, *"I've got to do better than that."*

Brutus was jarred from his reverie by a sharp wrap on the ticket booth window by the ticket man on the other side of the counter.

"'Scuse me, young man," he said with a smile, "Are you all right? Can I help you?"

Brutus shook his head slightly and cleared his throat. Maybe he didn't have to be cheerful, just reserved, unemotional. No need to over dramatize the adult-thing.

"Sir," Brutus said with composure and very articulately, "I wish to purchase a ticket to Kittanning." He pulled his wallet out of his back pocket. His expression was unsmiling and grave.

The clerk's smile faded a little. "Yes, my friend, let me see here." He averted his eyes and looked down at the counter where he ran his finger down a schedule of prices.

He stopped to look up and asked, "Is that one-way or round trip?"

"One way," Brutus said colorlessly.

"Yes, of course." The clerk looked back down at the schedule and without looking up this time said, "That will be 145 grankels."

Brutus had figured out by now that this meant it would take one green bill and a red one to cover the cost. He pulled these out of his wallet and gave them to the clerk. The clerk gave him a pink bill in exchange.

"The magnerail will be leaving in fifteen minutes. The departure dock is on your ticket. All docks are through that entrance." The clerk was pointing to the entranceway the woman and her children had passed through only minutes before.

Brutus nodded and turned. He made his way across the floor to the entranceway and stepped through. He was looking out onto an expansive, cavernous area that was covered with a high and arched ceiling. At the far end, the enclosure opened very widely, and he was able to see city buildings and distant clouds in a blue sky.

Brutus was standing on a broad platform. He walked out until he came to the far edge. It abruptly dropped off about five feet onto an earth floor. Extending out from the platform were several long, narrow docks, like piers jutting out into an ocean.

Brutus backed up several feet and looked up. There were signs overhead that marked each dock from 'A' to 'F' beginning on his left. He looked at his ticket. His magnerail was leaving on dock 'E' which, according to the signs, was the next to last dock on his right. When he looked in that direction, he realized he didn't need his ticket to know which one to go to; there was only one dock that had a magnerail parked along it.

The magnerail looked like a slender, silver tube with small, square windows along the sides. Brutus expected something like a train with a series of railcars hitched to one another. Instead, this was a single unit about a hundred feet in length and approximately thirty feet in diameter. Most remarkably, it hovered in mid-air while parked.

Through the windows, Brutus detected movement inside and was pleased to see that it did not look overly populated. He stepped off quickly, his footsteps and stick sounding very hollow as their echo died away somewhere high above near the roof. He found that dock 'E' ran along the side of the magnerail that faced away from him. He made his way down the dock, passing by the magnerail's windows which were now on his left. He discovered that there was only one way onto the metallic tube - a double door that opened out toward the dock.

There were steps that led up into the magnerail. A post divided the doorway. One boarded the magnerail to the right of the post and exited from the left.

Brutus walked up the steps and into the magnerail. Immediately the hollow echoes of the station were gone, and the voices of the passengers assumed their rich, solid tones again. A long aisle ran the length of the magnerail with seats to the left and right. At the far end to his right as he entered, Brutus observed that the aisle abruptly stopped before a closed door. He assumed this was the engineer's compartment. At the other end toward the back of the magnerail, the aisle led to an open area where there was a snack bar of sorts, and one could purchase a sandwich made to order and a drink. Midway, on either side of the aisle, were small restrooms.

Brutus was a little thirsty and decided to get something to drink. He had little difficulty ordering and paying for the drink with the correct bills. Making his way back into the magnerail, he chose a seat next to a window where the dock was located.

There was an official looking man dressed in a bright red uniform and yellow hat. He had walked up and down the aisle several times smiling, slapping palms, and conversing with the passengers. So far, Brutus had been able to avoid him, but his luck was about to run out.

"Welcome aboard the Commodore Mitchell. I will be your conductor for this ride." The conductor had spoken warmly and held up his hand.

Brutus stared at the hand for a moment before he grudgingly greeted the uniformed man. As he dropped his arm, the red mark on the back of his right hand became blatantly visible. It appeared to have become very sore and inflamed. In fact, however, Brutus felt nothing, and he took it as a sign that the wound was not a very serious one after all.

The conductor winced when he saw the spot. "Nasty little burn you have there. You ought to do something for it, and rather soon I should think. There are first aid kits in the restrooms, you know. If that isn't sufficient, we have a fuller supply of medical items in the engineer's cabin. I would be glad to get anything you need."

Brutus held the back of his hand before his face so he could observe it and said in an unconcerned and condescending voice, "I judge it is not as serious as you think. Sometimes these little burns look far worse than they really are."

Brutus looked back at the conductor with a smug expression. And to make the point, he smiled in such a way as to say, "Why don't you go on and mind your own business?"

The conductor was mildly taken aback by this but ignored it. "First time on the magnerail?" he asked cheerfully.

Brutus was growing impatient, but he surprised himself as he responded in a controlled, composed mood.

"Yes it is. I hope to have a pleasant journey. I trust that you will see to it that I, that is, we passengers will have such a pleasant journey."

"Oh, yes indeed my friend, that is my job you know."

Brutus remembered his ticket. He took it out of his pocket and offered it to the conductor. The conductor was puzzled at this gesture.

"Is there something wrong?" The conductor took the ticket and inspected it. "Indeed you are on the correct line. Is there a question about your ticket?"

Brutus had forgotten that, just like everything else in that world, there was no expectation of cheating or deception. The conductor's job was to assist the passengers in every way possible to ensure their safety and enjoyment of the trip. Collecting or even verifying the possession of a ticket was not a part of that job. It was always assumed the passenger had an authentic ticket.

Brutus had a ready response. "If you will notice in the upper right hand corner of the ticket the departure time is printed."

"Indeed, it is."

"May I assume that we will not be late in either departing or arriving?"

The conductor pulled his chain watch from his belt and looked at the time.

"It is now 10:40 PM, and we are scheduled to leave in five minutes." His voice was soothing and genuinely concerned. "So far, there is nothing that should keep us from meeting the departure time. As for arriving, unless there are delays along the way, we should arrive in Kittanning at 13:35 PM, likewise as scheduled. Please relax and enjoy the trip, my friend. The Commodore Mitchell has not missed a scheduled stop in over three years."

The conductor was about to move on when he stopped and said, "If you change your mind about medical assistance, just press that button." He pointed to a yellow button just below the window. The conductor smiled and continued on his way.

Brutus rested his cane in the crevice between the windowsill and the seat to his front. He sat back and closed his eyes. He immediately felt very drowsy as his internal clock rebelled against the forcing of his body to stay awake in spite of badly needed sleep. Bits and pieces of the events of the day involuntarily began to reel through his mind in no particular order: Froodly's white meerschaum pipe, the woman with the red hair, Bortamus's Kaiser roll hat, the flowers by the roadway, the grounds keeper and his walkie-talkie, the distant white building with the small dark square windows, the grill with the orange yank and red beef steaks, the sandpaper surface of the clay-baked pavement, the red-bricked main street, the yellow-orange eyes of that beastly lizard.

Brutus was asleep now, but he struggled in the grip of deep fear as those hypnotic, unblinking eyes stared into his. In a dream-like state, he struggled to free himself from that gaze. He pushed and kicked to retreat from the eyes, but nothing seemed to work. And then he began to hear a soft whipping, slapping sound that was soothing and irritating at the same time. He instantly recognized it and could feel himself, without effort on his part, extend his arm forward toward the eyes and slithering tongue. He struggled to pull it back but to no avail. The enticement of those eyes, the enchantment of that whipping tongue overpowered him and left him with little strength to resist.

Then a new entity entered the hallucination. It was an unfamiliar voice whose whisperings formulated familiar syllables strung together randomly and with no discernable meaning. There was something about those sounds that made them significant; as if they promised good or perhaps knowledge, perhaps wisdom or guidance or insight. If only he could unscramble and reorder them in a meaningful way.

He listened intently to the inflections and intonations of the nonsense words to discern meaning from them. As he did so he began to detect a few words that were intermixed but distinguishable. The word "mister" rose to the surface of that boiling cauldron of syllable and sound and then sunk. It happened again, more loudly and forcefully than before, but it likewise faded away. A third time he heard it as if it were spoken directly into his ear. At the same time, he could feel his arm grasped and shaken as if by a small, weak hand. Another shake and Brutus's dream began to dissolve. One more shake and Brutus opened his eyes.

He was sweating and tensely gripping the arms of his seat. As he looked straight ahead he saw only the back of the seat to his front and his walking stick reclining against the windowsill. He also saw something else, to his left. Slowly he moved his eyes in that direction anticipating with fear what he might see. It was the little girl that he frightened back at the station. She was tugging on his arm and saying "Mister, Mister, are you all right?"

Brutus closed his eyes and with an audible gush let out a breath he had been holding for the last thirty seconds. It was okay. It was only a dream. Everything was normal. He opened his eyes and looked out the window to see the landscape rushing by. He closed his eyes a second time and chuckled at himself like one might do when he realizes someone has played a joke on him.

He opened his eyes and once again looked at the little girl. He was still smiling in relief from his nightmare. She had released his arm and stood with blue eyes, blond hair, and the soft, smooth complexion of an innocent and harmless being. She was a little angel.

"Mister, are you all right?"

A sober expression slowly replaced the smile on Brutus's face. She addressed him as an adult. She called him "Mister." She made no distinction in her mind between him and any one of the other adult males on the magnerail. This was a discerning little girl. She understood him as he really was; not an immature youth as he had always been treated even by his own parents.

"Indeed I am, thank you. I was just having a little dream, and I thank you for waking me. Aren't you the one I frightened in the magnerail station before we left?"

"Oh, I wasn't frightened."

"But you ran away, didn't you?"

"I wanted to let mommy know. I thought you were sick or something. You made such a strange face when I looked up at you I thought there was something wrong. Then I saw you sitting here. You still don't look very well."

The little girl held a small stuffed dog with big floppy ears in her arms.

"Why, that is a cute little pet you have there. What's its name?"

She held it up with its big sad eyes facing Brutus and said, "His name is Sniffles. Would you like to give him a kiss?"

Brutus did not want to kiss a stuffed dog, especially one named Sniffles. But he knew that the polite or adult thing to do would be to humor the little girl. So he took the dog and kissed it on top of its head. The little girl giggled with glee. Brutus asked her if she would like to sit in the seat next to him to which she replied, "Sure."

"What's your name mister? My name is Dandy. That's short for Dandelion."

"My what a pretty name; a flower, and one of my favorites. My name is Bruce Malroye, but everyone calls me Brutus." Brutus held up his hand to greet the little girl, to which she responded with a tap of her palm.

"Tell me, is your mommy on the train?" Brutus, of course, knew that she was.

"Oh yes, she's over there. And that's my sister, Bluebell, but we just call her Blue." The little girl pointed toward a seat about eight rows down and on the other side of the aisle. Brutus looked in that direction and saw the woman from the station in Puddle Bottom West. Dandy's sister was sitting next to her.

"And to which city are you and your mother taking the magnerail?"

"We're going to Kittanning to visit my Aunt and Uncle."

"Kittanning? What a coincidence. I'm going there myself."

"Do you live there?"

"No, I'm visiting...let us say...family. In fact, I've never seen them, and they don't even know I'm coming. It's going to be a grand surprise," Brutus said with a flair of his hands. "Do you like surprises?" Dandy giggled signifying that she did.

Several minutes passed as they talked about a variety of things. Meanwhile, the magnerail raced along at 137.6 miles per hour. It slowed down several times as it passed through the smaller towns that had no station. For an observer from the outside, the magnerail looked like a silver arrow that glided ten feet off the ground above a set of three thick iron rails. One rail was directly beneath the bottom of the tube and the other two were about four feet on either side of the middle rail and about seven feet off the ground. These outer rails were broad, concave iron strips oriented in such a way that if the magnerail were to stop and rest, the round bottom of the silver tube would fit almost perfectly into these outer two rails. The rail directly beneath the tube provided the power while the outer two rails provided stability and direction.

The sun had gone down, and three full moons shone brightly above them. The lighting inside the magnerail was bright and made it a little difficult to see what lay along their route. When they passed through farm country, there was little to view except a few barns and houses that were accompanied by a single blue-white lamp affixed to a tall pole.

When they passed through the smaller towns, it was still early and the streets were not yet abandoned as they would be in another hour or two. Traffic was very light with an autobox here and there. Light that shone from street lamps or brightly illuminated windows and doorways cast a pale hue on the pedestrians that strolled along the quiet avenues.

Only in towns that were sizable enough to have a large magnerail station was there activity that bustled. In these towns, autoboxes with gleaming headlamps continued to fill the streets. Sidewalk and pedestrian alike were tinged in yellow, green, blue, and red from the effusion of energy that flowed from neon lights in the windows and signs of the buildings that lined the street. There were luxurious restaurants, halls of entertainment, sports arenas, and meeting places for recreation. They were all clean, wholesome, and elegant. They were places where men, women, and children gathered together to enjoy the company of one another and the good creation in a truly pleasant and beneficial atmosphere. The town was one big, harmonious, happy family.

Bluebell looked back at Dandy and Brutus. She turned to her mother and told her what she saw. Her mother looked back.

"Oh dear, I hope Dandy isn't bothering that young man," her mother said. "I think we need to make sure everything is okay."

The woman had Bluebell scoot out of her seat. Bluebell was two years older than her sister and had a purse that was a small replica of her mother's. She carried the purse with her everywhere she went. Bluebell followed her mother to where Dandy and the young man were sitting.

The lady approached Brutus with an apologetic smile. "I'm so sorry. Dandy is so outgoing. She loves to talk to people. I hope she hasn't been a bother."

"No, no ma'am, Dandy and I have been having a fine time talking things over." Brutus saw Bluebell just behind her mother. "And you must be Bluebell."

Bluebell, always the shy one, was embarrassed that Brutus noticed her. "Yes I am, but everyone calls me Blue."

"He knows that already," said Dandy, "I already told him." Everyone laughed.

Brutus noticed Bluebell's black play purse. "Well aren't you quite grown up."

Bluebell frowned.

"I mean that pretty purse that you've got there. It's such a nice and shiny thing, isn't it." He looked down at Dandy as he said this.

Dandy looked up with a big smile and giggled and said, "She takes her purse everywhere, even when she goes to sleep at night."

Bluebell blushed. "Not every night. And I put it on the floor by the bed; I don't really sleep with it in my bed." She laughed at such a silly idea.

The mother spoke up, "Well, if you grow weary of keeping up with a little seven year old, just let her know; isn't that right, Dandy?" The lady was looking directly at her daughter to make sure she heard what she said.

"Sure mommy, I don't want to bother Brutus. I just thought

he wasn't feeling well, and so I stopped to see."

"Oh, are you not feeling well young man?"

Brutus stiffened as he heard those words again. Can't this woman see that he was no longer a young man, that he had grown up? Can't she see what her little seven-year-old could see?

Brutus was careful to answer as politely as he could although, at the moment, he felt only disdain for this woman. "Yes, ma'am," he said steadily, "I am quite all right, and Dandy has been no inconvenience. I'm sure we'll enjoy the rest of the trip together."

At precisely that moment the conductor in the red uniform stepped into their conversation. "Is there anything wrong?" His arrival did not help Brutus's mood.

"It is nothing, sir," said Brutus. "We were just making acquaintances."

"He's just trying not to be a bother," the woman said admonishingly, an eye on Brutus. "We think he might not be feeling well."

Brutus opened his mouth to protest, but the conductor stepped in. Turning to Brutus he said, "Remember what I said? You should have that burn taken care of. It's a nasty little burn, nasty."

"Now, now, just show me," the woman said to Brutus in a sympathetic tone meant to appease a mere child, "Maybe I can help."

This extremely annoyed Brutus, and he rolled his eyes.

"Now don't you put up a fuss. I know how you young men are. You think you can endure anything. You should see some of the kids I've had to patch up after a rough game of greenchnik."

This was almost too much to take. There were those words again: "young men"; and now a new one, "kids." The flesh on Brutus face suddenly felt warm as his temper rose, but once again he suppressed it and remained calm. He extended his hand so that the red spot was exposed before them all.

The woman grimaced just as the conductor had done earlier.

"My, my, that *is* a nasty burn. How did you do it?"

"Froodly's," Brutus lied.

"Froodly's?"

"Froodly Frisber, the tobacconist back in Puddle Bottom East. I ventured into his shop today for a visit knowing that I would be leaving this evening. We are friends, Froodly and I. He and a few of his patrons were smoking cigars and having a jolly good time when one of them, Fratemore by name, accidentally tapped the red-hot ash of his cigar onto the back of my hand. They offered to take care of it right then, but I had to leave or I would miss my magnerail."

"You were in the tobacco shop?" the woman asked, surprised to hear this. "The shop must have been open late. Most shops have closed by that time."

"Indeed they do, ma'am, and so was Froodly's. It was a private gathering; they were celebrating the birthday of one of the patrons. It seems that, for them, a box of cigars is the most reasonable way to celebrate such an event."

The woman acknowledged that sometimes masculine habits carry with them certain hazards. In the meanwhile, the conductor had gone to the engineer's cabin for some medical items and returned. He offered them to the lady who picked out a tube of salve, a special bandage, and some tape.

"You are quite blessed that they have a very good selection of salves. This one is especially helpful for burns. We'll have this thing looking as good as new by morning."

The lady squeezed some of the salve onto a square patch of pinkish material. As the salve made contact with the material, it turned blue. The woman waited another half-minute after which the salve turned a bright yellow. The moment it did so, the lady quickly placed it over the wound and taped it down.

As she was finishing up the dressing of the wound she looked at Brutus and said, "You know, you don't talk like most kids your age. You speak as if you've been schooled very well in English grammar and diction."

"I speak as I am," said Brutus in a low voice.

The lady was not sure what he meant by that but gave it no more thought as Dandy interrupted her.

"Mommy, can I sit with Mr. Malroye."

"Why, I don't think that will be a problem if Mr. Malroye doesn't mind." She winked at Brutus as she played along with the "Mr. Malroye" theme. This, of course, rubbed Brutus quite the wrong way. He really, really wanted to say something, but held his tongue.

"No, ma'am, I rather enjoy the company of Dandy. She won't be a bother at all."

Brutus pasted a pleasant-looking smile on his face.

"Well then," Dandy's mother said, "if Mr. Malroye needs some time to himself, he will let you know. But anyway, I think you should come back and sit with us in about a half-hour. We should be arriving in Kittanning in about an hour or so, and I think we should give Mr. Malroye some time alone."

Dandy agreed, and her mother and sister turned to go back to their seats. Bluebell's purse had a long strap, and she was carrying it over her right shoulder. Brutus watched the purse all the way back to Bluebell's seat where she slipped it off and placed it in her lap as she sat down. It was such a pretty purse. A purse that every little girl, no matter the age, would desire.

"Isn't that a pretty purse your sister has?" said Brutus.

"Oh yes," Dandy replied, "She picked it out all by herself."

"Now I wonder what Blue would carry in such a pretty purse as that one?"

"Oh lots of things. She has a comb and brush; a wallet with a pink bill which mommy gave her on her birthday. A little bottle of cologne that she got at the ham and dom store,[8]

---

[8]That is, "five and ten store," but ham and dom are short for hamponk and domponk, the names for the coins worth five ponks and ten ponks respectively.

a little package of tissues, some makeup, and a pencil. She might have a pack of gum, but I think she took it out this morning before we left our house."

"My goodness, that is a lot of things. I never would have guessed that you could put so much...uh, stuff...into such a pretty purse as that. And how did you ever remember it all?"

Dandy thought a moment and said, "I guess because she's my sister, and we always do things together, and I see her take it out most every day. She's always taking something out, especially her makeup with the mirror." Dandy giggled at this.

"She uses the mirror a lot. She says girls should be as pretty as they can even if they aren't pretty. My sister doesn't think she's very pretty, but I do. I wish I had long dark hair like she does. But she says she wishes she had short blonde hair like I do." Dandy was glowing with that last thought.

Brutus also smiled. "It sounds like you and your sister have lots of fun together. Does she ever let you play with her purse?"

Dandy hesitated before answering. "Well, not really. I mean, sometimes she lets me put it on my shoulder the way she does and walk around our bedroom a little. But since it's for older people like her, I don't get to go outside with it. Besides, if I did, what would my sister do? She wouldn't have a purse."

"Who said it's for older people like your sister? Surely a delightful little girl such as yourself would look very nice with such a pretty purse."

"My mommy says it's for older kids. I'm too young. But when I get older, I can have one too." Bluebell looked back and waved. Dandy waved back, and Brutus smiled and nodded.

"Would you like a purse like that?" Brutus asked.

"Sure. I would love to have a purse like that. But I have to wait 'til I'm more grown up."

"I don't think you should have to wait. I think if you wanted a purse you should have one now. Why should your sister have one and not you?"

Dandy frowned at that suggestion. "You mean you think my mommy is wrong? She's all grown up like you, and she should know."

"Surely purses should be for little girls such as yourself. Maybe your mommy doesn't understand. Maybe she has forgotten what it was like when she was a little girl. I'll bet she would have liked a purse, too."

Dandy thought about this for a while. Her sister always looked so grown up when she had it. And sometimes she did wish she could wear it in public and be just like her. Now that she thought about it, there seemed to be no really good reason why she could not have one too. She would be happy even with a smaller purse and one not so shiny as her sister's. What would be wrong with that? Maybe Mr. Malroye was right, and her mother was wrong.

Now, to be sure, Dandy thought, her mother was not trying to be mean; she was just making a mistake. Even though her mother was quite smart, smarter than a lot of grown-ups for that matter, it was possible that she misjudged Dandy in thinking that she should be older. And would not her mother want Dandy to be just as happy as her sister? Maybe her mother did not know how much Dandy would love to have a purse just like her sister.

Brutus was delighted to see that Dandy was musing over this. He never realized how powerful simple suggestion really was. And he never knew how skilled he was in utilizing it. He had always thought that the fist was mightier than the word. But now he saw that the word was just as powerful as the fist. What was even more glorious about it all was that if the word did not work, there was still the fist.

"I'll bet," Brutus began, "that if you asked your sister, she might let you have it for the rest of the trip."

"I don't think so. She always keeps it close to her. She never lets it out of her sight."

"Go on, ask her. You'll never know unless you try."

"But my mommy says it's only for Blue. She wouldn't like it if I asked to have it."

"Well, what do you think? Do you think it's right for your sister to have a purse and you not to have one?" Brutus was very serious when he said this. The change of tone in his voice made Dandy look up at him curiously.

"I don't know. You're asking me to do something that I don't think my mommy would want me to do."

Brutus was not daunted by this response.

"But that's the whole point, Dandy. You don't know for sure what your mother would want. You're not demanding that you have the purse, you're just asking that you might have it, for a little while. Surely your mother would understand that, wouldn't she?"

Dandy knew that her mother was always fair and honest and that she loved her and Bluebell very much. It did seem that she would not be asking too much of her sister. And now that she thought about it, her mother never said that her sister was not allowed to share the purse just for a little while. It made more sense now that she thought about it.

Dandy slid out of her seat and made her way to her mother and sister. Brutus watched with satisfaction. The moment he first saw Bluebell's purse he had the urge to plant the idea in Dandy's head that she should have one, too. He was not completely sure why. Maybe it was to satisfy one of his most basic pleasures to be manipulative of another person, especially one so delightfully innocent and unsuspecting. Besides, he was still annoyed about how Dandy's mother spoke of him, as if he were a child like her daughters. This was matching his wits against hers; his authority as a special, mature, wise, ahead-of-his-years adult against her authority as a parent.

Dandy reached their row. Bluebell was sitting nearest the aisle. She paused and looked back at Brutus for reassurance. Brutus smiled and nodded for encouragement.

"Blue," Dandy said, "I was just wondering if I could carry

your purse for a while. Only until we get off the magnerail."

Their mother had been reading a book, but this caught her attention. Bluebell looked at her mother for guidance.

With an inquisitive look their mother said to Dandy, "Why do you want to carry your sister's purse? You have Sniffles."

"I...I thought it would be nice to have a purse just like Blue. She always gets to carry it."

"But it's her purse."

The lady looked back over the seat toward Brutus who pretended to be looking out the window.

She continued, "Would you be willing to let Blue have Sniffles while she let you carry her purse."

At this, Bluebell looked at her mother with dismay. "But Mom, I don't think I want to trade my purse for Sniffles. Sniffles is for little kids."

Dandy's mouth dropped open as she sucked in a breath. "Is that all you think I am?" asked Dandy in a pouting tone. "Just a little kid?" Dandy was hurt by that but not nearly as much as she pretended to be. "I'm your sister, you know."

The children's mother was very perplexed at this. Rarely was there a disagreement between the two. They had always played well together and always were willing to suffer loss for the benefit of the other.

"Well Bluebell, it's only for a little while. We'll be arriving in Kittanning soon. It wouldn't hurt to let your sister carry the purse till we get there, don't you think?"

Bluebell was in a quandary now. She wanted to do what her mother said, but she really didn't want to be seen with Sniffles. And all because her sister wanted her purse. She knew a purse was for someone older. It was probably because she wanted to impress that Mr. Malroye guy.

Bluebell looked back at Brutus and their eyes met. She looked quickly away. He was watching. What would he think of her if she kept the purse? What would he think of her if she took Sniffles? She looked back at her mother with an anguished expression.

Their mother now saw that this was going to be very difficult for Bluebell. Maybe this was an opportunity for her to be
kind when it was hard to be kind.

"Bluebell, she's your sister, and you love her, don't you?"

"Sure Mom, it's just Sniffles."

"You don't love Sniffles?" Dandy was truly hurt and didn't
feign any of it this time. "You say you love me, your sister, and
you don't care about Sniffles? Sniffles is my friend, you know.
How can you say you love me and not Sniffles?"

"But I didn't mean it that way, Dandy." Bluebell felt very
bad about this. "I mean, you know I love you, but Sniffles isn't
real; he's just a stuffed animal, a play toy. I'm too old for a play
toy."

"Then you're saying you're too old to play with me. You
think I'm silly because I have a 'play toy'." Dandy's voice had
a good dose of sarcasm in it.

"Now Dandy, don't talk like that to your sister. You know
that's not nice."

"Why don't you tell her to talk nice to me. She thinks I'm
stupid, just like she thinks Sniffles is stupid." Dandy's voice
was louder now and caught the attention of several of the other
passengers.

"Dandy," her mother said in as harsh a manner as possible
without appearing to be angry, "you know that she doesn't
think you're stupid."

Dandy stood there with a very stern expression and her
arms crossed. Then suddenly, she nabbed Bluebell's purse and
ran off toward the rear of the magnerail. Bluebell immediately
jumped out of her seat and ran after her. Their mother was
stunned. Everyone stood up to watch Dandy and Bluebell race
toward the refreshment bar. The woman got up to go after her
two daughters, but the aisle was now crowded and everyone
was astir over the fiasco.

Dandy was surprisingly fast for such a little girl. She managed to stay ahead of her sister as she burst into the open area next to the serving counter. At the same moment, there was one who had just bought a yankburger and a large fizz. He stepped back into the aisle just in front of the two sisters, and Dandy crashed into him with a full body slam. That knocked him off balance a little, but he managed to keep his burger and drink on the tray. But Bluebell was right behind Dandy, and her body slam did the job. The yankburger flew one way and the drink another. The man tripped and fell across the counter sending napkins, empty drinking cups, paper bags, salt and pepper shakers, pickles, relish, onions, and mustard on a trek across the counter and onto the floor. Bluebell had fallen on top of Dandy.

"Get off me! Get off me!" Dandy was pushing and shoving and kicking.

"Give me my purse! It's mine!"

They both had a good hold on the purse and were playing tug-of-war with it. Bluebell was the stronger and was gaining the upper hand when Dandy gave her a good kick in the arm, which made Bluebell release it.

Dandy got to her feet and started running back up the aisle when she saw the entire load of travelers pack the aisle and seats. There was no way through. She heard her sister from behind scream for her to give her purse back. Dandy knew she had gotten up and was going to get to her if she did not act fast.

To Dandy's right was a row of seats which held a package in the seat closest to the window. Dandy climbed onto the seat near the aisle and then stepped over the bag so that she was now straddling the bag with a foot on each armrest. Her sister caught her by a leg and proceeded to yank and tug to pull Dandy back down.

Now the next thing that happened is one of those things that one would say "You had to be there to believe it." To an observer, it would have been oddly humorous, and yet, shocking at the same time. Along the inside of the magnerail tube above the windows and near the ceiling, was a cord that ran the length of the aisle. This cord was for one purpose only - to stop the magnerail in an emergency. Dandy was struggling to be loose of Bluebell's hold on her leg. She was grabbing at anything she could get her hands on, and when she felt the cord, she grasped it with her free hand. At the same time, Bluebell managed to finally get both arms around Dandy's legs and used her full weight to pull Dandy down off the seat. Dandy instinctively dropped the purse and grabbed onto the cord with both hands. This resulted in a mighty tug of the cord and the silver tube came to a severe stop in three hundred thirty-four and one-half feet precisely. There was no screeching of wheels as there were no wheels. A sudden silent stop and everyone who stood in the aisle fell backwards like bowling pins that were bombarded for a strike. Anything on the shelves in the snack area came crashing to the floor. One individual in a restroom was slammed against the wall and, needless to say, made a mess of himself and the restroom.

Dandy and Bluebell were tossed forward. Dandy fell over the seat to her front where she banged her nose and made it bleed. Bluebell flew into the aisle where she slid and became partially wedged under a seat on the far side.

The scene was pure bedlam. People at the bottom of the pile began to push and yell at the ones on top to get off. The conductor was at the far end yelling out for everyone to calm down and not to panic.

Brutus had remained in his seat the whole time. He was inwardly enjoying every moment of this. What power he had! What potential! This was just a small sample of what he could accomplish. True, he did not expect it to end in such mayhem. He would have preferred that the sisters had gotten only into a spat so that their day would have been spent in bickering and picking on one another, not to mention the unpleasantries of discipline their mother would have surely rendered to their little behinds. But he figured that he would get better at it and would soon learn how to manipulate by suggestion or, if necessary, by threat many unsuspecting and unwilling participants to get whatever he wanted.

What *that* was he was not sure yet, but a very foggy notion was beginning to form in the recesses of his mind. If he could have ventured inward to the depths of his imagination he would have found that it was, in fact, something he had never dreamed of when he first laid foot on Eskathoer.

Chapter 9

A Visit to the Ferguson Farm

The trouble on the Commodore Mitchell came to a relatively peaceful conclusion. When their mother had finally climbed out of the pile and made her way to the back of the magnerail, she found Dandy crying because of her nose and Blue holding her ankle because she had twisted it. After ensuring that neither had been badly hurt, the mother took Dandy and Blue to the snack area and pulled the cloth curtain across the doorway. She did something she had never had to do before. She scolded them severely. She would have spanked them, but she didn't want to embarrass them in front of a tubeful of passengers. Dandy and Blue soon realized how foolishly they had behaved. Dandy apologized for taking the purse, and Blue apologized for chasing Dandy.

The whole episode lasted about fifteen minutes, after which the passengers settled back into their seats. There were only minor bumps and bruises except for one who appeared to have broken an arm. By the time they arrived in Kittanning, Blue and Dandy and their mother were back to their cheery dispositions once again. In fact, the mood among the load of passengers was generally pleasant after apologies had crisscrossed the length and breadth of the magnerail, and many a palm had been slapped.

This surprised and disappointed Brutus who had hoped that the unpleasant experience would cause the whole load to leave the magnerail in a very bad humor.

When they arrived in Kittanning, everyone disembarked

as if nothing had happened at all. The conductor was the only one who seemed disturbed. He took Brutus aside and spoke with him.

"I apologize for the late arrival," he said ruefully. He stood thoughtfully for a moment and then said curiously to himself, "Odd that it should happen on an evening when one of the passengers specifically asked about the promptness of the Commodore Mitchell." The mood of his voice was wary.

With the not-so-subtle reference to Brutus's remarks earlier that evening, Brutus was certain the conductor was suspicious. He answered with noticeable scorn.

"And what are you suggesting? Do you think I had anything to do with what happened? It was only a few children who simply got out of hand. That happens you know."

The conductor's demeanor suddenly changed, and he looked at Brutus in a most peculiar fashion with one eye squinting slightly as though he were looking through a microscope. "Sir," he began, "You...uh...seem to be...well, have you done anything with...with..." The conductor's voice trailed off, and he simply gazed at Brutus with suspicious yet surprised eyes.

There was indeed something different about Brutus. He still looked like Brutus, but there was an odd transformation about him. The conductor slowly shook his head, mystified. Was it possible he had mistaken him for a youth when he first met him that evening, for the Brutus that presently stood before him certainly did not look like one in his teens. He was much older.

The conductor puzzled over this when, suddenly, he remembered something about Brutus. He remembered how Brutus had spoken with a certain maturity and clarity that was often lacking among the younger sort. He spoke like one rather well educated and very particular about his speech. He had to admit to himself now that the memory of the evening, before the Bluebell and Dandelion debacle, was a little cloudy. Perhaps, after all, his recollection of Brutus's physical appearance was wrong. It had to be. That was the only explanation.

All the while the conductor pondered these things, Brutus had held the conductor's gaze with one of his own that was menacing. He did not at all like the way the conductor seemed to peer down his nose at him.

"What now?" Brutus asked with his lip slightly curled and a tighter grip on his stick. "You look at me as if there is something wrong." Brutus looked down at himself to see if perhaps there was something out of place or torn from the mishap on the magnerail.

"Nothing...Nothing really, my friend. I hope you have a good rest of the evening." With that, the conductor nodded and walked away tentatively, looking back over his shoulder every so often as if to make sure what he saw was not a trick of his eyes.

"What's going on?" Brutus asked himself in a whisper. Fleeting images of freakish faces and deformed bodies haunted him for a moment. He had to find out what was wrong with him. He needed to get to a mirror. He had to be sure that there was nothing that would rouse undue attention from others. There was a restroom across the station floor. Brutus made his way directly to it.

Only a few were inside, and they paid no mind to Brutus. There were no sinks, only several hollowed spaces in the walls. There was a mirror that ran the length of the wall, and Brutus immediately took advantage of it.

What he saw shocked him. The figure that looked back at him was no longer a fifteen year old. He moved his face to within inches of the glass and inspected it closely. Remarkably, he'd acquired a full day's growth of beard. Gone was the light hair that had required shaving only once a week or two. The skin on his face was no longer smooth like the skin he had when he awakened that morning. His face was youthful, but not boyish. It was the face of one in his mid-twenties. He was face to face with an image of himself that he had imagined on several occasions that day in his reactions to the rude remarks referring to him as a "young man" and "one of the kids."

A smile spread across Brutus's face. He could not explain the change, but he didn't care. His deepest desire at the moment was respect and recognition in the world of adults. He knew he was their equal and more. Were there any others on that planet who could change...grow...mature by sheer will as he had done?

Brutus gazed upon his face in admiration. Deep from within his bosom rose a feeling, a conviction, just as he had when he stood before the ticket booth. But it was more powerful this time. He sensed he was a very special human being. He had a destiny that he must pursue. A destiny that no one could change. This emboldened Brutus. He had purpose.

Brutus laid his walking stick against the wall, and examined his hands. He noticed that they were slightly soiled from the trip. He still had the bandage on the back of his hand that Dandy's mother had dressed. He removed it to examine the wound. The salve was already having an effect. The red spot was only pink now. One would think on Earth it had been healing for several days.

He assumed the empty hollows along the wall were wash basins. He placed his hands in one of the spaces and a soft, warm scented spray covered them. The spray was directed in such a way that only the bare flesh was touched. The hands were immediately cleansed; the dirt simply fell away into the rinse of the mist. Then the hollow glowed for a second. This resulted in a very pleasing sensation as if the hands were massaged by little warm fingers. When the glow vanished, Brutus pulled his hands out and examined them. They were as clean as if he had scrubbed them for an hour. And they were perfectly free of moisture.

Brutus picked up his stick and left the latrine to enter the station's hall once again. Through the translucent doors at the front of the building, he saw blurry outlines of several large blocks. He suspected they were autoboxes parked along the sidewalk, like taxis at a busy train station on Earth. They were all painted black and white like the squat police cars in those old late-night third-rate movies he watched on television as a young tyke. He had to sneak out of bed when his mom and dad were snoring too loudly to hear him. From the way they lined up along the curb, Brutus assumed they were taxies. He made a straight path through the front doors to solicit the first one in line.

As soon as he got to it, he opened the door and climbed into the back seat, shuffling his walking stick around so that he could lay it next to him. There was no protective screen or glass between him and the taxi driver. One more sign of the little concern for security in that world.

"G'evenin to you sir. Pleasant evening isn't it?"

Brutus was in no mood to exchange pleasantries. "Ferguson Farm," he said directly and very business-like.

The driver looked back over the front seat with a sideways glance. "Ferguson Farm, sir? Do yeh mean *the* Ferguson Farm, the one with the big house and all?"

"Is there any other?" Brutus asked in a dry monotone.

Looking back again, the driver said, "Well sir, that's a bit of a ride, know what I mean?" Switching to the mirror, he eyed Brutus and continued. "They're about twenty miles north on highway eleven. A bit of a distance fer a city taxi if yeh know what I mean. Don't mind takin' yeh, but it'll be expensive. At least fifty grankels, I'd say."

The taxi driver was a short balding man who wore a vest over a T-shirt. He had glasses which were stoutly perched on the bridge of his nose. The lenses were large and round and extremely thick. They magnified his eyes such that when he blinked, he looked like he was sending a signal.

"Tell me," said Brutus, "have you ever had any optic problems?"

"Optic problems?" The driver puzzled a second and then brightly chirped, "Oh no sir not me; I always opt for the best. I can make up my mind fairly well. I've got a nose for that sorta thing. Yes sir, if there's one thing that Mortimer T. Sneekums can do it's make up his mind in a hurry and live by it as well, know what I mean?"

Brutus cleared his throat. "No, no, you...uh...you misunderstood my meaning. Let me be frank. Have you ever had a problem seeing the road?"

With a quick turn of his head, Sneekums looked directly into Brutus's face. He blinked and said, "Why, no sir, what ever gave you that idea?"

"Oh...nothing. Never mind. Can you take me or not; or shall I have to get another taxi?" Judging from Mr. Sneekums attire, Brutus reasoned that the driver could use all the fares that came his way. To add pressure, Brutus looked impassively out of the window as if he cared little which taxi he took.

"Oh...I see. A little edgy are yeh? Not many of my clientele is edgy, know what I mean? Haven't had an edgy one in over...say...two years. And he, I mean his wife, was having a baby. Had to get him to the hospital in a wink, yeh know; guess he was a little nervous an' all, know what I mean?"

"Yes, yes," Brutus sniveled, "I know what you mean. Please...sir." Brutus closed his eyes and took a deep breath to compose himself. "Please, just...drive. And if you don't mind I prefer to be left in silence...if you know what I mean!"

"Ooooohhhh yes sir, I understand. Yes indeed you're an edgy one, but I understand; you must have some real important business...OH!"

Brutus flinched at the exclamation. "What now?"

"Of course, of course, makes perfect sense. You must be a pretty important person." Mortimer was spying Brutus in the mirror and, as if he happened upon a secret, asked with a sly look in his overblown eyes, "Did the Gov'nor send you?" He raised his eyebrows hinting that it was okay to tell him; he could be trusted.

Brutus simply sat in mystery wondering what this near-sighted fool was talking about. His silence was proof to Mortimer that he had guessed correctly.

"Never mind, never mind. None of my business. Just lettin' yeh know I understand now. Important business, I'll bet, between the Gov'nor and the Fergusons. Very important. Well, well, well."

Mortimer was mumbling to himself now, rubbing his palms together like a hungry hobo about to sit down at a feast, "I better get you there as quickly as I can."

The taxi driver fiddled with something that Brutus couldn't see and suddenly, without warning, a series of red, blue, and pink flashing lights around the roof of the taxi lit up like a dozen emergency vehicles at a twenty-car pile up. A shrill blast like an air-raid siren topped it off.

To an observer in the street it appeared that the driver turned the wheel sharply and pushed the gas pedal to the floor. In fact, Mr. Sneekums simply entered a few keystrokes on a keypad somewhere to his right and out of Brutus's view. The steering wheel turned, and the box took off on its own, speeding down the main avenue of the city. The automated traffic baskets changed conveniently as the autobox approached each intersection. In less than four minutes, the city lights were in the taxi's rearview mirror. The driver entered another series of keystrokes, and the flashing lights went out as he took control of the steering wheel.

"The company prefers that we turn off the TERS once we no longer need it, and since we just left the city limits, I 'spect we don't need it any more."

"TERS?" Brutus stated questioningly.

"Oh sorry, chap, that's kinda technical jargon that only us in the taxi business know. It stands for Taxi Emergency Response System. We turn it on in emergencies or for urgent matters like yours."

Brutus had been leaning forward a little but now sat back and closed his eyes. This strange new world was full of boneheads, he thought to himself. Twenty miles. It should not take long. He just hoped the driver would respect his request for silence.

"'Scuse me, sir."

"Now what?"

"Pardon me for sayin', but I suggest you try to get yourself together. You want to make a good impression, yeh know. The Fergusons have close ties with the Gov'nor, yeh know, and out of respec' fer the Gov'nor, you need to tidy up a bit."

Brutus caught a glimpse of the driver rubbing his cheek to indicate the obvious beard that Brutus had. Mortimer reached over to a compartment in the dash and pulled out a plastic package.

"Always carry a couple of spares with me in case I have to put in some overtime."

He handed Brutus the package. Brutus opened it and a pleasant, floral aroma filled the autobox. He looked up and made eye contact with the driver through the mirror. He had no idea what to do with the package.

"Go on, you can use it. It's clean, fresh from the factory. Them there shaving towels will do wonders for yeh, know what I mean?"

There was a large but very thin towel folded neatly inside the package. It was warm to the touch.

"I suggest, if you don't mind my saying, that you kinda cover your whole face with it, yeh know, give yerself the full treatment. Makes yeh feel like you just got a good snooze in, know what I mean?"

"That is a ridiculous idea. I would sooner wear mouse ears than ride around in the back of a taxi with my face covered in a towel. What if someone saw me?"

"Well, sir, I'm not the biggest drop o' rain that's fallen from the sky, but if you take a look around, I don't think you're right likely to be seen by anyone or anything 'ceptin maybe a portamuk[9] or a skunk or one of them yanks down there in the meadow."

From the moment they had left the city limits of Kittanning, there was nothing but country road with a few houses here and there and very few autoboxes. It was such a silly thing to do; and yet the warmth of the towel and the scent were very agreeable.

"Before now, have you ever, ever suggested to any of your passengers to actually take a shaving towel and wrap their face in it while riding in your taxi?"

"Yes sir, once. It was my brother, Bartholomew. Ol' Bart was late for a date, if you know what I mean. He pulled a double-shift and just got off work. Poor soul, his eyes had such dark rings under 'em, he looked like a raccoon. A bit like yours I might add. Well, I give him one of them towels and by the time he got to his girl's house he was lookin' fresh as a cucumber."

Brutus took one more look outside the speeding autobox just to reassure himself. He pulled the towel out and said, "Do not, I repeat, do not allow me to be seen by anyone with this ridiculous thing on my face."

Brutus unfolded the towel to its full length and wrapped his face in it. If one were to look at Brutus from the outside, his appearance was now as one hospitalized for multiple facial fractures. Brutus sat back with his head angled backward so that it lay on the top of the seat as the towel rested on his face.

"That's right sir, yeh got the idea. It'll be another ten minutes before we get there. Jus' sit back and relax. I'll let yeh know when we get there."

The driver finally shut up and Brutus relaxed. The towel was so soothing that Brutus dozed off without the slightest

---

[9] A portamuk is a floppy-eared animal the size of a deer that hops like a rabbit and barks like a dog. One of its peculiarities is its fondness for eating lilies and strawberries.

notion of a dream. But it soon ended when he was awakened ten minutes later by the honk of a horn. He jerked himself up and pulled the towel off his face. The towel was still warm and his face was clean-shaven. Brutus felt like a million bucks.

To their front was a gate that was opening apparently to the sound of the horn. Mr. Mortimer T. Sneekums, one of a long line of taxi drivers in his family, pulled through the gate and up the driveway that led to the front of a beautiful three-story mansion. Its beauty was enhanced by a series of floodlights that ran along the perimeter of the structure. The autobox came to rest in front of a wide sheltered porch that was reached by a flight of ten steps. Along each side of the stairway was a wall on which sat the figure of a lion.

The fare came to 58.80 grankels. Brutus gave the driver a red and blue bill worth seventy grankels and told him to keep the change. He also requested the driver to stay and let the meter run. He was not yet sure how this little family reunion was going to go.

Brutus, with the aid of his walking staff, ascended the steps and approached the front door. It was a large wooden door with an intricate floral design carved into the wood. To the right of the door there was a button three inches in diameter that had the word "Welcome" printed on it. Brutus pressed the button and somewhere above and behind him there rang out the unexpected *Dong! Dong!* of a heavy bell. Brutus turned around quickly and apprehensively peered up at the roof over the porch expecting to see huge church bells hanging over his head. The door suddenly opened behind him.

He was greeted cordially by one whom Brutus assumed to be the butler. The butler, in a very courteous manner, asked Brutus to state the purpose of his visit. Brutus sensed that Mortimer had his eyes and ears open and was observing the whole affair like a mother anxiously watching every move of her child in a play. He lied to the butler that he had an important message from the governor and wished to speak with the

Fergusons directly. The butler asked Brutus to step inside and wait while he would deliver the message.

Brutus looked back and found Sneekum's gaze locked onto him like a birddog's. Mortimer winked and gave him the thumbs up. Feeling quite foolish, Brutus returned the signal. His primary concern at the moment was to play along as agreeably as possible. He knew once inside the door he would no longer have to perpetuate the cover story that the taxi driver had unwittingly imposed on him. Brutus stepped through the door and the butler closed it behind him. Brutus relaxed now that he was out of sight.

Mr. Mortimer T. Sneekums muttered to himself, "I sure hope that shavin' towel did the trick," and sat back as he turned on the holobox[10] to relax. It was tuned to his favorite station, which played inspirational golden oldies thirty-two hours a day.

The butler left to inform Mr. Ferguson of the visitor. It was only another minute before the butler returned and told Brutus that Mr. Ferguson would meet with him in the library. Brutus followed the butler who led him down a brightly lit hallway. The library was on the right across from a dining room, and Brutus stepped in to wait for Mr. Ferguson.

The library was a large hall with a high ceiling from which there were suspended three chandeliers. One of these hung just inside the entranceway. The room was softly illuminated with two desk lamps on a desk to his right as he entered, two floor lamps that were positioned next to large cushiony reading chairs, and the chandelier near the entranceway. The desk had a clock that ticked quietly. In front of the desk that bore the lamps were two chairs that were clearly positioned in such a way that one could sit in them and comfortably converse with another who sat behind the desk.

The four walls were lined with shelves and shelves of books.

[10] The holobox is like a radio with a glass bubble. Inside the bubble one may watch a three dimensional performance of the artist while listening at the same time.

Two reading tables with unlit lamps were neatly centered in the middle of the room. Scattered here and there were other reading chairs, each of which had their own floor lamps that were at the present likewise unlit. On the wall opposite the desk, there was a fireplace and mantle which were not in use since the season was warm.

Over the doorway was an extremely large portrait of a distinguished looking male dressed in a white suit. He was seated at a desk that looked very much like the one in the library. He sat with his hands folded next to a sheet of writing paper. On the desk was an inkbottle in which there was placed a quill. Brutus suspected the quill was intended to place the portrait in a quaint and venerable atmosphere. The background of the portrait was shelved books that were remarkably similar to the set of books that were currently behind the desk before him. As Brutus compared the books in the portrait to the wall of books behind the desk, he realized that those in the portrait and those in the library were identical in size, position, color, and title (that is, those titles that were readable in the portrait). That was very peculiar. The portrait must have been done in the same library in which he now stood, and the books had not been removed or rearranged since then. That was an interesting curiosity to Brutus, but he immediately forgot about it when Mr. Ferguson entered the room.

Brutus was expecting an old man to greet him. Instead, he was greeted by one that didn't look a day over thirty. The children of Angus and Mary were aging well in this world. In fact, they looked like they could live on for another three or four hundred years. He remembered how Bortamus lamented that Henry and Ginny would probably pass away within a hundred years, but from all appearances that was entirely unlikely.

Brutus decided that if he was going to persuade Mr. Ferguson that he was an authentic human being from Earth, he would have to do something that secured his attention quickly. Mr. Ferguson held his palm up in greeting. Brutus hesitated and then responded by extending his hand as one does when greeting with a handshake. Mr. Ferguson was visibly affected by this as he lowered his hand slowly and grasped Brutus's hand.

"It has been years...decades...since I last saw my father greet another in this manner. And it was not on this planet. There is only one place in the whole universe where men greet one another in this fashion."

"Indeed there is, Mr. Ferguson." Brutus looked sternly into Mr. Ferguson's eyes. "My name is Brutus Malroye, and I am from that place. I am from Hampton, North Carolina, of the United States of America. I am from the planet Earth."

Mr. Ferguson numbly ambled to the desk and slowly collapsed into the seat behind it. He gestured for Brutus to sit down. Brutus did so in a pompously dignified manner as if he were royalty from another world. He laid the stick on the floor next to him. He now had the advantage. He decided he would come straight out with the story. He explained everything from the mystery of Griffin Farm to the escape he had made that morning from the governor's mansion.

Then he related what he thought was the key point in all of this, that he was kin to Henry and his sister. It was a little complicated, but Brutus stated it as plainly and bluntly as possible. He was a distant cousin of Henry and Ginny. Brutus's great, great, great grandmother, Virginia Malroye, was named after Henry and Ginny's aunt, who was also Virginia's grandmother.

In the whole story, there were two points that Brutus concealed by lying.

The first was the claim to have entered Eskathoer by the oak tree which had grown back. Brutus concocted that the existence of the farm and tree were unknown to the authorities on Earth and that he discovered their location through the piecing together of stories that were kept secret in his family. He mentioned nothing about the rediscovery of the oak leaves.

He thought it best to leave that fact unmentioned until he understood the significance of the leaves better.

The second point was his age. He claimed to be twenty-five and was pleased to see that Mr. Ferguson accepted it unquestioningly. Everything was going as hoped for. It was exhilarating to manipulate another by telling, of all things, the truth. There were the exceptions, of course, of the two minor issues regarding the oak leaves and his age.

Brutus pressed Henry for his help to counter the governor's plan to send him back to Earth. After a long pause, Henry spoke, "So, Mr. Malroye, you are asking for assistance from me and my sister to persuade the governor, Lord Bigsley, to allow you to stay in this world. Are you not familiar with..."

Mr. Ferguson was interrupted by the figure of his sister, Ginny, who just entered the room.

Flustered by her unexpected arrival, Henry stumbled for words, but recovered quickly and said, "Mr. Malroye, allow me to introduce you to my sister. Ginny, dear, this is Mr. Malroye. He is...uh...from out of town."

He motioned for his sister to come forward. As she did so, she stepped directly under the light of the chandelier. Ginny was stunningly beautiful. She greeted Brutus with open palm, and he returned the gesture.

"It is a pleasure to meet you ma'am. May I add that it is hard to conceive of anything more lovely than you in all of Eskathoer."

Ginny blushed and Mr. Ferguson frowned.

The butler now appeared in the doorway of the library.

"Mr. Ferguson, sir, there is an urgent visit for you in the interaction room."

"Urgent visit? Thank you, Desmond." Mr. Ferguson excused himself and quickly left.

"Desmond," Ginny said, "would you please bring us a pot of tokkofo[11] and sweets from the pantry? Don't forget a cup

[11] Tokkofo is a hot beverage similar to tea served with cinnamon.

for Henry."

"Yes, ma'am." Desmond immediately left.

Ginny spoke first. "I hesitate to ask what the occasion of your visit is since I am sure you have spent a good part of the last hour explaining that to my brother."

Brutus smiled and began loftily, "Indeed, it is a long story, and I am rather exhausted from the telling of it. But why don't you tell me about yourself. How is it that you have remained so long with your brother? I should think one as lovely as you would have had many suitors."

Ginny blushed again. "Mr. Malroye, you embarrass me. I am quite happy here. You mention suitors, which is another way of asking why I am not married. Marriage is not for everyone you know. The truth is, I am not permitted to marry."

"What!" Brutus was genuinely surprised and disturbed by this. "How could such a thing be?"

"I am not from this world as you know. My brother and I are not permitted to marry because we are descendants of Adam, the fallen one."

The remark disappointed Brutus. This beautiful, intelligent woman was speaking words that smacked of the superstition of an earlier age. To Brutus, such talk of sin and fallen humanity was sheer foolishness. He had outgrown these ideas on Earth long before he came to Eskathoer.

In spite of Ginny's presence, Brutus's thoughts began to drift. Strangely, and yet marvelously, Brutus felt that his understanding of what was really the truth had grown. He had always thought that such ideas as sin and a fallen humanity were absurd. He always had a firm conviction about their foolishness. But now, since his arrival in that world, the clarity of how unreasonable they were had intensified. Brutus could not quite put his finger on when and how, but everything was so much clearer now, as if he had stepped out of murky shadow into light.

Brutus realized now that this insight of the 'real truth' had been only an artificial one, like a spectator in the stands, not as one in the game. He had had an imperfect notion of the truth, as one has difficulty discerning figures through tinted and very wavy glass. But now he understood clearly. And not merely as one looking through crystal-clear glass, but as one on the other side of the glass. He understood as one on the inside and in the middle of it all. He realized that the great mysteries of where man came from and where he is going are summed up in this simple maxim: the universe is all that ever was, all that ever is, and all that ever will be. If there is a God, Brutus reasoned, surely he would have revealed himself.

"*No, no,*" Brutus thought to himself, "*the idea of a Supreme Being is lame.*" It was so anti-intellectual, so backward. It was a waste product from the desire of intelligent creatures to reach out to something beyond themselves. The sooner one recognizes that he controls his own fate the sooner he can take the next step toward reaching his full potential.

Man's hope is man himself. Humankind, regardless of what planet, is in a grand march toward a destiny that ultimately will lead straight into the halls of glory, power, and preeminence.

There had been many in Earth's history who appreciated this. Those who were disparaged as brutal, ruthless dictators were really those who had the greatest insight into these truths. They alone knew what man's potential was, and they were willing to sacrifice their bodies and their lives to bring humanity closer, albeit only a tiny step closer, to its final destiny. Admittedly, they often had to resort to brute force, but it was for the good of all. Some were destined to be sacrificed along the way. Only a few were destined to lead and make the hard decisions.

"*Yes,*" Brutus pondered inwardly, "*I have been a spectator far too long.*"

"Mr. Malroye, you seem lost in thought. Do I bore you?"

Ginny was not behaving rudely or trying to be sarcastic by

that remark. She simply asked an honest question.

Brutus's reverie evaporated, and he fumbled momentarily collecting himself. He resumed his lofty air.

"Indeed not, ma'am. I am just taken aback by the thought of your never having been able to socialize with anyone other than your brother. I assume you do not get out much."

"You are quite mistaken if you think I am a recluse. I and my brother often visit friends and travel."

"Ah, yes, but it is always with your brother, is it not? Have you ever been allowed to socialize with men other than your brother?

Ginny was hesitant in her answer. "Mr. Malroye, there is absolutely no need for me to socialize with men. I am quite happy as I am. Besides, there are a couple of possibilities that could bring an end to my spinsterhood." This last remark was intended as mild sarcasm.

"Really," said Brutus with equal sarcasm, "and what might those possibilities be?"

"For one, if there were ever a man from Earth who was fortunate enough to find his way into this world and be permitted to stay, he would be very eligible, provided of course he is not already married.

"And the second is so obvious that you would stumble over it trying to guess."

"That they change this ridiculous law?"

Ginny was surprised at Brutus's assessment of that law. "No, Mr. Malroye, it is not a ridiculous law. It is a very good law, in fact. The simple and obvious answer is that I return to Earth."

Brutus would have stumbled trying to guess. Why would anyone want to leave Eskathoer?

"And you would want to go back to Earth? After all these years on Eskathoer, I find it difficult to believe you could just get up and leave."

Ginny smiled. "Yes Mr. Malroye, you are quite right. It is

unlikely I would ever leave this beautiful world. But there is always that possibility. One should never count out even the most unlikely turn of events."

"And how would you go back? The same way you came?"

Brutus had asked this because he wanted some confirmation that the oak tree of Griffin Farm did, in fact, have something to do with the way in which Ginny and her family had arrived in Eskathoer. Henry's silence on Brutus's lie that he entered into that world through the oak tree was strong evidence supporting that confirmation. But he wanted more. The family's story of the oak tree always seemed a little dubious. And the plain truth was that he had not actually escaped Earth through the oak tree. The tree didn't exist. The only obvious possibility was the oak leaves. It just seemed too much of a coincidence in his mind that he was holding the leaves in his hand when that terrifying beam of light appeared and shot him right into Eskathoer.

"Indeed, I could, but it is completely unnecessary because - let us just say - there is another ride home."

"And what is that?" Brutus remembered Mortimer and that the meter was still running.

"The oerken leaves."

Brutus was stunned by this. There was a connection. The leaves must have had something to do with it. But how?

"Oerken leaves?"

"Yes. Sadly, as evidenced by your response, I see that the oerken leaves have faded away into a little known legend. But it is no legend. The oerken leaves are a powerful force. A force that could be used for much good. But they are largely regarded as legend because of the fact that one of the leaves is lost. Well, I don't really mean lost. In fact, it was hidden - by my father."

"Your father? Vicegerent Angus Ferguson?"

"Yes. There is one leaf that is still under the care and protection of the Governor of Brandenhelm Province. The other was placed under my father's care."

"But why were the leaves ever separated?" Brutus asked.

"My father suggested the idea. He feared that they could be used for evil instead of good. A single leaf itself has great potential for good...or evil. But the two leaves together have unimaginable potential. My father preferred to sacrifice their potential for good out of fear of their potential for evil."

"But who, in all of Eskathoer, would want to use them for evil?"

Brutus was partly humoring Ginny with this question. But he also thought it was a relevant question. It seemed to him that one born in Eskathoer tended to grow up into what one might call on Earth a hopeless Puritan. Who, in this beautiful, happy world, would ever think of using it for so-called evil? There was no one in this world, Brutus was sure, who truly understands what evil really means. Even on Earth, where so-called evil was rampant, few understood its true nature. There is a fine distinction between *evil* and those reasonable and necessary acts that have a higher goal for the benefit of all. Indeed, at times one must make no distinction between the highest good and evil.

Ginny responded, "No one in Eskathoer would ever use them in such a way unless, of course, they were deceived into doing so."

"Is there anyone that would ever seek to do such a horrible thing?" Brutus pretended to be dismayed at the thought.

"No Eskathoerian would do so." With a sigh of repugnance, she added, "But one from my home-world could easily pursue such a hideous ambition. I thank God that only I and my family are from that vile planet."

It was all falling into place now. Sweet, mysterious, glorious, merciful, gracious Fate was on Brutus's side. He could see it more clearly now than ever. Fate would have him to be the only genius his family had for generations. Fate pushed and pulled and wrestled with the reasoning of his inner man not to dismiss the stories of Chester and Clara as madness. Fate led him to the discovery in his attic of the old, yellowing map of Griffin Farm that identified the location of the missing leaf. Fate graciously facilitated every step of the way for his rediscovery of that leaf. And Fate most certainly, even with a kind of sense of humor, shot him into oblivion only to land in a world that was so innocent, so unsuspecting, so ripe for the picking.

"Nobody knows where the second leaf is?" Brutus asked. "That is fascinating. Tell me more; I have always been fond of a good mystery."

Ginny was amused by Brutus's enthusiasm. "There is not much to say. My father hid it and told no one where. It's just as simple as that." Ginny gave a little shrug for emphasis.

"And has no one ever tried to find it?"

Ginny frowned, "Why would anyone want to do that? It was the wish of my father, Vicegerent Ferguson mind you, that the leaf remain hidden. It would be disrespectful of anyone to go against those wishes."

This reminded Brutus of Bortamus, when he became so defensive about Brutus's calling the vicegerent, *Mr.* Ferguson.

"Indeed, Miss Ginny, that is what I would expect as well. Certainly, your father was confident that no one would try to discover the secret of its hiding place. Do you think it's possible he may have been a little over-confident? May he not have recorded the secret somewhere in his writings, thinking they were safe because no one would dare look for them?" Brutus was fishing for anything.

"Well Mr. Malroye, if you were up on the customs of high office, you would know that he was required to keep a record of all of his activities, even the most sensitive. And those records are open to public scrutiny. But search as you may, there is no mention of the secret."

"Then your father did not conform to custom, did he? A wise man I must say." Inwardly Brutus was cursing and blessing the vicegerent at the same time. If he had recorded the secret, it would be known by all. But without a record of it, how was he going to find out?

"On the contrary, I believe he did conform to the required custom, Mr. Malroye. He simply recorded it in a place that no one would look."

"But where could that possibly be?" Brutus was feverish. He felt so close; the little gem that he was seeking was just within reach.

"It seems to me," he continued, "that everything one writes can sooner or later be discovered and read by anyone who has a mind to. Unless, of course, such a document itself is hidden or locked up. If your father recorded the secret, as you think he did, then it has to be in an unofficial document. It would have to be a document that is not a matter of public record but still satisfies the obligation to bear witness to it."

Ginny nodded in agreement. "There is one document that would have provided my father with both the ability to comply with the custom and yet keep it a secret at the same time. It is a tradition to keep a diary for one who holds a position of authority such as my father did. The contents of that diary may not be disclosed to anyone until after the official dies. My father did keep such a diary. But it too is gone. We believe he recorded the location of the hiding place of the missing leaf in his diary, and for that reason, he hid it as well. We fear that he may have hid it with the leaf itself. That diary preserves the private history of his life. My father was a great man, Mr. Malroye. Great men should have their story told. That diary would tell his story well."

Brutus almost moaned out loud at this very disturbing revelation.

Ginny made an amused face and, as an afterthought, revealed, "My father once said, if you want to hide something from someone, just stick it right under his nose. He'll never think to look for it there. But I have never run across the diary in any place that I would consider to be 'right under my nose'."

That remark struck Brutus like a bolt of lightning. Perhaps the diary was indeed right under their noses. Perhaps it was in a place where it was easily seen but not actually noticed. The ideal hiding place for such a book would be a place in which it does not stand out, a place in which it is not obvious, and yet a place in which it is no surprise to find it there. There was only one place that Brutus could think of, and they were standing in the middle of it.

Chapter 10

In Search of a Diary

While Ginny and Brutus were talking about the laws and customs of high office and the whereabouts of the oerken leaves and Vicegerent Angus's diary, Ginny's brother, Henry, was in the interaction room taking an important visit.

The interaction room was not a common feature among the households of Eskathoer. A few were found in the homes of the affluent, but most of them were either in national government buildings or the homes of those who held high public office. The interaction room was more than just a simple phone booth. It was a room in which one could interact in a three-dimensional manner with another whose location was physically hundreds or even thousands of miles away. The spatial characteristics of each room were manipulated in such a way that they appeared to overlap and fuse.

Back at the governor's mansion, immediately after dismissing John, Josie, and Matt from the evening meal in the Blueberry room, Lord Bigsley visited the Ferguson Farm via the interaction room. As Henry entered the room in his own house, he was greeted by Lord Bigsley as though he were physically present. Likewise, in the interaction room at the governor's mansion, it appeared as if Henry had bodily walked into the room to meet Lord Bigsley.

Lord Bigsley, with a warm smile, held up his palm, which Henry, with equal cordiality, patted in greeting, though neither felt the slap from the other.

"It's good to see you, Henry. How is Ginny?" the governor asked.

"Ginny is doing well, Charles." The governor preferred to be addressed by his middle name among friends. "We are both doing fine. I see that you are doing quite well also."

"Indeed I am, Henry. This particular evening has been a very enjoyable one and yet a very grave one as well."

"Enjoyable and yet grave? Now that is a strange combination." Henry spoke in an amused manner, but he quickly realized that the governor was quite serious.

"Henry," Lord Bigsley said soberly, "Let us sit down."

The two sat down opposite one another, each in their own chair. Lord Bigsley had pulled his chair close to the center of the exchange knowing that the conversation might take a while. He wanted to be as comfortable as possible.

The governor spoke in a somewhat hushed tone but quite earnestly and deliberately, "I have to warn you, Henry, about something of which I'm not really sure how to begin, so I might as well begin with the events of a few days ago."

Lord Bigsley gave an account, in some detail, of the series of events that began with Brutus's ungraceful arrival via the oerken tree two days earlier, to his escape that morning. He also related how he obtained the help of John and his siblings, who were, as he put it, "very bright, behaved, and quite charming youngsters" from Earth. He skipped the part about how they got there, thinking it was not important at the moment. Finally, his face ashen and eyes dark, he explained the possibility, and the reason why, Brutus might try to contact Henry and his sister at Ferguson Farm.

"Charles," Henry said stiffly, "Brutus has already found us. He arrived only minutes ago."

"What? Already?" Lord Bigsley was so astounded by this that he shot up out of his chair.

"I underestimated that young whipper-snapper!" he said, pounding his fist into the palm of his other hand. "I thought it would take him at least a day or two before he'd make it your way."

"There you go again," said Henry with a very puzzled look on his face. "You keep referring to him as a youth, a boy, a young teen. The 'boy' that is in my library at this very moment does not look like a young whipper-snapper." Henry paused and faintly smiled as he recalled how his own father used to call him by that term whenever he got a little out of line as a young boy. He continued, "He claims to be twenty-five, and by all appearances, I would not judge him a liar. One could easily take him to be thirty."

Lord Bigsley was stymied and lost in thought over this. He looked up at Henry shaking his head and said, "I don't understand, Henry. The Brutus Malroye that escaped this morning was a youth of not more than 16 or 17 years. In fact, he told us he was fifteen Earth-years of age. Are you sure of what you saw?"

"As sure as anything, Charles. He must be the same person. He knows too much about us. Claims that two of his ancestors, an Aunt Clara and Uncle Chester by name, used to make frequent trips to Eskathoer, like a holiday. He says they used the 'oak' tree, which I assume is like the oerken tree on your estate."

"Did he mention their last name, this Clara and Chester couple?"

"Indeed, he did. Their name was Chester and Clara Wilson. His Aunt Clara was a Malroye."

The governor chuckled in a worrisome manner.

"Well, my friend, they both must be one and the same. No one else in Eskathoer would have known the names of those two. We kept a close eye on Chester and Clara, but they never required anything more than that. No one but Amos and Amy, and a few others of us, knew about them. The Buckwalters did a very good job in managing them. They prevented a serious crisis."

"Amos and Amy! Why how are they? How I miss those two. We haven't seen them since Dad's funeral."

"Well, don't feel too bad about it. If I judge correctly, you'll be seeing them again and quite soon. Now, listen, we need to confront Brutus as soon as possible, but I don't want to do it tonight. John and his brother and sister have had an exhausting day, not to mention star lag and a little culture shock. They need a good night's rest. Do you think you can keep Brutus there 'til morning?"

"I don't think that will be a problem at all. He came to us for help. I'm not completely sure, but I think it's a ninety percent likelihood he will take an offer to stay the night."

"Good. We will be there early in the morning. I'll get Amos to take us in one of his antiques. We should be there by 9:00 o'clock at the latest."

"One more thing, Charles," Henry said, his words spiked with nervousness. Lord Bigsley responded with a glance that said he was listening.

"I haven't told Ginny about Brutus. I mean, she doesn't know who he is or where he's from." Then with sudden alarm he said, "My goodness I had clean forgotten! I left them alone in the library!" In anguish, Henry looked away toward the door from where he entered the interaction room. "Charles, I need to get back right away!" Without waiting for an answer, Henry rose quickly to his feet, stumbled over his chair and ran out of the room.

"Hurry!" the governor called out after him, nodding in agreement as he followed his flight. When Henry was gone, he reached out and touched a little black box that was sitting on the table in front of him. He immediately disappeared as well as his chair and a few other pieces of furniture that appeared with him. The room fell dark. Henry was running down the hallway as fast as the polished floors allowed him with only one thing in his mind - to get back to the library as quickly as possible.

———

Josie and Matt had already bathed and gone to bed. Matt had been looking forward to the golden tub and its whirlpool bath ever since before dinner. But as it turned out, he was so tired that he skipped the whirlpool and simply took a quick shower and brushed his teeth before he crawled into bed.

"Wow and double-wow," he said as he slipped under the sheet and blanket and stretched himself out on the bed. It felt so much better, if that were possible, than it did earlier that day when the maid had first introduced them to their quarters. At that time, it had felt like a cloud; now he was certain it was a cloud. Never in his long ten Earth-years of existence had he felt as euphoric as he did now, lying under the deep, soft folds of the magnificent blankets. It was cool and airy and the mattress was cushiony. The instant he settled into it he went limp, as though the bed itself caused the body to relax and quickly fall into a drowsy, slumberous state. The last thing he saw through heavy and blinking lids as he slid off into blissful sleep was Michelangelo lying on the rug next to the bed. He and Michelangelo were becoming good buddies. Matt smiled over that thought.

After John made sure that his brother and sister had made it into bed, he likewise bathed and brushed his teeth. He was about to crawl into bed when he took a final look around their cozy room. The light was soft, so soft that it had a physically relaxing effect. It certainly didn't keep Matt from sleeping. His deep breathing told John that he had long drifted away. Michelangelo, lying on the floor next to Matt's bed, was snoozing soundly. No wonder, John figured. Michelangelo was probably one dog that could sleep under a brilliant noonday sun.

The light switch, like all switches in the mansion, was a glossy button, lemon-yellow, about midway up the wall next to the door which John had left open. John was about to punch it with his fist when he saw his book bag resting against the foot of his bed.

John couldn't help but think how insignificant the book

bag had become since his arrival in Eskathoer. He mentally tallied its contents. He had a notion to leave the coins for Amos as a souvenir from Earth, but then he realized that if Amos had built replicas of American cars, he surely had some American coins stashed away.

Now the camera was something else. He opened the bag, rummaged through it until his hand bumped into it, and pulled it out. He immediately took a picture of Michelangelo. He took another shot of Matt, now curled up under the fluffy blankets with a semi-smile on his face. John returned the camera to the book bag.

He saw the pocket Bible nestled against the two library books. The golden edges were darker now with wear and age. Strangely, its presence brought a sense of uneasiness in his midsection. The Bible was God's revelation of himself to a lost world, not a world like Eskathoer. How helpful was it going to be for him, especially in such a time as this? He pulled it out trying to think of some verse that would have meaning for him at that point in time and place in the universe.

"Hmm," John murmured pensively, "the universe." The vivid image of the galaxy on the back porch of Michelangelo's house in the oak on Griffin Farm suddenly seized John with awe. That galaxy was in deep, deep space. The recollection of the blackness all around the Starliner sent a chill down his spine. He knew how Matt must have felt when he took that first step to climb into the Studebaker. One slip and what would he have fallen into? Nothingness? A bottomless well?

John opened the pocket Bible to the New Testament and found a verse that reflected his thoughts:

> "For I am persuaded that neither
> death nor life, nor angels nor principali-
> ties nor powers, nor things present nor
> things to come, nor height nor depth..."

There it was, the word *depth*. As Earthlings, John and his brother and sister were in depths that they had never dreamed existed. John read on:

> "...nor depth, nor any other created thing, shall be able to separate us from the love of God which is in Christ Jesus our Lord."

A knock came to the door of their quarters. John closed the Bible and hurriedly slipped it back into the book bag. He stepped outside of the bedroom and closed the door gently. The knock came to the door once again. John hastened to the door and opened it. There he found Bentley standing with a large pitcher of warm milk and three glasses.

"Pardon me sir, but the governor has sent this for the three of you. It will help you to sleep well," he said in stiff butler-ese.

"Thank you," said John with a smile, "But I think you're a little late. Josie and Matt are lights out already."

"Lights out, sir?" Bentley asked, one eyebrow slightly lifted.

"You might want to write that one down, too," John suggested with a hint of laughter. "On Earth, at least where I come from, it means you're asleep. Comes from the idea that when you sleep, it's usually with the lights out."

"Why, I must make a note of that one. I'm sure the governor will be delighted to hear of it."

From somewhere deep within his emerald coat, Bentley found his notepad and pulled it out. He scribbled on it in little jerky strokes as he made an annotation about the expression. He read it back to himself silently, and with a satisfied nod indicating that he had captured its meaning sufficiently, he put it away. He looked back up at John who had watched in fascination, wondering what else Bentley kept in that little notepad.

"Shall I leave the yank milk anyway?"

"Yank milk?"

"Yes sir, yank milk. It's like cow's milk only sweeter and has a unique and quite robust flavor. When taken just before retiring, as you are soon to do I judge, it provides one with a most pleasant and refreshing sleep. It is a shame that your brother and sister have already gone to bed."

"Believe me," John said, "I don't think it would have made much difference. We are all pretty exhausted. I don't think sleep is going to be a problem for any of us."

"That is good, sir. The governor wants to be sure that you get a good night's rest. It looks as if your services will be needed sooner than we had expected."

The mention about his services reminded John of several bothersome things. It reminded him of the evening's experience in the Blueberry room where Lord Bigsley laid the burden of the fate of the whole planet on John. It reminded him that in spite of his importance, he felt so completely incompetent for the job. He knew how the governor was counting on him. Not just the governor. He recalled the reaction of the young woman at the gate when they first arrived, how she was so pleased at their arrival. He remembered the look on Amos's face back on Earth when he pointed with his pipe beyond the ruins of Griffin Farm and said to John that if he were looking for history, he'd have to look deeper into the woods.

John was sure that the governor was overestimating, by a wide margin, his ability to deal effectively with Brutus. His stomach felt that unpleasant ache once again, just as it had done earlier that evening.

"On second thought, I think I might need that milk. Please bring it in and leave it on the table over there."

Bentley, in a very deliberate fashion, as butlers are trained to do, walked to the table and gracefully laid the tray with the pitcher and glasses on it without a sound, not even a tinkle. Then he walked back to the door in the same butlerish manner and started to leave when he suddenly stopped and turned around.

"Sir, if I may, I would like to say something."

John poured himself a glass of yank milk and nodded to Bentley to continue.

"I know that you are very unsure of yourself. I know that you think that you are an insignificant nobody that stumbled into something way over your head. Well, it is good that you feel that way. It means that you will not take anything for granted. You won't be foolhardy. You will use your head. That is very important. You must not allow your emotions to rule over your head."

"Thank you," said John, "I will try to do that."

"And one more thing, sir. Don't worry. It is going to turn out well. I can sense those things." Bentley paused a moment and recalled something that Vicegerent Ferguson was fond of saying. He continued, "All things work together for good, as you well know. Keep that in mind. It's just that if things get a bit grim, don't lose your head. Keep your faith. If you do that, you'll get through this."

John wasn't sure if this was helping or making things worse. All the same, it was very thoughtful of Bentley to offer his concern and advice. And perhaps it was a simple rule that he could keep close by; something that would make the difference when the time came.

"Thank you again." John smiled appreciatively.

"Oh," said John suddenly. He reached down and poured another glass of yank milk.

"Here, take this and get a good night's rest yourself."

Bentley looked at the glass of milk and with a wave of his hand said, "No thank you, sir; never touch the stuff myself. I was raised on cow's milk." With that, Bentley stepped through the door, closed it, and was gone.

John lingered over Bentley's parting words about all things working together for good. He was certain they were from the same place in the Bible he was just reading before Bentley had brought the yank milk. And that reminded him of another verse in the same chapter. It was something that tied in very well with what Lord Bigsley had said during the evening meal, about how the universe had physically changed after Adam had sinned on Earth. John didn't need to look it up, he could recite it from memory:

> "...The creation itself also will be delivered from the bondage of corruption into the glorious liberty of the children of God. For we know that the whole creation groans and labors with birth pangs together until now."

John took a deep breath and let it out in a muffled whistle. God's word to the sinful world that he came from was as true in Eskathoer as it was in the oak tree on Earth. He must take heart. The present outlook was dark but John was reassured that it had not escaped the mind of God.

Henry arrived at the library at a dead run. Just before he reached the door he slowed down to catch his breath and compose himself. The door was almost closed. Just outside the room he paced up and down the hall several times, wringing his hands, going over in his mind what he was going to say to Brutus. On his fifth pass, he was still not sure how he was going to broach the subject, but decided to enter anyway. He quietly opened the door slightly more and peered in. Brutus and Ginny were standing under the chandelier, its radiance casting a romantic glow as each sipped tokkofo from a cup. Ginny had caught the slight movement of the door as it came ajar and somehow sensed who it was on the other side.

She was mildly puzzled at this behavior. With a trace of mirth in her voice she asked, "Henry, is that you? Do come in and have a cup of tokkofo with us. It should still be hot. Brutus and I have been getting acquainted. Who was it in the interaction room anyhow?" Ginny fired these off as quickly as they rumbled into her head.

Henry ignored the question about the interaction room and bluntly asked, "Mr. Malroye, how would you like to stay the evening with us? We have a guest room ready."

Brutus was inwardly delighted at the invitation and quickly agreed. "Please allow me to send the cab off," he said as he took a step toward the library's door.

Ginny and Henry looked at each other in surprise.

"You arrived in a taxi?" Ginny asked, falling out of here genteel manner a bit.

"Of course. I just arrived in Kittanning this evening. I have no other transportation. A taxi was the most convenient way to get here."

Henry saw this as a problem. He didn't want to allow Brutus out of his sight until he was in the guest room. The taxi was especially precarious since it afforded Brutus the chance to leave without warning. It occurred to Henry that Brutus had accepted his offer to stay too easily. Of course, it may have meant that he was sincere and fully appreciative of the offer. On the other hand, perhaps Brutus suspected something was up and feigned delight so as not to arouse suspicion. Henry couldn't take the chance.

"Allow me to have the butler send him away. I'm sorry you kept him waiting. That'll be quite a fare you've built up. We can take care of that."

"Henry is right," Ginny said, "we could easily have had one of our chauffeurs take you back to town. Let us take care of the fare."

"No need to worry about the fare," Brutus said quickly in an impromptu way, "that is no problem. It was...er...my decision to come without invitation if you remember. The fare is my responsibility. I will not allow you to pay for it."

Brutus was very adamant about that point; so much so, it made Henry and Ginny think that he would take it as an offense if they didn't allow him to pay the fare. They felt they had no choice but to let Brutus handle it himself.

It struck Henry now that Brutus must have obtained the money by stealing it. How else would he have gotten enough to cover such an expense so soon? He had just escaped that morning. The governor's misgivings about Brutus were turning out to be accurate.

"Well, allow me to escort you to the front door," Henry suggested. He wanted to keep Brutus under observation until he knew the taxi was gone.

"I know where the front door is," Brutus said light-heartedly, "no need to waste your time." For Brutus, it was absolutely imperative that he do this alone. His plans for the evening required him to have a moment in private with Sneekums.

Ginny's expression said that she more or less agreed with Brutus. If Henry persisted, he might have gotten Brutus to relent, but it was his sister that he was worried about. He didn't want to raise any questions that she might ask while Brutus was still present. He judged that Brutus had not yet revealed anything critical during his short absence. Henry relented and Brutus left the library, staff in hand, to settle the fare.

But Henry was still not ready to let Brutus go unobserved. As soon as Brutus stepped out of the library, Henry went to the doorway and surreptitiously peered around the corner. He watched until he saw Brutus turn the corner at the end of the hall. Henry quickly followed and watched him open the front door. As soon as he saw Brutus step out onto the porch, he made his way to the front window and watched him as he approached the taxi. Ginny was intrigued by all of this and had followed her brother.

"What are you doing Henry?" she asked in a troubled voice. "You act as if you don't trust this man."

"Ginny, you'll have to trust me when I say this, but Brutus is not who you think he is." Ginny said nothing. She was stymied over Henry's behavior. She held his eyes, trying to read meaning from them and would have laughed if it weren't for the deep worry she saw in them.

"Henry, I don't understand..."

Henry held his finger to his mouth and cast a furtive glance out the window. When he looked back at Ginny, she was glowering impatiently. She wanted to know what was going on, now!

A heavy sense of frustration fell over Henry, as little curious noises eeked from his throat giving away his struggle with the decision. Dare he tell her who Brutus was?

Henry averted his eyes and looked out the window again. "Quit looking at me like that," he said, almost growling, perturbed at her scowl. After a momentary silence, a quick glance revealed that Ginny's countenance had remained fixed.

"Oh...all right!" Henry said in a bluster, "I'll have to tell you sometime..." His voice trailed off in resignation.

"Ginny," he began in a whisper, "Brutus is from Earth and Lord Bigsley wants to send him back." In a louder tone he continued, "Of course, we can't force him to leave, but Charles wants to try to convince him that he should. He's going to be here in the morning. I just want to make sure Brutus doesn't leave before then."

Ginny was dumfounded. Was it really possible? Brutus was a man from Earth? She thought back on their conversation, and her face flushed slightly from embarrassing recollections. She remembered what she had told him about the ways in which her 'spinsterhood' could end.

An angry thought interrupted.

"The nerve of that man, pretending to be an Eskathoerian."

She clenched her fists.

"And he let me spout on about my feelings of marriage and how it might be remedied."

That thought afflicted Ginny with a fit of faster, shorter breaths. Henry caught it.

"Why, he must have been laughing at me all along, thinking what a fool I was to speak of such things in front of him like that."

Henry glanced out the window. Brutus was still occupied with the taxi. He turned back to Ginny and opened his mouth to speak, but Ginny held her hand up to stop him, eyes ablaze. Henry promptly closed his mouth.

"He has no business to ask me those questions. No business at all! Why, I'll bet he thinks I really want to be married!

That last thought lingered, and Ginny turned away from Henry. She realized it didn't matter if Brutus thought that about her or not. In her heart of hearts, she knew it was true, but she had never really faced it until now.

So what? Did it matter if it were true? It did not. It was simply out of the question. Brutus had no business in that world. His apparently uninvited presence and Charles's desire to get him back to Earth raised too many objections.

Henry looked out the window again. Brutus was handing the driver something, probably the fare. He would be returning soon.

"Ginny," Henry said urgently, "We need to get..."

Ginny didn't acknowledge, but began to move, slowly. Henry was relieved, and followed, trying to will her to move faster. Henry didn't notice, but Ginny's manner softened a bit as she made her way to leave the vestibule.

"Maybe Charles is wrong. Brutus certainly behaved as a gentleman and an attractive one to boot."

Ginny slipped into the hall with Henry just behind her; he thought he heard Brutus at the front door.

Ginny heard nothing. She wasn't listening for anything.

"If what Henry said were true, there was no denying the fact Brutus was a human being like she was. Could it be providence?

Could it be possible?

Henry stepped up beside Ginny and began to move her along by the arm. Ginny stopped abruptly, and Henry lost his hold.

"Oh, this is silly," Ginny thought, peering distractedly ahead unaware of the frantic look in Henry's eyes, *"I just met the man. And why should he care at all for me?"*

Henry grabbed Ginny by the hands, pulled her down the hall and yanked her into the library. He swung the door shut and hurried to seat himself behind the desk with the lamp.

Ginny plopped into the nearest reading chair. Her heart and mind swung wildly between anger and hope.

"I've got to stop this!" she thought recklessly. *"I've got to quit thinking like this!"*

But she simply could not banish the thoughts. Ginny continued to mull the possibilities, and as she did so, she realized more and more how much she wanted to settle down and marry just like any normal woman in the universe might do.

Mortimer had fallen asleep with the holobox still on and was snoring loudly. Brutus went around to the driver's side and rapped on the window with the stick. Mortimer didn't stir. Brutus rapped more loudly, but still Mortimer snored on.

"This lamebrain," Brutus muttered to himself. "Of all the taxi drivers in Eskathoer I had to pick one who sleeps like he's got anesthesia running through his veins."

Brutus opened the door and Mortimer's arm flopped out. Brutus shook it roughly and Mortimer began to smack his lips like one does when he begins to awaken from thirst. Brutus shook him again, and Mortimer finally opened his eyes.

"Sorry sir, I'm off duty; please see the fella in the taxi behind me." Mr. Sneekums smacked his dry lips as his eyes fell shut once more, and he began to snore again. Brutus stuck his head in the door, and in a very loud voice yelled, "Mortimer T. Sneekums, wake up!" This did the trick. Mortimer jumped and let out a cry as his eyes popped wide open to peer directly into the face of Brutus. His glasses hung from his head by one ear.

"What in the name o' common sense is the matter with you!" he cried. "I know I'm only a hunert and eighty-three years old, but you can give a fella a heart attack doing somethin' like that. Look at me," he continued as he held up his hand, "I'm a bundle o' raw nerves now. How d'yeh 'spect me to drive in this condition." Mortimer's hand was visibly shaking. He had difficulty resetting his glasses back on his nose and over his ears.

Brutus didn't care much whether Mortimer made it home or not except that he still needed him. Brutus took a deep breath and mustered enough resolve to start again, this time in a cool and civil manner.

"My dear friend Mr. Sneekums, I apologize for the...er...rude interruption. I do hope I haven't caused you much distress."

"Distress? You mean like the way one feels when he gets the blast of a horn in his ear? That's what it was like yeh know." Mortimer was very agitated and trying extremely hard to control his temper. He had lost it only once before, a little over a hundred years ago. He didn't want to lose it again, especially so soon.

"Mr. Sneekums," Brutus began again, "I have a proposition that will solve the problem of your...er...temporary incapacity to drive your taxi back to Kittanning and prove financially profitable as well."

Mortimer wasn't as concerned about the profitable part as he was about the state he was in and how it might affect his driving. He didn't want to drive far in his condition and Kittanning was just a little bit too far.

"Is there a motel nearby?"

"Is there a what?" Sneekums snorted.

"Is there a motel, a place where a traveler might stop and

spend the night?"

"Oh, you mean a motor hotel. Never heard 'em called a motel before. Makes sense if you combine the two words, you know the 'mo' from motor and..."

"Ah, yes, Mr. Sneekums, you are quite right, but I need you to do me a favor."

"Well, go on...OH!"

"What is it, Mr. Sneekums, and please hurry, I haven't much time."

"Why, I remember what this is all about." Sneekums looked intently into the face of Brutus and asked in a low voice, "How did it go? Did the shavin' towel do the trick? I mean, it's none of my business and all, but I was sure rootin' fer yeh."

"Yes, Mr. Sneekums, it went very well. I shall be staying for a while longer. In fact, they have asked me to stay the night, and I didn't want to disappoint them. But I have to get back to the governor's mansion as early as I can tomorrow. The problem is that I feel that I have already been too much of a burden to ask them to provide transportation for me to the magnerail in the morning; especially at the hour I will need to leave. By the way, do you know what the earliest departure time of the magnerail might be?"

Sneekums thought a moment. "Well I haven't worked the day shift in a while, but I'm purty sure there's one leavin' about 6:00 o'clock in the morning, well before sunrise, know what I mean?"

"Ah," lamented Brutus, "it is just as I thought. Indeed, it would be too much of an imposition on the Fergusons to see me off at such an early hour, not to mention the bother for the chauffeur. And my return to the Mansion at the earliest possible time is so critical." Brutus said this in a manner that convinced Mortimer that Brutus's business with the Fergusons was one of major consequence. A sense of duty and urgency seized Sneekums.

"Don't know what it is and don't care to know; none of

my business. But whatever it is, count me in. What can I do fer yeh?"

"The motel...I mean, the motor hotel. Where is the closest one?"

"Well, there's one prob'ly just a mile or two down the road. Never been there, but it looks like it might be a right nice place. Think they have a pool simulator too."

"Very good. I want you to go there and get a room. I'll cover the cost. Get yourself some rest and be back here at 4:30 in the morning sharp."

"Not a problem. That'll give me plenty o' sleep. Hope they have good mattresses. I have a minor back problem; comes from sitting and driving all day, know what I mean? A few stretches and twists and I get the kinks out right well like. Only, the mattress gives me fits sometimes, know what I mean?"

"Yes, Mr. Sneekums, I understand. But you must be sure to be here at 4:30 AM, not a minute later. If I'm not outside waiting for you, don't fret. I'll be out shortly. Oh, and as a matter of courtesy, do turn your lights out as you approach the house; no need to take the chance on waking them."

Brutus slipped two green bills worth 200 grankels to the taxi driver. Sneekums gave Brutus the thumbs up and took off. Brutus watched the taxi as it made its way down the lane to the gate where it made a left turn and out of sight. A moment later, the taxi came into view again until it rounded a curve and disappeared for good. The gate had closed on its own which disturbed Brutus. It meant that Sneekums would have to sound the horn to get the gate to open when he returned. But it probably didn't matter; it was probably too far away to wake anyone who might be sleeping in the house. The house was built solidly and well insulated from loud noises. Lights from the taxi's headlamps would be a greater risk and Sneekums was going to turn them off, assuming he didn't forget.

With the matter of Sneekums settled, Brutus immediately put all of this out of his mind. There were too many other things he had to worry about. The night was going to be one of stealthy, detective work.

When Brutus came back in after Mortimer and the taxi had left, he went back to the library where he found Henry and his sister. He declined an offer of food and drink saying that he was quite tired and preferred to retire for the night. The butler was called to escort Brutus to his room. Before the butler arrived, Brutus noticed that Ginny was strangely quiet. Perhaps a better word to describe her demeanor was 'shy.' She made no eye contact with him except when she said good night to him and the butler just as they were leaving. Brutus puzzled over this change of mood but again forced himself to put it out of his mind as well. He was going to have to put all his mental energy in the task that lay before him.

At about 1:00 AM, three and a half-hours before Sneekums was to return, Brutus awoke after a short three-hour nap. He would have slept through the night except for the chiming alarm clock that went off next to his bed. Moonlight came through the window casting a serene hue across the floor. The walking stick was propped up against the bedpost and wall where Brutus could easily reach it quickly if necessary. He rose, hurriedly shaved (his beard seemed heavier than it was when he last remembered it back at the magnerail station in Kittanning), bathed, and dressed completely except for his shoes. These he wrapped in a towel and carried them under his arm.

Brutus had a mind to take his staff also but decided it would be too much of a burden. Leaving it propped up by the bed, Brutus opened the door to his bedroom just a crack and took a peek out. It was very dark and quiet, and it was clear that neither Ginny nor Henry nor any of the household workers were awake. Brutus opened the door wider, put his head out into the hallway, and listened. It was completely silent except for a rare creaking or tapping that accompanies the natural settling of a domicile that large.

He pushed the door open further so that it was now wide enough for him to step through. Once on the other side he softly closed it behind him. Looking up and down the hallway there was nothing to see or hear. About thirty feet down the hall to the left, as he came out of his room, was the stairway that descended to the lower first floor. The hallway continued another sixty feet beyond the stairway where it ended at a tall window divided into several panes. The pale light of two of the moons that were still visible in the sky shone brightly through the sheer curtain onto the floor. Somewhere at that end of the hall, on either side, were the bedrooms of Ginny and Henry.

Several nightlights glowed softly. These were located on the lower part of the walls about a foot above the floor. Their dim, lustery radiance made it very easy for Brutus to sneak quietly to the stairway and make his descent to the first floor. He immediately headed for the library which he entered and quietly shut the door behind him. He stood motionless for several moments, and once he was convinced that he was still the only person not in bed, he took his shoes out of the towel and placed them on the floor. Then he placed the towel at the bottom of the door and blocked the space between the door and the floor. Satisfied that no possible light could be seen from the other side, he felt his way to the desk and turned on one of the desk lamps.

Looking back at the door he saw the switches that turned on the three chandeliers. Directly below them, on the floor, were his shoes. Brutus had no intention to wear them, but he wanted them close by in case of an unexpected change of plans.

Brutus walked over to the chandelier switches and placed his left hand over them. Before he turned on the chandeliers he closed his eyes and covered them with his right hand. With the flick of the switches, the chandeliers filled the library with a light that, in contrast to the darkness of only a moment before, now appeared to be like the noonday sun. Brutus could tell the room was very bright even though his eyes were closed. He removed his hand from his eyes, which he kept closed for a few moments to allow them to adjust to the light that penetrated the eyelids. Squinting, he barely opened his eyes and the objects in the room appeared to be distorted and hazy. As his eyes adjusted to the increase of light, he opened them a little wider. In this manner he was able, by degrees, in less than one minute, to open his eyes completely and view the room normally. It was important to see everything clearly and in their proper color. If he had not closed them or if he had opened them immediately after he had turned on the chandeliers, he would have spent too much precious time waiting for them to adjust and become useful.

The first thing Brutus did was pick his shoes up from the floor and bring them back to the desk. He placed them neatly on the corner of the desktop closest to the door.

Brutus made a quick scan of the four walls looking for anything unusual. The fireplace caught his attention right away. Above it were five shelves of books of various thicknesses and colors. He tried to discern a pattern: color, thickness, height, anything that looked like it may have had design or purpose in their positioning. Brutus reasoned that though the vicegerent wanted to hide the diary he also wanted not to do such a good job that he himself would lose track of its location. He wanted to make sure it was under their noses but not out of sight.

On the shelf just above the mantel there was a definite pattern - three thick volumes and then a thin one. This pattern continued halfway across the shelf and then reversed itself. The color of the books themselves generally followed a pattern as well; volumes whose covers were a very light shade were on the left and volumes of a very dark shade were on the right.

Brutus approached the mantel and began mentally to read the names of the titles. The third one he came to caught his eye straightaway, *Diary of a Little Known Politician*, by Norbin Poolether, First Chancellor of Vinthoeria, 1867-1985. Brutus pulled the thick volume from the shelf and opened it. It was not the original since it was produced by a printing press and not the cursive writing of a free hand. There was nothing extraordinary about it. It spoke of very mundane activities that seemed to differ very little from that of a commoner. Apparently the Chancellor was fond of dogs, in particular one of fame by the name of Michelangelo.

Brutus put it back on the shelf and continued to scan the titles. On the tenth volume he found another title, which again indicated that the book was a diary. Brutus hurried his scan and found two more like it. This encouraged Brutus and discouraged him at the same time. What a perfect place to hide a diary. It was like hiding a blade of grass in a meadow. And yet, the presence of so many diaries would make it even more difficult to spot the only diary that mattered.

To be sure, he had calculated that this was going to be difficult, but this new twist cast an extremely doubtful question mark over the possibility of a quick success. It now looked that it might take hours, if not some days, to find the cursed thing. Anxiety grew and the question as to whether it was even in the library loomed very large in Brutus's mind. It was that remark about placing the diary "right under the nose" which had resonated so well. It made very good sense to Brutus that the library was the most likely place to hide it. That conviction was now weaker, and Brutus forced himself to believe that it was just a matter of his simply missing something. He had to try and get a fresh start; take a new approach.

Brutus took a deep breath and closed his eyes. He began to recount the earlier events of the previous evening when he first stepped into the house and waited for the butler at the front door. He recalled how he was taken to the library and asked to wait. He remembered how the library was dimly lit as he stood near the desk with the two lamps on it. His first impression was the shelves and shelves of books that sat on the four walls of the library. Then he remembered the second thing that stuck in his mind. It was the portrait over the door.

Brutus opened his eyes and directed them to the door and the portrait that hung above it. Since the room was well lit now, the portrait was much clearer and the details were sharper. Brutus walked across the room and stood directly to the front of the portrait. The first time he stood before it, he was closer. But now he stood farther away and was able to take in the whole painting more easily. There was something about it that Brutus sensed to be significant, but he couldn't put his finger on it. As he gazed on it a little longer he recalled how peculiar it was that the books in the portrait were identical in size, location and color to the ones behind the actual desk in the library.

Brutus moved to the front of the desk where he judged that the artist must have stood when he originally made the painting. He took greater care this time as he compared the books behind the desk to the ones in the portrait. As he had observed the evening before, the books, in an uncanny way, were identical. You could pick out any book in the portrait and find one that matched it behind the desk. Of course, Brutus didn't have the time to compare all of the books, but he did so for several, and was convinced that the books behind the desk must have been exactly the same books that were present when the portrait was first painted. He was about to sit down in one of the chairs in front of the desk to think things over when it suddenly struck him what it was that he had not been able to put his finger on.

The eyes of the subject of most portraits, at least of all the ones that Brutus could ever remember, always appeared to look out on a level that was even with the horizon. Sometimes it appeared that the individual in the portrait was looking directly at you. At other times, the subject was looking off in another direction, but always on a line that went straight out, never up or down. This portrait was different. The distinguished individual was looking down and to his right. In fact, he was looking toward the shelves of books that were behind the desk.

This was very odd. That would have meant that the subject would have been looking down at the floor when posing for the portrait. That would only make sense if the intent was to make the individual in the painting to appear to be gazing upon the books behind the desk while the portrait hung above the doorway.

Brutus stood up quickly. He tried to imagine a line that would match up with the line of sight that ran from the eyes of the portrait to the books behind the desk. Brutus narrowed the terminus of this line to an area that took in about four or five books. He carefully compared these to the ones in the portrait when a thrill of discovery went through him like a shock. It was so obvious he couldn't imagine how he missed it before. There was one book sitting on the shelf behind the desk whose match in the portrait was identical in size, thickness, shape and title; but it was not identical in color. The one in the portrait was black. The one on the shelf was white.

As soon as he discovered this, another equally electrifying detail came to his attention. The quill, as it was painted in the portrait, sat in the inkwell at such an angle that it actually pointed to the black book in the painting. In fact, in the two-dimensional representation of the portrait, the very tip of the quill appeared to just touch the lower left corner of the book.

Brutus hurried to make his way behind the desk. He pulled the white volume from the shelf and opened it up. A blank expression crossed his face followed by dismal disappointment. The book was no diary at all. It was a novel of some sort which Brutus took no effort to skim or read the title. He threw it down on the desk in anger. He clenched his fists and pounded the books that lay on the shelf directly above the vacancy left by the book he removed. When he did so, the books moved inward on the shelf revealing that there was some space behind them.

Brutus slowly lowered his head and shoulders until he looked right into the vacancy on the shelf below. If the room had been dimly lit as it had been the evening before, he would have never noticed that there was something at the back of the shelf behind the books. It was situated almost imperceptibly behind the space left by the vacant book.

Brutus pulled two more books off the shelf and placed them on the desk with the white one. Then he reached in and grasped the object. It lay flat on its side, but Brutus turned it so that it stood upright. It was so thick he barely had room to pull it out through the space he had cleared. With both hands, Brutus held it up and clearly saw that it was worn and leather-bound with an embossed inscription on the front cover.

Brutus pushed away the other books on the desktop and laid the leather-bound book face up in front of him. The inscription was in untarnished gold indicating that it had been placed on the cover relatively recently. It read:

Diary of Angus Ferguson
Vicegerent of Cynthoeria
Former Inhabitant of Earth
1979 - 2116

Brutus's stomach had butterflies. He wanted to jump up, move around, do anything to extinguish the sudden nervous energy that shot through him as he read those words. He found it! He held the secret in his hands!

After a few deep breaths, and several suggestions to himself to calm down, Brutus evenly looked back down on the book. He read the inscription again, this time with less emotion and more reason. Apparently, Brutus concluded, old Angus knew his death was impending and had the title imprinted in time to hide the diary.

With a weak hand, he opened the diary to the first page. Brutus held it to his nose. The paper was remarkably fresh and pliant, not brittle or discolored or musty as are the pages of such old books on Earth. The script was written in black ink with a fountain pen. The characters were neat, legible, and evenly spaced. Here and there a word had a line drawn through it to strike it from the text. It was dated *Poerene (the Lord's Day), Wansor 16, 2018.*

Brutus was tempted to read, but knew he had little time for such inconsequential activity. He must find the secret of the hiding place of the missing oerken leaf. Brutus immediately turned to the back of the hefty diary where there were several blank pages that were destined to remain empty. Flipping the pages forward a few at a time, he quickly came to the last entry. Brutus took the time to read it in full:

Mapsor 7, 2121

This will be the last entry. The end is near and I must at last conceal the only written account of the second oerken leaf under my care. I cannot bring myself to destroy this diary, partly as a matter of pride and dignity, but primarily because I do not think it is the good will of the Living God to do such a thing. I cannot explain why, but I am convinced that there is a purpose that He alone has determined and will yet fulfill with the oerken leaves. Along with that conviction there is the confidence that this diary will play a vital role in it and that I should not make it impossible to find. Hence, my effort to conceal it is also accompanied by the establishment of certain clues to assist its recovery. Whether it is discovered through those clues or merely by providence, is not important to me. My hope is that this account will come to light once again. My prayer is that it will be discovered by the right person at the right time. If I am wrong in this, may God forgive me for my presumption. But I take heart; all things work together for good.

There was nothing more on the page. How ironic, Brutus thought. The hope and prayer of this obviously intelligent person had turned out to be an empty, misguided, self-deceptive illusion. More proof that God is a superstitious myth, a fantasy. A deep-throated guttural chuckle escaped his lips. So did another, but it was louder and more prolonged than the first. A third time, at the risk of drawing attention to his whereabouts, a full, sinister, dark, peal of laughter exploded from his lungs and echoed throughout the room. Yes indeed, Brutus thought to himself, Fate was gracious.

Brutus turned to the clock on the desk. It was 2:56 AM, an hour and a half before Sneekums was to arrive. This gave him time to return to the relative security of his room and study the diary for an hour or so. He planned to return the book before his departure. The mystery of the whereabouts of the missing diary hadn't been solved in two years, and Brutus had no reason to believe it would be solved by anyone else in the next two.

Brutus arranged the books on the desk in such a way that he could pick them up in a certain order with little thought and return them to their proper place on the shelf when the time came. After turning off the desk lamps, he retrieved his shoes once again and carried them to the door with his left hand; the diary he carried under his right arm. He turned off the chandeliers, removed the towel from the space under the door, and placed his shoes, along with the diary, in the towel in such a way that he could easily carry them over his shoulder. Brutus had selected the largest towel for this very purpose. After he left the library, he found his way back to his quarters with ease. Safely inside the room, he removed the shoes and diary from the towel and, once again, placed the towel under the door to conceal the light.

The room was furnished with a large cushiony reading chair and a reading lamp that suited Brutus's need perfectly. He found the last entry and began to page backwards searching for the entry that told the tale of the missing oerken leaf. He had long ago learned to control his dyslexia though he still could not scan a page as quickly as one without the problem. As he leafed backwards, he noted that often two or three days would appear on the same page. Often the entries were a single page and a few were more than a page. Only once did he find a day's account that exceeded three pages. Neither did he find an entry for every day. Sometimes a whole week would pass between recordings.

It took much longer than Brutus anticipated, and it was not until he turned to the sixty-eighth page from the end that Brutus caught a glimpse of the word 'oerken.' Though it was a few lines into the text, Brutus spotted it almost right away. He sat up with a jerk. This was it. This was the page he was looking for. The entry was a single page, and he quickly surveyed it from top to bottom. The word appeared at least twice more. This is how it read:

Danksor 20, 2119

Today I have completed the plans that I have been alluding to in these pages for the last month or so. I have not hitherto revealed the location of the leaf's hiding place, but I will reveal it now. The oerken leaf has been locked away in a gold chest and hidden in a little known cave on Mount Pisgah. The name of this cave is withheld from this entry, but its identity and location can be ascertained by an elderly gentleman, Brig Stokkleplat by name, who runs a small general store in the village of Pearl Springs at the base of the mountain. This individual has been instructed to take the bearer of a specific message to the cave. The message follows: "Mr. Buckwalter and his hound send you their greetings." Mr. Stokkleplat will respond by saying, "And what is the name of the hound?" The proper response to this is simply, "Michelangelo."

The golden chest bearing the oerken leaf is concealed in the wall at the back of the cave...

Brutus did not get to finish for the alarm of his clock chimed marking the time at 4:15 AM. Brutus had only fifteen minutes to return the book to its shelf and make it out the front door to meet Sneekums.

Chapter 11

The Cave on Mount Pisgah

Michelangelo was sleeping soundly beside the bed, just as Matt remembered him before he fell asleep the night before. Matt had slept very soundly, but was now in a light stage of sleep. A sharp knock on the door of his and John's room awakened him. He lifted his head to see if John heard it. The moonlight from the only window in their room revealed that John didn't stir. Matt scooted out of bed and stepped around Michelangelo to get to the door.

In a hoarse and drowsy voice Matt whispered, "Who is it?"

"It's me...Josie. We have to get up."

"Are you kidding me," said Matt as he looked out the window, "the sun's not even up. What time is it?"

"It's 6:30. I have no clue what time that is back home, but I think it's pretty early. Mr. Porter says it's time to get up."

"Whoever Mr. Porter is," said Matt, "shouldn't he still be sleeping?"

"He's the governor's head housekeeper. Come on, Matt, we have to get up. Something's going on."

Matt opened the door and let Josie in. Behind her stood Mr. Porter, a very austere looking man with bushy sideburns and spectacles. He waited outside the room. Josie walked over to John's bed and shook him till he woke. It took a moment to clear his sleepy, groggy mind.

"What's going on?" John said. He saw Mr. Porter standing beyond the door.

"We have to get up," Josie said. "Something's happening, and we have to be downstairs in the breakfast room in an hour."

John whispered, "Who's he?"

"Allow me to introduce myself, sir," Mr. Porter said rigidly. His temperament changed and for a few awkward moments he seemed to be suspended between conflicting impulses. This was disagreeable to Mr. Porter as he had no children of his own and found it difficult to act in a way that he thought appropriate in their presence. He finally concluded that it was wise to speak up and dispel the mystery of his appearance. He glued on a semi-cheery smile.

"I am Mr. Harvey Porter. I am Lord Bigsley's number one housekeeper. He has sent me since I am usually the only one who rises at such an uneskathoeric hour. I'm afraid there is a bit of urgent news."

"I know," said John, "the butler told me last night; you know, Mr..." John didn't remember his name, as did neither Josie nor Matt.

"Mr. Grahame, sir. The head butler's name is Merriweather Bentley Grahame. You can call him Merry or Sunshine or, as he himself prefers, Bentley. And please call me Harvey or simply...Harv," the housekeeper rolled his eyes upward, "it's all the same to me. Everyone gets on here by their first name or nickname after the first day. Except, of course, for the governor himself. I don't think it would be appropriate for you to call him Chuck." He finished in a deadpan expression.

After a moment's pause, Mr. Porter forcefully smiled at this and, as he intended, it lightened the mood a bit which made him feel less awkward and more confident. John chuckled, as well as Josie and Matt. John tumbled out of bed.

"Mr. Porter...Harvey...we will be downstairs in fifty minutes or so. I'm not sure where the breakfast room is. Can you meet us at the bottom of the staircase?"

"Yes sir, in fifty minutes then," Mr. Porter said in a lighter tone. He came to attention and made a slight bow before he turned and left. He picked up the pitcher of yank milk and the three glasses on his way out.

As soon as the door closed behind him, John started the ball rolling. "Okay everybody, it looks like the day is starting early. Let's get cleaned up. Matt, you first and don't be long."

Josie had started back to her room before John finished. The next forty-eight minutes was a frenzy of activity. The three took care of the typical necessities associated with cleaning, grooming, and getting dressed.

Attired in all-Eskathoerian clothing (which each thought was amazingly comfortable), at precisely twenty-two minutes past seven o'clock everyone, including Michelangelo who awakened as if on cue at the very last possible moment, was at the door poised to depart in search of the breakfast room. They were leaving behind three neatly made beds and a hamper full of dirty clothes.

They made their way down the hall to the top of the spiral staircase. They could see Mr. Porter waiting at the bottom. Michelangelo scooted to the front and led the way down the steps. Mr. Porter greeted Michelangelo by grasping him on both sides behind his head at the shoulders and giving him a good massage. Michelangelo fully enjoyed it. The head housekeeper then led them across the granite floor to the entrance of another hallway positioned directly opposite the one that took them to the Blueberry Room the night before.

This hall had no statues in it, but was filled with many paintings, mostly scenes from the countryside. There were also potted plants and indoor shrubbery along the walls, intermingled with reading chairs and lamps next to them; certainly an odd place, John thought, to read a good book. They came to a room on the left about a third of the way down from which a delicious aroma of scrambled eggs, bacon, hotcakes, and coffee floated into the corridor. They entered the room single file.

Inside were several tables that sat four to six persons comfortably. Amos was already there with Amy at his side; they were seated at a table that was set for six.

"How you'nes doin' this fine early mornin'," said Amos.

"Breakfast's jus' about ready. Gov'nor should be here soon." Amy likewise greeted them with a cheerful, "Morning dearies."

The greetings were no sooner spoken than Lord Bigsley entered the room. There was no fanfare as there was the night before. He appeared to be in good spirits; no hint of a difficult or arduous task ahead. The most unexpected feature was his apparel. He wore no tuxedo. He was dressed casually like one prepared to travel. The only aspect of his dress that remained unchanged was the color. He wore a silky pastel yellow shirt, open at the collar, and smooth green pants. The boots were black as well as his cap.

"Greetings my friends. I apologize for getting you all up at this early hour but to make a long story short, we've found Brutus."

John, Josie, and Matt made no response. Though they had not been told anything about the search for Brutus, they had, each on his own, suspected that such was the case. Now that it was confirmed, they were stymied by the thought of what was to happen next.

Curiously, that question was not answered right away. The governor insisted that they sit down immediately and have a good breakfast. In a remarkable way, the governor was able to turn what might have been a hasty and ungratifying meal into a very enjoyable and light-hearted one. This took the burden of the hour off their minds, especially for John. In spite of the cheery atmosphere, they all still ate in greater haste than usual, and the meal didn't last very long.

Wiping his mouth after the last bite of toast and swallow of coffee, the governor turned to Amos and said, "Well, what do you think, Amos, how would you like to try out one of your antiques today?"

Amos's face lit up and gave the governor a glance that enthusiastically said "Yes!"

"The Starliner's ready to go, but I'm athinkin' we might try somethin' new today."

"We don't need anything fancy, mind you," Lord Bigsley said, "something comfortable and roomy."

"Do we need to take to the air?" asked Amos.

"Good point. We will need to get to our destination rather quickly so air will be the most ideal. We're expected at 9:00 in Kittanning, and it is now..." the governor's eyes shifted upward to a clock on the wall, "...thirteen minutes after eight. How long do you think before we can get started?"

"If'n we all go to the garage together we kin leave from there, I reckon. I'll give 'em a heads up." With that, Amos rose and left the room. He was gone for only a minute before he came back.

"It's all set. I got 'em revvin' up the Edsel. It's roomy enough. Has a few extras too."

The governor chuckled, "Indeed Amos, I think you've put some extras into all of them."

They all rose to leave. Amy kissed Amos goodbye and told him not to be late for dinner. They were entertaining the Benton's who were dropping in from Garanland[12] that evening. Their doople[13], whose name was Leonardo, would be with them. Michelangelo and Leonardo got along very well.

The governor took the lead while the rest followed. He brought them to a side door that opened onto a veranda which overlooked a small plaza. The plaza contained a water fountain and pool bordered on one side by an elegant flower garden. Passing by the pool and garden, they made their way to the far side where there was a narrow walkway which wound its way through a lightly wooded forest.

Michelangelo took up his position just in front of Matt who brought up the rear. Michelangelo kept cadence and stayed in

[12] Garanland is a northern continent on Eskathoer. The winter season is so cold that only the southern third of the continent is inhabitable year round.

[13] A *doople* is a longhaired dog-like animal with long droopy ears, a very large blue nose, and extremely large paws. They are well suited for cold weather, but can get along in warmer climates as well.

line except once when he stunned them all (except for Amos) by chasing a chikalik[14] up a tree. It was only a brief interruption. Matt called him back, and Michelangelo obediently responded.

They walked along the path for a little over a minute when they came to a paved lane, which they followed for another two minutes. It took them around a curve and into the view of a large building whose front was glassed in on three sides. It was the "garage" which had a built-in showroom for Amos's favorite antiques. The Starliner was visible as well as the Edsel.

They entered a side door which led to a maintenance area where there were many vehicles, not all from Earth, in one stage or another of repair and inspection. A few were being fitted with some of the 'extras' that Amos liked to play around with.

"That's one o' my favorites over there," said Amos. "Don't git to drive it often. Needs two drivers." Suspended about eight feet above the floor was a lightly armored machine; narrow, sleek, and very speedy looking, like a bullet. It appeared to have rolled down a long hill covered with boulders. On the floor near it was another one. It too showed signs that it had a rough time of it. These were designed to hold two drivers, facing opposite directions, sitting at either end. The front and rear were identical. From a distance one could not tell if it was coming or going. It was primarily used in ricochet racing (akin to demolition derbies on Earth) which uses a three dimensional track where the traffic flow reverses often and randomly.

John spied a really old looking car, sitting in an area that was cordoned off.

"What's so special about that one over there?"

Amos looked and smiled nostalgically. "Thet ther's a Model T Ferd. Made it from the 'riginal blueprints"

[14] A chikalik is a bushy tailed rat. It oinks like a pig and grows about as big as a cat. Chikaliks are fond of hot coffee with liquefied cheese, preferably goat's cheese.

John whistled, "Wow, the original blueprints? How did you get those?"

"Well," Amos began, thumbs in the suspenders of his pants, "Me and Amy, we was on Earth once. Guess you'd call 'er an extended stay somewheres 'round 1921, Earth-time that is. We bumped into a feller by the name o' Chuck Wills. Said he knew another feller by the name o' Ferd, Harry Ferd, I think."

"Henry," John corrected, "It must have been Henry Ford."

"Yeh, right, 'twas Henry, jus' like yeh said. Anyway, this Chuck feller, him and Mr. Ferd came up with an idea of somethin' that was called horsliss...like a horsliss wagin or a horsliss coach, or somethin' like that there, can't 'member 'xactly now..."

"Carriage," John offered, "He probably said 'horseless carriage'."

"Yeh, tha's what he said. They made one o' them horsliss carriages and called it a Model T, like th' letter, yeh know. Anyway, t'make a long story short like, he give me somethin' called blueprints, and said it was an ol' version, one they never got to really make, an' all.

"Ol' Chuck said he liked some o' th' ideas I had fer his cars, like heat fer the winter, n' an automatic crank instead o' one yeh had to turn yerself. He thought they had possibilities, so he give me the blueprints as a gift like. Tol' him I was honored, I did, an' I was too.

"Anyway, even though the blueprints weren't nothin' they ever made, I could see th' ones they did make motorin' up and down the streets and alleys, an' all over the place, as a matter o' fact. So 'twas pritty easy to make one from th' blueprints. Only this here one kin go only 'bout a hundred lightyears before needin' more gas. An' it can't go no faster'n ten lightyears an hour though. Perty slow."

When they entered the showroom portion of the building, a sleepy-eyed mechanic dressed in satiny blue overalls was standing by the Edsel. Amos walked over to him and patted him on the shoulder.

"Thank yeh kindly, Garfy; we appreciate yeh gettin' the Edsel hummin'"

"Think nothing of it sir. Just so yeh know, I put five pellets in the fuel magazine. There are five more in the glove compartment. These are the thirty gallon ones, mind yeh. Gives yeh enough conventional liquid hydrogen to get to the moons and back. If yeh need to go any farther, yeh'll need to switch over to the atomizer. Once it's burned its fuel, you can use the extra pellets, but they won't do as well; they're not made for that kind of burnin'. They'll get yeh about a hundred light-years and back. If yeh run out of fuel, you'll need to call in. We can send a fuel flight right away as long as yer within three hundred light-years. Otherwise we'll need to get a longer range ship, but that might take a couple of hours more."

Amos was pleased with Garfield's thoroughness. "We're not leavin' the planit this time, Garfy. We're just takin a short skip up north to Kittanning. We just wanted somethin' with a little leg room that could get us there by nine o'clock."

Amos told Garfield to get back to his quarters and catch up on his sleep. Garfield nodded appreciatively and left.

They all got into the Edsel as it sat there in the showroom. The twins and their brother climbed in the back with Michelangelo somewhere in the middle. The governor sat up front in the passenger seat. Amos slipped in behind the wheel and rubbed his hands together in excitement. He needed no key. A voice activator that matched Amos's speech pattern had replaced it. There were fifteen other patterns that were programmed. The governor's was one of those.

"Giddy up!" commanded Amos.

The Edsel came to life and purred like a kitten. Amos pushed a button on the dash (it had far fewer buttons and lights than the Starliner) and the roof of the showroom opened up directly above them.

"Hold on to yer seats," Amos said. He pushed another button and the Edsel shot straight up five hundred feet and hovered momentarily. Amos hit a third button which gave him normal control of the car by way of the steering wheel, brakes, and licky pedal[15].

The trip to Ferguson Farm would take only seven minutes. It didn't give anyone time to think about what was coming. For John, that was a welcome respite. He didn't want to think about what he was getting into. So, just to get his mind off things, he asked Amos about the Edsel and the other antiques from Earth.

"We've built 'em to look like the ones on Earth. Mostly 'merican but a few Eurapeens as well."

"Why would you build them to look like cars on Earth. What's so special about them?" John thought a moment longer and then asked a more pressing question. "How do you know about them anyway? I thought Earth was off-limits."

"Well it's like this Johnny boy, me an' Amy's kinda like special agents of the government. We've been to yer planet several times, you know; kinda jus' drop in from time t' time jus' to keep up on things. I jus' like the American auto. Has a flare about it. That is, 'til the 1960's, on Earth. Then they started makin 'em outta tin foil and fiberglass. Yeh were afraid if it rained it'd put dents in the hood."

"You're government agents?" Matt asked in awe. "You mean like...spies?"

"Indeed they are," said Lord Bigsley. "They are experts in Earth affairs. They first took an interest in your planet at the time of the Reformation. The story goes they got pretty excited when they heard about Luther and his ninety-five theses." Lord Bigsley turned to Amos with a big smile. "Word has it they carried on as if the Yellow Hounds just scored big."

"Uh...the Yeller Hounds are the Puddle Bottom West Greenchnik team. They were jus' double-A back then, but they's since become triple-A. Lots o' their players go to the bigs, yeh know."

[15]Short for 'liquid hydrogen pedal.'

As interesting as all of this was, it didn't really help John take his mind off of Brutus. What the governor said next didn't help matters either.

"There's something you all need to know before we get there." Lord Bigsley said this as Amos maneuvered the Edsel down onto highway 11 a few miles south of the Ferguson Farm. He did so at the governor's orders who wanted to approach the farm by land and give everyone a chance to get accustomed to traveling over ground. It was the same route that Mortimer and Brutus had taken the night before. The Edsel passed through a small village that had a few stores, a fuel pellet station, an elementary school, and a motor hotel. The village was an unlikely location for the motor hotel, but since it was relatively close to Kittanning, the road was traveled well enough to give it sufficient business.

Lord Bigsley continued, "Don't be surprised if Brutus doesn't seem to be...er, Brutus."

"What do you mean, sir? Is he behaving differently?" Josie asked.

"Well, I'm a bit confused about it myself. But I summoned Mr. Ferguson...Henry, that is...I interacted with him last night, and he described Brutus as a bit older than you or I saw him last."

"Older," John said. "You mean like maybe seventeen or eighteen?"

"No, it's more like twenty-four or twenty-five. He looks like an adult."

"No way!" said Matt. "Does he have any more muscles? I mean, does he look any meaner than before?"

"Henry didn't go into a detailed description of him, but there was nothing extraordinarily unusual about him; at least, nothing that Henry mentioned. He just looked older."

They were only a half mile or so from the front gate.

"But what was Brutus like? Did he beat anybody up?" Matt's face showed worry.

"Shh, Matt, don't think about that right now. If he's with the Fergusons he's not out to get anybody...yet." Josie was annoyed, but she also felt a little sorry for Matt. She couldn't help but imagine what Brutus might look like now.

They were soon at the front gate of the Ferguson Farm. Nothing appeared unusual. The gate was closed and Amos was about to sound the horn when the gate opened on its own. They drove through, and as they approached the house, Henry and Ginny ran out the front door and down the steps to meet them. Their faces were filled with anguish. Amos pulled the Edsel next to them, and Henry opened Lord Bigsley's door. Before the governor was able to take a step or even speak, Henry cried, "He's gone! Clean gone, I tell you! And he knows where the leaf is."

Lord Bigsley sat in bewilderment as he pondered the news. Things were getting worse by the day. He turned to Henry and said, "Let's go inside, I want to hear the whole story."

They all got out of the Edsel and followed Henry and Ginny up the steps and into the library. The room was lit up by all three chandeliers. On the desk lay several books that obviously were taken from a couple of shelves just behind the desk. These were lying in short stacks around the edge and each one had a strip of paper between the pages like a bookmark. The stacks surrounded a lone book that lay open in the center of the desktop. This one appeared to contain handwritten lines on its pages and was, in fact, the diary of Angus Ferguson, the very one which Brutus had found only hours earlier.

The governor was still turning over the news in his mind that Henry had greeted him with and paid little attention to the desk and books. Lord Bigsley, Amos, and Henry sat in three sofa chairs which were located near a reading table where Ginny and the three took their seats. The butler remained standing after he ensured that all the appropriate lamps were turned on. As soon as they were all settled, Henry began to relate the events of that morning.

"I rose rather early not having slept very well. It was about 5:30. I got up and went to the kitchen to have a cup of tokkofo and think things over. I wanted to make sure every aspect of the coming meeting was clear in my mind. This brought me to the question of where the best place for the discussions might be and after pondering several possibilities I decided on the library. It was the place where Brutus met both Ginny and me and where he had related his story to me. So, I thought it would be a place where he might feel the most comfortable and least disagreeable.

"I went to the library to look it over and confirm if my notion of its suitability was reasonable. I turned on the chandeliers and surveyed the room. It was only a moment or so before I noticed something odd about the books behind the desk."

Henry gestured toward the shelves.

"This troubled me a little since Dad explicitly left orders that his library was not to be disturbed, that every book was to remain in its place for the next century. Indeed, it was an odd request, but we respected his wishes and were awaiting the day we could open the library to the public. To be sure, he didn't forbid the reading of the books; but they were not to leave the house, nor were they to be rearranged."

"What was it that caught your eye, Henry?"

"The shelf behind the desk. There were several books on it that were not in their proper place. Not that they had been rearranged. They were in the proper order. But they were very noticeably pushed back on the shelf. All the books should have been neatly flush with the edge of the shelf, just as Dad was always careful to do. But these looked as if someone had given them a good shove. I reconciled the problem and left the library to go back to the kitchen. Eventually I became drowsy, and since Ginny was still asleep, I went back to bed and fell asleep myself. I awoke again at about 8:15. Ginny was already up. Perhaps she can tell you some more."

Ginny began pensively. "I was also having a rough night of it but managed to fall asleep late only to awaken around 8:00 this morning. I got up and likewise went to the kitchen to ponder the events of the day. I was there for a little while when Henry came in. He immediately told me of what he had found in the library, about the books being pushed in on the shelf. We confirmed that neither of us had done it. And we knew that it was simply out of the question that any of the household workers would have done it. This left us with only one conclusion, and a rather obvious one. Only Mr. Malroye could have done it."

John and Josie looked at each other. To hear Brutus referred to as 'Mr. Malroye' was so absurd they almost laughed. Matt wasn't laughing. It struck him as another omen of Brutus's new dreadful personality.

"We debated whether to disturb Mr. Malroye. We finally decided to do so and went to his room directly. We thought it unnecessary to awaken Desmond."

Desmond, who was still standing by, interjected his thoughts, "Sir, you know I would have gladly gotten up."

"Yes, Desmond, I know," Henry said. "That's part of the reason why I didn't awaken you. You deserve a break now and then, don't you think?" Desmond acquiesced to Henry's kind thought and objected no further.

Ginny continued, "We were alarmed when Mr. Malroye didn't answer the door. Our first thought was that something was wrong, perhaps he was ill. But when we went in, we discovered Mr. Malroye gone. A quick but thorough search failed to find his whereabouts. How he was able to get away we don't know unless he had made prior arrangements."

Ginny looked sheepishly at Henry. He was right about not trusting Brutus, at least on that account.

Henry broke in, "We were able to open the door to his room easily enough, part way that is. About half way open it was obstructed by a towel on the floor arranged in such a way that it looked like it was meant to be there. We judged the towel was used as a barrier under the door to conceal the light while he was up and about before he left. It is strange that he would do that, however. He could easily have prepared to leave with the lights out. The moons were bright and that room is ideally situated to receive moonlight.

"We tried to make sense of it all. I asked Ginny if she had any idea what it was all about."

Ginny began again. "I told Henry about our...that is Mr. Malroye and I...our conversation while he was taking your visit, Charles, in the interaction room last evening.

"We were alone in the library and talked about many things. Somehow, our conversation turned to Dad and how he had hidden the oerken leaf and the reason why. Mr. Malroye was quite surprised at all of this and asked questions about it. I was sure he was sincere; I mean, he spoke so honestly and earnestly. He spoke as sincerely as one from Eskathoer or Prantathoer or any planet...except Earth. There was no reason to suspect him. That's why I was so puzzled at Henry's behavior when he followed Mr. Malroye to the front door. I caught up with him, and we watched from a window as Mr. Malroye handled the fare for the taxi."

"A taxi?" Lord Bigsley asked.

"Yes, we were surprised also."

"Henry," the governor said feverishly, "The taxi may have been how he got away. We must contact all the taxi companies of Kittanning and try to find the one who picked him up and where he took him."

Henry responded, "That may be unnecessary as we shall soon explain. But it still may prove valuable to us." He asked Desmond to get on it right away.

"Now Ginny," the governor began ardently, itching to get to the bottom of what happened, "can you tell us how you know that Brutus knows where the leaf is. Didn't your father hide the leaf?"

"Yes, he did."

"Then how could Brutus have learned the secret of its hiding place?"

"I'm afraid it was because of me," Ginny moaned.

"Now Ginny, I've explained to you already that you can't blame yourself for this. You didn't know who Brutus was."

"I know," Ginny said, "and I appreciate what you're trying to do, Henry. But if I hadn't brought the oerken leaf up in the first place, this would never have happened."

John finally spoke up. "Miss Ferguson, I know you feel bad about this, but you can take my word for it. No matter how much Brutus has changed, deep inside, he's the same person. He is a very bad person."

John's remark disturbed Ginny. With a harsh voice she said, "He is no more evil than you or I. Who are we to speak of him that way?"

Neither John nor anyone else expected Ginny to react that way. There was an awkward moment of silence when Lord Bigsley, in an obvious effort to change the subject, cleared his throat and said, "Ginny, please continue. Why do you think that Brutus knows where the oerken leaf is?"

Ginny spoke directly and without feeling, "He read it. It's over there on the desk. Take a look for yourself."

Henry was not so much displeased with what Ginny said as with how she said it. She was showing a temperament that he hadn't seen in her for many years; one that she had learned to control long ago on Eskathoer. Henry wondered what was going on in Ginny's head, why she had become defensive of Brutus.

The governor rose and went to the desk. The diary of Angus Ferguson lay open before him at the page that explained the whole matter of the cave and Brig Stokkleplat. He read it over twice.

"How did you find the diary?" he asked.

"We didn't discover it," Henry said, "Brutus did. He

reckoned it was in the library." Henry gave a little sigh, not sure how he was going to explain this gracefully. He avoided Ginny's eyes.

"As you'll soon see," he said meekly, "that's no surprise." He hesitated and then with an exasperated burst, "But what is really puzzling is how he managed to figure out exactly where it was in the library!"

The governor stood hunched with his arms folded across his chest, jaw fixed, musing over his next question. Sullenly, he spoke, "Earlier...you mentioned the books on the shelf behind the desk...that they were pushed back...that you restored them to their proper position."

Henry nodded.

Bigsley was not looking at Henry. He unfolded his arms and clasped his hands behind his back in a fidgety way.

"You mentioned nothing about finding the diary at that time or even suspecting that it was involved."

Henry nodded again.

The governor was clearly flustered. He released his hands and extended them toward Henry in a plea.

"Henry," he said, "how on Eskathoer is it that you came across the diary yourself?" Lord Bigsley was perplexed and was looking at Henry expectantly.

Henry fidgeted a little with the button on his coat.

"Now Ginny, I know you're going to blame yourself again, but please, dear sister, you're not to blame. But we do have to bring it up."

Everyone turned their head toward Ginny.

Ginny looked away. She almost didn't care now. She was still brooding over John's earlier remark.

Henry continued, "It's really nothing at all. Ginny just mentioned something to Brutus about what Dad used to say."

Henry paused.

"Well, go on, Henry, what was it that you're father used to say?"

"Well, he said that if you ever want to hide something from your children, just stick it right under their noses."

"And?" the governor asked, waiting for the rest.

"And...that's it; don't you get it. Dad had given us a clue all along, every time he said it. He said it so often that we were tiring of it. It was like a joke that was funny the first time, amusing the second time, and quite stale the third time."

Lord Bigsley smiled helplessly, "Henry, I still don't get it."

Henry took a deep breath and said, "Well I guess I can see how you might miss it. It's just that once we figured it out, it was so obvious."

By now, the governor, indeed everyone, having no clue what Henry was trying to say, was ready to jump up out of his seat and scream out, "What are you talking about!"

"Look," Henry said, "to answer the question of where would be the best place to hide a book under our noses, is to answer the question, 'Where is the best place to hide cookies?' Answer: in the cookie jar. One would reason that the cookie jar is the most obvious place to find a cookie so why would anyone bother to hide it there."

The governor's expression went from stunned, to amused, and then to laughter. No one else was laughing.

"Don't you all get it?" he said to Amos and the others, "He hid it in the library." With that the governor let out another burst of laughter. "That Angus, he was a tricky one wasn't he." The laughter continued a few moments longer before it settled into a gentle, quiet smile. "That Angus," he said softly to himself, shaking his head slowly and soberly, "he was such a prankster. How I miss him."

Henry explained how he reckoned that Brutus must have been looking for the book in the library. He wasn't sure what clues caused Brutus to narrow his search to the exact location. As for his own search, that location was narrowed by Brutus's carelessness. If Brutus had taken care to adjust the books that he shoved, they probably would not have found the diary, at least not so soon.

Henry was replacing the books on the shelf as he was speaking. The little strip of paper in each book identified its location to ensure it was put back in the exact place where it had come from.

Desmond returned and announced that he had gotten up with the taxi company. There were only three in all of Kittanning so it was not difficult to find the one they were looking for.

"What have you found, Desmond? Any good news?"

"We indeed have found the company, sir. The taxi driver is one, Mortimer T. Sneekums."

"Did you arrange to speak with him?"

"I'm afraid not, sir. Mr. Sneekums never returned to the station last evening and never reported in until this morning around 4:25. He reported that he was about to pick up a fare at the Ferguson Farm. He hasn't reported in since then. They don't know where he is."

The governor stood up.

"The diary reveals that Angus hid the oerken leaf in a cave on Mount Pisgah. We have to hurry. The mountain is more than one hundred fifty miles from here, but Brutus has had quite a head start assuming he left directly. The last fifty miles or so is slow highway so that might give us the edge. I say we leave immediately and retrieve the leaf before he does. The recovery of that leaf has now become more important than Brutus."

The governor and his party got up and started for the door. Henry and Ginny escorted them to their car. They were seated inside as before and ready to go when the governor rolled his window down to speak with Henry.

"Henry, you won't be able to contact us directly, but you can pass any news along to the mansion. They can relay it to me from there." Henry acknowledged and stepped back. Amos pushed a couple of buttons and the Edsel shot upwards as it did back at the showroom. Another second, and Henry watched it streak out of sight over a distant hill.

John sat back. Everyone was silent. Michelangelo lay quietly between Matt and Josie and surprisingly was awake. Amos had the seat refitted with cushioned panels for the backrest. There were three and each panel could be pushed in toward the rear of the car until it lay flat on the floor of the trunk behind the seat. The middle panel was open, and it gave Michelangelo ample room to sit or lie there comfortably without disturbing other passengers.

Matt broke the silence. "How long 'til we get there?"

Amos looked at the chronometer in the dash which indicated both the time they expended as well as the time remaining for their little trip. It indicated that there were three minutes left before they would arrive at the very peak of Mt. Pisgah. Amos explained that to Matt and the others.

John asked, "We're not going to land on top of the mountain, are we?"

"No, no, Johnny boy, that there peak's just a coordinate," Amos said.

"We have to get to the general store in Pearl Springs," the governor added.

"I'll put 'er down right close like to the store. It'll just take a shake of a stick t' find out if'n Brutus's made it before we'nes did. Should add only 'bout another minit. Assumin' we kin spot the store right away, that is."

As it turned out, they spotted the store on a fly-by and Amos was able to set the Edsel down into a space in the parking lot just as if he drove up to it. They got out and waited for the governor to decide what to do next.

Lord Bigsley looked around. There were several autoboxes parked neatly along the row nearest the store. John, Josie, and Matt had never seen an autobox and asked about them.

"Them there's autopods," said Amos. "Most o' the time they's called autoboxes on account o' their shape. They ain't built fer flyin', but they kin sure hug the road nice, like a new pair of greenchnik spikes."

There was one, partly hidden from their view, which was a two-tone black and white autobox. In the front seat, behind the wheel, sat the driver who was snoring loudly over a sports broadcast of the Yellow Hounds and the Mighty Yanks.

The governor almost missed it. As soon as he spotted it, he knew it was what he was looking for. His anxiety took another leap.

"There's a taxi over there." Everyone looked in the direction he was pointing. Only Amos picked it up since the three had no idea what distinguished a taxi from the other boxes.

Lord Bigsley quickly devised a plan that he related to the others. Amos made a few suggestions which the governor went along with. When they broke up, Amos and Lord Bigsley approached the autobox from the rear, one on each side. Amos stayed behind the taxi, and the governor continued around to the front. Josie, Matt, and Michelangelo stayed out in the parking lot just behind Amos. It was John's job to speak with whoever was inside the autobox.

John approached the door to the driver's side. The window was down, and he could hear a whistle blown in the game on the holobox. Behind the steering wheel was Mortimer, with his head resting on the back of the seat (there was no headrest). His lips vibrated loudly on every snore. John hated to awaken the unexpecting victim. He looked at Lord Bigsley who motioned to keep going. John looked back down at Mortimer and pushed on his shoulder. Mortimer snored on.

"Sir," John said, "Sir, excuse me." No movement except for the lips.

John shook Mortimer harder this time, making his head swivel across the top of the seat. No good. Mortimer continued his blissful snooze.

John was about to give up when an idea came to him. He reached in and gently but firmly squeezed Mortimer's nose shut. It only took a moment. Mortimer opened his eyes sputtering. John released his hold, withdrew his hand, and stood by looking as innocent as possible.

"Mr. Sneekums? Mr. Mortimer T. Sneekums, I presume."

Mortimer squinted at John who was extremely blurry. He reached down to the passenger seat next to him, found his glasses and put them on. He took another look at the figure standing outside his window.

"Mr. Sneekums, my name is John Eaton. I'm sorry to disturb you, but my friends and I need to ask you some questions."

Mortimer looked away from John to ponder what he just said. He, of course, had no idea who John was. At first, he thought John was the only one standing outside his door. But when he looked out his front window and saw the governor, Mortimer's eyes opened wide. He quickly shot his hand out of the door window and waved.

"Gov'nor, yer boy's here, at the store yonder." Mortimer was pointing up a steep climb of steps to a store that sat on a terraced section at the mountain's base. On the front of the store was a large sign which read:

Pearl Springs General Store
Brig Stokkleplat Owner/Operator

"How long have you been here?" asked John.

"How long?" Mortimer looked vacantly at his taxi's steering helm as he tried to determine an answer.

"Well, I been sleeping most o' the time since we got here," he said thoughtfully. "Had to leave early yeh know. Thought we was heading back to Kittannin' but your boy had a change o' plans. If twern't so important I mightta had to say no."

"But how long have you been here?" asked John again.

"Well, I can't reckon I can say...OH!"

Something jogged Mortimer's memory and John's eyebrows

shot up in anticipation of the news. But Mortimer just reached over and turned up the volume on the holobox.

"Let me see if I can get the time left in the game. Too bad this ain't a viddycast, I mighta been able to see a clock."

The broadcasters carried on at an excited tempo about "foot blasts" and "tackles" and "frontal bashes" and "popping bounces" until a foul stopped play and the broadcasters announced the time remaining: 18:02 was left on the clock in the third quarter.

"Aha, all right, I kin tell yeh...uh...let me see here." Mortimer closed his eyes and began to mutter words and numbers as he wrote in the air with his forefinger, "okay now...take away two and...uh...bring down...carry a minit here and scratch that...can't ferget to reckon on...now let's see, gotta divide by...and...okay, okay I got it."

He opened his eyes and in a clearer voice said, "According to my calculations, which should be pretty good since I was tops in math in sixth grade, I reckon we've been here 'bout oh, maybe, an hour and twenty-seven minits. Give or take a minit or two...maybe?"

"AN HOUR AND TWENTY-SEVEN MINITS!" wailed Lord Bigsley. "We're too late!"

All eyes turned toward the mountain. They strained to see anything that might confirm the governor's fears. There was nothing but tree and rock along the side that faced them. The climb was steep but not so steep one couldn't make it on foot. There was an exception, at about five or six hundred feet below the peak. It was there that the mountain turned into a sheer rock cliff for a hundred feet. Everything above and below that vertical face was traversable by foot.

"Amos!" Lord Bigsley shouted, "Crank up the Edsel. Everybody, back in the car."

In his mirror, Mortimer saw them all rush past a couple of rows of boxes and then out of sight. He opened the door and quickly got out to see what was going on. He lost track of them, but picked them up again at the far corner of the lot.

"Hey, hey, where yeh all goin'? My 'rithmetic might be a little off, know what I mean." Then he asked himself, "Too late fer what?"

The Edsel stirred a little and then began to rise. When its wheels cleared the tops of the parked autoboxes, it shot straight up a hundred feet. It hovered a moment and then sped away toward the mountain.

Mortimer watched all this utterly mystified. "Well if I ain't a toad," he said, "they jus' all upped an' left. Don't they know their boy ain't goin' no place without Mortimer T. Sneekums and his taxi?"

As they approached the peak they all strained to see anything that might look like a way into the heart of the mountain, but there was nothing.

"Try the other side, maybe the cave's there."

"Good idea there, Matt." Lord Bigsley motioned for Amos to take them around.

As they flew, the mountain was on Amos's left, and it was just as Matt suggested. There came into view a dark area at the bottom of the cliff that readily marked the opening of the cave. This gave new hope that there might be some time after all. It would take considerably longer to get to the cavern if Brutus had to climb to the other side of the mountain.

The cavernous hole was very dark; only the very edge of the opening was exposed to sunlight. Beyond that it was black. Amos eased the Edsel down to the front of the opening so that they were looking directly into it through the front window. It was large enough for the Edsel to fit into. The car was poised as if they were going to drive it into a garage.

There was no walkway or trail or any other kind of path that led to the cave. It was reachable, but one had to climb over rock and cranny to get to it. It was difficult to tell if any one had approached the cavern that morning. They waited silently a few moments. Amos was about to turn the headlamps on when suddenly a light came on, and the chamber lit up.

There were two figures. The storekeeper was standing near the wall to the right and waving as if to greet the hovering Edsel. Behind him was something that looked to John like a large snowmobile. The other figure had been so intent on his labor that he was unaware of the presence of the governor's party. He stood at the back of the cave facing the wall and was holding an object above his head with both hands. The spectacle was reminiscent of a victor in a close and hard fought game celebrating the World Greenchnik Cup in joyous triumph. The trophy in this figure's hands shone like a brilliant incandescent lamp generating wave after wave of intense heat and light. But its bearer showed no sign of discomfort or pain.

At the governor's direction, Amos sounded the horn of the Edsel. He had it replaced with an 'extra' so that, instead of a noisy attention-getting blast, it sounded like the trumpet call of a foxhunt. The governor rolled his eyes. It was not a very distinguished greeting.

The figure twirled around. It was difficult to discern any certain detail, but the stance and manner was Brutus's. The figure pulled the glowing object to his chest and shook his head as he formed the word 'No' on his lips. The Edsel hovered before him like a threatening police dog. Brutus closed his eyes as if in pain or intense concentration. The image of the governor and that old coot behind the wheel shattered Brutus's sense of destiny in an instant. How could this be? How could he have come this far? The precious, coveted leaf was in his hands and now he was about to lose it all. He was trapped.

Inexplicably, in that moment of desperation, Brutus recollected a long forgotten experience he once had on Earth. He recalled playing with a water balloon in his yard when a couple of the neighborhood kids saw him. They wanted the balloon and began to push and shove to make him give it to them. Brutus pushed and shoved back. It turned into a rather nasty scuffle but Brutus held on to the balloon the whole while. When he finally got away, they chased him into a dead-end alley. Panic seized him as he frantically looked around and found no place to hide. Then, in a completely involuntary and unmeditated reaction, Brutus threw the water balloon with all his might and struck the leader squarely in the face. It landed with such force that it knocked him down.

Michelangelo, now snoozing and oblivious, was jolted awake by the impact of the first balloon. Then came an onslaught of popping and splatting water balloons that smashed into the car from all sides. The pounding was so furious it seemed the glass would crack and shatter. Michelangelo whined and barked. Amos sat in disbelief and revolted at the thought of what the hood would have looked like had the Edsel been one of the original models.

When the deluge stopped, Amos turned the wipers on. Brutus was still standing with the precious leaf clutched to his chest. But the panic was gone. He was gazing on them in an astonished but confident manner. Mr. Stokkleplat came to the mouth of the hollow to get a better view. In absolute disbelief, he stood, mouth gaping and eyes wide open taking in the floating Edsel. There was water streaming off its sides and deflated torn balloons hanging haphazardly over the bumper and across the hood.

At the governor's direction, Amos pulled the Edsel into the chamber between the two figures. It was not a natural cave but one dug out of the mountainside. It was a grotto where an infrequent party of climbers might find shelter in a sudden storm. Other than that, it held no interest to the general public. Angus had picked the perfect place to hide the oerken leaf. But contrary to Angus's hope and prayer, the oerken leaf had fallen into the hands of an evil genius.

Chapter 12

A Shadow of Things to Come

Bigsley opened his door and stepped out of the Edsel. Brutus still held the glowing oerken leaf. It was encased in crystal just like the one at the governor's mansion.

The governor walked around the front of the Edsel to get to the other side where he could face Brutus. The machine that looked like a snowmobile caught his attention. It explained how Brutus had reached the cave so soon. He and Mr. Stokkleplat rode a state-of-the-art mechanized caterpillar up the side of the mountain straight to the mouth of the cave. The caterpillar had a bottom that gripped and conformed to the contours of the ground as it passed over it. It provided a sure-footed, smooth, and speedy means of covering difficult, even non-drivable terrain. On the floor of the caterpillar, and out of sight, lay Brutus's walking stick.

As the governor approached, Brutus shouted, "Stop there! Don't come any closer!" He held the oerken leaf out toward the governor as if it were a talisman charged with a magical power to ward off evil spirits. Lord Bigsley stopped abruptly. He and Amos cast glances at each other but said nothing. Lord Bigsley's face was somber and pallid in the dull light of the cave. He was so focused on Brutus that the skin on his brow squished together in wrinkles.

Though Brutus held the oerken leaf directly toward the governor, he was careful to keep everything else under his eye. He looked at the governor one moment and then at Amos the next. With another glance, he took account of the passengers in the back seat though he couldn't make out who they were. He did this for a little while when, finally, he lowered the leaf.

"I suppose," he began defiantly, "you have come to arrest me and take me back to the mansion."

The governor spoke cautiously and said, "Mr. Malroye, we have not come here to arrest you, and we have no intention of forcing you to do anything or go anywhere."

Brutus didn't believe the governor one whit.

"Uh...yeah...I'm sure. Fancy that," Brutus sneered, lapsing into his tough-boy drawl. It was just the way John remembered him back on Earth.

Brutus smacked his forehead with his free hand in mock wonder. "Why, I can't believe it. You mean to tell me that you came all the way from the Big House just to tell me that!"

The words dropped out of his mouth in sniping, sarcastic utterances. A clink like the latch on a gate distracted him.

John opened his door and slowly got out. For the first time since they arrived on Eskathoer, John and Brutus came face to face. Brutus's face turned ashen even in the pale light of the cavern.

"No! It can't be. How could it..." Brutus didn't finish, the revelation was so overwhelming. He clutched the oerken to his chest. With words that seemed to stick to his tongue, Brutus tried again, in a hoarse whisper, "What are you doing here?"

Brutus's mind was in such a whirl he had to close his eyes to keep his focus. He slumped backward against the stone wall, hope seeping away like water through a crack. No longer defiant and confident, the oerken leaf dimmed to a dull, dark amber, like an ember just about to burn out.

"Lord Bigsley isn't lying to you, Brutus. Nobody is going to force you to do anything. We came here to...uh...to ask you to come back to Earth...with me."

"Wait a minute," Brutus said in a contemptuous snigger, "are you telling me that they brought you all the way across the universe to a galaxy far, far away, to convince me that I should go home with you?" Brutus's lips were upturned at the corners ready to break out in rude laughter.

John's mouth suddenly became dry. The whole notion of

Brutus acceding to such a request was absurd beyond comprehension. Who could ever have thought that this would work.

"Well, kinda...I guess."

Brutus shook his head in wonder and stiffened. "Did you happen to tell them how buddy-buddy we were back home? Give me one good reason why I should go back."

"One good reason?" John thought, *"are you kidding?"* The answer was obvious; John spoke without hesitating.

"Because you don't belong here, just like I don't belong here. We're not like they are. We're not the good guys, they are. And we need to keep it that way."

This surge of boldness amused Brutus.

"Oh, really," said Brutus. "Then please explain to me why Angus Ferguson and company were allowed to stay. What makes them so different?" Brutus expected that question to fluster John since he reckoned that John knew nothing about the Fergusons.

"Angus and Mary, and Henry and Ginny for that matter, have proven themselves capable of living in this world in spite of themselves, not because of themselves."

That response was unexpected. That John knew the Fergusons by their first names surprised Brutus. That he knew the children by name stunned him. Oddly, the mention of Ginny's name brought back a recollection of the evening before, how she suddenly became aloof, as though he embarrassed her.

Brutus curled his lips, and his nose shot into the air. "What are you talking about, Eaton?" he asked derisively. "Are you saying that because we're humans, Earth-humans if you please, that we are different than the humans, or whatever they are, around here?"

"I know you don't understand this, Brutus, I can't expect you to. But if we allow ourselves to stay here, we can cause a lot of problems." With that last thought, an idea came to John.

"Tell me, Brutus, where did you get the money to pay the

taxi fare?"

Brutus was alarmed at the question. As quickly as he could, he pondered it from every side possible. He couldn't think of any lie that would be convincing. So he said nothing, expressing his guilt no less lucidly than if he told them outright that he stole it.

"Don't you see Brutus, we don't belong here. We need to go back home."

The confidence Brutus gained at the end of the bombardment of water balloons was now waning. He was quickly coming to the conclusion that he was not going to be able to talk his way out of this. The oerken leaf began to glow furiously again in his hand. Matt ducked down.

And then a thought came to Brutus and the leaf dimmed once again. He turned to the governor and said, "What do you mean you have no intention of forcing me to go anywhere or do anything?" Then with a sideways look, he asked, "Are you saying that I am free?"

The governor stiffened and said with unwilling words, "That's exactly what I am saying. By law, you cannot be forced to leave this world for one year, one Eskathoer year, that is. It is called sanctuary status."

Brutus was stunned. Shock ran from head to toe. He struggled to comprehend it and mentally rehearsed each word back to himself to make sure he got it right. No matter which way he played it, it said the same thing. The governor was telling him that he was free. Brutus suddenly forgot all about the business of acting like an adult who was to become the new man of a destiny handed to him graciously from Fate. He wanted to tear away the façade, leap into the air and click his heels. Ridiculous, silly thoughts ran through his mind, *"Scooooore!...Ladies and gentlemen - he has snatched victory out of the jaws of defeat...Can you believe it, Brutus is on the comeback trail...Oh yeah, baby, there's plenty of time left in the game...Yes sirree, Brutus old boy, it just goes to show you, it ain't over 'til it's over...You're the man; YOU ARE THE MAN..."*

Brutus shook off the reverie and barely regained his composure. The juvenile thoughts scattered away. He had to be convincing now more than ever. He faced the governor once again. As calmly and believably as he ever told any lie, he said, "I thank you, fine sir, for your honesty. I assure you, I will not be a problem. I confess that I have slipped a little but just give me a chance. I will prove myself."

John's heart fell. Brutus was not going to leave. He had failed. And yet, did he really expect it to be any different? Isn't that what he told the governor?

John looked at the governor who was obviously disappointed. Even so, he gave John a sympathetic nod telling him that he understood and that it was not John himself that caused the disappointment. The governor faced Brutus again.

"Mr. Malroye, please understand that we will have to keep an eye on you. Though we cannot make you leave, we can intervene when necessary. And let me make it perfectly clear; I am the one who will make the final decision whether you leave or stay. As it stands now, you can expect to be on your way home the instant your sanctuary runs out."

That last remark stung Brutus, and his temper flared inwardly. The oerken flashed and then promptly died out. That little burst of light was like a slap in the face to John, jolting him awake. What was to be done with the oerken leaf? Certainly the governor would say something about it. Weren't there any restrictions - was Brutus allowed to do whatever he pleased with it? Shouldn't he be required to report its whereabouts at all times? Shouldn't he be held responsible for its safekeeping?

John looked helplessly at the governor expecting him to open his mouth at any moment and answer all these questions. But he remained silent. John thought of saying something himself, but what good would that have done? If anything was to be said, the governor would have already said it.

Hence, the confrontation between John and Brutus which everyone had anticipated, turned out not to be much of a confrontation after all. In fact, it was a relatively mild and superficial debate that resolved nothing. The precarious situation continued.

John was mulling this over as he got back into the Edsel. The governor likewise had gotten back in and Amos backed the antique out of the cavern. They hovered in front of the opening, lights on, and watched Brutus place the golden chest, which now held the oerken leaf, onto the floor of the caterpillar next to the staff. Then he and Mr. Stokkleplat mounted. A moment later, the caterpillar made its way to the edge of the cave and fell slowly forward onto the sloping mountainside.

As soon as the vehicle touched the surface, a sucking sound accompanied the protrusion of the flat underbelly as it shaped itself around the rock, stone, gouges, bumps, and debris of the ground. It reminded John of packing putty thickly in a hole or around a peg. Then the underbelly, like a treadmill, pulled itself and the upper body along the ground. Amazingly, as the bottom jolted and jerked making sucking and popping sounds, the upper carriage remained smooth and level.

To make his point about keeping an eye on Brutus, Lord Bigsley had Amos keep the Edsel only a few hundred feet above the caterpillar as it clambered down the mountainside. John wondered how long it would take. He noted that the caterpillar was moving along fairly quickly. Still, it would probably take a half-hour or so before they got back to the general store and the parking lot.

This gave John some time to think about what had happened. He asked the governor why he said nothing about the oerken leaf.

"Indeed, I would have if I had authority to do so, but I couldn't."

"You mean sanctuary status allows him to keep anything he finds?"

"No, it's not that. It was the diary. Angus, who was the guardian of the leaf, and therefore the only one who could legally dictate how it was to be treated, stipulated that if the leaf was ever found, it became the property of the one who found it."

Amos spoke up and said, "That boy's gonna be trouble, yeh kin jus' smell it."

Matt sat quietly. He had seen Brutus in a way that he never thought possible. "I didn't think he was so tough. Back home he would have just walked over to you guys and started swinging. Instead, he just did...nothing. Well, he talked a lot, as if he thought that was going to help him." Then something else about the encounter struck Matt.

"Remember just before Lord Bigsley told him about being able to stay and all?"

Josie thought about it but wasn't sure what Matt was referring to. "The only thing I remember was that Brutus asked what the governor was talking about earlier, if it meant he was free."

"No, no, not that," Matt said, "The leaf. It got real bright all of a sudden, like a sparkler on the Fourth of July...like it was going to do something."

"Was that why you ducked down?" Josie asked.

"Yeah! I wasn't taking any chances, you know!" Matt looked at Josie as if she had seriously asked him if he would jump out of the way of a charging bull.

"It probably wouldn't have mattered though," Matt continued. "It probably would have been something else instead of water balloons. He probably would have melted us all with Z rays."

Josie rolled her eyes. "Oh, come on, Matt, you still think Brutus is out to get us all? Can't you see that he's changed?"

Everyone turned and looked at Josie, except Amos of course, who used the rearview mirror.

"What are you talking about?" John asked, wondering how Josie could even think Brutus would change on his own. "You mean you don't think he's as bad as he was before?"

"Oh no, you got me wrong," she said, waving her hand

and shaking her head. "I think he's as bad as before, all right. In fact, somehow I think he might be worse, if that's possible. I mean, it's as if something has happened to him, changed him into another person. Not for good, mind you."

She thought a little, looking for a way to explain what she meant. "He's still bad, but not in the same way. I think he's smarter now. He's not the stupid bully he was on Earth where he'd just go around pushing and shoving. I think he's got other things up his sleeve. I think he's going to be trickier."

John contemplated what Josie had just said. "You're right."

Facing Lord Bigsley, he said, "You were right, sir. Brutus doesn't look like Brutus. He did look older, and he acted like he was older. He even talked like he was older."

Looking back at Josie, "Maybe it's not as bad as we think. I mean, even if he is worse than before, he seems to be using his head, you know, controls his temper, doesn't do like what Matt said; he doesn't just start swinging."

"Well, if you'nes don't mind me puttin' in my three ponks worth," said Amos, "seems to me that means he's playin' smart now. I think yeh'd rather have 'im start swingin' all the time; at least wise, yeh know what t' spect from him. But now, ain't tellin' what he's goin' to do. If'n yeh can't figger him out, yer gonna have real problems. 'Sides all that, everybody's got a boilin' point. A guy like that, he'll stay cool only fer so long. Things have a might curious way of abuildin' up inside. Then all suddenly like, he goes bonkers. I seen it a hunert times on Earth."

"Hmm, yes Amos," said the governor, nodding his head faintly, "you have a good point there. We have got to watch that boy. And that's going to be a difficult thing to do."

Back at the Ferguson Farm, Ginny and Henry were waiting anxiously for news. They had gone to the kitchen to calm themselves over a cup of tokkofo and some sweets from the pantry. In fact, this was usually a favorite pastime. They often sat in the kitchen talking about the recent trips they had taken or what they planned to do for the coming day. Sometimes they took the refreshments out onto the back veranda, especially in the summer months when it was shady and cool. Oddly, as often as they did this, they never seemed to gain a single pound. In fact, the people of that world were uncommonly slim. Only a few, like Lord Bigsley, gained some extra pounds. And Henry could think of one, maybe two, that he ever met whom he considered to be anything close to obese.

The kitchen setting was familiar, of course, but the mood kept them from enjoying the snack. They spoke mostly of what had happened the night before. As they did so, Henry sensed that there was something disturbing Ginny. It became so obvious that he finally had to stop and blatantly ask her what was wrong. Ginny had tried hard to conceal her troubled heart. But now that she knew she had failed, she decided to confide in Henry.

Speaking frankly, she said, "Henry, I'll tell you what the problem is. I don't want to remain unmarried my whole life." Ginny's jaw was set, and her face was stern.

Henry didn't become angry. In fact, he smiled and kindly said, "Ginny, I know how you feel. I've been there too. But we have chosen..."

"But I don't want to go along with it anymore," Ginny said sharply.

Once again, Henry was troubled by the tone of Ginny's voice. She didn't want to argue the point; she just wanted her way. Until now, he and Ginny had been able to discuss any matter that they disagreed on without resorting to quarrelsome language or threatening attitudes. But this was different, and Henry knew there was more that Ginny was concealing, and it was causing her to behave in a very unbecoming manner. It now seemed more than ever to Henry, that Brutus's arrival and Ginny's change was more than mere coincidence.

"It's Mr. Malroye, isn't it? Ginny, how can you even consider..."

"Who are you to tell me what I may consider or not consider. It's my life. I think I should be able to do with it as I please." Ginny looked away stubbornly.

Henry continued to speak in a calm manner. "Ginny, you know that is not true. We are not our own, we've been bought with a price. We have been marked just as surely as if we had been branded on the back of our hand. We do not belong to ourselves or any other creature for that matter."

"He can change. We all can change. Why can't he?"

"But the only change that he is capable of is an outward change. He can appear to be good, but that doesn't mean he is good."

Ginny wasn't listening.

"Ginny," Henry said firmly, "listen to me. Where do you think Brutus got the money to pay the taxi fare? He escaped from Yellow House only yesterday morning. There is only one way that he could have come into that money."

"But he was frantic. He thought he was being persecuted. He had never heard of sanctuary. Tell me Henry, if the tables were turned and they showed up on our doorstep with the news that they were sending you back to Earth, no questions asked, how would you respond?"

Henry felt suddenly uncomfortable. He would resist it, that is certain. But would he flee and become a renegade as Brutus had?

"Of course, I would oppose it. But that's the difference between Brutus and me; Brutus won't go by the rules no matter what the cost. I would do everything permissible to stop my being sent back, but if they insisted, in the end I would give in...I know I would." The thought of actually having to go back to Earth produced an extremely knotty sensation in the pit of his stomach.

Henry tried another tack. "Ginny, you are a beautiful woman. Mr. Malroye was obviously stunned by it. Even if he showed any interest, do you think it would be for the right reasons."

"Are you saying that beauty should have no part in it?"

"No, not at all. God created beautiful things. And beauty such as yours is suited perfectly for marriage. But Mr. Malroye hardly sees you in that light. What if he became so accustomed to your beauty that he simply grew tired of you? How do you think he would treat you then? What about when you grow old and your beauty fades? For that matter, do you think he could remain faithful to one woman? From everything we know about the man he can't be trusted; especially on matters, such as marriage, that affect the rest of your life."

Ginny struggled within. She knew Henry was right. And deep inside she wanted to do what was right. But, oh, the desire to be joined to another. To be complete as God intended her to be. To be like most of the women she ever knew. The conflict within overcame her, and Ginny broke down and sobbed. Henry laid his hand on her shoulder; he, too, now saw how much she had been suppressing that desire all those years. It only took the appearance of one man to change all that. Why did that man have to be Brutus Malroye?

The caterpillar popped and suctioned its way across the parking lot to the taxi next to Sneekums who had gotten out to stretch. The greenchnik game had ended only minutes earlier, so the time had passed quickly. The Yellow Hounds had their first loss of the year by a single goal.

Amos set the Edsel down in the same spot Mortimer saw them leave an hour earlier. They all got out, except for Michelangelo, and walked over to the taxi. Brutus had gotten off the caterpillar and held the golden chest in his hands.

On his way back from the cave, Brutus had begun to plot. It was not about how he was going to keep from being sent back to Earth. That thought never occurred to him because his ultimate goal would preclude that.

His first step was to ensure he retained possession of the oerken leaf and to master its power. He was pretty confident that the leaf was not going to be taken from him or it would have happened already. As for the power of the leaf, he only had a few experiences. The leaf in the golden chest and the two that he had on Earth at Griffin Farm were nearly identical in shape and condition. He was certain now that his arrival in Eskathoer was because of the oak leaves. They were Earth's version of the oerken leaf.

He remembered how the beam of light that burst out of the rock, had sucked him up into some kind of wormhole (or, for all he knew, maybe it was a yet-to-be-discovered phenomenon of the universe) that transferred him directly to Eskathoer with no passage of time. That was his first experience. His second was the water balloons back at the cave. Brutus examined both incidents in detail and tried to find something common between them. It was not until they were almost back at the parking lot when it struck Brutus what that common point was.

In both cases, Brutus was under intense emotional strain. At the Griffin Farm, he was so feverishly excited over the discovery of the leaf and his zeal to discover the same world that Chester and Clara had found, that his desire became reality. Likewise for the deluge at the cave. His imagination coupled with intense emotion created the water balloons. Brutus admitted to himself that there was really no comparison to the time he plastered the neighborhood kid with a single balloon and the massive attack on the Edsel. But that only meant a lack of control and concentration. He would learn to use the oerken leaf at will. And the sooner the better.

Michelangelo woke up suddenly. He felt uneasy, an emotion he didn't quite understand. What was it like? Was it like those rare times when Amos was late in getting his daily ration of milkbones to him? No, that was just a little hunger mixed in with a lot of impatience.

Perhaps, Michelangelo thought, it was like earlier that morning when he chased the chikalik up the tree, and they called him back before he was ready to quit. No, that wasn't it either. That was just having your fun spoiled. Sure, there was an inner whimper that, if it could be heard, or better, if it could be felt by those who made him come back, they would know firsthand the cruel disappointments of a dog's life. But disappointment was not the same thing as that uncomfortable feeling right now.

It was like that night at old doc Mason's house. Everyone was nice to him; everyone except that mean old cat, with those deep yellow-orange eyes. That cat should have been chased right out of the house he was so troublesome. Threatening was more like it. It had such a horrible, ferocious hiss. Couldn't even get up and stretch without that cat raising its back, narrowing its eyes, and then hissing like a snake. And then, after all that, it would crouch down low on its belly and slither away like a lizard and hide. No telling when it would come back and do it all over again. Michelangelo recalled how little sleep he got that night.

He poked his head up over the front seat and looked around. No one else was in the Edsel. He pawed his way to the door window to see what was going on outside. Matt was there, not far away. That was comforting. Michelangelo relaxed a little.

The rest were a good deal farther away. Michelangelo saw them crowded around a vehicle that he could barely see. There was a new face, a funny looking man with big thick glasses. He must have been important, because everyone was looking at him, and he was the only one who seemed to be doing the talking. There was another next to him, holding a big stick in one hand, while extending the other hand toward the man with the glasses.

Hmm, that one with the stick was different. Strange, Michelangelo thought; can almost see that eerie strangeness, like a dull aura. Need to be careful about him. Yes, yes, something strange, something dark. Better forget about him, or there might be bad dreams ahead. Look for somebody familiar, quickly now; look for another comforting face. Who else? Oh, the governor's there, and...who's that other one there?...not sure...hmm, it looks like...ah yes, it's Amos. Well, well, seems like everything is quite normal after all...but that was such an odd feeling, and it's still not quite gone. Oh well, just put it out of mind. Probably nothing that should cause one to pass up a chance for a good snooze.

The events that Michelangelo observed in the parking lot were extraordinary, although he had no inkling of it. Brutus had gone over to the taxi and stood by the door with the golden chest under one arm, the staff in the other. Mortimer looked at him wondering why he just didn't get into the taxi. Then the chest caught his attention. It was really the way Brutus was holding it. He held it close to him. And he was very deliberate in his movement so as not to allow the chest to suffer even the most minute scratch. Mortimer was fairly certain that the chest was what all the hubbub was about. He guessed the governor and his party must not have been late after all. And just as he predicted, their boy wasn't going anywhere without him and his taxi.

Brutus continued to stand by the door and Mortimer listlessly did the same. *"What is wrong with this guy?"* Brutus thought. *"Can't he see that I can't open the door?"*

"Mr. Sneekums," Brutus said politely but icily, "Could you kindly open the door? I seem to be a little disadvantaged at the moment." Brutus held his stick up a few inches from Mortimer's face to make the point more obvious.

Mortimer got the point. As he took the door handle and gave it a twist to open, the sunlight struck his glasses in such a way that they momentarily flashed in Brutus's eyes. The image of that flash stuck in Brutus's head, and it gave him an inspiration. He laid the chest inside the taxi on the seat, but instead of getting in himself, he withdrew.

This was going to be a gamble. Brutus had no good reason to expect his idea to really work. But it wasn't reason that was driving him. It was the sense of pre-eminence, the New Man feel, that assured him of what he was about to do would succeed. That feeling had come away with him from the pond just outside of Puddle Bottom West. That seemed so long ago, and yet it was only yesterday evening. Perhaps the long days made the experience seem distant. Regardless, the images of that pond and gloom were still fresh; most of all, the image of that...well, he preferred not to think of it directly. He could feel the mark on the back of his hand stinging. The mark was now quite faded but still noticeable.

The stinging, of course, was all in his head. But he knew he was different now. Not so much in his inner nature but in power and wisdom. He had gained a vision, a perception of his destiny. He had a purpose that was going to bring him greatness. His insight into what was truly good would play an important role. He would be one of many who started from humble beginnings and rise to a position of excellence and domination; he would gain the respect, even reverence, of all.

But the world had to be convinced. True, he had been exposed to only a small part of that world, but anyone who has attained greatness had to have a beginning. And what better way to convince an unbeliever than through a sensational and extraordinary event? What better way than by miracle?

"Mr. Sneekums, may I see your glasses please?"

"My glasses? Well, I don't know, it's my only pair, know what I mean? I'm careful like about these glasses. Anything happens to them and you'll be adrivin', yeh know?" Mortimer grinned uncertainly.

"Mr. Sneekums," Brutus said firmly and authoritatively,

"your glasses please."

Mortimer looked at the governor for guidance, but he just shrugged his shoulders. Mortimer changed the subject.

"Yeh know, I've been carting yeh all over creation, and I don't even know yer name? Seems to me that fellers like us that have been through so much should be on a first name basis, know what I mean?"

"Yes...Mortimer...I agree. My name is Bruce Malroye, but I prefer Brutus. Now, will you please take off your glasses and give them to me!"

Reluctantly, Mortimer reached up, took his glasses off and laid them in the palm of Brutus's hand. Mortimer was now squinting fiercely. In fact, Squinteye was his nickname, one that he didn't really care for and therefore never brought up.

Indeed, there was a time when Squinteye was the more familiar name. Even within his own family, he rarely went by 'Mortimer'. The name came about one day when he and the neighborhood kids were playing something like the game of cowboys and Indians[16]. Mortimer was an Indian that day, and he was squinting, because he had misplaced his glasses and showed up to play without them. Just as well, he thought; who ever heard of an Indian wearing glasses? Indians never had such inventions. As names were doled out for the game, he was dubbed Squinteye by unanimous choice, and it stuck with him from that day forward.

Brutus theatrically dropped the spectacles on the ground,

---

[16] Remarkably, almost every planet in the universe has such a childhood game. The only difference is that on Earth, the cowboys fight with the Indians. On all the other planets, cowboys and Indians are friends. The Indians, however, are an imaginary people who speak and live in primitive conditions. By primitive, we don't mean poor or inferior or underprivileged. Primitive means exactly that. The 'Indians' are people who live as they did in the early history of the universe, before all the new inventions and comforts of modern life came along. As their culture was primitive so was the language; at least, that is how the children who play the game imagine it to be.

stepped on them, and smashed them into pieces of glass and crumpled metal. Everyone gasped, except Mortimer who couldn't see what was happening. Brutus called John over to stand by his side. John didn't want to, but he did so only to coddle Brutus. Then Brutus opened the door of the taxi, pulled out the golden chest, and placed it in the hands of John. This in itself was chancy, Brutus thought. John could easily have stolen away with it. But it would prove once and for all to himself, as well as the others, that the leaf was now his.

Brutus opened the box and reached in to pull out the oerken leaf. The moment he touched it, it began to brighten. When he pulled it out into the broad light of day, the oerken leaf flashed brilliantly and then settled into a warm glow.

Brutus instructed John to place the chest on the ground near his feet and then to back away. John did so, and took up a position next to Josie and Matt.

"What's going on, John?" Josie asked. "I don't like the way this looks."

John nodded in agreement. Matt looked at him with that fear-of-Brutus-look in his eyes again. He was expecting the Z rays. The governor and Amos were several yards away and beyond the earshot of a whisper. But they too were wary.

"All who can hear my voice," cried Brutus, "take heed, for today you will see a marvel which I, Brutus Malroye, the new bearer of the leaf, master of the secret arts, shall perform before your very eyes." Brutus, one by one, looked on the face of each that stood by. A few bystanders had walked over to see what the commotion was about. Several at the top of the steps that led to Mr. Stokkleplat's store likewise stopped to see what was going on below them in the parking lot.

As Brutus closed his eyes and began to concentrate, several more curious onlookers walked over and gathered round. Brutus summoned an image in his mind of two figures, the one clearly a magnificently and lavishly dressed miracle worker, the other the recipient of the miracle. The miracle worker wore a dark cape adorned with brilliant jewels and intricate needle-work. In his right hand, he held a wooden scepter overlaid with silver and tipped with a crystalline object that glowed. Around these two figures he pictured a multitude of bystanders in the thralls of wild cheering and applause. The entire scene was exactly what he desired, but the vividness and detail were far from what he wanted to imagine.

Brutus's concentration deepened as he intently focused all his thoughts on this single image. The effort was strenuous and sweat began to form on his temple. To the spectator, however, nothing notable appeared to be going on. Mortimer simply stood there, squinting savagely, trying to catch anything that would give him a clue of what was happening. Brutus, however, was locked in a trance and began to shake. His face contorted in a monstrous and inhuman manner, twitching, sneering, shaking, and screwed up to the point that many let out little muffled shrieks. A sense of dread came over the witnesses; a sense that something unnatural and horror-filled was about to happen before their very eyes.

Then, unexpectedly, the encrystaled leaf began to sparkle and flash. A few cries of astonishment from the crowd made Mortimer ask, "What? What's wrong? What's going on?"

In Brutus's struggle to formulate the crowning mental picture, he slowly but surely summoned the image into clearer and clearer resolution. This toil continued until there came a moment in which the mental image was perfect. At precisely that moment, Brutus cried out in a loud and pompous voice, "Abbra! Cadabbra! Kalamazoo! SHAZAM!"

A soundless explosion of smoke engulfed the two of them and, for a moment, they were obscured from view. The smoke billowed skyward in large blood-red puffs. Everyone was certain that Brutus and Mortimer would be stained crimson from head to toe, but as the smoke cleared, it unveiled the very two figures of Brutus's imagination.

Brutus, unscathed and untouched by the smoke, stood

stunningly bedecked in a flowing hooded cape with a high collar that came around the sides of his head whose tips turned out like two sharp petals of an unnatural black flower.

Sewn into the back of the cape with intricate detail was a decorative figure which had the likeness of a reptile whose eyes were two yellow-orange gems. Brutus's silvery walking stick radiated dazzling streaks of light under the brilliant sun. On the tip there was a crystal orb which held the oerken leaf. The leaf shone with a pulsating glow and flashing sparkles.

"Oh!" cried Mortimer as his hands shot up to cover his eyes. "My eyes! My eyes! They burn! What's happening? Help me!" Mortimer fell to his knees, his face twisted in pain. The crowd rushed in and began to tug and pull at him to lift him up and carry him away to relief.

Then Mortimer suddenly stopped screaming and became perfectly still. The burning was gone. He slowly moved his hands from his face and lowered them with his eyes still closed. The crowd backed away and stood by motionlessly, quietly. No sound was heard except the rustle of the wind and the faint, distant bellow of a yank.

Mortimer opened his eyes and blinked. He could see! Not blurry images, but objects whose features were crisp and clear. He quickly rubbed his eyes and then opened them again. His eyes were greeted with a panorama of crystal clear detail.

"I can see," he said in a whisper of disbelief. "I can see," he said more excitedly. A third time he cried out, "I can see! I can see! NO MORE SQUINTEYE!"

Mortimer looked up toward the heavens and in a prayer mouthed the words, "Thank you." Ooh's and aah's flittered above the band of witnesses. Brutus, radiant and smiling, exuberantly swished back his mantle and extended his arm toward Mortimer in the way the host of a rock concert might introduce the star performer.

John looked at Josie and Matt. They stood, mouth open, astonished like the others. He whispered to them, "Are you kidding me? I don't believe it."

Josie whispered back, "This is like a magic show."

"That Brutus!" John spat, "Brutus is learning to use the oerken leaf." He cast a dark look at Brutus who was smiling and waving to the cheers.

John muttered desperately, "This is more than just the leaf. Something else is in this too, I can just feel it. There's something mysterious and unnatural about this...something supernatural."

"Look at him," Matt said, his face lined with contempt, "Look at him standing there like some hotshot."

"He did this for the attention," Josie said, hands on her hips. "He's up to something. Look at the governor; he sees it, too."

John glanced over at the governor who was tight-lipped and grim-faced. Amos simply shook his head mumbling something that was lost in the commotion of the noise that had gone up from the crowd.

The small throng rushed in to gather round Mortimer, patting his back, slapping palms, laughing and howling over the great wonder they had just witnessed.

From inside his cloak, Brutus pulled out a fitted cloth and covered the orb. Then he stood smugly as he peered across the clamor to where the governor stood. Their eyes met for a moment before the governor looked away in dismay. He knew something was amiss. And yet, what could he say? The jubilant assembly had just witnessed a marvel that none had ever seen or heard before. A marvel that had all the appearances of goodness and compassion.

All now looked to Brutus like the ancient Romans may have done, as if he were a god who came down from Olympus. But the Eskathoerians knew there were no such gods. There was only one true God. From time to time, the true God had sent one among them, just as he had done on Earth, to enlighten them, reassure them of his goodness and his care for them. It was through such men that they learned that the sin of the first parents of Earth brought a curse not only upon that world but also upon the entire universe as well. These men revealed how the creation and all its inhabitants throughout the billions and billions of galaxies, because of that sin, were presently subject to the discomforts of life, even pain and sorrow. Most importantly, they learned that the Son of the Living God had become a man like themselves and went to Earth to suffer and die so that the curse would some day be broken. Indeed, so these special men taught, there was a day coming in which the creation would no longer groan under the curse of that world's sin. But none of those spokesmen had performed a single miracle as Brutus had done. This was something new, something marvelous and wonderful.

John cast an anxious glance toward Brutus. There he stood, the oerken staff in hand, the leaf itself covered as if to hide its light from the onlookers. What a catastrophe, John thought. The oerken had been hidden away for safekeeping and now it was in the hands of an evil genius. John almost laughed at the expression as it came to mind. 'Evil Genius.' Those were words reserved for a melodrama, not this. This was real. The oerken was real, and its power was in the hands of one whose wicked character John had seen and experienced first hand. But John had never seen Brutus in this new role of miracle worker. What an absurd thought - Brutus, a benevolent worker of kindnesses and benign miracles. Ridiculous! Did anyone really know the full depth of Brutus's dark nature?

Then a thought struck John that made him shiver under the warmth of the Eskathoerian sun. How did all of this happen anyway? Was there purpose behind this? Certainly not God's, but perhaps something or someone else. Of course, God was in control, that's what John had always been taught in church and Sunday School, and he believed that with all his heart. But that didn't mean none ever dared to oppose Him. The Adversary had been at work since the garden, opposing God at every step of the calamitous history of man. Was he at work now, in this world? John looked up into the bright blue sky. A perfect day in an almost perfect world. Could what happened on Earth happen here?

Another thought. What about the other oerken, the one at the mansion? Was it safe? John quickly looked around to find the governor. He saw him on the other side of the small clump of onlookers that had gathered on their side of the parking lot. As though the governor knew John was eyeing him, he looked John's way, and their eyes locked. John opened his mouth, but nothing came out. He faintly shook his head realizing that he was not at all sure what to say. Even if he were, was this the right time and place to mention his concern over the other leaf? He closed his mouth, and a slight frown crossed the governor's brow.

What were the next few days or weeks going to bring? John hoped he wouldn't have to face Brutus again, but if not, would that mean the governor would send him and his brother and sister home? After all, that was why they were summoned, and he had failed. Anxiety swept over him and without realizing what he was doing, John stole another glance of the governor. He wanted to catch anything in his expression that might answer that perplexing question.

John's gloomy spirit was broken by a round of cheers that went up again from the crowd. There was no denying it. Brutus had done something spectacular. He had come as close as one could in giving sight to the blind. John surveyed the crowd, wondering if they had any idea what they just witnessed and who this figure in the flowing hooded cape was. It made him sick. The question that was asked long ago on Earth of the True Miracle Worker was sooner or later going to have to be faced by each person in the throng...perhaps by each person on the whole planet - "Who is this man?"

An excerpt from the book 2 of the Trilogy, *The Traveler-King*.

"How are you doing Mr. Malroye," the driver said in a deep bass voice and with very articulate syllables. This was not the voice of Mortimer. "That 'miracle' you performed this morning was a nice touch I must say. And the cape and staff were perfect." The driver turned and looked back at Brutus. It was Sneekums, but a different Sneekums. The face was certainly that of Mortimer's but the features were exaggerated and grotesque, like a gargoyle's. Brutus reacted with a quick sucking breath of air. Was this real? Was he dreaming?

The driver chuckled. "Is this unpleasant? I can try something different?" With that, the driver's face protruded so that his nose and mouth pushed outward and his eyes moved to the sides and became yellow with diamond-shaped pupils. When the transformation was complete, the features were reptilian, a bit like a lizard or snake, but more beastly and dragon-like than anything else that Brutus could think of. It was frightening and threatening; Brutus wanted it to go away.

Brutus gulped. "No, no, you were fine...er...the first way."

The driver reassumed the face of the Sneekums gargoyle.

"Mr. Malroye," the gargoyle said, "do you know who I am?"

Brutus imagined many things including ghosts, evil wizards, dead spirits, and even Lucifer himself. He believed in none of these, but what he just saw was something that had no reasonable, ordinary, or natural explanation. It was unnatural. Brutus was tempted to think of it as supernatural. But then again, he didn't believe in the supernatural, which was a bit of a dilemma for him. Of late, he had the vivid notion, or better, the deep and heavy feeling, that he himself was not completely ordinary. He was a human being, of course, but there was something mysterious about his existence, his presence in this new world.

The back of his hand, the one with the mark, suddenly stung like a bee-sting.

"Ow!" Brutus winced and brought the back of his hand up to his face. The mark was quite visible again, appearing in a vivid red, just as it did when he pulled his arm out of the dismal pond by the walking trail.

Sneekums looked back once again, smiling hideously and literally from ear to ear. "Perhaps that will jog your memory, my dear Brutus."

I knew that if my father authored this section, the reader would get just the facts: "Thomas Booher is married and the father of two children. He currently resides in Sanford, North Carolina". While factual, it lacks the sentiment that I believe an 'about the author' section commands, which is why I've decided to step in. Without sounding like I'm providing a "my-dad's-the-best-dad-in-the-whole-world" essay, I want to inform you, the reader, about the author. He instilled in me a passion for the written word beginning when he taught me to read C. S. Lewis books before I entered my first year in school. Looking back on my childhood, I now notice how his desire to write was evident even when I was a little girl. He read to me stories that he began writing for the sole purpose of my entertainment. (They would have been more entertaining had any of them been finished works;

instead, I have several unresolved storylines that have been swimming in my head for years, but I digress…). His passion for completing stories became most apparent this past year when he wrote this trilogy. My brother and I have known for years that Dad should be telling stories. Relentlessly, we pester him to the point of reluctant compliance to our requests for him to tell us stories from his childhood, despite our having heard them several times before. We do this because, when he tells them, they never get old. Now he shares the first of three (relatively) completed books with all of us, and my brother and I hope you are as entertained as we both have been over the years.

- Carrie S. Booher

www.ingramcontent.com/pod-product-compliance
Lightning Source LLC
Chambersburg PA
CBHW051549030726
47592CB00001B/200